Praise for Miranda Dickinson

'A proper lovely romance, and a fabulous spirit-lifter'
Ruth Jones

'Heart-warming and believable.
This is Miranda Dickinson at her very best'
Sarah Morgan

'Perfection in page form. A book that seeps into your soul,
warms your heart and makes your brain sigh'
Milly Johnson

'Miranda is such a big-
full of warr
Jenny

'A story about love, fear, trust,
this is a big warm-hearted hug of a book'
Prima

'This love story has everything we want from a
classic rom-com – the perfect pick-me-up read'
Woman & Home

'Oh my heart, this book! What a story. It's so achingly tender
and bittersweet, and a spark of true joy. I adored every page'
Josie Silver

'This story will have you championing the pair all the way'
Sun

Miranda Dickinson is the author of fifteen books, including six *Sunday Times* bestsellers. Her books have been translated into sixteen languages, selling over a million copies worldwide. She has been shortlisted for the RNA Novel of the Year, Contemporary Novel of the Year and Popular Romantic Novel of the Year awards and is the winner of the 26 Project Writer award. She is the founder of *WriteFoxy* and the host of the online show *Fab Night in Chatty Thing*. Miranda lives in the Black Country with her husband and daughter.

Also by Miranda Dickinson

Things We Do For Love
All My Love
The Start of Something
Our Story
The Day We Meet Again
Somewhere Beyond the Sea
Searching for a Silver Lining
A Parcel for Anna Browne
I'll Take New York
Take a Look at Me Now
When I Fall in Love
It Started with a Kiss
Welcome to My World
Fairytale of New York

Miranda Dickinson

and then there was you

ONE PLACE. MANY STORIES

HQ
An imprint of HarperCollins*Publishers* Ltd
1 London Bridge Street
London SE1 9GF

www.harpercollins.co.uk

HarperCollins*Publishers*
Macken House, 39/40 Mayor Street Upper
Dublin 1, D01 C9W8, Ireland
This edition 2025

2
First published in Great Britain by HQ,
an imprint of HarperCollins*Publishers* Ltd 2025

ISBN: 9780008590055

Set in Adobe Caslon Pro by HarperCollins*Publishers* India

Printed and bound in the UK using 100% Renewable
Electricity at CPI Group (UK) Ltd

For more information visit: www.harpercollins.co.uk/green

To Levi French
for teaching me to play piano
and for our many, many chats!

'Where there is love, there is life'
Mahatma Gandhi (1869–1948)

PART ONE

'Brand New Day' (Radio Edit)

– Joshua Radin

One

MERRYN

Summer nights in St Ives are strange beasts. Vivid and raucous, joy-filled and stressful. And busy. Always busy.

But tonight is a good one.

There's a rare lull in the crowds, most holidaymakers tucked into their overpriced fishermen's cottages that no fisherman could ever afford to live in now. The bars have kicked out their patrons – most of them, anyway, a few stragglers still clinging stubbornly to their pints as the bar staff will them to leave. It's a warm evening, as the last twelve days have been, but tonight there's a cool breeze blowing in from the sea. It makes the rows of tiny white lights dance over Fore Street, the loose curls lift and sway around my face. Beyond, the ink-black waters of the harbour are almost at full tide, lapping against the harbour walls and rising up the slipway that leads to the lifeboat station. Light-trails of reflection from the restaurants, bars, shops and houses of the town dance over the waves, magical as ever.

And I'm happy.

Content.

Bone-tired, after a long day at work, of course. But peaceful.

There was a time in my life, not so long ago, when I didn't think I'd ever feel like this again. When pain and betrayal and worry eclipsed everything else.

But I'm here. Alive. Thriving. And tonight St Ives is hugging my heart.

'You're quiet.'

Seth Hartley, my best friend, ever the observant one. He walks beside me, swaying a little after the unwise tequila shot he chose to end the night with, the slap of his ever-present flip-flops echoing around the darkened buildings of St Ives' main shopping street. He's funny when he's drunk. He'll be funnier still tomorrow morning, when the impending hangover kicks in. And I love him for it.

'I'm just taking it in,' I reply, giggling when he bumps side-wards against me. 'Unlike you.'

'Hey, I'm the biggest fan of the amb . . . ambi . . . *vibe* of the town,' he insists, bottom lip jutting out at the word that escapes him. 'I just choose to find it in liquid form.'

'You'll regret it tomorrow.'

'Abso-*bleddy*-lutely.' He sniggers. 'Might as well make the most of the crime before I pay the price for it.'

I grin at him as he loops his arm through mine. 'I'll bring you a strong coffee first thing.'

'And that, Merryn Rowe, is why you're my heaven-sent angel.' His words dance and blur, sounding more like *hevnnsenanggel*. He probably won't remember this conversation tomorrow, which is just as well. Seth famously believes he is a titan when it comes to holding his drink. None of his friends have the heart to correct him. It's far more fun watching his misplaced pride at play, knowing what a lightweight he was the night before.

The journey home is slow but tonight I don't mind. We natter about unimportant things, giggle and fall silent as the constant burr of the sea and chatter of seagulls carries us.

We're just taking a short cut along North Terrace when I see it.

Out on the pavement. The last thing I expected to see.

Seth is still chuckling about a drunk woman we passed a while back, not realising he is on a similar level of inebriation. 'Did you see her legs? Cooked spaghetti! No way she'll make it up that hill . . .'

'Seth.'

'Wibbly wobbly woman . . .'

'*Seth*.' I grab his sleeve.

'Wasson?'

'Look!'

His eyes follow my pointing finger. 'What? Who put that there?'

I can hardly believe it. But it's real.

A piano.

Just left on the pavement, in the almost-midnight gloom.

I hurry over, my fingers meeting the warm wood of the instrument. It's old, scratched a little along the side, and the varnish has worn away along the edge of the lid, where countless fingers have lifted and closed it. But the scent of the wood – musky and sweet with dust, age and ancient polish – brings a thousand buried memories back to the surface.

I look to my left to see which building it's come from. The three-storey house in whose shadow it rests is boarded up, a large *Brotherson Developments* sign nailed to the chipboard covering the front bay window.

Brotherson Developments – everyone in town knows them. Whenever one of the larger houses comes up for sale, you can bet Bill Brotherson and his team of developers will get their hands on it.

They don't deal with old pianos, though.

'It's probably broken,' Seth says, rounding the piano. 'Probably sounds like it should live in a Wild West saloon.'

'It might be okay.'

Gently, I lift the lid, revealing the keys. None of the veneers are missing, all the keys intact and aligned. Yellowed with age, certainly, but far from broken. My fingers hover over the keys, the long shadows they cast in the moonlight stretching over ivory and ebony. But they shrink back, just before they make contact, like before. Like every time since . . .

My heart contracts with them, as an age-old rush of defeat joins the assault. I start to lower the lid – but Seth's hands find the keys, a haphazard chord ringing out into the night. The tuning isn't perfect, but it's a clear, sure tone.

Seth grins. 'Sounds good to me.'

I rest my hand on the piano's side. 'Why would anyone throw this out?'

'They probably just want rid. Can't see Bill Brotherson knockin' out a few tunes for his demolition team.' He peers closer, pulling up a sheet of paper that's been taped to the front of the piano. 'Yep, they definitely want rid.'

I move to his side to read the message hastily scrawled across the paper in thick marker ink:

FREE TO A GOOD HOME

And maybe it's because of the memories the piano brings back, or maybe it's the weariness of a long work day making me emotional, but in that instant, my mind is set.

'I want it.'

'What?'

'*Free to a good home* – my home.' I beam at my friend, who stares back.

'Be serious.'

'I *am* serious. Nobody wants this, but I do. We could wheel it back to mine . . .'

'Mer, you're insane.'

But I'm not. I am thinking more clearly than I can ever remember, my heart swelling as I imagine this beautiful, old, forgotten instrument finding its forever home. In *my* home.

'Help me push it back.'

'Giss on! Where do you think you've room for this gert thing?'

'It'll fit, I know it will.' I beam my brightest smile at him, willing him to relent. 'Come on, Seth? Help me?'

Maybe I'll regret this tomorrow. But tonight the unexpected magic of finding the piano is impossible to ignore.

Seth snorts, shaking his head. 'Whatever. Grab that end, then.'

'Yes! I love you!'

I don't hug him like I want to, for fear he'll change his mind in the time it takes to happen. So I hurry to the other side of the instrument and take hold of the edge of the case.

Together, we ease the piano carefully off the high kerb onto the road. The old wheels squeal and creak in protest, but they move, and once we have a little momentum the instrument glides over the sand-dusted tarmac. Every bump registers with a metallic reverberation inside the piano's upright frame; I wince with each one.

I remember once, long ago, watching a piano being manoeuvred into a room. Two surly men huffing and puffing while a third barked orders at them.

Watch the side! Steady now! This is a delicate instrument, not a wooden box . . .

Seth and I are far from delicate, but moving the piano to the bend in the road and getting it down a narrower pathway requires significant effort. The creaks and squeaks and metallic groans of the piano continue as we swing it over cobbles and kerbs, narrowly miss plastered stone walls and avoid discarded chip papers picked clean by seagulls.

It doesn't help that Seth is already three sheets to the wind or that neither of us has ever attempted to move a piano before. But we make clunky, bumpy progress through the streets of St Ives, giggling as we go.

It feels audacious. Exhilarating. Magical, in a completely loopy way.

Finally, we bumble down a narrow alleyway and emerge in Star Court. It's quieter here, the only café on it closed since five p.m.

My café.

My home, too.

My whole world in one slightly wonky, delightfully quirky little building.

Sweet Reverie, my café, snuggles between two similarly eccentric buildings – Porthia Surf on the left – Seth's surf shop – and Dydh Da deli on the right (currently being renovated by a middle-aged couple called Gi and Heather). Unlike Seth, who has a flat higher up in town, just off Tregenna Hill, I live in the tiny apartment above my shop. I feel beyond lucky to live here, even though the building has seen better days and there's barely enough room to swing a guinea pig in my home, let alone a cat.

As for a piano . . .

Seth helps me rest the piano on the thin strip of pavement outside and heads to the front door.

'Nope.'

'What?'

'Not possible, Mer. You might just get this thing into the café, but there's no way it'll go up the steps to your place.'

My heart crashes to the pavement. Why didn't I think of that?

The staircase to my home is super narrow and steep, so much so that the only way to safely navigate it is to brace your hands on either side and duck where the stairs turn under the ground-floor ceiling to take you up the last few steps to the first floor. It's a feature of the fisherman's cottage it once was, endearing and quirky but tricky at the best of times. And absolutely, resolutely impassable to elderly dark wooden pianos.

Crestfallen, I stare at the almost-midnight piano.

I should accept defeat and wheel it back to the derelict house for someone else to find. But I can't shake the feeling that *it* chose *me*.

I know how daft that sounds.

The warmth of Seth's arm meets my shoulders. 'I'm sorry, lovely. It's a lush old thing.'

'It is.'

What was I thinking? I might find a home for it, but I couldn't ever play it. I've tried, in the years since the piano I remember from my past was taken away from my childhood home. But it's as if waves of pain wash in between my fingers and the keys, sending them scurrying back for safety.

Tears well, despite my willing them not to.

I just thought . . . I hoped . . . this time might be different.

Seth gives my shoulders a squeeze, his other hand tapping the piano's lid. He doesn't like seeing anyone upset, especially not a woman and definitely not me. The tapping becomes impatient, the squeeze just a little tight.

'I'm okay . . .' I begin.

'No!' he exclaims, sniggering tipsily when his word echoes around the darkened street. 'Hang on – it won't get in the front door, but I reckon we could squeeze it in *there* . . .'

He's grinning at the side gate, half-hidden by the tangle of honeysuckle and ivy that blurs the line between my building and Seth's shop. It leads down the side of the café to a covered courtyard at the back.

The courtyard! Of course!

'We could make it a *Play Me* piano!'

'Yes!' Seth replies, the idea blossoming between us. 'And paint it!'

'Yes! With bright colours or waves, or . . .'

'. . . Flowers! Like the Surprise Song piano!'

I stare back at him, but he's unrepentant.

'What? I'm just a happy little Swiftie. The Eras Tour was *magic* . . . And you could bring the magic here – with *this* . . .' He pats the piano. 'So let's get this baby to its new home.'

It takes several anxious attempts to coax the piano through the gateway and round the side of the café, the final two stone steps up to the covered courtyard almost scuppering its journey.

But we make it, with only the smallest of scrapes along the bottom of the wood.

Delighted and out of breath from the effort, we wheel the piano between the café tables to a space against the far wall. Task thus completed, we collapse beside it.

'I'm going to think this was a tequila-induced fever dream tomorrow,' Seth says.

'I'm not sure it isn't.' I lean my head against his shoulder. 'Cheers for indulging me, dude.'

'Pleasure, bird.' He reaches over and ruffles my hair. 'You know, you could always get someone in to play it when you open for bistro nights . . .'

I don't hide my groan. 'Not this again . . .'

'No – hear me out, yeah? Where's the place all our mates come to get away from the emmets in the summer?'

Emmet. An old Cornish word for ant, and local people's favourite not-so-charming term for the tourists on whose business we all depend. It's a local joke, the ant thing, and I can see what they mean about the summer tourists who swarm about wherever they like, with little thought for whose livelihoods they're trampling over. At times it can feel like Cornwall is laid siege to every summer. But the truth is, we need them. All of us do.

'The Leopard,' I say, knowing full well this is merely a deflection and unlikely to deter him.

'Giss on! The only folk drinking in The Leopard are incomers pretendin' to be local. Everyone we know comes *here* – for the last hour of the day. And they'd hang around longer, too, if you didn't turf 'em out at six.'

'I can't afford to do evenings . . .'

'Four hours extra, just a few nights a week,' he insists. 'They'd flock here – you know they would. And if someone was playin' *this* old girl . . . You'd be quids in.'

I don't want him to make a good point, but he does. Truth is, I've been considering it for a while. I'd need extra staff for the night service, and a limited menu to keep costs down. Probably a bring-your-own-bottle policy, too, as the café isn't licensed. It's a ton of work, but plenty of other businesses in town have late-opening hours during the summer.

'I need to think about it,' I begin.

But that's enough for Seth. He jumps up and twirls me around, narrowly missing chairs and tables, until the effects of his enthusiastic night drinking catch up with him and he stops, breathless and dizzy.

'Bleddy hell, I need to be home.'

Still giggling, I lead him back along the side passage to the street. 'Thanks for tonight.'

'It was a good 'un. Weird as, but good.' He grins tipsily. 'And this, dear maid, is where I leave you.' He exacts a wobbly bow that, on the street cobbles, is very brave indeed.

'Will you be okay to get up the hill?' I ask.

He dismisses my question with an overblown wave of his hand. 'No problem, s'just a stagger . . .' His big loony grin makes me smile.

'Right, nighty-night, then.' I cup my hands around his face and plant a kiss on his forehead. 'Take care.'

'Don't I always?' He chuckles, backing away and bumping into a lamppost. 'Oops, 'scuse me, Lampy.'

Raising a hand in farewell, he heads back up the street towards home.

I watch until he disappears from view, then head back to the covered courtyard.

The piano is there.

Old. Battered in places. Scuffed in others.

But wonderful.

And *mine*.

It's way past midnight, and I'm due to get up at five-thirty. Tiredness battles with elation, calling me to bed. But as I open the door to head inside, I sneak one last look back.

Possibility sparkles in the air, like the strings of fairy lights illuminating the courtyard. I love how it feels.

'Night, piano,' I whisper, the thrill of it carrying me all the way to bed.

Two

ZACH

'I'm sorry, mate. There's nothing I can do.'

I don't doubt Sid Martyn's apology, but I can hear nerves in every word.

Somewhere out of view, *she's* watching. Eva. The girlfriend doing everything she can to drag my friend away from the surfing community for good. She's already binned his second-best board, and the only good thing about that is she doesn't yet know about his best one, stashed safely away in the back of St Ives Surf Club's building. But it's only a matter of time before she finds out and bins that, too.

It happens. I've seen it countless times before.

I just never thought it would happen to Sid.

'Don't sweat it,' I reply, swinging my rucksack onto my shoulder. 'Thanks for having me, yeah?'

We hand-clasp and I make my way out. I can practically feel Eva's triumph as I vacate the property.

Fine.

Let her crow over evicting me.

It was only supposed to be temporary, anyway.

My heart hits the cobbles of The Digey when Sid's front door shuts behind me. My whole life is temporary right now.

I could find a holiday rental, despite my noble statements about that being the death of Cornwall, but with the ridiculous prices they hike up for July and August, I'd barely afford a few days. If the weather's good I could kip on the beach for a couple of nights, but I learned long ago never to trust the forecast here in summer.

The sun is just rising as I walk slowly towards Fore Street, washing everything in hopeful golden light. A rush of love assaults me, as it always does in this town, despite living here being a challenge most of the year. And especially now, when St Ives is packed with holidaymakers and all the seasonal jobs are taken.

I can't help it: St Ives has my heart.

It doesn't matter what kind of day I'm having, what trouble is stalking me along the cobbled streets, being in this place always lifts me.

Even if I'm broke and, now, officially homeless . . .

I could always head to the legendary Becca's Bar, see if the good lady herself needs any extra help. Becca's known for taking in waifs and strays and it wouldn't be the first time she's given me work. But the summer season's already underway and she'll likely have her full contingent of bar staff sorted. Plus, my busted knee might not last a night shift.

I've called in all the favours I can think of, commandeered the sofas and spare beds of all the surfing buddies I know are in town. I'm running out of ideas – and money.

I'll think of something.

I always do.

But it's hard to be proactive at five-thirty in the morning, when you're knackered and hungry and you've just lost your bed for the night.

Bloody Eva.

Bloody *knee.*

I need to think. And I need coffee. And I know one place badass enough to be serving it before six.

I head down Fore Street, past Chy-an-Chy and up to Norway, the street whose name my mum always loved. 'That's it, I'm off to Norway!' she'd sing-song when she was popping to the small corner shop that lies at the end of it. The shop is still there, a TARDIS of a place packed with a surprising array of groceries, cakes, artisan breads and cheeses. Not a straight shelf in the place, which amused Mum, too.

The shop is still there, but Mum isn't.

I kick at the stab of pain that always attacks me when I think of her.

She's the reason I'm back here, five years after her passing. When my knee was injured, taking my pro-surfing career with it, St Ives was my best hope. I needed to be near to her, even though she isn't here anymore. Her heart is still here, I think. I feel it everywhere in this town, as real as the cobbled streets and as loud as the gulls.

She didn't leave a home for me when she passed away – she had to give it up when she went into the hospice. But St Ives was her home, for most of her life. So now, it's mine.

I duck down Porthmeor Road, the crash of the waves on the beach beyond its row of huddled fishermen's cottages unmistakable. There's a blast of salt-laden, sea-sodden air as I pass the gap between the buildings leading to the beach, then respite as the bulk of St Nicholas Court shelters me.

I can't face Porthmeor today. The surf's up and everyone will be out in the waves.

Instead, I skirt the Island car park – where a particularly optimistic four-by-four is camping out in the hope of a parking space. The driver – pale-faced and bug-eyed, clearly a tourist – is staring at the crowded rows of cars as if he thinks one of them might vanish. A frazzled-looking woman in the passenger seat and two sleepy kids crashed out in the back complete the set.

I wish them well, I do.

But in the summer season they've got more chance of unearthing the Holy Grail in between the stubbornly stationary vehicles here than ever finding a parking space.

As I pass the car park, another beach swings into view. Much smaller than Porthmeor but perfectly formed, with soft, pale fudge-coloured sand, dark grey rocks and a gentle slope of a bay beloved by families in the summer and early morning swimmers all year round.

The steep path that leads down to Porthgwidden Beach brings a rush of sound, a stiff sea breeze and the unmistakable aroma of the best beach coffee in town. My instincts proved right, I head for the small whitewashed building that presides over the beach. The door is ajar when I reach it, an invitation lovelier than I can express.

'Bleddy hell, look what the wind blew in!'

Aggie Keats turns from the shiny chrome coffee machine – revealing a burgeoning belly straining at the sides of her stone-coloured cotton dungarees.

'Hey, Aggs. What are you doing working? Aren't you due soon?'

'Cheek!' She chucks a tea towel at me. 'Is that the only

question anyone can ask me? I'm *eight-and-a-quarter months*, Zachary, so plenty of time before this lot arrive.'

'How many do you have in there?' I chuckle.

'Feels like a bleddy herd of rhino right now.' She carefully manoeuvres her impressive bump through the hatch in the counter and blesses me with a bear hug. 'Two, officially. Though I wouldn't be surprised if they've smuggled a mate in.'

'You're looking fab,' I say with a grin, kissing her cheek.

'You look like crap.' Her pierced eyebrow rises. 'No offence or nothin'.'

'None taken.'

'What you doing out this early? You're not hittin' the surf, are you?' Her gaze drops to my knee, as it does with everyone who knows me.

'I need coffee,' I reply. 'And you're the only bird mad enough to be making it so early.'

'Yeah, well, my swimmin' lads and ladies need something hot when they come out of the sea, don't they? Plus, I can't sleep. So it's all good. What'll it be, then?'

'Anything you like, as long as it's strong.'

Aggie sniggers as she returns behind the counter, fills a coffee arm with freshly ground espresso and cranks it into the machine. 'Like that, is it?'

'You have no idea.' I take a seat at the carved oak bar, only now feeling how tired my body is. Sleeping on sofas significantly shorter than your body length for weeks on end does nothing for you, I've discovered. I've forgotten what it feels like to stretch out flat in a bed.

'Where are you staying?'

I sigh. There's no point hiding the truth from Agatha Keats.

She'll uncover it in minutes, knowing the town grapevine as well as she does. 'I *was* staying at Sid Martyn's, until about twenty minutes ago.'

'Stick-up-her-arse Eva Price chucked you out then? No surprise there. She'd have Sid chained to the cobbles to keep him from the sea, if she could.' She shakes her head, spiral curls bobbling around her face as she does so. 'I've seen it too many times. But she's the worst in a while.'

'I never thought Sid would put up with it, but he's smitten.'

'Sid Martyn is a soft touch. Everyone knows it. Here you go, lovely.' She slides a huge mug of dark, smoky coffee to my waiting hands.

It's the most wonderful thing I've seen for days.

Aggie watches while I drink, wiping the bar with a cloth as she observes me. Beyond the walls of the coffee hut, the strengthening wind whistles as the surf continues to rise. There are a thousand things that should concern me right now: contingencies to be put in place, doors to be knocked, worries to address. But this one, simple moment, enjoying coffee by the beach before the rest of the town is even awake, is such a gift that I can't rush it.

I've learned to appreciate small moments like this. An injury will do that to you. For years I lived for the highs, the drama and the big events. I couldn't even count the smaller moments I let pass by while waiting for the big stuff. Like all the waves you dismiss when you're in the water, waiting for that one, perfect swell. Lately, I've had to pay attention to the smaller things because my world has shrunk. It's become about loose change and small serendipities, taking each day as it comes instead of racing ahead of the calendar to the next major event.

I no longer have the luxury of control over my life. And that hurts. I've always surfed my way out of lean times, trusting the next competition to solve the woes created by the last. But now, I have no firm plan, no forward schedule – and it scares me.

'So, what's the plan, Zachy?' Aggie leans on the counter, her gaze fixed on me.

'There isn't one.' It sucks to admit it, but it's Aggie asking. 'I need to find work so I can pay for somewhere to stay. You don't have anything going here, do you?'

Aggie's look of compassion both comforts and stings me.

'I wish I did, lover. I'm strugglin' to afford the staff I've got. Even with the summer rush comin' . . .'

'No worries.' I retreat to the comfort of Aggie's excellent coffee. I didn't expect her to be able to help. She has enough to deal with here and with her imminent arrivals. But asking for work has become such an instant thing that my request was out before I could stop it.

I hate this: the feeling of being behoven to my friends, of every acquaintance being a potential route to find work or a place to sleep. I'd never asked anyone for anything until my knee gave up on me. Now it seems it's all I do.

Aggie grabs a cloth and stabs at a coffee spill on the counter. Her brows knot as she does so – an expression I recognise. She's done it for as long as I've known her: the Aggie Keats Thinking Frown. The only time she's quiet, unless she's sleeping. She's a problem-solver, one of life's fixers. If she's turning something over in that brilliant mind of hers, the issue she's looking to solve is already history.

'Know what, Zachy? If you're stuck for a place to stay, Kieran has a room, on the side of his studio. He's not there at night, unless he's editin' a big photo job. There's a fold-out bed, little kitchen, a loo. Shower out in the yard behind it. I mean it isn't much, but . . .'

'Yes!' I rush, because I've long since abandoned pride in favour of open doors. 'That would be amazing. Would you ask him, Aggs?'

'I'll do better than that, babe.' She reaches over the counter and squeezes my hand. 'I'll *tell* him. Stick with me and we'll get you sorted, okay?'

It's all I can do not to yell out loud.

Three

MERRYN

It's six a.m. My body protests as I cross the flagged floor of the courtyard, carrying the old paint-stained dustsheet I've just rescued from the cellar, and an armful of paint pots.

There are a million and one things I should be doing to prepare for the day.

But they can all wait.

Because of *this*.

In daylight, the piano looks even older and more battle-worn than it did last night. But beneath the dust, dirt and scratches, the nut-brown wood glows. The loveliest pink-gold light is streaming in around me and everything feels fresh and new.

As I settle cross-legged on the dustsheet, I surround myself with paint pots in a palette of shades that capture the colours of St Ives in the summer. I wonder how many of the crowds of summer tourists will see the colours this morning, will stop to take it all in. How many heart-stopping sunrises will be missed as they sleep in their holiday cottage beds? How many subtle shade-shifts of the sea will be ignored in the crush of bodies along Wharf Road or the rush to secure a spot on the town beaches?

How can you come somewhere so beautiful and miss what makes it special?

Not here, I say to myself, facing the piano. *We see the magic, despite everything*.

It didn't occur to me to paint the piano until Seth suggested it. I wonder how his poor head is this morning, whether he's awake already or whether the hangover has forced him to seek refuge in bed. I'll take his coffee later, when the morning is underway and he's had a chance to ingest painkillers.

The tequila shot last night wasn't a brilliant idea. But painting the piano is.

So, what do I paint?

I'm grateful for the bright tester pots of colour surrounding me. I bought them months ago, when I was debating which colour to paint the walls of the courtyard. In the end, I opted for a soft yellow, the colour of rock samphire flowers that edge the cliff path around the Island in late summer. Which I love. But the unused tester pots have watched me from their box on the shelf behind the counter ever since, as if seeking their time to shine.

This is their moment.

But what shall I paint?

I have an hour before I have to start the morning jobs in the café, so I need to get started straight away. Seth suggested flowers – in a nod to his beloved Taylor Swift – so that seems as good a place as any to begin. Maybe I'll add more to the design when I've had time to think about it.

I pull a pencil from the messy bun my hair is pinned up in and set to work. I make light strokes on the aged wood back panel of the piano, the marks shining silver where they catch the light. I won't paint it all today, of course, but if I can get the basic design sketched out I'll be happy.

So the outlines of blushing roses and tiny daisies, sea pinks and blue agapanthus begin to appear, my heart lifting with the thought of how they'll look painted in. I picture where I've seen them in St Ives: climbing over walls, covering ancient stones, clinging to wind-tossed cliff paths and leaning against white-washed cottages. Flowers I see every day, colours I never want to take for granted. It's exuberant and freeing, this act of creation on this lovely instrument that's arrived in my life and home. My face aches with the smile I wear. I can't remember when something so trivial, so unimportant to my everyday life, felt so momentous.

It's another unexpected blessing in a week I didn't expect any. And it means so much more than I'll admit to anyone.

Truth is, I didn't just want the piano because it had been abandoned, or because I thought it would make a great addition to my home.

I wanted it because of *him*.

A face from my earliest years, the image faded and cracked with time, like an old photograph passed from pocket to pocket. The person who introduced me to music, to hope, and to the wonder of a piano.

Grant Henderson. The closest person to a father I've ever known.

Last night, long after I'd returned to the café, I searched for him again. It's been a constant thing since I moved into this place – the search saved on my phone with an ever-dwindling list of websites to try. On my own again after an acrimonious divorce, I finally felt free to start looking for him again. My ex always dissuaded me when we were together and the arguments that ensued became too much to risk looking. But now it's something I do almost every day.

Problem is, I'm running out of places to look. So instead, I repeat the same searches in soulless monotony, daring to hope that *this time* I'll have a breakthrough.

Grant was in my life for just over two years. But the change he made to it was seismic.

I grew up in a succession of rented homes around Penzance, the only child of a mother so caught up in her own eddies that she hardly noticed the storms around me. I never knew my father, only that when Mum told him she was pregnant, he gave her a wad of banknotes to travel to Truro for an abortion. Instead she used it to rent a tiny one-bed flat for us. She tried her best in the beginning, I think. But, as the years went by, her own thoughts and needs and demons demanded more of her time than she could ever give to me.

In many ways, I had to be the adult in our family, from a very early age. And that's how it was when Mum met Grant.

He worked in the local bar as a manager, and walked Mum home one night when she'd had too much to drink and his boss wanted her evicted. Grant's kindness struck a chord in Mum, in her battered heart so used to tumbling from one careless handler to the next. They got together very quickly, and Grant moved in three weeks later, bringing two bags, a box of books – and his piano.

That's when everything changed.

I was seven when he arrived. And it was like all my Christmas and birthday presents turned up at once.

I'd heard kids at school talk about their fathers, about weekends spent on the beach or out on the water, about after-school ice creams in the summer and bright, tinsel-strewn adventures at Christmas. And I never understood what any of those things could mean until Grant arrived in my life.

We'd walk along Penzance promenade, shooting the breeze and spotting tiny fish in the bay at high tide; visit the fishmongers in neighbouring Newlyn to score just-caught mackerel to roast over beach fires; and explore the town looking for *pirates in disguise* – Grant's favourite people-watching game, where we'd dream up seaworthy lives for passers-by. And in the evenings, when Mum went to bed early with a hangover or sadness or just a need to get away from the world, Grant would play lullabies and snippets of classical music on his piano.

It was those times I loved most.

I would sit on the old rag rug that followed us from house to house shedding scraps of colour-worn fabric as it went, caught up in the melodies that filled our small living room. The music brought colour and life and so much joy into that cramped space. It transported me to endlessly wide oceans, exciting landscapes and calming vistas. It opened an escape route I'd never found before.

Grant taught me to play, in the final months he was with us, although I didn't know then how close his leaving would be. My favourite of all the pieces he played was 'Time Wears Awa', an old Scottish folk song he would return to when he was working through his repertoire. Loving the tune, I begged him to show me the notes.

Eventually, he relented – as he always did – his broad smile as he taught me the chords and melody still bright whenever I think of him.

But then, without warning, Mum found somebody else.

And Grant had to leave.

He offered to give me the piano, but Mum said she'd hack it to firewood if he did. She wanted him – and all traces of what he'd brought into our lives – gone. And no amount of pleading and tears from me could sway her decision.

On the day he left, I watched from the grubby glass of my bedroom window, knees hugged tight to my chin, world crashing around me, as Grant Henderson wheeled his beloved instrument down the road and out of my life.

It's why I can't touch the keys of this piano now; why its presence is immediately soothing, but its melody is too painful to play.

I know exactly why. If I play it without him, I'm saying goodbye.

I didn't say goodbye when he left, believing, in my own naive way, that not saying it would leave a door open for him to return. To touch the piano keys now feels like slamming that door. I'm not ready to do it – even if the endless dead ends of my ongoing search for Grant suggest it's all in vain.

I work for almost an hour, not wanting to leave. But the clock above the serving counter marks the minutes with its tick, reverberating around the quiet courtyard through the open door to the café.

Ruthie, my café assistant, will be here soon. I have tasks to complete before she arrives, if we want to be ready in time to open at eight a.m.

Reluctantly, I put down my pencil. The sketched design is as complete as I can make it for now. I smile at the promise of the silvery-grey outlines, at the flowers that will soon bloom over the rescued instrument. Over *my* rescued piano.

I like how that sounds.

I gather up the paint pots, cover the piano with the dustsheet and pat its lid before I return to the café.

'You're going to look wonderful,' I say. 'Just you wait and see.'

*

'*What* is *that*?'

My assistant's expression doesn't mirror mine, when I show her my latest find.

'*That* is a piano,' I reply, the very word lifting my heart.

Ruthie edges round the instrument, inspecting it as if it's a dubious relic. 'Where did you dig it up from?'

'I didn't dig it up. Seth and I found it on the street, last night.'

Her pierced eyebrow makes a bid for the courtyard's canopy. 'You and Seth? Was he drunk?'

'Maybe a little.'

'Were you?'

'No!' I place a protective hand on the lid of the old instrument. The wood warms beneath my palm. 'It's serendipity we found it. Kismet.'

'It's a hunk of junk,' she retorts. 'And you're painting it?'

'It'll look good in the courtyard. I thought it could be one of those *Play Me* pianos, like the one we saw in Truro last summer.'

'So we get bombarded by five hundred renditions of "Chopsticks" every day?' Ruthie shakes her head. 'If that happens I'll need a pay rise.'

I offer her a grin. 'If we get more customers, I might be able to afford it.'

My assistant is far from convinced. 'Or they could pay us to *not* play it. Might be a quicker way of making money . . .'

'Oh *shush*,' I return, covering the piano up with the dust-sheet again as if the thick dusty fabric will protect it from her disparaging comments. 'We need to get cracking, or we'll have no customers at all.'

We set about preparing the café for the morning crowd, firing up the coffee machine, refilling sugar pots and placing fresh flowers in little painted jam jars on every table. I put on the café playlist I compiled last week, a laid-back, breezy collection of songs that evoke the spirit of summer. I hope it encourages our customers to linger a little, maybe order another coffee or treat themselves to one of the tempting cakes displayed under glass cloches on the counter.

Or maybe it will just keep Ruthie and me in a summery mood as we serve the seasonal crowds.

Either way, it helps.

No matter how I look at it this morning, things are on the up.

Our first customers are waiting by the door when I flip the CLOSED sign to OPEN. Another promising portent for the season ahead.

'Merryn Rowe, tell me the coffee is ready?' a bright-eyed man pleads as I let him in.

'It is, Jack, and I have a fresh delivery of pain aux raisins that you can be the first to test.'

Jack Dixon gives me the biggest hug, then blushes a little as he steps back. 'Apologies. I just really need coffee and carbs this morning.'

'Bill Brotherson keeping you busy, is he?' I ask, heading behind the counter to prepare his order.

Jack grimaces. 'And then some. Since he started developing the properties on North Terrace the timescales have been shrinking weekly. Not that I'm complaining.'

'Perish the thought.'

The controversial property developer Jack works for has ruffled a fair few feathers in the town before, but his choice of project manager seems to have had surprising effects on his recent developments. A lot of that has to do with Jack, I think. I can't imagine anyone not warming to his laid-back nature and whip-smart humour. If he wasn't happily settled with his girlfriend, I reckon half the town would be queuing up for him – he certainly elicits smiles from my customers whenever he comes here.

'I love the work,' he admits happily. 'But don't tell Bill. He's letting us keep all the period detail, none of his usual demolish-the-lot-and-rebuild rubbish. It's quite a revelation.'

'What have you done to the man?'

'Maybe I'm a good influence on him.' He chuckles. 'Or maybe he's worked out he can sell the places for twice the value of one of his boring *avant-garde* boxes.'

'Sounds more likely.' I pass him an extra-large travel cup of hot, smoky coffee and reach for the pastry tongs. 'So, one of these pastries?'

'Better make it two. No, *three*. Seren and Nessie are popping over at eleven. Ness will skin me alive if she finds out I had one of these without her.'

The mention of Jack's family warms my heart. He was widowed a few years ago, leaving him caring for his young daughter, Nessie. Then he met Seren McArthur – one of the loveliest people in this town – and the way they met is the stuff of local legend. Seaglass stars made over on Gwithian Beach, each of them making and completing them without knowing the identity of the other . . . It's beautiful. And now they're happier than I've ever seen them.

A familiar pang of loss sneaks in while I'm not looking.

I hate when my heart does that.

I don't begrudge anyone a moment's happiness. But when I think of seaglass, I remember another meeting, five years ago, down at the water's edge on Harbour Beach. Two hands reaching for the same beautiful piece of deep blue, sea-smoothed glass, half-hidden in the tumble of seaweed and tideline shingle. A shared look of surprise that quickly became something else . . .

No. I'm not revisiting that memory today.

It only leads one way and I'm not travelling there again.

'Three it is,' I say, handing Jack a brown paper bag with the still-warm pastries safe inside.

'You're a lifesaver.' He grins, tapping his card against the reader. 'You still on for the beach clean on Sunday?'

'Wouldn't miss it.'

'Great, I'll tell Seren. Cheers an' gone!'

Ruthie joins me as we watch Jack leave.

'Now *that* is the kind of man you don't kick out of bed for eating pasties.'

'Ruthie!'

She shrugs, unlikely to ever be dissuaded by anything I say. 'Well, where else am I going to get my eye candy? It's slim pickings around here, especially in summer. Unless I shack up with an emmet – and that's never a good plan.'

'Hasn't stopped you before,' I return, ducking to miss the

tea towel she aims at my head. Ruthie's summer flings are well documented, my assistant responsible for shattered hearts right across the south-west and beyond. It's a shame she doesn't seem to notice a certain good-looking surf shop owner, right next door, who has been holding a candle for her for three years . . .

Twenty minutes later, the morning rush begins in earnest. A line of locals awaiting takeaway coffee and pastries, another line of early-rising tourists queuing for tables. It's noisy and bustling and it keeps us on our toes, but it makes the time pass quickly and I'm glad of every sale. Summer is the time all of the businesses in St Ives make the most money – takings that have to sustain us through the quieter months of autumn and winter.

We're not on the main tourist drag, so visitors tend to stumble across us as they're exploring the winding backstreets of the town, unless they've found us before. I can't imagine how manic the coffee shops and bars are on Wharf Road this morning, the harbour-front attracting the lion's share of visitors and day-trippers. Once again, I'm glad I could never have afforded to set up a business there. It's beautiful, and the view across the harbour is the iconic St Ives setting, but in the summer it's a never-ending crush of jostling, impatient holidaymakers. I don't think my new business would have survived its first year, let alone made it to its third, as we have here.

At half past ten there's a lull in the queues, so I fill a large cup with a three-shot coffee, tip two packets of brown sugar into it and turn to my assistant.

'I'm just nipping out for five minutes.'

'Is that for His Nibs?' she asks, knowing me too well.

'I think he might need it.'

'It'll take more than a three-shot Americano to sort Seth Hartley out,' Ruthie observes, dismissing me with a wave of her order pad. 'Go. Attend to the poor lamb. I'm good here.'

'Cheers, lovely. Back soon.'

I leave her serving a young family with her famous loaded milkshakes, their gasps of delight the loveliest sound as I walk out of the café.

Porthia Surf is busy next door, its rainbow of surfboards and bodyboards flanking the entrance attracting the attention of a group of damp-haired, barefooted teens, fresh off the beach. T-shirts and wetsuits dance in the gentle morning breeze from their hooks across the shop's bay windows and rows of beach shoes, buckets, spades and crabbing reels line the boundary between the shopfront and the pavement. A line of sand leads from the *Surf's Up!* doormat into the heart of the shop, as it does in most of the businesses in town. Running a business here is a constant battle with beach sand carried in on the shoes and bare feet of visitors.

There's no sign of Seth when I enter, blinking in the low light of the shop after the brightness of outside. Behind the vintage surfboard-topped counter, a young man with a veil of dark hair raises a hand.

'Hey, M. Medicine run?'

I smile as I approach, holding the coffee cup aloft. 'As always, Flynn. How bad is it?'

'*Monumental*, dude. What did you let him drink last night?'

'Tequila. Which wasn't my idea.'

'Never is when Seth's involved.'

'Where is he?'

'In the back,' Flynn Rawlins replies, miming quotation marks in the air with the index and middle fingers of both hands, '*stocktaking*.'

'Ah.' It's worse than I expected. 'I'd better get this to him.'

'Please. Because if he doesn't stop growling soon, he'll scare our customers away.'

Stocktaking, it turns out, entails a row of boxes pulled together with a foam bodyboard laid on top, upon which a softly moaning Seth Hartley is currently lying.

'Coffee,' I whisper, stifling a grin at the groan he makes in reply.

'I hate my *head* . . .'

'Come on, you poor thing. Get up.'

'I can't.'

'Well, if you want this magical elixir that will solve all your ills, you'll have to.'

'You sound like my mum.'

'I'll take that as a compliment.'

I watch him struggle upright, then gently deliver the travel cup to his grateful hands. As he takes a sip, I sit beside him on the boogie board bed.

'I started painting the piano.'

Eyes screwed tight against the pain, Seth manages something between a smile and a grimace 'You did?'

'Sketching the design, at least. I think it's going to look amazing.'

'What did you go for?'

'Flowers, mostly. So a certain surf-shop Swiftie would be happy.'

'Aww.' He leans his head against my shoulder. 'I love you. Did you know?'

'You only love me for my coffee.'

'This mornin', yes. But for lots of other reasons when my head isn't trying to murder me.' He opens one eye to look at his cup. 'This is amazin', Mer. Thank you.'

'My pleasure. I'd better get back – I've left Ruthie on her own.'

'How is the lovely Ruthie this mornin'?'

'As *Ruthie* as she always is. And still single. . .'

He winces at the mention of it. 'I know what you're gettin' at, Mer, but I can't even think of it while my head's murderous.'

'It'll keep,' I concede, with a smile. 'I should get going, anyway.'

'Busy day?'

'Very. You?'

He winces when he tries to laugh. 'I wouldn't know. Flynn's pretty much run things this mornin'. Did you know he's leavin' soon?'

'At lunchtime?'

'No, leavin' this place. For good.'

This is a surprise. Flynn's been Seth's right-hand man for four years since he finished his college course. He started as a Saturday kid on his sixteenth birthday and never really left. 'Where's he going?'

'Surf comps.' The face Seth pulls tells me exactly what his opinion of Flynn's career choice is. 'I've told him it's a mug's game, but his heart is set.'

I've watched Flynn competing in the local surf meets at Porthmeor and Gwithian. He's good, whatever Seth says. According to Flynn's mum, he's been on a board pretty much since he started walking. Kids round here do that, the surf school on Porthmeor Beach a regular haunt for hordes of young surfers.

If I'd grown up in the town, instead of Penzance, I would have loved to go to a surf club. Problem was, my mum hated the water and did her level best to keep me away from it, too.

'He'll be great at that,' I offer, despite Seth's pained eye-roll. 'He *will*.'

'Maybe. I'm just so used to him bein' here. He knows the shop better than I do, can sell boards to anyone. What am I goin' to do without him?'

'Maybe *not* drink tequila on a school night?'

He groans again. 'You're not helpin'.'

'As long as the coffee is, that's all that matters.' I stand and pat his shoulder. 'I'm going to do more piano painting this evening, after I finish for the day, if you fancy it?'

'Yeah, go on.'

'Cheers.'

'Pleasure, bird. And anyway, if I'm helpin' you I can't be repeatin' past sins at the bar, can I? Besides, it'll give me a chance to bend your ear about the evenin' openings again.'

Of course it will. Even with a hangover from hell, Seth won't let me off the hook.

I leave him nursing his coffee and say goodbye to Flynn on my way out.

I don't mind Seth nagging me: evening hours are something I've thought a lot about. It makes sense. I think I just need a push to make it happen.

And if we can use the piano as a centrepiece, maybe it could attract diners in. Another reason its arrival in my life is serendipitous.

My café is sparkling in the mid-morning sunshine that's finally broken through the cloud. I pause for a moment on the pavement, gazing up at it. I like how positive everything feels today. I want to bottle this feeling, so I can dole it out on days when the clouds don't break and the customers don't arrive.

I've waited too long to have a day like this. I'm determined to enjoy it for as long as I can.

Seeing Ruthie beckoning me urgently through the window, I treat myself to one last inhale of the sweet, salty air before I head inside.

Four

ZACH

Kieran Macklin is watching me like a seagull eyeing a pasty.

It's unnerving.

But the tiny studio apartment is perfect.

I take my time looking around, which, to be honest, hardly requires any time at all. Like Aggie said, it's a room off Kieran's photo studio with a bed and an old wooden chest that serves as a bedside table, a storage space for clothes and a lampstand. There's a loo and a washbasin in an alcove behind a sliding door in the far wall. In the studio itself is a squashy orange velvet sofa that appears to have been sat on by the entire population of St Ives, and a dusty flatscreen TV fixed to the wall opposite. Behind the sofa is a run of three kitchen units, one with a microwave on it, one with a kettle and a toaster and the last one with a single-ring electric hob. The shower is outside in the yard, shielded from view by an L-shaped brick enclosure.

But it might as well be a suite of state rooms at The Ritz for what it means for me.

That's if I pass the Kieran Macklin Test.

Which, considering the way he's scowling at me, feels like a bloody big *if* . . .

'If an overnight job comes in for me you'll have to keep out of the way,' Kieran says, watching my slow navigation of his studio.

'Of course.'

'And you'd act as night security for this place.'

'Happy to.'

'I mean the kit in here is worth tens of thousands.'

'It looks great, man.'

'. . . Which you're not to touch. *Ever.*' He winces as an elbow connects sharply with his ribs.

'As if he's likely to,' Aggie returns, scowling at her partner. 'Admit it, Kier, you need him. When these nippers are here, you can't go off workin' all hours. We'll need you at home.'

That sounds a lot more threatening than Aggie thinks it does.

I hide my smile. I can't stuff up this interview. It's this place or sleeping on the beach.

'I'll stay out of your way,' I assure him. 'You won't even know I'm here. And I'll make sure the studio is safe. Honestly, man, you'd be doing me a huge favour.'

Aggie glares at Kieran.

I hold my breath and try not to look like I'm desperate.

Kieran groans. 'Okay. You can move in tomorrow and we'll review as we go.'

'He'll move in *now* and we'll bring him dinner later to celebrate,' Aggie corrects, a terrifying edge to her voice. I've never wanted to get on the wrong side of her in all the years we've been friends; to do it when she's eight-and-a-quarter-months pregnant would be fatal. 'Right, darlin'?'

'I was going to suggest that,' he bristles.

'Aw, ain't he a babe, Zachy?' Aggie purrs, stroking Kieran's hair like he's her favourite kitten. 'Our little 'uns are goin' to have the best daddy.'

Kieran flushes, his smile tighter than a sail at full tilt.

I don't dare exhale until they're outside.

I look down at the scuffed rucksack at my feet, containing the only belongings I have to move in. For a while I hated that I could carry everything I owned on my back. I grieved the stuff I had back in my flat in Padstow, the possessions I had to surrender when I lost the means to pay my rent. But the more I've moved around since I left the surfing circuit – and the more sofas I've crashed on – the more relieved I am not to be burdened by it all.

It's just *stuff*. The things you tell yourself you'd never manage without, which quickly become costly millstones around your neck when you no longer have anywhere to put them. I miss my books. I miss my camera. I miss music. I miss all the photos from years of competition that I just binned because I couldn't drag them all around with me. But when you're hungry and you need somewhere to sleep, things like that become meaningless.

I still have my memories, and they don't require living space.

All the same, my scuffed red rucksack looks pathetically small here.

I look around my new digs.

I can make this work. As long as Aggie stops Kieran from killing me.

Talking of work, now I have a place to crash, I need to find a way of making money. Aggie might have persuaded her partner not to charge me rent for this place, but I still have to eat.

I join them in the car park outside the studio and accept

a set of keys and a lukewarm handshake from Kieran. Then I head into St Ives, determined to find somewhere that can use my services. As I walk, I make a mental list of places to try: bars along Wharf Road that sometimes need casual staff, a couple of newer beach goods shops that might be looking for help and a handful of surf shops that might appreciate my skills.

The thought of working so closely with the kit I used every day isn't easy, but I'll take what I can get. And surfing is the one thing I really know anything about. Maybe my experience will swing it for me.

I work my way through potential places, getting the same refusals in varying shades of politeness. It's the wrong time to be looking, the summer season jobs long since doled out. The story is the same, everywhere I go. *We filled the positions a month ago . . . We're fully staffed till September . . . Come back in October when the season ends?*

I can't wait until then.

I meet a former surfing mate standing outside Cornish Bakery with a plate of pasty samples, and enjoy a few while we briefly natter. He sneaks me a *buy one, get one free* discount card when his boss isn't looking, but even with that the change in my pocket barely covers the treat.

Stuff it, I'm hungry. I haven't eaten since Aggie blessed me with breakfast. At least I know I have dinner tonight. I can't remember the last time I had three meals in one day.

I'd better make the most of it, though, because the search for a job is not looking good.

After I've exhausted the main shopping areas, I have to think outside the box. The tiny indoor market proves fruitless; the bloke in the cinema just laughs when I ask; and the shops in Cyril Noall Square's cobbled courtyard are too tiny to need anyone else.

Why did I ever think this would work?

Despondent and suddenly bone-tired, I start to retrace my steps. Maybe if I can grab a couple of hours' sleep at the studio, I'll be able to think more clearly.

The crowds have swelled in the time I've been job-hunting, swarming over the roads and holding up frazzled motorists daring to drive down to the harbour. The noise and clamour is too much for my weary brain to process, so I decide to be more creative in my homeward journey.

I wind through the backstreets, taking a zig-zag route that runs parallel to the busier roads. It's one blessing of knowing the geography of the town – no matter how packed the most popular streets are, you can always find a way around them. Narrow flights of stone steps that sneak off from the crowds, tiny alleyways snaking between rows of whitewashed former fishermen's cottages, half-cobbled backstreets that pass unnoticed behind the more popular parts of town – all of these are your friends if you know where to find them.

'Excuse me.'

I look up to see a woman, inches from me. I've wandered into her path, too busy looking up at the buildings that line the narrow street to notice her approach. She's wearing a sea-green apron, a striped orange and white T-shirt and pale blue jeans cut off at the knee beneath it. A brass star suspended from a black leather lace catches the light where it rests on her collarbone. It has a swirl like a sea eddy at its centre. Her hair is scooped up into a messy bun at the back of her head, the way my sister Elowen fixes hers up when she's working. The sight of that makes me think of family – of *home*: something I've missed since we lost Mum.

'Sorry,' I rush, raising my hands in apology.

I move to my left, but so does she; a move to my right is mirrored, too. Embarrassed, I take another step left and sweep my hand out in invitation. 'After you.'

Instead of pushing past immediately, she smiles at me.

It's like the sun coming out.

It's totally unexpected, and it steals the breath from my body.

Her dark eyes shine as she draws level with me. 'Thanks for the dance.'

'I – you're welcome . . .' I manage.

And then she's gone. I'm left gawping after her like a gormless fish in her wake.

Proof, I guess, that this town always has the capacity to surprise you.

I turn back – shaken but buzzing – and notice an archway ahead, leading to a small courtyard. Drawn by its colour, I walk towards it.

A stack of brightly coloured surfboards outside a bay-windowed shop comes into view. Porthia Surf – have I seen it before? Shops change so quickly in St Ives, often replaced by almost identical businesses, so it isn't easy to tell. This one looks promising, though, and the sight of the boards is so lovely that I can't resist heading in.

The place is busy, a mix of holidaymakers and local kids out of school for the summer wandering around the clothing racks and shelves. It's what I love most about surf shops: the universal appeal. Whether or not any of the tourists buying brightly coloured branded surf-wear and bodyboards will ever make it out onto the water is immaterial. It's all about the dream. People from all walks of life come here, sit on the clotted-cream-fudge-coloured sand of Porthmeor Beach watching the bods out on the waves, and think: *I could do that*.

And here's the bonus: if they can't *do that*, they can still look like a surfer in the right gear. Available to everyone, for the right price.

I think back to when I got my first sponsorship deal with a Cornwall-based surf brand. Their stuff was amazing, the kind of thing I'd lusted over in surf shops for years. Wearing it at competition meets and swaggering around town was the best feeling.

I still have the first hoodie they gave me, with a unique back print that marked me out as their pro surfer. My name over the design and everything. I don't wear it out much now. Only if I'm on the beach first thing or if it's cold where I'm crashing. I don't want people to know I'm . . .

'Zach Trevelyan!' A shout sounds, making me jump. 'Bleddy legend!'

No, not now . . .

Amused glances from the browsing shoppers greet me as I search for the source of the call. Is it someone I know? I don't recognise the voice, but I've been out of the loop for a while and it's scary how quickly I've forgotten people.

A young, impressively muscled bloke with a shoulder-length mop of dark hair, wearing ocean-print board shorts, a bright orange vest and scuffed Havaianas, lopes towards me, offering me his fist to bump.

'Hi,' I say, praying to St Ia that this guy tells me his name. My memory isn't the greatest at the best of times – *all that seawater sloshing around up there*, Mum used to say – but after the whirlwind of events today I haven't a hope of recall.

'I watched you on the circuit for years, man,' the guy rushes. 'I can't believe you're here!'

'Good to meet you . . . ?' I reply, hoping he'll fill the gap.

'S-sorry, Flynn. Flynn Rawlins? I'm a massive fan.'

'Well, cheers, Flynn.'

'So what brings you to St Ives? You doing a masterclass down the surf school?'

'Er, no, I . . .'

'. . . Cos, *oh my life*, what I'd give to be part of that.'

Customers are watching now, their interest piqued by Flynn's fulsome praise. Months ago, I would have loved this. But today it makes my toes bunch in my sneakers. He thinks I'm here to teach, or compete. He doesn't know I'm off the circuit. And somehow, I have to ask this bright-eyed, starstruck young dude for a job because I have no money. It makes everything a million times worse.

'No, just hanging out, you know.'

Flynn nods excitedly. 'Yeah, I get it. Checking out the competition, right? And the girls . . .'

My attempt at laughter comes out like a strained squeak, stress hissing in my ears.

'Just trying to relax, brother.'

'Yeah, yeah, totally. Hey, my boss is out back. He'll be stoked you're here! Surf ledge in our shop? Manic! Wait here – I'll go get him . . .'

Before I can reply, he's racing through the shop to an open doorway behind the counter.

This is a disaster. He's going to drag his boss out and then

I'll have to tell both of them that not only am I no longer a surf pro but I'm also on the scrounge for work. Worse still, the commotion Flynn has caused means there's now an audience gathering, one of whom is fiddling with their phone like they're about to take a photo . . .

This was a mistake. I can't ask for a job here. I just can't. Not after the rejection I've had today. I'd rather go and leave this kid believing one of his surf heroes is still out there, doing his thing.

I hurry back outside, the murmurs of the shoppers rising behind me like an ocean swell. I pull the peak of my cap low over my eyes, not wanting to attract any further attention. But the street is suddenly crammed with people – a German tour party with cameras and guidebooks and rucksacks, their frazzled-looking tour guide doing her best to steer them over the cobbles. I can't get past them – and now I can hear the young guy from Porthia Surf calling my name.

In desperation, I turn to the next shop. There's what looks like a side passage between it and the surf shop building, its entrance under an arching honeysuckle and ivy canopy, its gate open. I could duck down there, but I don't know how far it goes and whether it leads to a dead end or not. If I try to hide there, I might be found.

Instead, I make for the entrance to the shop itself, slamming the door behind me.

The scent of fresh coffee and sweet pastries immediately greets me, the hum of conversation blocking out the sounds from the street.

A tiny café.

It's packed, every table occupied and a line of four people queuing for takeaway food and drink. There's no room for me to hide anywhere and precious little room to even stand. If I wait here, I'll be blocking the entrance and will be discovered the moment someone tries to come in.

I look back through the glass panels of the door to see the kid from the surf shop and a taller, broader bloke with a riot of red curls and a scowl like he's battling a headache, peering around the slow-moving tour party.

Looking for me.

I can't leave. I can't stay. I'm stuck here, by the door, in a café I never intended to visit.

'All right, lover?'

A young woman behind the counter is grinning at me. She has a ring in her eyebrow, rainbow-tipped hair in kooky-looking bunches and a spectacular tattoo of a gecko walking up her left forearm.

'Hi, I'm not . . .'

'We're rammed in here, soz, but if it's a table for one you're after, there's a little 'un in the courtyard?' She jabs her thumb towards the back of the café, where an arched door is open, bright sunlight streaming in from outside.

'Zach? Zach Trevelyan?'

They're calling my name beyond the glass. It sounds closer now, as if they might be approaching the café . . .

'Yeah, cheers,' I reply, a plan rapidly forming.

I've less than two quid in my pocket – not enough to afford even a cup of tea in this place, judging by the prices on the hand-chalked menu board above the counter – but if they're busy they might not get to me for a while. I can hunker at a table out in the courtyard for ten minutes till the coast is clear, then escape down the greenery-covered side passage I just saw.

I edge around the busy tables towards the warm glow of daylight, stepping out into the sweet little courtyard. The tables are occupied here, too, save for a small, round bistro-style table with a single wrought-iron chair tucked underneath, beside a large object covered with what looks like a dustsheet. Cosy is not the word for it – and navigating the limited space with my long legs is a task in itself. Being six feet three inches tall has its advantages, but is a distinct disadvantage when attempting to fit in enclosed spaces.

It would help if the bulky *thing* beside the table wasn't here, jabbing into my leg.

What is it, anyway?

I catch the edge of its paint-splattered covering with my foot and edge it aside, revealing a dusty castor and an elegantly shaped panel of wood. Glancing up at the rest of its shape beneath the sheet, realisation dawns.

A piano.

Old, admittedly. Past its prime, most definitely. But unmistakable.

My heart contracts as I let the sheet fall back into place.

It isn't like mine – not the one I used to have. That was the colour of clotted cream, pale wood with a mother-of-pearl inlay of flowers across its front. But the ache this piano brings is the same I've felt whenever I've seen one in a bar or a restaurant, or in the window of a house I pass in the street.

I've learned to deal with the loss of my Padstow flat. But giving up my piano was the hardest thing. I'd had it for years, inherited from my aunt who went off travelling the world in her sixties and ended up settling in Australia. She'd been a music teacher all her life and she taught me from the age of six. And while I was often away competing, the piano was always waiting for me when I got home, the first thing I did after chucking my bags on the floor. Sit down. Play something. Feel the knots and the tension and the aches from my battered body melting away . . .

Does this piano play?

I wonder what it sounds like – its *voice*, as Auntie Sue always called it.

Every piano and every human has their own unique voice, Zachary. The magic is when one meets the other. A love match of keys and vocals, tone and breath. Find that, and you'll never feel alone.

Her memory summons a bittersweet smile. I wonder what Sue would make of this piano. Did it ever find its love match?

It's in a pretty sorry state, judging by the part of it I've seen. And the paint-stained dustsheet is hardly adequate protection for it out here, where the canopy overhead provides little shelter from the elements on the courtyard's two open sides.

Maybe it's a relic from the business that occupied this space before?

It could be.

The café looks pretty established, though. Usually you can tell if a business is new in this town, the smell of fresh paint and furniture polish a dead giveaway. Not here.

The piano might not even play. Some of the businesses in St Ives love the shabby-chic look, with old and antique furniture repurposed to add to the aesthetic. I remember one neighbourhood acquaintance whose grandfather took out all the inner workings of an old piano and installed a sound system inside instead. Auntie Sue never forgave them. The thought of such vandalism chills my skin even now, but could this piano have suffered a similar fate?

Whatever the truth – and despite the way the instrument encroaches on the little available space I have – its presence calms me. I'd never admit this aloud, of course, but it's almost as if I'm not here alone.

Daft, I know.

But I'll take it.

If Auntie Sue is watching, I reckon she'll be impressed with me.

'O-kay, what can I get you?' The woman from the counter is beside my table, arriving like a silent ninja. How did she do that? And how has she got here so quickly when there were so many customers before me waiting to be served?

'I – um – I don't have a menu,' I reply, warmth spreading up the back of my neck.

The woman hefts a sigh and turns to the next table. 'Mind if I borrow this, lovers? Cheers.' She swings back to my table and offers me the menu. The prices swim in my vision.

'Just a tea, please,' I manage, squashing down the panic that rises inside. I don't have enough change to buy this and I can't risk using my credit card, either.

'Mug or a pot?'

Which will delay her longest? I just need five minutes.

'Pot, please. And a biscuit plate,' I add, glancing at the list of options on the menu.

She scribbles my order on her notebook and blesses me with a harassed smile.

'Right y'are. Might be a few, okay?'

'You on your own today?' I ask, hoping that prolonging the

conversation will buy enough time for Flynn and his grizzled-looking employer to abandon their search.

'My boss is due back any mo.' She rolls her eyes. 'Milk delivery was wrong again this morning, so she's legged it to the Co-op.'

'Busy day, huh?'

'Busy *month*. Not that I'm complainin', mind. But these emmets . . .' She blesses the neighbouring table with a beatific smile as if she hasn't just insulted them, then lowers her voice. 'I swear they hide in the street, waitin' till one of us leaves before they all pile in.'

'Keeps the town going, though,' I reply, the standard cover-all statement that accompanies every business owner's moans about the stupidly busy high season. *Cornish optimism*, Mum called it: *like pessimism with a smile at the end.*

Everyone in St Ives and the other harbour towns and villages dotting the Cornish coastline accepts that tourists are essential for the economy, even if the summer months see more visitors than the local infrastructure can ever hope to cope with. But it still feels like we lose something for them being here. The town isn't ours until the winter months, the houses priced so high due to the holiday home market that local people haven't a hope of ever affording property, and we're essentially barred from the beaches, bars and streets while the visitors occupy them.

'Definitely that.' She gives me a cheeky smile, which makes what I'm about to do feel evil. 'Sit tight and I'll bring it over.'

I wait until she's woven her way back around the maze of tables and diners, then make myself stay at the mosaic-topped table for another couple of minutes before I slide out from my chair. As I do so, my hand bumps the covered lid of the piano, a faintly metallic sigh sounding from the internal strings in reply.

For a moment, I'm tempted to stay, beside this lovely old thing.

But then I see the young woman loading a pot onto a tray. Panic firing through me, I duck through the gap that leads to the side passage and hurry down it. I daren't risk looking back as I dash out onto the street, pushing and dodging my way back past the surf shop and on to Tregenna Hill. I don't stop running until I reach the summit, where the road snakes away up towards Tregenna Castle. Instead of following its upward trajectory, I take the small road leading down to the train station car park and the steps beyond to the beach.

It's only when I reach the lush gardens that border Porthminster Beach that I allow myself to slow, my lungs burning from my escape.

She'll be back at the table now, cursing the tall guy who legged it.

Maybe she'll tell her boss.

I'll just be one more rude, entitled git who thinks he owns St Ives and can treat those working in the town's businesses with contempt. She'll forget the joke and the cheeky smile and the moment of connection that proved I wasn't an emmet.

But am I one of them now?

No permanent abode here, only finding somewhere to live until I exhaust Aggie and Kieran's generosity, as I seem to have done with everyone else who's helped me out.

No. I can't think like that. Today is a good day, despite what the young woman in the tiny courtyard café thinks of me. If I don't celebrate the good stuff, I'll be lost.

I walk along the path through the gardens until it becomes sand. Porthminster is rammed as always, the beautiful stretch of pale gold beach forever a draw to anyone who visits St Ives. Bodies are clamouring for space, stakes claimed in tiny kingdoms from here to the sea. I kick off my sneakers and stalk barefoot across the warm sand, skirting towels and tents and old-fashioned stripy windbreaks, ignoring them all.

The ocean is cold when I reach the water's edge, the gentle lap of waves over my feet a reminder of everything I love. The sea is where I work it all out, my body small and insignificant in the vastness of the water and my problems brought into wide perspective. I wade in until I'm up to my knees, the shouts and laughter and delighted squeals of holidaymakers around me fading into the insistent, ever-present rumble of the waves.

In the sea I find myself, and what makes me who I am. That hasn't changed.

The sea and me are as present now as we ever were. I'm anchored here. It's where I belong.

And I have a place to sleep tonight. And food later.

I just need to work out the rest.

Five

MERRYN

'A pot of tea. A whole bleddy pot! *And* a plate of biscuits.'

Hours after the incident in question, Ruthie is still furious. I returned from my emergency dash to buy more milk to find her fuming behind the counter. Even an extra-long break and the last two slices of our Carthew Chocolate Cake haven't pacified her.

'Maybe he had an emergency,' I suggest, upending chairs and sliding the seats onto the café tables.

'Maybe he had a *God complex*.'

'Ruthie . . .'

'Well, what would you call placin' an order and then leggin' it without payin'?'

'Something that just happened. One little blip in a great day of trading.'

'A *little blip*? He didn't pay!'

'He didn't take the stuff, either. So we wasted one pot of tea and two teabags. It's not a big deal.'

My assistant glares back from the coffee machine she's cleaning. 'You're too nice to 'em – that's your problem, Mer.'

'They pay our bills . . .' I offer, but Ruthie is determined to rant.

'They're all the same: think we're some bleddy theme park they can just take for granted. Never think we might have livelihoods that depend on them. Entitled, arrogant emmets!'

'One pot of tea,' I repeat, tuning out my assistant's still-glowing fury. I understand her frustration – in this job the smallest problem can often unlock the floodgates – but dwelling on it achieves nothing.

Besides, I'm determined to hang on to my good mood today. The awkward doh-si-doh I did with the good-looking bloke in the street on my way out to get milk is still amusing me, adding to the buzz I've felt about the piano and my plans for it. He was lovely – a slightly blushing, sandy-haired serendipity in my day, with the bluest eyes I've ever seen . . .

Not that I'll tell Ruthie about him. That one was just for me.

It's another sign that I'm surrounded by hope here. St Ives seems full of it today, despite the crowds. I like the positivity, bright like the summer sun. I'm buzzing with ideas for the piano, too: not only of what I'll paint on it but how it will transform the courtyard with its presence.

A piano is a welcoming thing, its keys inviting anyone and everyone to play. I've seen it in action with the *Play Me* piano Ruthie and I spotted in Truro last summer, near the cathedral. People of all ages, from all walks of life, drawn to the instrument to hear others playing it or have a go themselves. Musical talent didn't matter there: single-fingered tunes, plonky keyboard experiments, shakily remembered melodies and confident, elaborate recitals sat side by side. It was wonderful.

Our piano will bring that same open welcome to everyone who visits Sweet Reverie. I can't wait to see it in action.

I complete my regular routine of end-of-day jobs, until the café is cleaned and ready for tomorrow's trading, and my assistant is standing by the door, ready to leave.

'Are you sure you don't fancy helping me paint the piano?' I ask.

'Safer not to,' she replies with the smallest hint of a smile as she opens the door. 'Mood I'm in the thing would be covered with daggers and skulls.'

Knowing my assistant, this would be a very real possibility . . .

I laugh to myself as I unlock the chain across the stairs and go up to my flat. The soothing sight of my home lifts my heart, as it always does. At first, I was hesitant about living above my business, concerned that the temptation to spend all hours downstairs might be too great, leaving little time for rest. But it's been one of the loveliest decisions I've made. When I'm exhausted after a day's work, having only twelve steps to get home is such a blessing. And while my home is small, with hardly any storage space, and feels crowded with more than one person in it, it's calm, comfortable and always welcoming.

I painted its walls white and chose furnishings in shades of the sea – blues, greens and greys, with a dash of lilac and gorse-flower yellow here and there to remind me of cliff path hues. When I open the old wooden sash windows I hear seagulls and, when there's a lull in their squawking, I can just catch the distant sound of the sea. There's a small wood burner that keeps the place toasty in colder months and the thickly plastered stone walls keep it cool in the summer. Rugs cover the floors, cushions rest on the sofa and rescued armchair, and books nestle in an old bookcase the previous owner abandoned. It's more than a home; it's my sanctuary.

And it arrived at the perfect time. Just like the piano.

Going through a divorce I never saw coming and losing the home I'd invested years in making was a blow I didn't think I'd recover from. But then Seth told me this place was up for rent – falling to bits and unable to keep a tenant for longer than six months – and with his help I secured it.

I'm so glad I took the chance then. Could opening in the evenings be the next step I need? I think I already know the answer, my decision poised at the edge, ready to jump in.

I shower and change into the old clothes I wear for beach cleans and decorating. The dungarees are my favourites, Cornish blue with shiny orange buttons at the side, worn for everything since I left university. The T-shirt underneath is an old band T-shirt that's more holes than shirt now, but so soft after years of washing and wearing that I can't bear to part with it. I chuck a pink and white striped shirt over the top, buttons open and sleeves rolled up, that I found in a St Ives charity shop last year and fell in love with. Then I make tea in my biggest mug and head back down to the café.

It's time to paint the piano.

It's the treat I've promised myself all day, and I can't stop smiling as I collect the paint things on my way to the courtyard. I'm secretly glad Ruthie declined the invitation to join me this evening. Painting the rescued instrument feels like a privilege and I want to make the most of it.

I move a small bistro table and chair aside to gently wheel the piano out into the space between the courtyard and the main café. My sketches from this morning catch the light as

I pull the dustsheet off and pool it around the piano's castors, and my heart lifts again. Hope – that wonderful, much-missed feeling – returns.

I settle at the foot of the instrument and select the first colour to apply. A sage green for the foliage and leaves. I'll add darker green accents later, together with white highlights to look like the flowers are basking in the warm Cornish sun.

My paintbrush pauses centimetres away from the old, time-worn wood. I take a breath, surprised to find it shaky. Once the paint is applied, there's no going back.

The piano we rescued last night is now a firm part of my café. And it sounds strange to admit it, but I feel like this instrument represents the beginning of a new chapter, for my business and for me. I can't explain why, but neither can I deny the feeling.

In the past three years, signs have become important: any move forward worthy of celebration. I started at rock bottom, everything I'd trusted snatched away. Step by faltering step, inch by inch, I've pulled myself up and slowly, painstakingly, rebuilt my life. This feels like another move forward.

I gather up my nerves, steady my hand, and set to work.

The first strokes go on like a dream and soon an hour passes as leaves, stalks and foliage appear. Paint covers the scratches, bumps and chips time has bestowed on the piano, the freshness of colour against the nut-brown wood ultimately satisfying.

'Shop!'

Seth bounds into the courtyard from the side passage I left unlocked in case he decided to join me.

'How's the head?'

'Better.' He grins. 'That thing about three p.m. deadlines for hangovers is surprisingly accurate. How's the masterpiece?'

'Coming on well.'

He rounds the piano and takes a moment to survey my work. 'Lookin' good, bird!'

'Thank you.'

'Welcome. Hungry?'

Now that he mentions it, I am. I didn't have a break at midday, what with the lunch rush, milk emergency and Ruthie's post non-paying customer meltdown. My stomach leaves me in no doubt of its opinion of skipping a meal. 'Very.'

'Good job I took a detour to Jasmine Garden, then.' He holds up a white carrier bag, food container edges jutting out of its sides, crowned with a rolled-top brown paper bag I know will contain freshly made prawn crackers.

'You star!' I rush, leaving the paint things around the piano as I stand.

'Can't have you starvin' for your art.'

We trade grins.

'How much food did you buy?' I ask, amazed at the selection emerging from the takeaway bag that Seth is unpacking on a nearby table.

'I wasn't sure what to get, so I just got everythin' I fancied.'

'How hungry were you?'

He's unapologetic. 'Ravenous. Considerin' my head stopped me eatin' most of the day. And I'm guessin' you skipped lunch today, after your mercy visit to me and the dash out for milk.'

'How do you know about that?'

'Ruthie popped in on her way home. Asked me to feed you.'

God bless my assistant and her pesky care of me. I'm supposed to be her boss, but many times I'm left wondering if she's the one in charge. It's sweet – not that she'd welcome me telling her that.

I make my excuses anyway, feeling like I should. I don't want anyone thinking I can't take care of myself, least of all Seth. 'It was just busy today. I didn't have time.'

'Well, you have time now.' He lifts a chair from one of the tables and swings it down beside the Chinese food feast like a magician producing a rabbit from his hat. 'So *sit*.'

The sight and scent of the food is the only persuasion I need. I thank my lucky stars for friends who watch out for me. In this town, it matters.

Seth joins me and we eat in companiable silence for a while. 'You missed our celebrity shopper today.'

'Oh?'

He helps himself to another tangle of noodles. 'Pro surfer. Just wandered in, apparently. Flynn nearly lost his mind over it.'

'That's a coup for the shop, then.'

'It would have been, if he'd stuck around.'

Sensing a story, I put down my fork. 'Okay, now I need the details.'

'Chap came in, chatted with Flynn, seemed to like the shop, but when Flynn headed into the back to fetch me, the bloke did a runner.'

'Who was he?'

Seth frowns. 'Zach someone-or-other? Can't say I was payin' much attention. My head was too busy killin' me to focus. Flynn was gutted, though. Bloke's a bit of a hero of his, apparently, huge on the pro-surf circuit. I couldn't get more than three words out of him for the rest of the day.'

I think about my assistant and how nice it would be if she

decided to go quiet for a shift. 'You're lucky. I had Ruthie bending my ear all afternoon, after . . .' The coincidence hits me. 'We had a disappearing customer, too.'

'What? When?'

'While I was out getting milk. Came in, ordered tea and biscuits, then when Ruthie took it over, he'd gone.'

Seth chuckles. 'Maybe it was the same bloke.'

I laugh too, because what are the odds of that happening? 'Maybe it's just the day for runaway customers.'

'You're probably right.' Seth sits back in his seat, patting his stomach. 'I am *stuffed*, bird. You'd best get me paintin' that instrument before I crash right here.'

So, we set to work. And as petals burst into bloom around the green stalks and leaves I painted before, the piano begins to glow with colour. The visible signs of time and carelessness become invisible, the wood shining between the newly painted features. We're surrounded by possibility, the beauty of what we're creating inspiring new additions to the design. Snaking speedwell flowers and ivy around the piano's base, honeysuckle and lavender creeping around the side of the piano from the mural on its back, with a collection of seashells and a series of curling waves in four shades of blue along the pedal board to mirror the landscape in which it now resides.

I find a small pot of pale gold paint in between the tester pots. I can't remember where it came from, but its discovery brings inspiration. Just above the line of multi-blue waves, I add a tiny golden star with a spiral at its heart.

Seth smiles when he sees it. 'Your star charm? Nice.'

My fingers move to the small brass star at my neck that hangs from a black leather lace. I wear it every day, a link to

61

my past that very few people know. That Seth recognises its importance speaks volumes about how close we are.

I don't tell many people because the reason behind it isn't easy to share. I wear the star with its own chimera at its heart to remind me that I can always escape; that I can find peace above it all. In recent years, it's become my talisman, my tangible proof that better things exist beyond the crises. It represents the escapes I found for myself as a kid whenever dealing with Mum got too much.

The things that saved me then were the sea, the stars and music, wherever I could find them. As a teenager, I would climb out of my bedroom window, head to the beach and watch the stars when I needed to escape. The sound of the sea and the spectacular night sky unhindered by light pollution calmed me, gave me hope, anchored me to the landscape in a way that no birthright could ever do.

So it's fitting that I honour the piano with the star that has guided me to safe harbours, time and again.

My thoughts return to Grant, as they always do, and the search that looks less and less likely to ever bear fruit. Maybe acknowledging it with the star on the piano – both symbols of my childhood – will be enough. Maybe returning the piano's sound to my life, here, in my café, will fill the missing gap I'd hoped the search would.

'This looks so cool.' Seth puts his brush down and scrambles up from the dustsheet to get a better view. 'You know what we need to do now.'

'What?' I put the final touches to the pale gold star and stand beside him. It looks wonderful and the still-bare wood around the design makes the flowers, foliage, shells and waves stand out.

His eyes sparkle despite the heavy smudges of tiredness beneath them. 'Play it.'

'Seth . . .'

But he's grabbed my hand and is pulling me around the piano. 'Come on, it's been here a whole twenty-four hours and we haven't even heard how it sounds in its new home.'

'I don't think we should . . .' I rush, panic building. I know what he's doing, and the heart behind it is admirable. But I can't touch the keys. I've tried and failed every time. Tonight has been so perfect, the happiest I've felt in forever. I don't want anything to spoil it.

He's set a chair beside the painted piano, ready for me to play. And now his free hand is reaching for the lid . . .

'Stop!'

Seth drops my hand in surprise.

The courtyard carries the last reverberation of my shout.

I didn't mean to yell out loud and now I'm backtracking as my best friend stares at me.

'Wasson, Mer?'

'Nothing. I'm sorry, I . . . It's late. We're both dead on our feet. And . . . I think we should let the paint dry first.'

His gaze narrows as he looks between me and the piano. 'We didn't paint the lid.'

'We painted round it. From the side of the piano . . .' Lamely, I point at the few glossy green ivy leaves curling around the edge of the piano, willing him to buy the excuse. 'If we lift the lid, it will rest against the ivy leaves and smudge them.'

'I guess . . .' He's far from convinced, but it's all I can offer. Because how could I ever admit the rest? 'But tomorrow, yeah? We should get the gang over. Christen this baby with beers.'

'Maybe.' Keen to move the conversation to safer ground, I squeeze his arm. 'Come on, it's late and we should be in bed.'

'Bleddy hell, bird! Help you paint a piano and you're invitin' me upstairs?' When I blush, Seth's laugh booms loud around the empty café.

'You should be so lucky.' I'm laughing now, embarrassed but relieved at least to be discussing something else.

'Nah, we'd end up murderin' each other,' he says.

It's true. We've often been mistaken for a couple but I love him like the brother I never had. Besides, I know his heart lies elsewhere.

'Of course, if a certain *someone else* in this café made you an offer . . .'

He reddens on sight. 'Now hang on, Mer . . .'

'I'm just saying, you'll never know if you don't ask her.'

'That's my cue to leave.'

'You and Ruthie would be amazing together,' I rush, knowing exactly what I'm doing.

'Okay, I'm off! Here I go!' As expected, at the mention of his secret crush, Seth blesses me with a swift kiss on my cheek before he dashes out of the café.

When he's gone, a stillness settles. I'm glad of it: exhilarated by the work we've done but exhausted by the barrage of memories and thoughts that have returned tonight. Maybe now the piano is finished and I can reveal it to my customers, it will pacify the ghosts from my past. Perhaps then I can just remember Grant and that brief period of childhood stability and forget the rest that has always accompanied the memory.

Carefully, I wheel the piano to the place I've decided it will live – opposite the entrance from the side passage, leaning against the wall. I shift a few of the courtyard tables around to give it space. It fits like a dream. I knew it would.

Maybe I should open a couple of nights a week. I could certainly use the extra takings, even if I have to pay for more staff to cover the new hours. And seeing the piano in its permanent home makes me want to show it off. An evening opening would lend itself more to musical accompaniment, and if we offered a tapas-style menu it wouldn't be that much of a stretch from what we already serve during the day. If we invite diners to bring their own drinks, too, it could make Sweet Reverie an enticing location for the evening crowd.

I imagine somebody sitting at the piano, some guests gathered around, as I serve small plates of delicious bites inspired by the Mediterranean. On a summer's night, with music and laughter and conversation accompanied by good food, Sweet Reverie could be the perfect place to be.

I'll do some costings tomorrow, maybe mention it to Seth for his input, too.

But not tonight.

Gathering the paint things together, I take one last look at my beautiful, flower-strewn piano in its new place of honour, before I switch off the strings of white lights over the courtyard and head to bed.

Six

ZACH

The first light of the day floods into Kieran's studio, a strip of golden light traversing the white-tiled floor to the chair where I've been sitting since five a.m.

I couldn't sleep: the adrenaline of the day refusing to leave my body, my limbs and mind restless as the night hours dragged past. I found an old Daphne Du Maurier compendium underneath the bed, the kind of thing postal book clubs used to produce, so loved by my gran. It's a chunk of a book, but in the too-quiet, still-unfamiliar surroundings of my latest temporary digs, I found its presence comforting.

Fact is, I'm waiting for things to go wrong.

Twelve months ago, I would have laughed at myself for this. I was always the one with audacious hope, with unwise belief that anything and everything I encountered would work out in my favour. And maybe that ridiculous confidence made the good stuff appear. Because for years I danced around situations that would have made most sane people baulk. The crap I avoided, the near-misses I chalked up – it led my fellow surf buddies to believe I was charmed.

I should have known it would all catch up with me.

I fold the page of *Jamaica Inn* to mark my place and drop the book on the small coffee table beside a potted palm I'm still not certain is real. My eyes ache from lack of sleep. Rubbing them only serves to confirm the fact.

I hit the screen of my phone beside the book, still charging from last night: 7.10 a.m. No point going back to bed now.

Before he left last night, Kieran informed me he has a project to work on this morning and will be in at eight. I should make myself scarce as soon as I can. I know Aggie's twisted his arm to make my staying here possible, but I'm very aware how shaky that particular ground is. Last night, over a takeaway from the wood-fired oven pizza van on the harbour-front, I was aware of Kieran's eyes on me. Aggie might think she's convinced him of my trustworthiness, but I can tell he's far from sold.

When I go to fetch my shoes from the doormat, I find a twenty-pound note folded up inside one of them, a handwritten note around it.

> *Make sure you eat, Z.*
> *And go and ask at Downalong Bakery for*
> *Matt.*
> *Tell him I sent you.*
> *He should have some work to chuck your*
> *way.*
> *A x*

Aggie Keats, my unexpected guardian angel.

That's my first destination of the morning sorted, then, allowing me to kill two birds with one stone. I can grab some breakfast and ask about work. Feeling more positive than I was expecting to, I collect my phone, wallet and keys and leave the studio.

It's a gorgeous morning. Calm, dew-damp and the slightest chill in the air, the already glowing pale-blue sky offering the promise of heat to come. Not many tourists are up yet, so it's one of the rare summer moments when the town feels like it's ours again. Delivery vans are parked on the narrow streets, their orange hazard lights blinking, while the clatter of post trolley wheels and sharp slam of doors echo around the buildings, as the distant cries of gulls rise above it all. I could close my eyes now and know exactly where I was, the unique shape of the town's roads and buildings crafting the air in a way that only they can.

Downalong Bakery is one of the places that's become iconic in town. I don't know the guy who owns it, but I know what a draw the single large display window is to anyone who passes. It's filled with shelf upon shelf of baked delights, from sourdough loaves and pillowy focaccias to traybakes, scones, pasties, trendy twisted cronuts and the largest strawberry meringues I've ever seen. My sister Elowen always says you can put on ten pounds just by gazing in the window. It's one of the three places she heads straight for when she comes back here on holiday – ice cream from Moomaid of Zennor on Street-an-Pol, books from tiny St Ives Bookseller and pretty much whatever she can get her hands on from Downalong Bakery. The Holy Holiday Trinity, she calls it.

I miss her, even though we weren't very close when we were growing up. She's ten years my senior, now running a successful B&B up in Bourton-on-the-Water in the Cotswolds, meaning I don't get to see her often. But that old adage about absence making your heart grow fonder is true for us. When we do manage to get our diaries to align, we have the best time.

She doesn't know how precarious my life has been lately. I prefer it that way. Perhaps when my foundations are less shaky, my job prospects improved and I've worked out what I want for my future, I'll call her. Until then, I have to focus on getting back on my feet.

My stomach grumbles as I watch freshly baked pastries, breads and treats being loaded onto the shelves. The twenty quid in my pocket promises me a feast. I like how that feels. Today already looks brighter than it did at five a.m.

The bakery is open early, as it will be right through the summer, local people visiting on their way to work and the small percentage of early-rising tourists who are in the know making the pilgrimage for baked goods to take back to their swanky holiday cottages for perfectly Instagrammable breakfasts.

I'll order first and ask about work after, I think. At least there isn't a queue yet, although knowing this place and its policy of closing as soon as it's sold the day's baking, it won't be long before there is.

All the same, the prospect of asking for work fills me with dread.

Come on, I chide myself, *just do it.*

I take a breath and walk inside.

The bakery counter is tiny, squeezed into the small space and surrounded by even more shelves of tantalisingly tasty delights. A young woman is serving there, doing her best to stifle her yawns as she attends to the customers ahead of me. I wonder if she's a university or college student working a summer here. Plenty of summer workers in the town are students – that's what makes finding casual work so difficult once the season has begun.

'What can I get you?' she asks, when I reach the counter.

'A rosemary focaccia and a cinnamon bun, please,' I reply. I made my decision only a split second before, opting for the largest things I could see. The cinnamon bun is bigger than my handspan so I'll get at least two meals out of it; the focaccia wide and deep and so moist with olive oil and honey that it will easily last for a couple of days.

She packs them up for me in brown paper bags, the bakery's logo already dotting with grease spots as soon as it comes into contact with the delicious contents. As I'm handing over money and waiting for my change, I seize the moment to ask.

'Is Matt in? Aggie Keats sent me.'

A knowing smile banishes the weariness from her expression. 'Hang on a mo, I'll call him.'

She thrusts the change into my hand and walks to a door at the back of the shop. 'Matt! Aggie's mate's here!'

I offer another silent thank you to the force of nature I'm lucky to call my friend. Has she sorted this for me already before I've even talked to the bakery's owner?

The young server lifts a hatch in the counter. 'Pop through here and wait. He's on his way.'

I smile despite my nerves. My sister is going to lose her mind when I tell her I've stood behind the counter in this hallowed place.

A minute later a huge bear of a bloke strides in. He has an impressive full beard and one arm covered with high-colour tattoos, with muscles that could only have come from kneading as much bread as he does daily. He wears a white T-shirt beneath a flour-dusted dark blue denim apron, with faded grey jeans and a pair of painted Doc Marten boots.

'You must be Zach.' He beams, his handshake almost crushing my hand. 'Come on through.'

I follow him through a low door into the bakery kitchen. Industrial steel preparation tables and baking racks filled with loaves and cakes cram into the small space, the rickety beams overhead revealing the age of the building and somehow making it appear even more magical.

He pulls out a stool at one of the prep tables and invites me to sit. 'Take a load off. Fancy a coffee?'

'Love one, please,' I reply, perching as confidently as I can on the narrow stool.

''Ansum.' He grins and moves to a coffee machine on the far side of the kitchen. Rich, dark coffee is waiting in a percolator jug underneath, which Matt pours into two branded mugs. He hands one to me, then fetches another stool to join me at the table.

'Thanks for seeing me,' I offer, the scent of the coffee and newly baked bread impossibly delicious around me.

'When Aggie's involved, you don't get much choice.'

I grin back. 'Well, cheers for not wanting to upset her.'

'More than my life's worth, upsetting Ms Keats.' He laughs and pulls a notebook and pen from the pocket of his apron. 'Right. Do you have a driving licence?'

Straight in, then.

'Yes.'

'Clean?'

'It is.'

'Ever driven a van?'

'A few, over the years.'

'I need a delivery driver, three days a week. Five a.m. start, working through till midday, maybe an hour the other side if we're busy in the shop. Hourly rate is this . . .' He scribbles a figure on a blank notebook page and swings it round to face me.

It's better than I'd get in any of the bars or shops I visited yesterday.

'That works for me,' I reply, hoping I don't sound too shaky, despite the whole of my body reverberating now.

'Great. Ag says you were a pro surfer?'

'I was. Busted my knee.'

'Harsh, mate.' Matt gives a solemn nod. 'Did it myself for eighteen months. Knackered my ankle, so I feel your pain – literally.'

'Is that what got you into baking?'

'Only other thing I could do.' He takes a swig of coffee – and his mouth must be asbestos-lined because I've already burned my tongue on the morning brew. 'Surfing and sourdough: those were my only two skills. I joined a branch of Kernow Bakery, did a bakery apprenticeship, despite being beardy and about fifteen years older than anyone else on the course. Then I started in my own kitchen, expanded when I took on this place and here we are.'

'Impressive. I really appreciate this.'

'My pleasure. I get the struggle. Besides, if Aggie Keats is vouching for you, I know you've got to be good.'

It's the break I needed. And while three days a week won't be enough by itself, I am so much further down the road to surviving here than I was yesterday. With a job in hand, it might even be easier to find extra shifts to fill the gaps. Employers trust you more when someone else has already taken you on.

Any way I look at it, this is a step up.

'When do I start?' I ask.

'Tomorrow morning, five a.m. sharp. Oh and we've misfires in that basket over there. Goods that aren't quite perfect. They're free for anyone to take, so grab some before you go.'

And the blessings keep coming.

I shake Matt's hand and take the large brown bag he offers me to collect some tasty treats from the not-so-perfect basket. They all look perfect to me, but then I'm hungry and not in charge of a bakery. I think I'm going to like it here.

I leave the bakery and wander slowly through the town, keeping to the narrower streets to deter any beady-eyed seagulls from swooping down on my breakfast. In the small memorial garden beside St Ia's Church near the harbour, I find a bench shielded from passing gulls by the low overhanging branches of a yew tree, and enjoy a celebratory meal, saying hello to Flakey, the legendary white cat who likes to hang out here.

This is perfect. I can take my time now and keep out of Kieran's way while he works in the studio. I still have money and the day is looking like a beautiful one. Maybe I'll head to the beach for a few hours, or visit the surf school to catch up with some mates there. Today is mine now, the need to find work already addressed.

It's going to be a good day.

Seven

MERRYN

The morning rush is so busy I barely have time to catch my breath. Ruthie and I weave and dance around one another as we prepare and serve breakfasts to our café and takeaway customers. The gorgeous scent of coffee and bacon fills the air, while the beep of the card reader and ring of the till are the loveliest sounds to hear.

Every year, I worry that people won't find us at the start of the summer season, that another, newer, shinier coffee shop will lure visitors away. We aren't in the most central place, so many of our customers come here either because of a recommendation or because they stumble upon us while exploring the town. We get a large proportion of locals, too, although mostly at weekends, unless they have family and friends visiting from other parts of the UK.

Judging by the line of customers to the door and the packed café tables this morning, my fears for this season seem to be unfounded.

Already, customers are admiring the piano in the courtyard. It has a *DON'T TOUCH – WET PAINT* sign still propped against its lid, partly to make sure that all the work Seth and I did last night doesn't get smudged, but also because I want its first playing to be at the grand unveiling.

I decided last night that the event where I'll officially welcome the piano to its new home will also be our first evening opening. It will be a good test of how much interest there might be and a soft launch to iron out any niggles before I go for it officially. I haven't told Ruthie or Seth yet, but the knowledge of it fires my heart in the whirlwind of the breakfast rush.

'I'm so glad you're open again this year,' a lady with a baby in a carry sling says, as I'm taking her order. 'So many places we went to last summer have closed.'

'It's always like that here,' I reply, ignoring the shiver of nerves that passes over me. It's the stock answer we all give when asked about the high turnover of businesses in town, but the truth is it's been worse in recent years. Everyone worries about it, even if business is good. The pressure to make money in the holiday season, the ever-rising shop rents and the constant competition are too much for many to bear. I've lost several friends and neighbours who have closed their businesses and moved away. Every year we're open is a blessing, one I'm determined never to take for granted.

'All the same, we're happy to visit you again.' She smiles, the baby stretching one chubby arm out of the sling. 'And with any luck, this one will be visiting for many more!'

Ruthie carries the tray over to the woman's table for her and I turn back to the queue, my smile instantly appearing when I greet the next customer.

'Pot of your finest tea and double toast, please,' Lou Helmsworth booms. He's a bit of a legend in town, a business owner and leader of pretty much every community committee going. If you need something doing, Lou's your best bet of making it happen, even if his constant bluster and tendency to take everything far more seriously than it needs to be makes his involvement both comical and frustrating.

'Lovely to see you, Lou,' I say, filling a large teapot with hot water. 'How's everything?'

He blows out his cheeks. 'Busy, busy. My wife keeps callin' me Lord Lucan because I'm always disappearin'. I hope I can count on you for the beach clean tomorrow?'

'Of course.'

Lou slaps a hand to his heart. 'An angel as ever, Merryn. It's gettin' harder to drag people out for the clean-ups. They're all suddenly busy the moment you ask.'

'Well, I'll be there, and Seth from next door is coming, too.'

'Fabulous. We've even scored a sponsor for it.'

'A sponsor?'

Lou nods happily. 'New bar openin' up over by Harbour Beach. Chap who co-owns it used to be a cub scout when my Margie was a pack leader, way back when. Payin' for the lot, he is – bin bags, proper gloves, litter pickers, fluorescent jackets, the whole shebang!'

'Wow, that's impressive. How did you swing that?'

He beams. 'Never underestimate the power of the Scouts, Merryn. Also it means he gets some good photos for his BookyFace page.'

A snigger sounds behind him as my assistant returns to the counter. 'What about you, Ruthie?'

'Beach clean tomorrow morning,' I prompt, when she looks mystified.

'No fear! Draggin' myself down before dawn to clean up someone else's rubbish? I don't think so.'

Lou's face reddens. 'You see? That's what I'm up against. The attitude of youth . . .'

'No offence, Lou, but some people have better things to do.'

'Better than protectin' the environmental wellbein' of the town?'

Ruthie considers this, then nods. 'Yeah.'

Lou stares blankly back.

'Extra butter on your toast?' I ask, keen to move the conversation along.

'Reckon I'll need it after that.'

I watch Lou drift over to a vacant table, still befuddled by Ruthie's reply, then turn to my assistant.

'What?' she says, clearly unrepentant.

'You could have just said you were busy.'

'And miss the chance to wind up Lou Helmsworth? Not likely!'

The busy period lasts until two-thirty p.m., when there's a lull and we finally get a chance to breathe. Only a few tables are occupied now, the customers there relishing the opportunity to sit down. I don't mind if they take their time over their tea and scones – part of what I love most about my café is its relaxed, welcoming atmosphere. I've worked hard to create a space people want to spend time in – and hopefully return to.

Will the evening openings create the same kind of atmosphere?

Handing Ruthie a steaming mug of tea, I decide to bite the bullet.

'I've been thinking . . .' I begin.

'Always dangerous,' she quips, fast as a whip.

'Funny. No, I've been thinking about opening some evenings.'

My assistant's pierced eyebrow rises. 'Seth finally got to you, has he?'

'He made a lot of sense.'

'That's a first.' Seeing my frown, she relents. 'It's a good idea. We've been sayin' so for ages. How many nights are you goin' to do?'

'Two, to start. Saturday nights and maybe Wednesday evenings?'

She considers this, tapping her nails against her mug. 'Might be confusin' for customers, though. How about Wednesday, Thursday and Friday? Most people round here do those nights. Saturdays are okay, but you'll have a lot of competition from the places on Wharf Road.'

It makes sense, but it takes me a moment to recalibrate the idea I've spent time considering. The fearful side of me insists three nights from the off are too many, the risk too great. But then I think of the possibility of regular customers being drawn here – enjoying the summer under the rows of white lights in the courtyard while candles glow on tables and music from the piano warms the space. The image is impossibly lovely.

It'll be so much work. Exhausting, too. And it could be a drain on finances if people don't come.

'Would you be up for working some of the evening shifts?' I ask, crossing everything that she might be.

'Couldn't do Wednesdays,' she replies. 'Thursdays and Fridays would be okay. But you'll need more staff to cover day shifts. I mean, I love you, Mer, but I'm not doin' a full day and night, too.'

I kick myself for not considering this. 'I'll put a card in the window.'

My assistant hefts a sigh, as if I'm a burden on her soul. 'Window cards are for amateurs. What you need is a *Lou*.'

I follow her nod to the beach clean poster Lou Helmsworth left for us to put up on our noticeboard. 'Brilliant, Ruthie! I'll ask him at the beach clean tomorrow.' I risk a bit of fun. 'Of course, it would be so much easier to broach the subject with him if I had my second-in-command beside me . . .'

Ruthie's smile immediately vanishes. 'Don't push it, boss.'

Oh well, it was worth a try.

But at least I have a firm way forward now: open for three consecutive nights a week to build local support, and recruit the unofficial Eyes and Ears of St Ives to assist me in finding new staff.

For the first time, the evening openings feel like a real possibility. The next brave step for the business I built from nothing. I like how positive that feels.

Onwards and upwards . . .

Eight

ZACH

Kieran takes the news of my new early morning job with surprising positivity, given his gruffness towards me since I moved into the studio. He even jokes about me 'bringing my work home occasionally', meaning sneaking baked goods back to the studio for him. Maybe I should, to keep him onside.

It's a good start, the first step to rebuilding my life. What else might be possible for me?

With the rest of the day mine to spend how I wish, I take a long, lazy walk through town, emerging onto Harbour Road. The tide is out, leaving the harbour a wide, welcoming sweep of pale golden sand and a cluster of boats resting on their sides as if they're enjoying a late morning snooze. It's beautiful, and the vision of the sand glowing in the strengthening sun calls to me like a siren from the sea. I'm powerless to resist, the call of the waves far out beyond Smeaton's Pier a distant thunder drawing me out towards it.

The moment I'm down on the sand and picking my way over the brightly coloured mooring ropes that crisscross the beach, I feel at home. Out here, right now, nobody cares whether I'm a visitor or a local, whether I have a holiday home to return to or am relying on the kindness of friends to keep a roof over my head. I'm just a bloke walking across the rippled sand of a wide, sea-empty harbour. I have no past and no sense of future. I exist right here, right now, in this moment. And for the first time in longer than I can remember, I'm at peace.

The knowledge of this strengthens my spine as I walk towards the sea, the breaking white curls of surf over waves turning turquoise as they curve over the shore so familiar and longed for. I have spent half my life in the sea – probably longer. It's where I work everything out; where life becomes neatly boxed into *pre-surf* and *post-surf.*

I need to get back out there. Soon.

The tide is powerful today. It pummels the wide golden sand beyond the harbour walls. Too uncertain for surfers, though. Too unpredictable. Too much energy that could become your enemy in a heartbeat if you don't pay attention. There's bound to be one or two either inexperienced or daft surfers trying their luck, but that's a mug's game.

'Bleddy Zach Trevelyan!'

A shout to my left makes my heart sink like a rock in the ocean. All I wanted was to be by the sea. But I turn anyway, because there's no escape now unless I wade straight into the waves.

The huge smile that greets me blows away all my concern.

'Jakey! Man, it's good to see you!'

Jakey Lowen greets me with a high hand-grasp, our shoulders bumping together. I haven't seen him for a couple of years, the last time at Boardmasters up on Newquay's Fistral

Beach. We joined the circuit together a few months apart and, while we didn't always compete in the same locations, we invariably ended up hanging out at surf meets across the UK and Europe.

He looks older, of course, the first hint of silver edging the dark waves of his hair where they meet his temples. I wonder how I look to him. Can he see the toll of recent years etched into my skin?

'When did you blow back into town?' he asks.

'Couple of months ago. I've been sofa-surfing with a few mates.'

'Hard times, dude.'

'Yeah, but, you know, I'm getting back on my feet.'

Jakey nods. 'Tough job, but I reckon you'll be okay. Trev the Comeback King can't be kept down for long.'

'Cheers,' I say, cringing a little at the mention of my former nickname, from a time when my surf mates believed I was invincible. 'So what are you up to now?'

'Teaching, over at the surf school.'

I laugh, because he's the absolute last person I ever expected to want to teach kids. Jakey was never one for rules and systems, always carving his own, unconventional path through the waves. 'And they *let* you?'

'Yeah, yeah, laugh it up, Trev. I'm one of their most popular instructors, actually.'

'Heaven help the circuit when your protégés hit it in a few years.'

Jakey bats this away. 'Maybe they'll shake it up a bit. Talking of which, you should come down one lesson. Show the nippers how a real pro does it.'

The old fear instantly returns. 'I don't think so . . .'

'Oh come on, Trev, you'd ace it.' He studies my expression and I will the flood of panic to hide from my face. 'Is this because of your knee?'

Everything is because of my knee. Before the injury that killed my career, I never worried about showing off my skills to anyone, never hesitated to throw myself into situations that scared me. I hate that I can't escape it now. It's why I haven't ventured out with my board since the injury.

'I just don't think I can, okay?'

'You can still surf, though?'

'Yeah, of course.' Can I? I think I can, but unless I get back in the water, how will I ever know?

'So come and hang with us. Doesn't matter if you aren't firing on all cylinders. You love the waves.' He gazes out at the rolling surf, sparkling where the sunlight illuminates the spray above each crest. 'You want to be out there, right?'

You can't kid a surfer. The instinct remains strong, the pull on your heart impossible to fight, even when your body isn't up to the task like it once was.

'Yeah,' I admit. 'I haven't been out for months.' Longer than that, but *months* sounds better.

'So, come hang with me. Soon. We'll get you back out there.' When I seem less than convinced, he grins up at me. 'I teach five-year-olds, Trev. You'll be no challenge.'

It makes me laugh, despite everything else. 'Maybe.'

'Yes! Date in the diary, Zachy-boy! So, what are you doing for work?'

I tell him about the job I've scored at Downalong Bakery – amused when Jakey's eyes glaze over at the thought of *that* window display – and the temporary home I've found in Kieran Macklin's studio. 'I need to find something else, though – and no, not teaching, thank you.'

'We wouldn't take you anyway,' he jokes, laughing when I roll my eyes. 'You should try that new place on the harbour.'

'Which one?'

He looks back at the town and points over towards The Sloop pub and the Aspects Holidays office beyond it. 'The one with the stripes across its hoarding. Can't miss it.'

Sure enough, I see it, beyond the glow from the exposed sand of the harbour. A double length of boarding with a door cut at its centre, the boards painted in alternate Cornish blue and white stripes, like the popular crockery synonymous with the county. A large banner draped across the top of the boards has a message printed on it, but from here I can't see what it says.

Jakey stands by my elbow. 'Going to be a bar and restaurant, apparently. Used to be a gallery with a pub next door. The owners have bought both and are knocking them together.'

'They're not painting the thing blue and white, are they?'

'Not unless they fancy being sued by Cornishware,' Jakey grins. 'They're chucking money around, though. I reckon you could score some shifts there, if that's your thing.'

We turn back to the sea, our conversation drifting back to memories of the surf circuit and the people we competed alongside. It's great to catch up with him. The small glimpse of normality feels like a gift.

When we part – having swapped numbers and promises to hit the waves soon – I stalk back across the sand towards the town. I round the end of Smeaton's Pier and follow its dark grey barnacled stone brickwork towards the arches and the iconic pink house at Kitty's Corner. Then I walk up the stone ramp to the promenade, its upturned rowboats lying in a horizonal guard of honour.

I can see it now, the wording on the banner clear at close quarters.

PENGELLY'S IS COMING TO ST IVES.

NEW BAR & SEAFOOD
RESTAURANT OPENING SOON.

On the rough-cut door in the centre of the striped boards is a smaller sign, handwritten in thick, slanting lines of black pen:

Bar staff and servers required
Flexible shifts available
Apply within.

It's the invitation I need. That and the fact that the makeshift entrance door is already ajar.

I never believed in signs until my life fell apart. Lately, I've been seeking them out. The serendipity of meeting Jakey Lowen after years apart, and his mentioning of this place that I somehow missed on my job-seeking rounds of the town the other day, are too many coincidences to ignore.

Seize the day or whatever you can grab, as Mum used to say.

I kick the sand from my shoes and gingerly push the striped door. It swings open with a creak far older than its years.

It's dark inside. My eyes take a few moments to adjust after the brightness of the beach. When I blink away the ghost-image of Cornish light, I see a half-constructed bar at the centre of the two former buildings, dustsheets covering most of its length. The scar of the old partitioning wall rises up and over it, a newly installed rolled steel joist supporting the weight of the floors above. Dust hangs in the air, catching the back of my throat as I walk in.

I wonder how long it will take to transform this space into a high-spec new bar and restaurant. They don't have long if they want to start their business with the summer trade. But at least if they're a few weeks away, there may still be jobs going.

A man seated by the bar looks up from a roll of plans spread out across its dusty surface.

'Can I help you?'

'Er, yeah. I've come about the jobs?'

'Excellent.' He claps his hands, sending more dust spinning up into the gloomy air, jumping down from his stool and striding across the floor towards me. 'You're our first enquirer.'

'Oh, great. I'm Zach Trevelyan,' I rush, remembering my manners.

When the man reaches me he shakes my hand with considerable grip. 'Luke Pengelly. I'm the co-founder of this place. My business partner, Scott, is out at the moment. Let me find us some chairs and we'll have a chat, yeah?'

I like him immediately, his forthrightness and confidence infectious. We move past the bar into an area that looks like it might soon be a kitchen. It's a world away from the ordered, stainless steel-furnished kitchen at Downalong Bakery, but about three times the size. I imagine when it's complete it will be impressive.

In the centre of the space is a metal garden table and two bistro chairs. A sudden memory of a similar table by a dust-sheet-covered piano and an embarrassing retreat invades my thoughts. I shelve it immediately. This isn't going to be like that. I won't be running away from here. I keep my smile front and centre, hoping Luke can't see the sudden dip in my confidence as we sit.

He shuffles a pile of papers on the pale yellow tabletop. 'O-kay, so . . . A bit about us. We own three successful restaurants across the south-west, employing around seventy-five people. Two of our restaurants are in development as boutique hotels. This one won't be: we're hoping to establish it as our flagship restaurant, hence the large space. I co-owned a restaurant here a few years ago and when it closed – through no fault of the business – I vowed I'd be back when the market was right.' He beams a super-confident smile as I take this in.

He's slick: that much I'm sure of. And he believes in his business empire. Especially so, considering the cost of creating this place in St Ives. He has the kind of unquestioning belief and moxie that I wish I could have. I wonder if he ever doubts anything he's done? Even having history of a failed business in town (whatever he says about that) hasn't dented his self-confidence about returning to try again. Perhaps working alongside him will inspire more of that in me.

If I get the job.

Spiel over, he folds his hands on the stack of papers and looks me dead in the eye. 'But enough about me. Tell me about yourself. Do you have hospitality experience?'

'I've worked in bars, pubs and restaurants since I was sixteen,' I say, which sounds like more of a career path than it actually is. 'I supported myself through college and when I was starting out in the competitive surf scene, until I found a sponsor to be able to compete full-time.'

Luke appears impressed by this – although the smile he seems to wear permanently makes it difficult to gauge any change in his mood. 'A pro surfer? Cool. You still compete?'

It's a valid question but it still stings to hear it. Also, would I really be doorstepping new businesses in town looking for casual work if I were? I brighten my smile to match his. 'No, unfortunately. I suffered a knee injury thirteen months ago. Hence looking for work now.'

He nods – and I give up trying to read his expression. His smile bars everything else. 'Well, we have daytime shifts and night shifts available. Bar work and front-of-house food service. Do you have kitchen experience?'

'Not restaurant-standard,' I admit. 'I've helped prepare meals in smaller cafés and bar snacks in pubs, but I'm not trained.'

'Fair enough. Do you have any references?'

That might be a push, given the number of places I've scored short-term work at over the last five years. 'I can find some for you.'

'Okay. Any preference for day or night?'

Nights would make sense, I think, but then I remember Kieran and his current photography project, for which he needed me to be out of the studio. 'Day shifts, if possible. But I'm happy to consider either,' I add, a jolt of fear demanding a clarification. I don't want anything to dissuade Luke from employing me.

'Any other work or time commitments?'

'I'm working at Downalong Bakery, three mornings a week.'

'Days?'

'Mondays, Thursdays and Saturdays.'

'And what time would that finish?'

'One p.m.,' I reply, thinking of what Matt said about occasionally working an extra hour in the bakery shop if they're busy.

'Probably best to avoid them, then . . .' He flips the papers until he finds what looks like a timesheet, a mostly blank grid with a few names already written in the left-hand column. 'How about we start on three days a week, working behind the bar initially with maybe some lunch service when required? Say, Tuesdays, Wednesdays and Fridays? Then if you're happy and we're happy, we could look into adding more shifts.'

It's perfect. I'll be knackered and my knee will hate me, but that would be work covered most days.

'That works for me,' I say, trying – and probably failing – to keep my cool.

This will keep Kieran happy, will keep me and my brain busy and bring in some decent money. Talking of which . . .

'What's the hourly rate?' I ask, kicking myself that I didn't think to check before now.

'Thirteen pounds per hour.'

That'll do!

'Great. When do you want me to start?'

Luke laughs. 'When we have a restaurant instead of a construction site. We open in three weeks, believe it or not. Throwing everything at it to get it ready – and if there are delays we'll still pay the team for all hours worked in the interim. Even if that's just keeping Scott and me from losing our heads over it all.'

'I reckon I can do that.'

'Great. Let me take your details and we'll be in touch.'

I'm buzzing when I walk away from what will soon be Pengelly's. Today has been a day of good things, none of which I woke up expecting. That's new – and will take some getting used to. I've been firefighting for too long, scrutinising every detail for its potential to kick me.

If this proves to be the turning point, as I hope it will, coming back to St Ives might just be my best decision in months . . .

Nine

MERRYN

We meet on Porthmeor Beach at five a.m., a small but happy band of volunteers bundled up against the Atlantic chill. The weather forecast promises temperatures will rise once the sun is up, but nobody's told Porthmeor that yet. We gather by the large black rocks just opposite the ramp that leads down from the road by Tate St Ives, past the St Ives Surf School building and onto the beach.

When we arrive, Lou is noisily checking items on the clipboard he brandishes like a shield.

'Right, when I say your name, please make yourselves known,' he barks. 'Then we can divvy up the bin bags and grabbers and get crackin'.'

'*Bin bags and Grabbers* – name of my new grunge band,' Seth whispers beside me, causing me to stuff my giggles behind my summer scarf when Lou sends me a sharp look.

It feels like the school trips I remember as a kid, all of us now supplied with fluorescent yellow gilets so we can be seen and being corralled by a stern-faced Lou as best he can. His seriousness, coupled with the early hour, makes the urge to muck about strong. Muffled sniggers and conspiratorial grins pass between the beach clean volunteers while Lou hands us rolls of bin bags, thick red rubber gloves and metal litter pickers – which, of course, instantly become duelling swords and lightsabers, depending upon your weapon of choice.

In the pre-dawn blue the pale sand glows beneath our feet almost as bright as the gilets we wear. The wind whips at our hair, the thunder of the outgoing tide competing with our chatter as we greet one another.

I recognise several of the volunteers – Seth, of course, whose good-natured grumbling looks set to be my constant companion this morning; Aggie Keats, who owns the coffee hut on Porthgwidden Beach and is bustling around despite being very pregnant; Cerrie Austin, a schoolteacher who's always part of Lou's various community initiatives; and Cerrie's boyfriend, Tom, who bears more than a passing resemblance to Thor from the Marvel movies. Jack Dixon is here, too, with his girlfriend Seren and his totally brilliant daughter, Nessie. Despite the early hour, she is full of energy, her dark curls dancing in the wind as she skips around Jack and Seren.

I'm tired after a broken night of sleep, plans and contingencies for the evening openings racing around my brain. I'll ask Lou for his help once the beach clean is underway. The thought of it chills me more than the early morning breeze. But the fun in this group and the potential for hilarity is the perfect antidote to my nerves.

'Now, before you all begin, we need to say a huge thank you to the sponsors of the beach clean this mornin'. In fact, the local business supplyin' all the equipment you're usin' have agreed to sponsor the beach cleans for the rest of the year!'

This is met by genuine applause. We might all poke fun at Lou's officiousness, but we know how hard he works to raise funds for the many community projects he champions. Lou practically sparkles with the reception to his news. He lets the applause last for a while, then raises his clipboard for quiet.

'Thank you, thank you kindly, all. So let's all thank the very generous Scott Mayfield, co-owner of Pengelly's, the brand-new restaurant openin' soon on the harbour . . .'

Applause swells around me, but I'm frozen. Seth isn't clapping, his concerned stare warm against my cheek.

I've seen the construction boards around the former pub overlooking Harbour Beach – painted in Cornish blue and white stripes like the iconic Cornishware pottery; they were impossible to miss. But the business had no name – until Lou confirmed it.

Pengelly's.

It's possible it's a coincidence. But there's only one Pengelly likely to be setting up a restaurant in St Ives.

There used to be two, before I reclaimed my maiden name when my divorce finalised, three years ago.

I feel sick.

'It might not be him,' Seth whispers, glancing at the other beach volunteers who have now started to cotton on.

'Who else could it be?' I hiss back.

Last I heard, Luke Pengelly was opening a licensed restaurant in Falmouth, with the intention of developing the entire building in which it was housed into a boutique hotel. He planned to then repeat the development with properties in Sennen Cove and St Just. Why deviate from that plan to come back here?

Especially after what happened.

The last time I saw my ex-husband was to sign the final settlement papers of our divorce. That day he made no secret of his dislike of St Ives and his hurry to be out of the town. We met in The Hub overlooking the harbour, our solicitors tucking into their breakfasts while ours went untouched. The restaurant we'd opened together had sold faster than we'd hoped, meaning that funds from the sale could be split at the same time as our divorce was nearing finalisation. My *decree nisi* had arrived that morning and the short sentence declaring the intended dissolution of our three-year marriage had hit me like a speeding train. Dismissing our commitment, our hopes and dreams as mere formalities, the court casting it all away as easily as Luke had. He'd left me for someone else: walking out on our home and our business, leaving me to deal with the emotional and financial fallout, and a furious team of staff finding themselves suddenly unemployed. The money from the sale of the building did little to compensate for the horrific time I'd had dealing with it all.

'Thank you, everyone,' Scott is saying now, his voice almost lost in the strengthening wind from the sea. 'We're happy to help. Pengelly's will be opening in two weeks' time and I hope we can welcome you all for fine dining and the best selection of spirits in St Ives.'

'Says he,' Seth mutters, glancing at a man beside us I recognise from one of the established bars in town. The man catches Seth's eye and shakes his head. No doubt the other bar owners and restaurateurs will have similar reactions, if they've been in St Ives for more than a few years. People here have long memories: they remember the mess Luke Pengelly left in his wake.

'Are you joining us for the beach clean, then, Scott?' one of the volunteers asks, the friendly question edged with the smallest hint of sarcasm.

Lou's smile tightens. I can see what's coming a mile off.

'Scotty has places to be,' he rushes, before Scott can reply. 'We all know the craziness of openin' a new business, right? But I'm sure we'll tempt him down for a future beach clean, right?'

'I mean, we'll do our best.' Scott's nod is less than convincing. 'We'll be doing press, though,' he offers. 'Really getting the word out about the initiative. Rallying the troops and all that.'

'Talkin' of which,' Lou interrupts, 'we should get crackin'. The sun'll be fully up soon and this beach won't clean itself!'

There's a definite atmosphere between the volunteers as we disperse over the beach to begin the clean. Seth joins me without waiting for an invitation and we work in silence for the first few minutes. I know he's biding his time and I'm grateful for the pause it affords me. Because, honestly, my head is a mess. I don't know how to feel about this – about any of it. For the last three years, I've patrolled my mind for thoughts of my ex, clamping down on any I encounter. It does me no good to give them room.

I thought I was free of him, physically at least, when he ended our marriage with so little concern for what we'd had. Knowing St Ives was a safe place, one he'd sworn never to return to, gave me confidence to carve out the new chapter of my life here. And I love the life I've established in this place. I'm proud of what I've achieved, of my café that I founded from bare bones and the community it's created. We aren't just surviving as a business, we're thriving – which is no mean feat given the intense competition and high turnover of businesses here.

But if I have to enter each new day with the possibility of seeing Luke again – and the woman he so easily left me for – it will change everything.

I don't love him anymore. Being kicked to the kerb by someone who had so loudly declared his lifelong commitment was a pretty effective way to kill any love I had left. But I know Luke. He isn't one to hide in the shadows. He'll flaunt his new business and new life for all it's worth, with no thought of how that might make me feel.

'You're overthinkin' it,' Seth says, when we're carrying the first bin bags back to the rocks.

'Am I? He said he was never coming back here.'

'He said a lot of things he reneged on.' It stings, but it's true. 'One thing's for certain: if he sent his lackey down here, it means we won't see him. He's keepin' his head down and with bleddy good reason. Besides, Luke never gets out of bed before eight a.m. I doubt he even knows this time of day exists.'

I love Seth for trying, but my mood is set and no amount of his kind jokes will shift it. I can't believe Lou didn't think to mention the identity of his 'sponsor'. With his near-encyclo-paedic knowledge of everyone and everything in the town, how did he fail to clock the link with the surname? He knew me first as Merryn Pengelly – as most of the traders did in town.

I shudder now at the memory of that name, at the ghost of me who carried it.

'Lou could have warned me.'

'Yes, he could,' Seth concedes. 'But he's been desperate for a sponsor for the beach cleans for months.'

'That doesn't make it okay.' I know I'm being unreasonable now, but I can't see past this. Lou knows me and he knows what I went through when Luke left. 'A word of warning when he came into the café yesterday would have been enough.'

Seth drops the bin bag in the growing pile by the rocks and hands me a new bag. 'Would it, though, Mer?'

I meet his knowing stare with a sigh. 'No.'

We walk slowly away to resume our litter picking, any conversation we might have had stolen by the revelation.

The quietness between us makes me face facts. The truth is, I'm angry with Lou because today was the day I'd planned to ask for his help finding staff for the evening openings. I was so excited to share the news, but the bombshell of Luke being back in town has stolen it. I feel like Luke has robbed me again, and I'm as powerless to prevent it as I was before. When I look at how far I've come in the last three years, I've always measured it by two things: how confident I feel and how much distance I've put between Luke Pengelly and me. This morning, he stamped right back into view, making that achievement as good as nothing.

'I wanted to ask Lou to help me find more staff,' I confess, when my anger has receded a little.

Seth brightens immediately. 'You mean . . . ?'

'Three nights a week, to begin with,' I say, catching the excitement I see in my friend. 'Wednesdays, Thursdays and Fridays, right through the summer.'

'You beauty!' Seth scoops me up in a hug so tight it almost

lifts my feet from the sand. It elicits amused looks from our fellow volunteers as he lifts me bodily and twirls me around. In the middle of the confusion, of the questions I never wanted to consider again, it's a moment of sudden light.

I let him spin us on the sand, welcoming in his excitement like a breath of salt air. And as he does, I make a promise to myself. I'm going to hang on to the celebration of this decision. I won't allow Luke Pengelly – or anyone else – to rob me of it.

'We'll find staff,' Seth says, breathless from his endeavours. 'And I'll work the shifts Ruthie can't do.'

It's a kind offer, but he's already working so hard running the surf shop.

'I can't ask you to do that,' I begin, but Seth won't let me finish.

'That's why I'm offerin'. Come on, Mer, this is going to be amazin'. And you wouldn't be doin' it if it weren't for my naggin'.' There's pure mischief in his smile.

'Is that so?' I take off one of my rubber gloves and brandish it like a missile.

'You know it, babe.' He grins back, pulling off his glove, too. 'Total brains behind the operation, me.'

The game arrives as easy as breathing. I flick my glove against his arm and take off across the beach, laughing when he gives chase, swinging his glove at my back. We duck and weave, sometimes dodging glove slaps, sometimes catching them. Our friends watch with amusement, shouting encouragement to the side they've chosen to root for. It's like we're kids again, kicking out across the line of pebbles and shells left by high tide before dawn. The energy and fun dislodges the hurt from my heart, just as sunlight breaks across the waves beside us.

I have to hold on to this, I decide in that moment, not let fear steal it. The only things Luke Pengelly can grab from me now are the things I let him take. He took my past and five years of my life. I won't allow him to take my future.

Ten

ZACH

Early mornings when you're determined to catch the first waves of the day are easy.

Early mornings when you start work at five a.m., lugging enormous crates of bread and pastries in and out of a van across south-west Cornwall, *hurt*.

My knee hates me.

The rest of my body isn't keen on me, either.

The van is new and drives like a dream, but it's wider than I'm used to. And pre-dawn, narrow, twisty Cornish country roads are pretty scary to navigate in an expensive vehicle belonging to your brand-new employer.

My route follows the coast from St Ives to Carbis Bay and Hayle, then inland to Camborne, and down to Mousehole, Newlyn, Penzance and Marazion in Mount's Bay. A mix of cafés, corner shops, hotels and pubs form my drop-offs. The people are friendly enough – as friendly as anyone is before the sun rises. And the more times I visit, the greater my repertoire of small talk becomes.

I like it. It isn't what I imagined doing with my life, but then none of where I currently find myself is.

A week into my rounds, I start to settle into some kind of routine. I even score a couple of extra shifts – one afternoon serving in the bakery shop and an after-closing run with Matt to deliver unsold bread to a local homeless shelter in Penzance. He seems happy with me and I like what I'm doing.

Kieran's happy, too. Well, as happy as Kieran ever gets where I'm concerned. He comes into the studio to work after I've left for my shift and I stay out until three or four in the afternoon, meaning the most time we spend in the same space is a couple of hours. Aggie checks in regularly, which helps. I'm glad I have her on my side. She was fearsome enough before, but pregnancy has added a whole new level of scariness. Kieran's terrified to cross her and I don't blame him.

It works for now. But when their babies come along and the summer season ends, who knows?

I need to think about what happens next, about what I want this new chapter of my life to look like. I'll save as much as I can this summer and keep thinking as I work. With any luck, I might find the answer before the season is over.

Staying out of the studio on the days I'm not at the bakery means filling as many hours as possible with whatever I can find. I catch a couple of films at the tiny Royal St Ives Cinema in Royal Square, wander the streets of the town as long as my knee allows, or just take a flask and a book and sit on one of St Ives' lovely beaches. On rainy days I make a coffee last as long as possible in Aggie's place on Porthgwidden Beach, then wander slowly back through the town, ducking into shops as I go.

It's Friday today, so no early start at the bakery. And for once this week, the sun is shining. Bored with my usual route around the streets, I choose an alleyway that seems vaguely familiar – and stop dead when I realise why.

The surf shop. And the little café next door.

I shouldn't be here. If the young guy sees me, or worse, that waitress from the café . . . I turn to leave the way I came, but something stops me.

A woman, walking out of the café.

Instantly, I recognise her. She's the one I had the awkward pavement-dance with, the day I made my ill-fated visit to the surf shop and the café next door.

Her café.

The café she works in, at any rate.

She carries a blackboard, painted with those chalk pens that allow elaborate designs to remain on the surface, no matter what the weather throws at it. Does she just work here, like the other waitress, or could she own it? As she nears me, I notice the pocket in the front of her apron contains a hammer and two screwdrivers – not the kind of tools I would expect a waitress to have. So, the owner, then?

She walks along to the side passage where I made my escape before, stopping beside the gate. Then she holds the painted blackboard up, moving it from side to side to gauge the right location for it.

As the blackboard lifts into place, I can see a message surrounded by yellow flowers and trailing ivy painted in chalks across it:

GRAND EVENING OPENING.
CELEBRATE WITH US!
SAMPLE OUR NEW MENU AND

The piano. The one I found myself hiding next to.

I've kept thinking about it as I've driven around my bakery route, the quietness of the roads and the slowly emerging dawn presenting the perfect opportunity to mull things over.

I don't know why it's still in my thoughts. I wasn't next to it for very long – twenty minutes at most before I fled. But it's caused an inexplicable ache within me that I can't shake off.

There was a time, in my teens, when the piano gave me a way of expressing the huge emotional swings I experienced. When I couldn't get to the sea to surf, I played our old family piano instead. It was ancient and so chronically out of tune that it would have sounded more at home in a Wild West saloon, but even its honky-tonk tone could connect with feelings I couldn't express. It was why I jumped at the chance to have Auntie Sue's piano, when I got my own place and she left for Australia. It didn't matter that for months I couldn't play it while I was travelling around to competitions. As soon as I returned, I'd head straight for the keys.

When I lost Mum, the piano was where I expressed my grief, spending hours playing when words failed me. I remember her delight as she listened to me play, perched on the end of the piano stool she found for me in an antique shop in Truro. When she passed away, it was where I felt closest to her.

Parting with it, when I had to leave my flat, was like losing a part of myself and losing Mum all over again.

I watch the woman fixing the sign to the wall. She's smiling as she works. It's as striking as it was when I first encountered her – I feel compelled to see it. Is she thinking about the event advertised on the blackboard, imagining the celebration to come? Or is she thinking of their *new-old* piano having its debut?

Merlin.

Who calls a piano Merlin?

Is it a magic piano? The thought is endearing – and seems to suit the woman hanging the blackboard sign. Was *Merlin* her idea? It fits her, crazy as that sounds. It's hopeful and whimsical, born out of a sense of fun, with a cheeky reference to the Arthurian legend's wizard so synonymous with Cornwall. She has a spark to her. I see it in the way she gazes at the blackboard sign as she secures it to the wall. In the rise and fall of her chest, as if she's feeling a rush of nerves and hope.

This has to be her idea.

To be fair, it's a great one.

I hope people are drawn into the café by the piano. If I hadn't burned my bridges there by abandoning my order the other day, I'd be tempted to go, too.

What would the café look like at night? When I was there before, I noticed strings of lightbulbs across the canopy that partially covered the courtyard. If they were illuminated over that cosy space, I imagine it would look magical. And add the woman's smile and the soothing tones of the piano to the picture . . .

My heart contracts.

It sounds like the kind of place I'd head to one evening, if I hadn't stuffed everything up by dashing out of there without paying.

I'm about to leave, when she turns. A tiny wrinkle appears between her eyebrows and then she smiles. It's as lovely as before. She raises her hand and I do the same. One shy wave is exchanged and then she heads back into her café, gone before I can scramble a greeting together.

I should have said hello. Or asked for her name. I should follow her into the café now . . . except the other waitress might be there, and she'll definitely remember me.

My face flushes as I drag my gaze back to the new sign by the side passage gate.

CELEBRATE WITH US!

Could I?

I'd wondered what the piano would sound like when I was huddled next to it. And now I'm wondering what it would be like to talk to the beautiful woman in the café. This could be my opportunity to find out. *Could have been*, if I hadn't embarrassed myself enough already. And I don't know why, but the knowledge of that bites at my heels as I duck between the milling tourists and hurry on my way.

Eleven

MERRYN

Everything is ready.

Flyers have gone out, Seth has delivered posters to as many businesses in the town as he could manage in his lunch break and Ruthie painted the blackboard sign so that I could fix it to the wall of the café beside the courtyard entrance.

I have two new members of staff starting with us for tomorrow's opening night, who will then share the shifts Ruthie can't do. Jenna Tilson, a local teenager who's on a year out before she goes to university in Cambridge next September, is a total sweetheart. She's a trainee lifeboat volunteer, too, so we have an agreement that if the alarm is raised, she's free to race to the lifeboat station on the harbour. And then there's Arthur Murphy, known to everyone as Murph. He's one of the Penwith Lifeguards serving on Porthmeor Beach during the day and wanted evening work to supplement his summer income.

They're both lifesavers in every sense of the word – and I'm delighted to have them on the team.

My *team*.

The word both thrills and terrifies me.

I'm nervous about more livelihoods depending on Sweet Reverie for support. Seth assures me my nerves are natural but unnecessary.

'You've just reached an upward step, bird. It happens with every business, mine included. You're nervous because it'll change what you're comfortable with. But remember, that was uncomfortable at the beginnin'.'

I know he's right. But the butterflies that have laid siege to my stomach for the last week refuse to be pacified.

I've planned as much as I can. I've covered every eventuality, imagined every scenario we might encounter.

There's just one thing I haven't done.

'You've not played it yet?' Ruthie demands, hands on hips.

'No,' I reply, avoiding her incredulous stare. I won't go into the reasons why with her, no matter how hard she pushes. But I know it must sound ridiculous. I was the one who wanted the piano, the one who cajoled a rather drunk Seth to help me rescue it from North Terrace. I'm the person who has built a whole new section of her business around it being in the courtyard, and the one who lovingly painted its exterior to give it maximum appeal.

Working on Merlin has kept memories of Grant Henderson close in my thoughts. Ruthie doesn't know about him, or the searches I continue in vain most nights. I'm not going to explain it all now. But I had hoped that the piano finding its place might finally unlock my fear of playing the keys. That it might be easier to let him go, now Merlin is here.

I tried to play, last night. Hours after closing, I unlocked the back door, switched on the string of lights over the courtyard and approached the piano bathed in their soft white glow. I settled myself on the faded red velvet seat of the piano stool, and gently rested my hands on Merlin's lid. The newly painted wood felt cool and smooth beneath my palms. Inviting. Welcoming. I cast my mind back to the first time I sat at a piano, recalling the thrill of being allowed to lift the lid to reveal the black and white keys beneath. The creak of the hinges. The rush of scent – dust and old wood – and memories of discovering music written years before I was born.

The lid creaked open as Grant's piano had all those years ago. A startlingly similar sound that caused my breath to catch. And the keys, the white ones yellowed with age and use, the black ones faded to a deep, dark brown at their edges, just as inviting as they had been then.

And I thought I was going to do it. To break the jinx of too many years of hurt and loss and fear. My fingers found the keys . . . but sprang back again.

Even this piano – this serendipitous entity that arrived so magnificently in my life and made the next stage of my business dream possible – was too much to touch. And the worst thing is that I don't know why.

I waited for Grant's return, firm in the belief that he would come back one day: that the brief period of stability and happiness I'd enjoyed in my young life was just a precursor to more. I dreamed of seeing him wheeling his piano back down our street. Of Mum welcoming him home for good.

It never happened. Mum lurched from one disastrous relationship to the next, her chosen beaus a depressing procession of losers, thugs and wastes of space. If I ever dared to question her choice of partners she'd fly into a rage that bruised and stung for days, grudges being the only consistent thing Mum could hold in her life.

I'm not that kid now, waiting for the fairy-tale ending that never arrives. I know I'll never see Grant Henderson again. If the last three years have taught me anything, it's to pursue my own happiness, not place all my hopes on someone else making it happen. So I should be able to play Merlin, finally letting Grant go in peace.

But the little girl in me is still watching, waiting to see him again.

Knowing Luke is back in St Ives has brought it all back to the surface. I've been on shaky ground since the beach clean, and no amount of throwing myself into preparations for the evening openings has been able to take it away.

Maybe it's nerves about the next big step for my business agitating the waters, dredging up old rubbish from deep beneath the surface, exposing my vulnerabilities. Maybe, once the evening openings are under way, everything will settle again.

But right now, it all feels precarious, as if one wrong move might bring the lot crashing down around me.

'It's easy,' Ruthie insists now. 'You lift the piano lid and play it. What's the problem?'

'There's too much to do,' I lie, keen to escape her questions.

'We've prepped everything. The staff are sorted. The flyers are out. Twenty customers have RSVP'd. What else do we need to do?'

When I don't answer, she groans and marches out to the courtyard. I follow her, hating the image she must have of me, scurrying in her wake. She goes to the piano, lifts the lid and starts to play.

It's . . . *beautiful*.

All I can do is watch, my heart simultaneously full and

splintering as the courtyard floods with the voice of my piano. For the first time, I hear its tone – warm and true, despite everything it's endured in its journey to us. It tugs at my heart, a voice shrouded in the mists of my memory.

Ruthie plays a few more bars, then stops. 'There. Played. Was that so hard?'

'Where did you learn to play like that?'

'Mum forced lessons on me as a kid.' She shrugs. 'I don't miss them.'

I struggle to pack away my shock at both her hidden talent and the sound of the piano. 'You should play tomorrow night.'

'No fear! I don't play in public. Maybe *you* should do it.'

'I'll be busy.' It's the truth, but I know it for the deflection it is.

She stares at me, hand on hip, exasperation high. 'Whatever. Can I go now?'

'Of course.' The café is cleaned, all the end-of-day jobs complete. Tomorrow will be a long day and both of us need to prepare for it. 'Thanks, Ruthie.'

'Cheers.' She closes Merlin's lid and walks back into the café, pausing to pat my shoulder as she passes. She collects her things from behind the counter, raises a hand in farewell, then unlocks the door and leaves.

As end-of-day stillness settles over my café, I hug my arms to myself. Ruthie's playing was wonderful – effortless and easy, like it used to be for me when Grant was with us. But the starkness of that ease set against my own inability to touch the keys is too much to bear.

I walk to Merlin, its bright, hopeful colours like a beacon. *Merlin* the magical piano. Seth's idea, of course.

And although I found it hilarious at first, the more I thought about it the more perfect the name became. I don't know if I believe in magic, but I'm learning to believe in possibility. Since I made the decision to rebuild my life after my divorce, there have been too many tiny serendipities to ignore. The piano is the biggest of those, so granting it a magical name seems apt.

And it makes me smile whenever I think of it, which has to be a good thing.

Slowly, I sit beside it and rest my hand on the smooth wood of the lid.

My mind returns to a sunlit moment in a small living room, the shafts of golden light streaming in through the single sash window bleaching out the grubbiness of the nets, the spatter of black mould rising from the skirting boards and the threadbare carpet worn down to its backing cloth. A rare day at home – my school closed to act as a polling station for local elections – and Grant off work to look after me.

I don't remember Mum being there. Where was she? Out drinking, maybe? Or holed up in the prison of her room, a headache or a hangover banishing her to her bed . . .

Grant sitting at the piano. Me seated on a cushion on the floor. And music everywhere: sheet music books strewn across the top of the piano and gathered around my feet like elegant resting birds.

'Find me a tune, Merry.'

My favourite game. Searching through the music books with names of composers I didn't know and often couldn't pronounce, following the lines of notes that danced across the staves. The magic that happened when I passed my chosen piece to Grant and the dancing notes became music beneath his hands. Classical pieces, ragtime, jazz, Beatles songs, movie music – every one a new adventure, a door opened to worlds so different from my own . . .

I pull my phone from my apron pocket, open the saved search page and run it again. His name, my estimate at his age based on half-remembered conversations and memories. We celebrated his birthday in the spring, but the month and date elude me.

NO MATCHES FOUND

I change the terms slightly: a different year, a different month.

Did you mean GRANT HENSON?
GARETH HANSON? GEORGE ENSON?

I close one search window, open another. My heart sits like rock within me. I already know what the result will be. What it always has been, ever since I started searching, days after Luke left me. He'd always dissuaded me when I'd mentioned looking for Grant, insisting it was foolish. When he left me, searching for Grant was my only form of retaliation.

It's become a ritual in my day. The hope that summons me to the search window, followed by the heavy hit of another slammed door. I know I should leave this now, but the arrival of Merlin has spurred me to try again.

I stare at the closed lid, the urge to lift it strong. But my fingers falter the moment I try.

It's too much.

Tears filling my eyes, I hurry upstairs.

Twelve

ZACH

'Zach? Hey, it's Luke Pengelly.'

I scramble upright, rubbing sleep from my eyes. I got back to the studio from an extra bakery run an hour ago, Matt calling me in for a double shift because his other regular weekend driver was ill. I was glad of the work but my knee disagreed, especially when I hit a huge tailback of tourist traffic as I was returning to St Ives and had to drive at ten miles per hour all the way home.

I don't remember falling asleep on the sofa in the studio, but then I don't remember much since getting back from the bakery. Kieran isn't coming here today, so that's a blessing. But my whole body protests as I stand.

'Luke, hi.'

'I have a shift schedule for you and I was wondering if you could come in today to collect it? Give you a chance to meet the rest of the team and see what we've done with the place since you last saw it.'

'Today?' I repeat, my head fuzzy from the sudden awakening.

'If that suits?'

'Sure. What time?'

'In about half an hour?'

Wow. Nothing like giving me warning, Luke.

'Um, yeah, sure.'

'Great. See you soon.'

The call ends as suddenly as it arrived. I stare at my phone, the rest of my body glaring at me for agreeing to get it moving again so soon.

It isn't how I'd expected to spend my Saturday. But more work is worth disrupting my plans for. Even if my poor, exhausted body hates me. So I leave the comfort of the studio and the quiet afternoon I'd promised myself and force my reluctant body back out onto the packed weekend streets of St Ives.

The tide is in, so I can't take a short cut across the harbour sand. Instead, I duck between groups of slow-moving visitors along Fore Street, my knee burning with every twist and turn I have to make. St Ives seems busier this weekend, the crush of bodies denser, spilling into more of the backstreets. It's been a while since I spent a full summer here, always just breezing in for competitions while I was on the circuit rather than living in the town. It's a bit of a culture shock. Good for business, though, I guess, especially for Aggie's coffee hut, Matt's bakery and Luke's soon-to-be restaurant.

And the piano café.

I think of the hopeful woman I saw outside it. I've thought about her a lot, actually. That smile of hers. The way her face illuminated when she hung the sign. The way I felt when she looked at me. Hope and positivity – things I get glimpses of now I'm starting to find my feet again, that she seems to embody.

I know it's daft. And there are probably a hundred other

things that should occupy my mind. But their grand evening opening event is tonight. I should want to give Sweet Reverie as wide a berth as possible. But the truth is, I want to go back there.

I want to hear what the piano sounds like.

And I want to see *her* again. I want to watch her celebrating her brave new venture and see just how bright her smile becomes . . .

'Do you mind?' A raised voice and a sudden shove to my left shoulder drags me back to the gauntlet of jostling bodies. A bald-headed bloke in vest, shorts and flip-flops is barrelling through the crowd around me, scowl firmly fixed as people jump out of his way.

I watch him forge ahead down Fore Street towards the shell shop, and exchange a rueful smile with the lady nearest to me who Angry Bloke inadvertently used as a battering ram into my shoulder.

'Joys of holidaymakers, eh?'

'Happy beggars, one an' all,' she replies. 'You okay?'

'Good thanks. You?'

'I'll live. You have a better day than old mardy bum down there, lover.'

Her blessing makes me smile all the way to Pengelly's.

The transformation of the business in such a short space of time is incredible. Where builders' lamps provided the only light before, a constellation of small halogen spotlights now sparkle from the newly plastered ceiling. Everything has been painted white, apart from the wide bar that glows beneath a wash of sea blue varnish. The floor is Cornish slate, blue-grey with natural lines and contours running along each piece that mirror the waves in the harbour. Pale wood tables, the colour of Porthmeor sand, have been placed alongside the full-length windows that run the width of the restaurant, each one flanked by chairs with seats upholstered in deep blue denim. It's as if the view from inside continues out onto Harbour Beach, an uninterrupted line from Pengelly's to the landscape beyond.

And at the centre, Luke Pengelly is holding court with a group of nervous-looking, mostly young people. I feel old just approaching them.

'Zach! Great to see you!' he calls, beckoning me over. 'Everyone, this is Zach Trevelyan. He's joining the team.'

'Hi,' I reply, fist-bumping and shaking hands around the group.

I smile as the introductions happen, knowing I won't remember any of the names they're telling me. *Seawater for brains*, Mum used to say. I just haven't the best memory for people's names. Never have had. *Mate* and *dude* serve me well enough, most of the time. I hope that'll work here, too.

Luke waits for the round of introductions to end, then commands our attention with a loud clap of his hands that echoes around the newly decorated space. 'Great, thanks. So, my purpose for bringing you all in today is twofold: firstly, to check you're okay with day-to-day stuff like working the till and card readers, pulling pints, making coffee and serving food; and secondly, to let you know that we're bringing the opening forward by a week. Got to make the most of these lovely rich tourists, eh?'

We smile politely and he waits for a moment, his own smile noticeably tight. Is he waiting for laughter? Applause?

Just as the pause starts to become uncomfortable, Luke snaps back into his spiel. 'We're as good to go as we can be and

I want us to hit the ground running. Really make our mark, show the town we've arrived. I believe Pengelly's is going to be *the* destination restaurant in St Ives. We may be new, but we're going to be the name on everyone's lips. So, let's get cracking and demonstrate what a crack team we'll be!'

As we wait in line to do the food and drink serving tests, a tall, lanky kid with a trendy beard and a tattoo of an anchor on his right forearm turns to me and grins.

'Ready to work for Captain Cliché?'

I relax as I chuckle, glad it wasn't just me who noted Luke's apparent deep love of well-worn phrases. 'Reckon we need bingo cards to tick them off as we hear them.'

'I'm up for that. Might have to design some . . .'

'Shh!' the young woman with a knot of strawberry blonde plaits on the top of her head admonishes us. When we drop our gazes like two cheeky schoolkids, she snorts with laughter. 'There's some serious ground-hitting with running happening here.'

'Blue-sky thinking, that is,' says the girl beside her, the joke filtering along the queue ahead.

I think I'm going to like it here. I'm going to like the money even more.

The news of the new opening date is a surprise, having seen the state of the place before, but it'll be good for my bank account. Having shifts here that dovetail with my Downalong Bakery deliveries will fill my days and allow me to save a little – something I haven't been able to do for years. Six weeks here at the lowest estimate – eight, if I'm lucky and the work continues into September. It'll give me money to live on while working out what I want to do with the next part of my life.

The food and drink service tests are a breeze. Pulling pints is like riding a bike – once you know how it's done, it becomes instinctive. My barista skills are a little rustier, it being at least four years since I last used them. But I pass and Luke appears impressed. The till and card reader are straightforward enough and, like everything in my new occupations, will become second nature by repetition.

To our collective surprise, Luke hands us each forty quid in pristine new notes at the end of our session, doling out the money with the flair of a casino croupier dealing cards.

'As a token of my thanks,' he informs us, displaying his trademark grin.

We leave as a happy band of soon-to-be servers, considerably richer than we arrived.

A win, any way I look at it.

It's calmer in town as I walk back to Kieran's studio. A natural lull, where day-trippers have left via train or car, and holidaymakers have gone back to their rented apartments, cottages and houses to rest before their evening adventures begin.

I like this time of day, when the sun hangs lower in the sky and the town dares to take a breath. I should grab something to eat back at the studio, taking full advantage of a night there without Kieran. I will – but not yet.

It's just over an hour until Sweet Reverie's grand evening opening begins.

Even if I hadn't been toying with the idea of sneaking in, I wouldn't be able to miss details of it. In almost every shop I pass along Fore Street now, I see posters for the event. Even if I tried not to notice one, there would be another ten further along my route. The owner must be popular with fellow businesses in

St Ives; either that or they've bribed a heck of a lot of people to display the posters.

I should go home.

But I want to hear the piano.

And I want to see her again . . .

Thirteen

MERRYN

'Stop worryin'.'

'I'm not worrying.'

'Tell it to your hands.'

I glance down at my fidgeting fingers and relent as Seth's laugh warms my cheek.

'There's just so much at stake,' I admit, because the closer we've got to the grand opening, the more mountainous the occasion has felt to me. I see it now, looming ahead, a near-vertical climb to a place I'm not certain Sweet Reverie is ready to go.

'There's so much to *celebrate*.' His hand at my back steadies me. 'Look how far you've come, Mer. You built this place from the ground up and now it's ready to go further than you ever thought possible.'

'But if it fails . . .'

'It won't.'

'But if it does . . . No, Seth, it's a real concern. It isn't just my livelihood depending on the evening openings now. I have a team . . .'

'. . . Who are all thrilled to be here. And who would all find other jobs in town no problem if the evenin' hours don't work. But they *will* work. So stop bleddy worryin'!'

I know he's right. Of course I do. I just wish that my nerves weren't trying to scupper the new opening hours before we've even begun. I'll be happier once people arrive for the celebration, I tell myself. When the café and courtyard are filled with conversation and laughter and the sound of Merlin being played.

Tonight, Seth's younger sister Mhairi is playing for us. She's just passed her Grade 8 piano and plays with a local jazz trio. It will mean a steady supply of relaxed, beautiful music welcoming everyone into the café in its new evening guise. Then, as promised, I'll invite the celebration guests to play towards the end of the event, when everyone is relaxed and more likely to have a go.

Mhairi arrives just before seven and I settle her at the piano with a generous supply of snacks to sustain her. I wait while she warms up with scales, enjoying the sound and warmth of the piano at last. Now the initial bittersweet moment of hearing Merlin for the first time is over – thanks to Ruthie – I can start to see my vision of the piano in Sweet Reverie. It's more perfect than I could have hoped, the natural reverberation of the courtyard and walls adding depth and substance to the sound.

Mhairi smiles as she plays. 'It has a great tone.'

'Doesn't it?' I agree, as proud as a mother hen.

'Seth says you found it outside?'

'Yes – on North Terrace, left by a house that's being renovated.'

She completes another scale and pauses to have a drink. 'You'd never guess from the quality of the sound. I'm going to enjoy hanging out with this magic boy tonight!'

Ruthie arrives with Jenna and Murph just as the first guests are walking in. They greet one another in the doorway, walking in as one happy, chatty party. While Ruthie and my new team members hurry behind the counter to help ready the trays of canapés and tiny bites we prepared this afternoon, Seth lights the tea-light candles in painted jam jars on every table and Mhairi starts to play out in the courtyard.

As more guests arrive, I see it: the vision of what an evening opening in Sweet Reverie could be, like I first imagined when Seth and I found the piano. Soft candlelight, soothing music, good-natured conversation and the sense of a community coming together. It's beautiful – and the sight of it all happening around me blows away every last concern from my mind.

'It looks amazing,' Jack says, while Seren and Nessie gaze around in delight.

'There's a piano!' Nessie breathes, dark brown curls bouncing around her face as she gazes at Merlin.

'You have a go on it later, if you like,' I tell her, rewarded immediately by a squeal of delight.

Seren laughs. 'I think that's a yes.'

'Boss, where do you want these?' Murph arrives at my side with a tray of mini white and dark chocolate bites. 'There's no room left on the counter.'

'Start handing them around,' I say, waving at Jack, Seren and Nessie as they move out into the courtyard. 'I don't think anyone's going to mind if they have savoury and sweet canapés together.'

'Should I try one? You know, just so I know what I'm delivering?' His smile is pure mischief.

'Nice try. I tell you what, if you deliver all of those, I'll let you have the box of extras after the event.'

'Deal!' Murph is off like a greyhound, delivering sweet treats like a pro.

I stand by the counter, where Ruthie is in charge of drinks – non-alcoholic fruit punch garnished with sweet sage leaves and strawberries – and let my gaze travel across the café. People are chatting together, good-natured laughter filling the space. Some standing in groups, others gathered around the tables. As Mhairi's beautiful playing fills the air, the extra fairy lights we added behind the counter and around the door to the courtyard bestow a welcoming glow. It feels different to our usual day service. Special. Like we've created a space that's never existed before.

And there it is: the hope that I've caught hold of since I found the piano. I look at my café and I see the physical embodiment of the feeling I've carried. Friends, regular customers, tourists who are here because of Ruthie's beautiful sign, and my café, proving beyond a shadow of a doubt what its potential could be.

I have so much to do, but for one small moment I let myself feel this. Drink it all in. And let it settle in my soul: I built this, from a broken place where I thought I might never find my way back.

It's beautiful. It's hopeful.

And at the centre of it all, the piano sings.

Fourteen

ZACH

The gate is wide open.

I hoped it might be.

Light glows from the café's windows, the rumble of chatter and laughter sounding inside. But I don't intend to enter by the front door.

Beneath its dense canopy of honeysuckle and ivy, the wrought-iron gateway is shrouded in shadow. Checking nobody is watching, I duck between the buildings, leaving the street behind.

I hear it as soon as I'm in the passageway, flattening my back against the wall of the café building to listen for a moment.

The piano is playing.

A lilting, laid-back piece of jazz, perfect for a summer night. I don't recognise the tune, but the tone of the instrument feels like the fond-remembered voice of an old, old friend.

I've missed it. That sound. It's bittersweet: the music that reminds me of so many hours sitting by my own piano, against the memory of all I've lost. The sound makes me miss Mum, more now than ever. She loved to hear me play, insisting I perform for her whenever I visited, on the old, out-of-tune instrument she kept at home.

In the months before Mum moved into the hospice, I played for her for hours a day. It settled her mind, she said, took her attention away from the pain. It didn't feel like nearly enough, but it made her smile – and I wanted her to smile more than anything in the world.

I miss the connection between the melody in my mind and the feeling of the keys beneath my fingers. I miss the pieces I would return to whenever I needed to play. The ones that came as naturally as breathing, the muscle memory of years of practice clicking into action.

Feeling brave, I dare to move a little further towards the end of the passageway, where light spills out from the courtyard ahead of me. I want more. Not just the distant sound of a beautiful piano. I want to see the effect it has on the café customers, to be in the room, surrounded by the music. I'm already further in than I thought I'd get, but now it isn't enough.

I want to see the courtyard, with those lights illuminated across it.

I want to be surrounded by people: be in the thick of small talk and raucous jokes, feel like I belong and have roots like they do, instead of basically surviving on my own.

And I want to see her – the lovely, hopeful woman who's danced through my thoughts like we danced on the pavement, the first time I saw her. If my instinct is correct and this is her place, I know that her hope and delight will only be magnified. I want to see what that looks like.

So I edge along the wall, taking my time, halting when a burst of laughter sounds, too close for comfort. I only stop when I'm at the point where the wall at my back gives way to the entrance of the courtyard, my heart thudding as hard as if I've just ridden a championship wave.

I peer around the corner, the nearest side of the courtyard swinging into view.

And there she is . . .

She's leaning against the counter of the café, looking out towards the courtyard. I keep close to the edge of the courtyard entrance, but she isn't looking over here. I follow her gaze to where it rests on the piano, now painted with flowers and foliage, waves and shells, sending its gorgeous music out to fill the space. She looks blissfully happy – and as I watch her wistful smile and obvious pride, I catch that emotion, too.

Maybe she's taking this moment to celebrate the good stuff because it's a highlight in the constant slog of everything else. Or maybe she's one of those rare creatures who manages to be happy all the time. I never really believed they existed before, but perhaps she disproves my theory.

My attention swings to the piano.

I had to see it tonight. And even though my vantage point is precarious and my welcome may be short, I'm so glad I risked this visit. The song ends and the courtyard rings with applause. I'm tempted to applaud, too. But I can't give away my vantage point. I've seen the other café worker – the one who served me before – circulating tonight. She has the kind of look about her that suggests she never forgets a face. If she sees me here . . .

Wait – the lady I wanted to see is leaving the bar . . .

She's heading this way.

Instinctively, I pull the hood of my sweatshirt up, safer in the anonymity it gives me. It makes no sense at all, considering how many people are here tonight and the fact that I'm currently peering around the courtyard entrance wall. But I don't want anyone to see me. It feels risky enough without attracting undue attention to myself.

She claps her hands and the café customers hush.

'Hi, everyone. I'm Merryn Rowe, owner of Sweet Reverie.'

A loud whoop sounds, causing a ripple of laughter from the customers. When I look in the direction it comes from, I see the other bloke from the surf shop – the young guy's boss, who was searching the street for me last time I saw him with a face like thunder. He's grinning now, but that would change in seconds if he saw me. He's gazing at the woman – *Merryn* – like all his birthdays arrived at once. Are they together?

'Thanks, Seth,' Merryn says, blushing a little.

If they're not together yet, I reckon they could be after tonight.

I slump a little against the wall as Merryn continues.

'I just want to thank you all for coming. This evening is the first of what we hope will be many. Sweet Reverie will be opening late on Wednesday, Thursday and Friday evenings from next week.'

A cheer erupts from the café. I'm suddenly aware of a huge swell of love in the room, rolling like a summer tide towards her. They're all here for her, aren't they? All these people, supporting her business. Were they drawn to her hopefulness and light like I was?

I don't know Merryn Rowe. But I'm inexplicably glad for her. Glad that she has people around her who love and support her. It shouldn't matter to me, a complete stranger hiding on the periphery of this event, but I'm surprised to find it does.

Somehow, the piano she now stands by seems to embody her hope for the café. Did she paint it? The flowers and waves, shells and stars across its body have been created with care and love. It's just an old piano, but it seems to represent more than that – for me, as well as her.

I should go.

This is Merryn's moment. Her business, her piano.

But my feet won't listen to my brain.

So I stay where I am, rooted to the spot, while Merryn tells a story of rescuing the piano from the street, of a crazy late-night dash to bring it back, and of the reason it now lives here, in the courtyard of her café.

'I hadn't even considered the stairs,' she says, to a swell of laughter from the room. 'I was just so excited to get it home. But actually, I think the courtyard is the perfect place for Merlin. Because now I get to share the piano with all of you.'

The warm murmurs of approval this elicits feel like an audible embrace.

The more she talks, the more I'm drawn in. To her story, to the unsurprisingly generous heart revealed by her words. And to her firm belief that the piano is central to all the good things now happening for her business.

'And so, this is the moment I know several of you have been waiting for. Part of the reason Merlin is here is that I want it to be available to everyone to play. I want it to be ours, as a community. So come on, don't be shy. Come and play our piano!'

Her invitation sets the kid in me tugging at my arm, wide-eyed and insistent, begging me to play. And then, my feet are moving, my body overriding any shred of common sense I have as the empty piano stool beckons ahead.

What am I doing? I shouldn't even be here!

An old familiar ache floods my hands, the need to play, greater than I've felt it in months. I thought I'd surrendered the urge when I sold my piano and watched it being wheeled out of my Padstow flat. I thought I'd packed it up with the music books I gave to its new owner, knowing I had no use for them anymore.

I'm in the courtyard now, taking the two steps that lead up from the passageway, the shadow across my body surrendering to the warm, white glow of the lights overhead. The keys are still without a player, the piano almost within reach.

And then something slams hard into my right arm. The suddenness of the blow steals my balance and I tumble towards an empty bistro chair at the table beside the piano. It clatters as I grab it, a young girl with dark curls yelping a panicked apology as she jumps onto the piano stool and starts to play.

I feel hands around me, helping me to my feet – and when I look up, I see her. She's right in front of me, her fingers soft and gentle where they take my hands.

'Are you okay?'

'I – I'm good, thanks . . .'

Concern has stolen her smile, but I see recognition fire in her dark eyes. 'I'm so glad you came.'

I'm upright now, shaken and unsure what to do or say. But Merryn Rowe is here and she's beautiful, and I can't stop looking at her.

'*You!*'

The shout shakes me out of my thoughts. It's the waitress from my first visit, bearing down on me like a storm swell. I glance back at Merryn, whose hands still lightly enclose mine. I want to stay, but the other waitress is pushing her way through the customers towards us.

I don't wait for her to reach me. Pulling my hands away from Merryn's, I crash my way out, the shouts and shock reverberating in my wake. As I reach the corner of the building, I hear the furious waitress yell, '*Seth!*'

Seth – the name of the tall bloke who was searching for me last time.

Porthia Surf's Seth.

Merryn's Seth?

'Oi!' he yells, too close behind me.

I don't look back.

I just run.

Fifteen

MERRYN

It was *him* – the man I saw beside my café when I was hanging the sign. The one I thanked for our awkward dance around each other in the street before. He had his hood up, masking much of his face, but I would have recognised him anywhere. The blue eyes, the warm smile . . .

Why didn't I stop him leaving?

It's a drama I didn't want tonight, but I hate that he was scared away. Most of the customers have gone back to their celebrating now, thank goodness, the unexpected floor show over. At least tonight won't be remembered for this.

But still, I don't want anyone to feel they can't come here.

Especially not him.

Nessie is still playing the piano, apparently unruffled by the drama.

My heart is thudding hard as I assure my friends I'm fine.

'I'm so sorry,' Jack rushes. 'I've told Ness to watch where she's going, but . . .'

'She was excited,' I counter, keen now to move on. 'It was an accident.'

'It was that bleddy bloke again,' Ruthie insists, still glaring in the direction where Seth just ran. 'The one who left without payin'.'

Was he?

'You don't know that, Ruthie.'

'Yes, I do! Look what happened. Moment I called him out, he legged it! Creepy as, if you ask me.'

He didn't seem creepy. He looked lost. But many people who come to St Ives are searching for something. The sea is a pull to people who need reassurance, hope, something bigger than their own problems to give them perspective. I can attest to that. Besides, if he did run out on his order, like Ruthie insists, why would I have seen him in Star Court the other day? Surely he'd avoid this place after that?

'He was probably embarrassed,' Jack offers, even though Ruthie is unlikely to be denied her fury so easily. 'I know I would be.'

'*You* wouldn't order a pot of tea and a biscuit plate and then beggar off without payin' for them,' she retorts.

This is ridiculous. I've heard enough.

'Ruthie, let it go. We have customers to serve and a celebration to enjoy.'

'Boss is right,' Murph interjects, arriving by my side and nodding as if he's been part of the conversation from the beginning. 'No telling how many nutters we're likely to serve this summer. Best to get the first one out of the way, I reckon.'

Not exactly the solidarity I was hoping for, but I'll take it.

Seth returns, red-cheeked and breathless, a moment later. 'Lost him on Tregenna Hill. Little coward went dashin' for the station. I hope he gets the last train and doesn't come back.'

'You didn't have to chase him.'

'Yes, I did. See, this is why you need a padlock for that side gate, Mer. It isn't safe with creepy gits like that around.'

'The gate was open anyway,' I argue back. 'And the poor guy was embarrassed, not creepy. This place is for everyone, whether they're confident about being here or not.'

A cheer goes up as Nessie completes her bravura rendition of 'The Entertainer' and stands to take a bow. We join in, the drama finally abandoned. As Cerrie Austin and her hunky Australian boyfriend sit at the piano, I return behind the counter.

I hope the guy who ran away is okay. I can only imagine his embarrassment. If I'd fallen in front of a crowded café, I'd be mortified. I probably would think twice before setting foot in there again. I hope he doesn't feel that way. It was lovely to see him. Sweet Reverie should be his place, too, whatever Seth and Ruthie think.

Drama aside, the celebration is just what I hoped it would be. Forty-two guests, all of whom eat and drink and chat and laugh, bringing the courtyard alive in a way I've never seen before. As the evening passes, I see the potential of Sweet Reverie made real.

And at the centre of it all, is the piano.

It tempts reluctant fingers to traverse its keys. It sends beautiful music out into the night air. It even survives some of my not-so-musical customers' attempts to play it. We hear 'Chopsticks' and 'Blue Moon' more times than perhaps is necessary – and some tunes I couldn't place if my happy future depended upon it. But it *works*. That's what I wanted to see.

By ten, some people are starting to leave. By eleven, only three remain.

'Can I come back and play?' Nessie asks, stifling a yawn.

'Any time,' I reply.

Her dad hugs her to him. 'Thanks for tonight, Merryn. And congratulations.'

'Thanks for coming, all of you.'

'We wouldn't have missed it.' Seren smiles, then pulls something from her pocket. 'This is for you.'

She places a package wrapped in sea-green tissue paper in my hand. Surprised, I open it, my breath catching when I see what's inside.

A bracelet, delicate and hand-made, with silver-wire-wrapped pieces of pale blue, white and green beachcombed seaglass, joined by silver links.

'Oh wow! Is this one of yours?'

She smiles with pride. 'A new venture needs the blessing of some mermaid magic.' I see the look that passes between Seren and Nessie when she says this. Seaglass was so much a part of them finding each other, making this gift even more special.

'Mermaid treasure for luck,' Jack says.

'Just what we need. Thanks so much, Seren.'

'My pleasure. Now *we* need to get a certain celebrated piano player home to bed.'

'But I'm not tired,' Nessie insists, as they walk out, her argument scuppered by her immediate yawn.

I wave as they leave, my heart full.

Mermaid treasure for luck.

I'll take all the luck I can get.

*

I wake early next morning, despite it being Sunday and licence, if it was needed, for a lie-in. Bright sunlight floods my bedroom, too tempting to close my eyes and ignore. The need to be outside is strong, pulling me out of bed, into the shower and then into my comfiest clothes. I make coffee in a travel mug, sling my bag over my shoulder and head out into the early morning streets.

I love early summer mornings, when the day is filled with promise and the cobbles are still damp with dew. Hardly anyone is up yet, most shops and cafés not opening until ten a.m. But the air is sweet and cool, the promised heat not due to arrive until later in the day.

I take a zig-zag path across town, climbing hills and winding along impossibly perfect backstreets between white-painted fishermen's cottages. There are flowers everywhere: crazy white and pink Mexican fleabane daisy-like blooms spilling over stone walls; hanging baskets laden with fuchsia, yellow osteospermum, petunias and trails of white and purple lobelia; seaside planters of agapanthus and bright pink cosmos; and hydrangeas bustling between buildings. Scent and colour and the always present sound of the sea.

Working and living in St Ives means you have to make time to enjoy all the beauty around you. When I took on Sweet Reverie and moved into the flat above it, I made a promise to myself to get outside as often as possible. It's been my saving grace, especially when the demands of running a business become overwhelming. Sometimes a fifteen-minute walk along a beach or over the cliff path towards Clodgy Point can make all the difference.

Today, I'm giving myself an hour. We're due to open at ten-thirty a.m., so I have plenty of time. Murph will be arriving just after ten. He agreed to work today so Ruthie can have a rest – something she insisted she didn't need, but I saw how tired she was by the end of the celebration last night. Besides, I'm looking forward to a shift without lectures from her about creepy customers.

I think about the man in the hoodie as I skirt the Island car park and take the footpath across the lush grass up towards the coastguard station and the chapel above it. I hope he's okay this morning. Whatever Seth and Ruthie's opinions on the matter, I think he was just joining the celebration, like all our other guests. The blackboard sign I hung by the gate to the side passage was an invitation to everyone, including strangers who haven't visited us before.

Maybe he was intimidated by the number of the people there who appeared to know one another. It's an aspect of the café that I'm most proud of: that local residents find it as welcoming as the passing tourist trade. There are precious few places in St Ives that local people can count as their own during the summer. We surrender so much because we want visitors here. That both tourists and locals enjoy Sweet Reverie's atmosphere means the world to me.

I know we complain occasionally (some more than others). And it can be relentlessly busy in the six weeks of summer. But people choosing to visit our town from all over the world is a wonderful thing. Their holidays in St Ives allow me to have the business I've worked so hard to establish. That's cause for celebration, even if parking is a nightmare and some visitors are less than polite.

I don't know if the man in the hoodie was a visitor or a local. It doesn't matter either way; only that if he is a holidaymaker, I hope he feels able to come back before his stay in St Ives is over.

I reach the summit of the hill and sit on one of the steps

leading to St Nicholas Chapel, gazing down at the gorgeous spread of St Ives below. From here I can see the long stretch of Porthmeor Beach leading to the curved white building of Tate St Ives to my right, the higgledy-piggledy roofs of Downalong ahead, and the honey-coloured curve of Porthgwidden Beach to my left. This is my favourite vantage point, the place I come when I need perspective, or just to breathe.

I sip my coffee and drink in the view.

I needed this.

'You always came here when you needed to think.'

The voice cuts through my thoughts, jarring and unwelcome.

When I look to my right, Luke Pengelly is walking towards me.

No.

Not now . . .

He must have come up from the Island path on the Porthmeor side, scaling the steepest part of the hill. How did I miss his approach?

I can't ignore him, or walk away. Which is the worst thing.

He's sitting beside me before I can summon my body to move.

'That's what I'm trying to do,' I say, turning back to the spread of St Ives, determined not to meet his stare.

'That's it? No *what the hell are you doing here*? No *get out of my town*?'

'There are plenty of other places you could sit.'

'True. But I wanted to see you.'

Why is he here?

When I don't reply, he sniffs and brushes sand from the side of his calf. 'I was running on the Island path and I saw you walk up here. Thought it was best to get the awkward greeting out of the way.'

'Well, now you have.'

There's a pause and I know he's waiting for me to look at him. It's what he always did when we were together – inject deliberate pauses into our arguments, believing that the moment I gave him my attention, he'd win.

I won't give him the satisfaction today.

'I'm opening a place. On the harbour. Bigger and better than we had before.'

No, I'm not rising to it. The restaurant we had for exactly six months, before he announced he was leaving me and closing the business, was the biggest venture we'd taken on. His idea, not mine. That he felt comfortable in a restaurant far larger than the café I now own speaks volumes. It's all for show: big, overblown gestures he can retract in a heartbeat.

I give him six months with Pengelly's before he starts itching for a different challenge.

But that's no longer my problem.

I take a slow, deliberate sip of coffee, eyes resolutely forward, as he carries on, spinning his tales about his new business.

'We've just recruited the team, actually. Great bunch of kids. And the building work was completed faster than Scott or I had hoped. We open next weekend.' I can feel his eyes on me. 'I hope we'll see you there?'

'It's our busiest time.'

'Oh, it will be ours, too. So many covers, but with our prime location we'll have no trouble filling tables. We expect to be packed out all summer.' That pause again, as if the second time will prove lucky for him. 'All the same, I'd like to see you . . .'

'What do you want, Luke?' I'm glaring at him before I can stop myself. Infuriated that I've fallen into his trap, I prepare for a fight, the old impulses from before still surprisingly active after three years of no use.

'A civil conversation would be a start.'

'I have nothing to say to you.'

'Maybe.' He shrugs. 'I don't know, I just thought after three years you'd be over this.'

Over this? Like the three years of painstakingly piecing my life back together, of carving out a new space and life and business in the town I'd always believed we'd share our lives in, is no more than a trivial injustice?

It takes every ounce of strength I have to remain calm. Luke wants a shouting match – he always did. Because the moment I retaliate, he has me. Words yelled in anger reveal vulnerabilities and truths he can take advantage of. But I know better now.

'Oh, I'm over *you*,' I say, cool strength on the surface masking the shaking beneath it.

The slightest flicker in his expression is my reward.

'That's . . . that's not what I meant.'

I say nothing.

'Look, how things ended with us, it wasn't planned, okay? It wasn't how I wanted it. And maybe three years away from everything has made me think about that. I want to move on. Put all of the mess behind me.'

'Then why come back?'

It's more revealing than I want it to be. But it's the question I've wrestled with since I found out about Pengelly's. He swore he would never return here, making a life somewhere else in the Duchy with the woman he left me for. The things he said about St Ives on the last day I saw him were the kind of things you don't just renege on. What's changed?

'I missed this.'

It's ambiguous and I don't trust it. Missed St Ives? Missed fighting with me? I don't want to know if it's the latter. I haven't mended my heart just for him to smash it again. I don't love Luke anymore. But it took time to rid my heart of him.

'Nobody wants you here, Luke. People in the town have long memories and you betrayed so many.'

'I know. I *know*.' He's irritated now. Truth hurts. 'I get that I have to work hard to make amends. I know they won't accept me back easily. But if you put in a word for me . . .'

I want to say I can't believe this, but I can. 'No.'

'Oh come on, Mer. You know they'll listen to you.'

'You've no right to ask me.'

He shrugs, as if frustration isn't writ large across his face. 'Maybe I'll just say it, anyway.'

'Do what you want,' I say, standing up. I need to be away from this.

'Hey, I didn't mean it. Sorry. *Sorry*, Mer. It's just the stress of getting the business up and running. Look, why don't I drop by your place in a week or so? I hear you're doing well.'

'Please don't.' When he stares up at me, I continue. 'We're nothing to each other, Luke. So open your business and enjoy being back in St Ives. I wish you success. But stay out of my life.'

I don't give him the opportunity to reply as I leave the chapel steps and power back down the hill.

Sixteen

ZACH

I am such an idiot.

I can't believe I've run away from Merryn's café *twice*.

She tried to help me, but I still ran.

Now that Seth bloke and the thunder-faced waitress will be gunning for me. And who could blame them? First I skip out without paying, then I make an almighty spectacle of myself in front of a café full of people, leaving a mess in my wake.

And what about Merryn? She probably thinks I'm a weirdo. Or she isn't thinking of me at all. I'm not sure which is worse.

I never wanted any of this.

I just wanted to play the piano. And see Merryn again.

This morning everything feels precarious once more. Will I ever find steady ground?

Worst of all, it's Sunday. A day when I have nothing to distract my mind from regurgitating all the crap from last night. No bakery shifts, no work at Pengelly's till next week. No imminent arrival of Kieran, either, as he's taking Aggie shopping for baby stuff in Truro today. I don't want to head into town, in case anyone who witnessed my fall in Sweet Reverie recognises me.

I'm stuck within these four walls. Feeling like I threw away an important chance.

I know it'll pass. But it's too raw right now. If I'm not careful, my regret over last night will join hands with all the other mind-crap that's followed me around since I quit the surf scene.

I try to read, but my focus is gone.

I scan the groceries I've stocked the cupboards with, but nothing appeals.

I don't want to look at my phone because nothing I scroll will soothe my head today.

Why is nothing helping?

Pacing the studio, my thoughts make an inevitable return to the life I've lost. I need to find a way back to who I was before. The confident me, the Zach who never questioned where he was going or cared to look too far ahead. This endless questioning is not me. It never was.

This is ridiculous. I need air.

Defying the voice telling me to hide away, I head outside.

I've wasted most of the morning stuck in my own head, meaning the streets are busy when I reach the centre of town. I'll be okay as long as I avoid the street where Sweet Reverie and Porthia Surf are. St Ives might be small, but there are enough alternative routes available to me to be able to avoid that area.

It's another gorgeous day, the recent run of sunny weather a blessing in every sense. Good for visitors, good for businesses, good for me. Despite the heaviness of my mood, sunshine warms my limbs and spine as I climb up steeper streets to the hill at the back of the town.

The harbour sparkles far below as I rise above the rooflines, the ache in my calves gratifying. I don't do well cooped up inside. Never did. Mum used to joke that I'd be happier with a human-sized kennel in the garden than a room in the house. 'That way you'd never have to be separated from fresh air.'

Man, I miss her.

There were so many years when I was competing that I never gave Mum a second thought. She was such a force of nature that I assumed she'd be there forever. I thought it was a given, as much as the air or the sea or the land are always here.

Since I lost everything, Mum's returned to my mind often. I wonder what she'd make of me now, kicking my life back into touch after it fell apart.

I loved her with every breath, but I was never one for hanging around. She was content to love me from a distance. Always there if I needed her, happy to wait until I did. That's why moving back to take care of her three years ago almost broke us. She hated that I had to be there and I hated that she was going through it. We muddled through, enough for her to see out her final months with dignity and some level of humour. I guess I should be grateful for that time. I missed six months of the competitive circuit surf meets, but I was there for her when it mattered. Five and a half months taking care of her at her house, followed by two weeks pretty much living by her hospice bedside.

During that time, she lectured me whenever she was lucid. *Go back to the circuit, Zachary, win all the trophies you want, but start to think about life afterwards. Be ready for it, sweetheart, because life changes before you know it.*

I thought I had another five years to think about that – and I told her so. Little did I know that, just over a year later, my injury would kick me out of my career for good, and Mum's words would follow me as I lost my home and headed for the place where she no longer was.

Not that she would ever have let me wallow if she was here.

Chin up, boots on. Or probably flip-flops where you're concerned...

I laugh, despite my gloom, looking down at the trusty Havaianas I chose to wear today.

Okay, Mum. Let's do this your way.

I *am* making progress. Slower than I'd like, but I have two jobs and a roof over my head for the next few months at least. I'll just keep being reminded of missteps until I sort everything else out, but now I'm in St Ives I can work out what I want next.

I expect Mum would have plenty to say about that.

I reach the end of a steep footpath and cross the road. There's a bench here, at the edge of Trenwith car park, that I always sat on whenever I arrived in town for a surf meet, my first breath of St Ives air taken after too long in the stuffy confines of my car.

I find it now, the wood warm when I sit.

The breath I take feels like my first proper inhale since the mess of last night.

St Ives Bay stretches out across the horizon, the beaches that line the contours of the land small streaks of gold edging the blue. It's achingly familiar and startlingly new at once, the ever-changing colours of the sea making sure that no view of the bay is ever the same. Maybe that's why St Ives is the way it is: its historic buildings set in stone, yet restless and ever-changing in what they contain.

How long has Sweet Reverie been there? I try to spot the location of Star Court in the knot of streets below. I don't remember seeing it when I visited the town for competitions, but was I ever really looking then? So much seems to have passed me by while my life was consumed by surfing. What else have I missed?

I'll get past what happened last night. The sting of its memory will lessen as time moves on. But today I have to acknowledge it as an unwanted companion, an angry dog biting at my heels.

I was an idiot for running away.

I won't make that mistake again.

If I'm going to move on, I have to stop thinking about the piano, and stay the hell away from Sweet Reverie. I don't want to be reminded of what happened there. It would do me no good to return.

Taking a last look at the view, I set my sights on the road rising further out of town and start walking.

Seventeen

MERRYN

Sunday opening is a blessing after my run-in with Luke. The café is packed with people making the most of the day, lingering over coffee and brunch, the vibe laid-back and calm, as Murph and I sail from table to table. Lazy Sundays are my favourite and the familiar pace of service soothes me.

For once, I'm glad Ruthie isn't in today. Murph is a joy, a typical laid-back Cornish dude who does everything at his own speed but is so affable that nobody seems to mind. He feels like a great fit for our steadily expanding team and I'm grateful he's here.

I let him leave at three p.m., when trade eases a little, holding the fort alone for the last hour. A customer playing a lovely Brahms piece on Merlin and the gentle breeze blowing in from the open front door are balms to my soul.

But the moment the café is quiet and the customers are gone, fury returns from my early morning encounter, joining my lingering frustration with Ruthie and Seth for how they handled the man who ran away last night.

I don't remember much of the journey back here from the Island this morning, only that when I unlocked the front door

I noticed furious red half-moon scars in my palms where my clenched fists had driven my fingernails in.

I am *done* with people assuming they know what's best for me. Everything I now have is here because *I* made it happen. The insinuation that I can't cope alone, or that I need someone else to tell me what to do, stings my soul. I survived the toughest of childhoods to put myself through college and university. I kept myself together when Luke blew my world apart with his betrayal. And I'm here, now, builder of a successful business that is growing, expanding my initial vision beyond anything I could have imagined.

Weariness hits me as soon as the door is locked, the final tasks of the workday done. I wander through my café, the chairs up on the tables ready for tomorrow's trading and the space eerily silent after the bustle and life that's filled it today. I move to the courtyard and gently replace Merlin's cover, hesitating for just a moment to stare at the closed piano lid before covering it completely.

Ruthie found it so easy to play. So did Nessie and twenty or more of last night's guests. Just walked up, took a seat on the old piano stool and played. Like it was simple.

Why can't I do that?

I could try, here, now, in the silent surroundings of my closed café, with nobody to witness my playing. It's just Merlin and me in the afternoon sun that fills the courtyard and warms my skin.

Safe in the knowledge that I'm alone, I'm tempted.

Gingerly, I pick up one side of the cover again, lifting the piano's lid beneath to reveal the keys.

One note. That's all I need to play to break the spell.

One note to send the painful memories scattering, to reclaim my right to make music on these aged keys. One note to accept I will probably never find Grant. One note to reconcile what I lost then with what I've found now. One note to prove to myself that the only person who owns my past is me.

I sit slowly on the old piano stool, watching dust motes spinning in the shaft of afternoon sun pouring into the courtyard. If ever there was a perfect time to play, it's now. Nerves flutter, but peace calms me.

If Grant were here now, he'd tell me to play.

What if playing is the best tribute I can give him?

My fingers hover just above the keys, in a C chord, the first chord Grant taught me. The slightest movement will bring them down upon the keys.

We start with C. And then we'll see . . .

My heart lurches at the memory of Grant's words.

No sharps or flats to worry about here, birdie. Just plain sailing, straight up the scale . . .

This time, I won't let fear stop me. Merlin is my piano, brought into my life by a gentle serendipity: it should be mine to play.

I take a breath, and . . .

'The gate was wide open. Again!'

Seth's bark behind me sends my hands flying up from the keys, like startled seagulls flapping away from an angry shout.

'How did you get in?' I demand.

'The *side gate*,' he repeats, 'which you always forget to lock.'

My hackles are up already, his rude interruption having robbed me of the chance to play.

'It's not even five minutes since I closed the front door.'

'The side gate should be first.'

'Says who?'

'Me.'

I close Merlin's lid. 'It's my gate.'

He stares at me like I've just claimed ownership of the waves in the harbour. 'What the hell does it matter? You need to be safe.'

I jump up from the piano stool, the cover dropping over Merlin as I let go. 'And you need to butt out!'

'I'm tryin' to help you, Mer! Don't bite my head off!'

'I'm not the one stomping in here, yelling about the gate!'

I don't care if he was expecting a fight or not. I needed a target for the anger I've repressed all day and Seth just stepped into range.

'Can't I be worried about you? Can't I be concerned after what happened last night?'

I've heard enough. '*What happened* last night was an innocent accident made into a completely unnecessary drama by you!'

Seth reddens and I brace for his reply.

'He could have been anyone. He could have caused trouble.'

'Or he could have been a first-time visitor, embarrassed about bumping into Nessie and scared out of his wits by you chasing him away.'

'It wasn't his first time,' he bites back, as I realise my mistake. 'Ruthie said he was the customer who skipped out without payin' last week.'

'Oh *so what*? One pot of tea and a plate of biscuits, Seth, not the entire day's takings. Did you think he'd come back to do it again?'

'He could cause you grief, bird! He could be casin' up the café to steal more than biscuits.'

149

'Then why did he run away, hm? If he's this master criminal, casing up the joint to rob me blind, why be scared by you?'

'You think I couldn't handle him?'

Now he's just being ridiculous.

'This isn't about you. Because, believe it or not, I have more important things to consider than whether you could beat up a stranger.'

'Yeah? Like what?'

I square up to him, chin high, knowing that my reply will snuff out his anger. 'I saw Luke.'

The name steals his thunder. He blinks, winded. 'When?'

'This morning.'

'Where?'

'Up on the Island.'

'Oh, bird. How was it?'

'Like I thought it would be. Him boasting about all the success he's going to have, and asking me to vouch for him.'

'What?'

'With the town traders. He thinks I should be over what he did by now, so I can make his life easier for him by giving in to his every whim.'

'*Shit*, Mer.'

I round on him, determined not to let up. 'I am so tired of people thinking they can override my desires and decisions as if they don't matter. So you'll forgive me if I don't want you, or Luke, or anyone in St Ives telling me what I should and shouldn't do. *My* café. *My* business. *My* life. Not his. Or yours.'

He's silent for a moment. When he speaks again, the fire is gone entirely. 'I'm not tryin' to tell you what to do.'

'You just marched in here shouting at me about the side gate.'

He can't argue with that and he knows it. He drops his gaze to the floor. 'I care about you, Mer.'

'So trust me to look after myself. Please.'

'I do trust you. Whatever you think.' Seth reaches into his pocket and pulls out an object. He reaches past me, placing it on the top of the piano. 'I got you this. You should use it.' As he moves back, he pauses, close to me. 'I don't want to fight with you. I just want to keep you safe.'

'I'll be fine,' I reply. 'Thanks for your concern.'

I'm still rattled when he leaves. I hate arguing with Seth, but today has been a battle I was unprepared to encounter. I've fought so hard to carve out my own space, so it's only right I defend it.

Looking back at the piano, I see what he left there.

A padlock.

A completely overblown device, with combination lock and thick, steel base where the key fits. The kind of thing that should be bolted to an industrial unit, not the curling wrought iron of Sweet Reverie's side gate.

Instantly, I'm fuming again.

If the man who ran from the celebration last night were ever to return and see this monstrosity fixed to the gate he entered by, what message would it send? Sweet Reverie should be welcoming for everyone, not just the people Seth Hartley deems worthy to enter. And what gives him the right to decide who is and isn't allowed into *my* business anyway?

I snatch up the padlock and storm back into the café, throwing it into the bin behind the counter. It lands with a satisfyingly heavy clunk.

Nobody tells me what to do with my business. With my life.

Not Luke. Not Seth. Not Ruthie. Or anyone else.

I fetch the chalk paint pens and open the café door, the early evening sunshine flooding the space. Its warmth soothes me, the golden light it paints the front of Sweet Reverie lifting my heart.

The blackboard sign is where I fixed it last week, the message about the evening opening celebration gone after Murph cleaned it this morning. Time for a new invitation to live there: one that will be open to all, but I hope might be seen by one.

Steadying my hand, I write.

Welcome to Sweet Reverie.
Our piano is waiting in the courtyard,
if you want to play.

I surround the words with music notes and add a small gold heart above the name of my café.

It's the invitation I imagined when we found Merlin on the street and it looks completely at home on the blackboard sign now. This is what I want visitors to see when they visit Sweet Reverie, not a forbidding padlock.

I don't lock the side gate, just pull it closed and leave it on its latch. I've never had anyone use the side passage to gain after-hours entry to the café in the three years I've been trading and I won't start to worry about it now. A huge padlock is a challenge, suggesting the building is worth robbing. The gate remaining as it always has been draws no attention. That's how I want it to be. The locks on the back door of the café are secure and I feel safe here at night. Seth's overprotectiveness and Ruthie's dire imaginings are not going to change that.

The man who ran last night will probably never return.

But at least this stops anyone else from feeling too scared to visit my café.

I'm tired, and my heart hurts. I need food, a bath and an early night. Tomorrow will be brighter. I know it will.

Tonight, I need to hide away and let the sound of the sea lull me to sleep.

Eighteen

ZACH

Everything aches.

I walked much further than I'd intended, taking the road past Leach Pottery up into the windswept countryside above St Ives. It was beautiful and quiet, which made me want to keep walking, a blessing after the crowds and noise down in the town. It was only when my stomach protested its emptiness that I thought to turn back – realising how far I'd walked.

By the time I return to Kieran's studio – hungry, thirsty and bone-tired – it's well past six p.m.

And Kieran is waiting for me.

'Where have you been?' he demands, blocking the entrance.

'I went out,' I reply.

'Where?'

'For a walk.' I'm taken aback by his attitude. What business is it of his what I do when I'm out of the building? Wasn't he the one who told me to make myself scarce during the day?

'I've been calling you for *hours*,' he growls, still not relinquishing his position to let me inside. 'And then, when I get here, your phone is on the table.'

'I didn't need it.'

What is his problem? Nobody was going to call me today – or so I thought.

'Well *I* needed *you*.'

'I'm here now. Can I come in?'

He deigns to grant me entry, eyeballing me as I pass. 'We had a break-in.'

The air is instantly sucked from my lungs. 'When?'

'Sometime this morning. Presumably while you were off on your *walk*.' He says the word like it's a lame excuse I've given him, thrown back at me as an accusation of something else.

'What did they take?'

'Nothing that I can see. But they messed up the workstation and left *that* on the wall.'

I see it a heartbeat before Kieran says it. An ugly mess of spray paint tags on the wall beside the workstation, one discarded can lying in a lime green paint puddle staining the laminate floor beneath.

'I can get that off,' I rush, my heart thudding to my Havaianas.

'You wouldn't have to,' Kieran growls, 'if you'd been here . . .'

I'm not having that. It sucks that kids got in but what does he expect me to do? Become a hermit here?

'Mate, look, I could have been at work. I could have had a meeting with someone. How was I to know somebody was going to break in? In daylight?'

His eyes don't leave me. 'I said you could stay to keep an eye on the place.'

'You told me to make myself scarce during the day!' I don't need to antagonise my temporary landlord, but I won't be accused of something I haven't done. If this is how it ends, so be it. I don't know where else I'd go, but that's immaterial. I refuse to let Kieran Macklin use me for his own private punchbag whenever Aggie isn't there to keep him in check.

He relents a little, knowing I'm right. But I don't dare hope it's enough to pacify him. 'If you're security for this place you have to be here.'

'I work three days a week, more when Pengelly's opens next weekend. I can't stay in here twenty-four-seven. And maybe you need a better lock on the door, or CCTV or something.'

He hefts a sigh and shakes his head. 'That's what I don't understand: there was no damage to the door. Or the window in the back. No scratches where they used a screwdriver or something to prise the door open.'

'That's odd.'

'And they didn't take anything. Just made a mess and left.'

'Maybe that's what they were after. Chance to break in and leave a mess, rather than steal anything.'

'I have to hope so. Unless they went to get their mates to come back.'

It's a scary thought, but I sense a lessening of the taut atmosphere between us. 'I'm sorry they got in. Truly, Kieran. But I can't be here all the time. I've got to work.'

He raises a hand. 'Yeah, I know. I just need you to be contactable, at least. You should keep your phone with you.'

My gaze shifts to my phone on the low table. I left it behind because I didn't want to be chained to it. I've wasted far too many hours of my life endlessly scrolling social media whenever I've felt lonely, or on edge. I didn't need its constant pull of nothingness today. I just needed to walk.

But Kieran has a point about me staying contactable. He

might need me, or my sis might break the habit of a lifetime and call me instead of text. Or Matt or Luke might need me to work at short notice, neither of whom I should turn down, given my still-precarious personal finances.

'I will do,' I relent. 'But I think you should get some stronger locks for this place.'

'Already on it. Locksmith will be in tomorrow morning – I know you'll be at work, so I'll deal with that. Just keep your phone on, yeah?'

'No problem.'

I watch as he stands, stuffing his anger away in overflowing pockets. I don't ever think we'll be best buddies, but him not yelling at me is a start.

I fall on the food supplies the tiny fridge holds as soon as Kieran leaves. As first meals of the day at almost seven o'clock in the evening go, it isn't the prettiest, but the cheap frozen pizza and microwave mash with cheese I heap onto my plate feels like the biggest, most desirable feast. When I'm finished, I wash up my plate and the cooking stuff and collapse on the sofa. I'm so tired I can't keep my eyes open.

When I bump awake, not even realising I'd fallen asleep, the room is in darkness. I snap on a light and squint at my watch, shocked to find it's almost midnight. Groaning, I coax my weary body away from the cushions and reluctantly rise to my feet.

I move through to the small bedroom and throw back the duvet. But a sudden, metallic thud close by stops me climbing in.

What was that?

I look down to scan the floor for whatever fell – and can't believe what I see.

My keys.

They must have been on the bed, disturbed when I pulled the duvet back. But this is the first time I've been in here since I returned from my walk.

Which means . . .

My head swims.

Which means I didn't take them with me. And I couldn't have locked the door without them.

Shit.

I left Kieran's studio without locking the door, meaning that whoever 'broke in' to the studio didn't have to break anything to enter. I practically invited them in.

How did I let this happen?

I wasn't thinking straight this morning, the mortification from last night dominating my mind. I walked out of the studio without locking the door, without even checking it as I've always done. My keys were in here – available to anyone who came looking. They didn't take anything, but it could have been so much worse . . .

Why didn't I check I had my keys before I left? Why did it never cross my mind?

Kieran didn't want me to stay here in the first place, and I'll take a wild guess that he spent most of today wishing he'd never acquiesced.

I've just spectacularly proved his point, haven't I?

Despite the bullet I know I've dodged, I feel awful.

The peace and calm my walk brought me is gone, the gnawing ache returned to replace it. Am I ever going to find myself in this new life? Vulnerability scares me – and where most of my life I've chased my own fears, here I'm powerless to fight them.

So little from my former life remains. Even the clothes I'm

wearing now I bought after leaving my flat. There's nothing to show the Zach Trevelyan from before ever existed.

I should get back in the water. I haven't tried for months, since my last attempt ended in agony. My knee just can't flex like it used to, so all of the moves that came naturally to me don't work anymore. To have a hope of surfing again, I'll have to relearn from scratch, working with what I have now instead of the ability I enjoyed before. That seems like an insurmountable wave, towering high above me.

And why would I even attempt it? When I started surfing I was chasing a dream, every setback and issue another challenge on the road to where I wanted to be. My reason for getting back on the board was what I could see, way ahead, just out of my reach. Even when I turned pro, the dream remained just ahead of me, like chasing a rainbow across the sea. There were always new titles, higher scores and bigger prizes to aim for.

What would relearning my sport offer me now?

Jakey Lowen said he could get me back on my board when I met him on the beach. I could ask for his help, but how much of a comedown would that be? I coached him for six months after an injury and I remember him saying he had to bite his own pride to let me do it. Of all my former surfing mates, he'd be the one who'd understand. But I don't know if I can bring myself to be taught by someone who once looked up to me. Especially not surrounded by kids learning in the surf school.

I catch my train of thought before it thunders wildly off-track. No good will come of wrestling with this now. I should just go to bed and sleep it all off.

Except I'm too awake.

Hurting and alone, with nobody to call.

Suddenly, the four walls I've been so grateful to claim a place within become stifling. Worse than this morning. They crowd me in, stealing my air.

I need to get out again.

This time I shrug on a hoodie and ensure I have my phone and keys, as if being prepared will undo the damage of the day. I check the front door three times to ensure it's locked, and duck out into the night.

I tell myself I don't have a destination, that I'm just wandering the deserted streets in an aimless manner to distract my mind. But I know where my feet are taking me. I'm laying the ghosts of yesterday to rest, in the one place I've promised myself I'll never revisit.

Even though the café will be closed and the people inside it will long since have gone to their beds. Even though the three buildings in Star Court will be in darkness. If I can return there, my fears can be allayed and I might just have a chance of sleep tonight.

Nearing the narrow alleyway that leads to my destination, I finally admit to myself what I'm here to do. I'll just stand by the café, my feet completing a loop from when they ran from it yesterday. The act of returning will prove to myself that yesterday was one day in ten thousand; that the mistake I made here doesn't define me or bar me from ever coming back.

It wouldn't make sense to anyone else, but the rush of adrenaline I feel as I enter the street confirms my actions. I just want to feel like me again. The old me would have returned immediately this morning. The old me would never have run last night.

Mum called it 'inexplicable necessity'. *Sometimes you have to do something inexplicably odd to meet your needs. It doesn't have to make sense: it's symbolic only to you. But it's necessary for whatever your strange, unique, unconventional mind needs to deal with.*

She lived that theory, often dragging Elowen and me out to random places to do things like laying a pile of pebbles, or splashing her hands in a stream, or eating ice creams on the blusteriest beaches in the dead of winter. Tiny, incomprehensible acts that changed her outlook for the better.

Why have I forgotten this until now?

I reach the darkened building and stand outside. It's still, its windows blank shadows. The glass pane in the door reveals the *CLOSED* sign. There's no movement anywhere, not in the café, the surf shop or the empty deli. Checking nobody is approaching from either end of the street, I take a step forward, flattening my palm against the cool wood of the door.

'I'm sorry,' I whisper, because it makes sense in this inexplicable necessity of mine. 'I just wanted to play.'

Maybe the building will absorb my apology, pacifying the restless ghosts of last night with my words. Or maybe, when Merryn arrives to open up tomorrow morning, she'll think kindly of me. Not that I know what she thinks of me. I didn't stop to check her expression before I fled.

But it's said. And oddly, I feel calmer.

Wherever Mum is, I hope she's laughing her head off at me.

I step back – and something catches my eye. A glint of gold to my left, along the café wall. Whatever's making it is catching the white light from the streetlight opposite. Intrigued, I move closer.

It's a heart. A small, hand-drawn heart in sparkly gold paint, drawn on the blackboard sign I saw Merryn fixing in place a week ago. It's surrounded by pink and green music notes forming a border to a message.

The words stop me in my tracks.

Welcome to Sweet Reverie.
Our piano is waiting in the courtyard,
if you want to play.

Did she write this for everyone, or is it meant for me?

My heartbeat thunders in my ears, the shock of the message so soon after the building witnessed my apology too intriguing to ignore.

The invitation swims in my vision. I rub the saltwater away. I'm tired and at the end of myself. But *this* . . .

My gaze passes to the left of the sign, to the wrought-iron gate across the entrance to the side passage leading to the courtyard. Last night it was unlocked, my hands fumbling with the latch in my desperation to get out.

What if . . . ?

I glance back at the windows of Sweet Reverie. There's no light visible in the ground floor or the storey above. There are no drawn curtains, or signs of life. If the gate is locked, I'll go home, the message enough to soothe my battered head.

But if it's open . . .

I can't resist the invitation.

I approach the gate, searching its edge for any sign of a lock beyond the latch. Nothing. Just the gently curving filigrees of iron curling around the arch. Honeysuckle trails over the top, its scent strong in the still night air. It's magical in the white glow of the streetlight. Like a partially hidden entrance to a secret world.

If the gate opens, I'll accept Merryn's invitation. The piano is in the courtyard and there's no gate or barrier to it beyond this one. I can slip in, play a little, then leave.

My fingers find the latch, cold in the still-warm night.

So close to a discovery, I hesitate. Should I be doing this? What if the invitation only applies during trading hours?

But I don't know if I can return when the café is open yet. Coming here tonight was enough of a risk. And to play a piano now would bring me the one thing I crave: a connection with who I was.

It only needs to be for a few minutes. I'll go as soon as I've played.

In that moment, it's all I want.

I try the latch, willing it to move . . . and it does.

Nineteen

MERRYN

I wake suddenly, eyes blinking open in my darkened bedroom.

The room is silent, but my body is tense beneath the sheets, an uncomfortable heat beneath me. I must have been restless in my sleep, although I can't remember dreaming. My limbs are numb, almost not feeling like my own, as I untangle myself from the bedclothes and sit up.

The red display on my alarm clock stings my eyes as they slowly focus: 12.19 a.m.

Groaning, I flop back against my pillow. If there was ever a night I needed sleep, it's this one. After the emotional roller-coaster of yesterday, sleep was all I wanted. It's probably why I was restless – the aftermath of drama still playing out in my subconscious mind. But what just dragged me from sleep?

And then, I hear it.

Music.

A gentle, soft sound, from a direction I can't work out.

It isn't like the music I sometimes hear drifting into the street from a nearby pub. There's nobody in the upper storeys of either Porthia Surf or Dydh Da. Seth sometimes stays in the flat above his shop in high season when he rents out his place to holidaymakers, but he won't be doing that until next week.

There's no beat to the music, only melody. And as I listen, the notes begin to form a familiar pattern. A song from somewhere before. Music I haven't heard for years.

Not since . . .

Heart beating wildly, I scramble out of bed and throw on a sweatshirt over my vest top and pyjama shorts, grabbing a heavy torch I've kept on my bedside table since St Ives was hit by a raft of power cuts, caused by storms, back in the spring.

As soon as I'm at the top of the stairs, I know where the music is coming from.

And what is playing it.

But that's not possible, is it?

The tune is unmistakable now, a melody I know like my own breath. My hands shake as I hold the torch, unlit, like a weapon. I reach the bottom step and my breath stalls as the source of the music becomes clear.

Someone is playing Merlin.

And the song I've missed since Grant Henderson moved out of my life.

'Time Wears Awa' – an old Scottish folk song that tells of two people reflecting back on a lifetime of loving one another. Grant sang it to Mum, hoping maybe they would have a similar love story. Or perhaps because he knew they wouldn't – that Mum wasn't capable of loving someone the way the couple in the song do.

The music dances and spins around the tiny courtyard, a beautiful, beguiling melody that draws me in. It isn't how

Grant played it, but the notes flow with emotion that sweeps me into the tune.

I move quietly through the darkened café to the back door, turning the key as softly as I can. The door swings open silently, the barrier between the music and me gone.

And I see him.

A sandy-haired man, dressed in a faded blue hoodie and jeans, his head bent a little as his fingers travel across the keys, his eyes closed and the gentlest smile on his lips. It's mesmerising: I can't tear my gaze away.

Because I know him.

The man I danced with in the street, and saw outside the café. The man who ran from the opening celebration last night. Did he see the new message on the sign? Is that why he's come back?

Now I know my trust in him was justified. Seth was wrong: he isn't creepy or out to steal anything from me. He just wanted to play. I saw it in his expression, seconds before Nessie Dixon collided with him. That longing. I recognised it immediately because I feel it, too, every time I pass the piano. Only unlike me, he can play.

The smile he wears tells a million tales. Relief, joy, connection, a sense of finding something precious that was lost. Everything I want to feel if I can ever dare to touch the keys.

I slip out into the courtyard and sit on the step that marks the border between the outside and inside spaces of Sweet Reverie. The man remains lost in the music he's making, unaware that he has an audience tonight. I can't stop watching the movement of his fingers, the emotions playing across his face.

I would sometimes sneak out of bed when Grant was with us, perching halfway down the stairs and peering through the cracked and peeling wooden spindles of the banister to watch him play. From my vantage point I could see one edge of the piano and his right shoulder through the open living-room door. When the melody rose to the upper realms of the keys it would thrill me to see his hand appear, a musical game of hide-and-seek that made me feel at home for the first time in my young life. Music was the connection, the identity, the expression of love and safety neither of us could speak out loud.

I feel it now: that thrill as the tune lifts, the melody holding us both captive – him as the player and me as the listener. It's a moment out of time, a stunning serendipity I could never have imagined would happen here, in the darkened courtyard, hours before dawn.

In that moment, I forget everything. The drama, the concern, the impossibly late hour, the chill of the courtyard and the trespasser who really shouldn't be here. All that matters is the music.

He plays as if the piano is his lifeline, as if every modulation and improvisation he weaves around the tune my heart knows so well brings him closer to where his heart wants to be.

It's all in the heart, Grant told me once. *You can teach anyone to play what's written in the music, but you can't teach them to feel it. That has to come from the heart. You'll always tell a melody played from the heart because you feel it, here.*

His hand had tapped his chest above where his own heart was beating.

I place my hand on my heart now, feeling it race as the man at the piano plays.

It's all in the heart.

My heart feels fuller than I can ever remember.

And then, the song ends. The man sits back, rubs his eyes – and looks over his shoulder.

Instantly, he's on his feet, wide-eyed with shock, his hand reaching out as if to hold back an invisible tide.

'I'm sorry . . . I shouldn't have . . . I didn't know anyone was here.'

I jump up, my own hands outstretched. 'No, it's okay.'

'Don't call the police.'

'I won't.'

'I'm going now. I'm sorry.'

'Don't go. That was beautiful. I love your playing.' When he stares back, uncertainty focused on me, I press on. 'Stay. Please?'

'It's stupid o'clock. I'm sorry to wake you. The sign . . .'

'. . . was for you,' I rush. I can't let him leave thinking this was a mistake.

'For me?'

'I hoped you might see it.'

'Why?'

'Because I know you wanted to play. At the celebration? I'm so sorry if you felt unwelcome last night. The piano – Merlin – is for everyone.'

'I shouldn't have come.'

'Yes, you should.' I don't know if he trusts what I'm saying. I hope he does. 'I'm Merryn Rowe. I own Sweet Reverie.'

He considers my outstretched hand for a moment, then takes it. The meeting of his skin and mine is like a long-forgotten welcome.

'Zach . . .' He clears his throat, staring at my hand in his. 'I'm Zach Trevelyan.'

'You play from the heart,' I say, the words spilling out, encouraged by the warmth of our joined hands.

'What?'

'Someone I used to know, someone special, said that the best way to play is from the heart. That it makes all the difference to the music.'

'They sound wise.' He's staring back at me now, as if he can't quite believe we're here. 'Playing helps. Always has.'

I nod like I understand. Because I do, in theory. I know if I could get over this insurmountable barrier between my hands and the keys, I'd find peace at the piano. 'Play whenever you like.'

A hint of a smile dances on his lips. 'Maybe not after midnight, though, right?'

'It's an interesting choice.'

'Yeah.' Zach releases my hand, folding his arms as if a chill has entered the courtyard. 'I couldn't sleep. And it's been so long since I could play.'

'You don't have a piano at home?'

'I don't have a home.' My heart contracts at the sadness in his smile. 'Not a permanent one, anyway. I had to leave my last place, sell everything. My piano couldn't come with me.'

Is that what happened with Merlin's previous owner? The question presents itself and I wonder why I've never considered it before. Whoever lived in the property in North Terrace before it was sold to the developer must have had good reason to leave the piano behind. Was it their decision to sell the house, or did their landlord decide it? How much time did they have to find somewhere else to live? Was the piano a casualty of the move? Or was it a legacy from an earlier occupant, discarded by someone who didn't appreciate its worth?

'I'm sorry that happened to you,' I say.

'Um, thanks.'

I wonder if anyone has ever said that to him before. The way he receives it from me, with a combination of surprise and cautiousness, suggests maybe it's the first time.

'You can play here, Zach, whenever you like. I mean it.'

'If I did—' he holds my gaze, '—would you listen?'

A ripple of excitement passes across my shoulders. 'I'd love to.'

When he smiles, it's like sunshine breaking over the sea. 'Then I will.'

Twenty

ZACH

Merryn Rowe is a shock to my system.

I didn't know she lived above her café, and when I realised she was watching me, I just wanted to get out of there. But as I watch a smile bloom on her lovely face, my world tilts.

She's beautiful: not just as she appears before me, with her sleep-ruffled hair and flushed cheeks; but in the words she chooses so carefully and the heart beating behind them. I caught it when I first saw her, like a glint of sun on the waves, but standing opposite her now I'm captured by her light. She's luminous, in her crumpled sweatshirt and striped pyjama shorts.

And she's just given me the gift of her permission to play this piano.

Before I knew she was there, before I was aware of my audience of one, I found peace in this small, dark courtyard. The moment my fingers met the keys of the old piano, the release I've longed for arrived. The first song I played was an old Scottish folk tune my grandpa taught me, before dementia stole the music from his mind. Playing made it all feel better, even just for a few minutes.

'I should let you get back to bed,' I say, suddenly aware of how little time we'll both have to catch any sleep before our Mondays begin.

'Probably.'

We share an awkward pause before Merryn makes the first move, walking to the side of the courtyard that leads to the passage. I follow her down the narrow path towards the iron gate.

At the boundary between the gate and the street beyond it, she stops walking and looks up at me, her eyes bright despite the shadows.

'Thanks for the music,' she says.

'Thanks for the invitation,' I reply.

Her smile when I leave will stay with me long past tonight. It will call me back like the pull of the piano, stronger now than it was before.

*

'Bleddy hell, Zach, who did you fight for glory last night?'

Matt is irritatingly chipper at five a.m., all jokes and gentle digs I'm too knackered to spot. But then you can't expect anything less from a bloke who gets up at three a.m. to bake every morning.

'I didn't sleep much,' I reply adding the last loaf to the crate I'm filling, hefting it off the stainless steel prep table with a groan.

'Evidently. You okay to drive?'

'Yeah no worries. I have coffee.'

A frown furrows Matt's brow. 'What kind of coffee?'

'Instant. In a flask.'

If I'd said Matt's bread was filled with sawdust I couldn't receive as damning a look as he sends me now. 'Hand it over.'

'I just put it in the van.'

'Then *bring it out*.'

He's deadly serious. I don't have the will – or physical ability – to argue, so I trot out like an obedient puppy to the half-packed van parked on the cobbles outside the bakery, the orange flashes from its hazard lights bouncing off the neighbouring whitewashed buildings.

When I hand my flask to Matt, he opens the lid, takes a disparaging sniff, then deposits the lot in the wide sink beneath the window.

'I need that!' I wail.

'Trust me, Z-man, you do *not* need that in your life.' He rinses the inside with tap water and reaches for the glass percolator jug on the machine in the corner, pouring glossy, dark coffee into my waiting flask. The scent that surrounds us is something else. '*This* is what you need. And don't insult my business by bringing in that freeze-dried pap again.'

At least he's smiling when he says this. And I am not likely to turn down free coffee this morning, whatever its source.

'Cheers, boss.'

'Hang on . . .' He grabs two thick slices of sausage roll from a tray on the multi-shelved baking trolley, wrapping them in a length of tinfoil and handing the deliciously warm package to me. 'Eat as you go. I don't want you veering off the road due to low blood sugar.'

He's terrifying when he's being funny, but I can't fault his generosity. Other employers might have sent me packing for turning up to work looking like a sleep-deprived zombie, but not Matt. It's a blessing I won't forget to count.

And it's not alone.

As I drive the van along my route, my thoughts stray to Merryn. She was incredible last night. It's only now I'm navigating the twists and turns of the country roads that the danger of what I did hits me. She could have been terrified to find me in the courtyard. She would have been well within her rights to call the police, or demand I leave. Why didn't I consider her in the equation when I was staring at the gate, tempted to enter?

Truth is, I wasn't thinking straight. But the building was in darkness, with no drawn curtains on the first floor to suggest anybody lived there. I went to the courtyard because I believed I was alone. Thought I could sneak in, play and leave, with nobody any the wiser.

I didn't bank on Merryn Rowe.

The invitation was for you . . .

Have I remembered that correctly? Or has my sleep-starved mind added that embellishment? Did Merryn deliberately leave the message on the board for me to see? And what about the unlocked side gate? Was that part of her invitation, too?

'Lovely day for it,' Eric Cuthbert quips, as I unload the delivery for The Water Mill pub.

He says it every morning I visit, but I've learned it's his version of a twenty-minute chat.

'It is indeed, Eric. You expecting a busy one?'

'Don't we always?' he chuckles, despite his eye-roll. 'You take care now, boy.'

I wonder if he looks forward to our five-line conversation each delivery day, as I do.

I love it, I'll admit. It's acceptance: none of the scrutiny and unmasked suspicion I was greeted with by nearly everyone during my first two shifts. Two weeks in, I'm practically family.

Still-a-bit-distant family, that is, but I'm happy with it.

Trust is hard won in Cornwall. If you get even a glimpse of it, you're in.

Matt's superior coffee and excellent slices of sausage roll sustain me as I continue on my round. I'm glad I appalled him with my woeful beverage offering if this is the replacement I get. I can't do this tomorrow, but then I don't plan on playing piano in a stolen session for a lovely woman tonight.

A *beautiful* woman . . .

The dawn arrives, more sparkling and clear than any I've seen on my rounds since I started this job. Or is that my imagination because of what happened at Sweet Reverie last night?

I don't care.

The combination of playing piano at last and the unexpected company I had has lifted me from wherever the hell I was yesterday. I feel lighter, calmer, as I will the van up steep, single-track roads to reach my drop-offs in faster time. I'm learning short cuts, some suggested by customers, some discovered by trial, error and winding up in unfamiliar farmyard dead ends.

Yesterday, I couldn't imagine feeling positive about my life again.

This morning, I can't wait to find out what happens next.

The piano changed that. And Merryn.

I need to go back to Sweet Reverie. Soon.

The question is, when?

PART TWO

'Find Me'

– Sigma feat. Birdy

Twenty-One

MERRYN

'Merryn?'

I'm cleaning the chrome front of our espresso machine, watching the shine build with every stroke. Everything looks brighter this morning, from the sparkling sunshine flooding Sweet Reverie to the new batch of cakes that our supplier just delivered. The lemon, strawberry and cherry glazes gracing each four-layered sponge cake glisten as they sit on the counter, waiting for us to divide them into slices and place under the glass cloches.

'Earth to Merryn . . . ?'

I feel brighter, too. Despite falling back into bed just before three a.m. and my alarm rousing me at six. Despite every muscle in my body protesting. I ache, but I don't care. All I can think about is last night . . .

'I mean, I could try semaphore if it would be easier . . .'

. . . And Zach Trevelyan. I wanted the man who ran to feel welcomed back, but I couldn't have dreamed he would bring so much with him. That song, the one I haven't heard for years that's played in endless loops whenever I've thought of Grant. And the surprise of Zach himself. His story, which I still don't know all of. His heart, flowing through the melody as he played our piano like it was his lifeline.

'. . . Or Morse code? Maybe I could summon aliens to spell out the phrase *HEY BOSS* in the sky?'

I blink. 'Aliens?'

Ruthie is beside me, arms folded, judgement in full swing. 'I knew you weren't listenin' to me.'

I offer her a sheepish smile by way of apology. 'Sorry, Ruthie. I was miles away.'

'Tell me about it. What's got into you?'

'Nothing. I just didn't sleep well.'

My assistant's eyes narrow. 'Well the sleep you got was enough to power that big, dopey smile you're wearin'.'

Am I smiling?

Okay, I know the answer – the fact of which only makes me smile more.

'I don't have a dopey smile.'

'You do this mornin'. Also cotton wool in your ears, apparently.'

I snort-laugh at this. It's such an old-fashioned phrase for my very modern, absolutely Gen Z colleague to choose. 'I just need sleep.'

'You need *somethin'* . . .' She stares into my soul. 'You met someone?'

'No.'

She catches the note of uncertainty that sneaks into my reply. 'You have! Who is he?'

'You've got this all wrong.'

'I know a moonin' face when I see one, Mer, and yours is the mooniest one I've seen in a while.'

'Can we drop this?'

'Only if you give me his name.' Her eyes sparkle as another thought occurs. 'Or did you even catch his name?'

'What's that supposed to mean?'

'Well, if you had a cheeky one-nighter, perhaps there wasn't time . . .'

'*Ruthie!*'

She laughs, holding out a hand to me. 'Listen, bird, fair play to you if you did. I mean, it's been a while and a half, hasn't it? If anyone's earned a bit of horizontal boppin', it's you.'

This line of questioning is making me want to run from the café. How could I ever explain what happened when Ruthie's already made up her mind?

'Enough now,' I say, the sharpness of my words cutting the jovial atmosphere dead.

'Suit yourself.' She huffs and starts to restock the jar of mini marshmallows. It's a shocking masterclass in passive-aggressive confectionery handling.

If this was a different time, I might have confided in her. In Seth, too, before yesterday afternoon. It's still early, and Mondays are traditionally quiet first thing, even in the summer, but I've heard nothing from him. No apologetic or bullish texts. No missed calls or grudging voicemails. He was furious with me when he left and, to be honest, I was furious with him too.

If he finds out Zach not only gained entry to the courtyard last night through the gate I purposefully didn't lock but also roused me from my bed with his piano playing, Seth will hit the roof.

So I keep it to myself, loving the thrill of knowing something about my life that others don't.

Leaving the side gate accessible was the right thing for me to do.

But Seth believes he did the right thing, too, by insisting on greater security.

And so we stand at an impasse – or we will if he ever decides to speak to me again.

My mind drifts back to shadowy, intimate images from last night. Of how Zach's head bent a little as he played, like he was about to whisper secrets to the piano; of how his fingers coaxed the loveliest melodies from the keys, like they had been designed for his hands to touch. And of how he looked at me, startled and amazed, when we held hands.

He promised to return. But he left without saying *when*.

Which gives me a dilemma: do I change the sign tonight, extending the invitation again? And leave the gate lightly on its latch?

It's dangerous and thrilling and quite unlike anything I've done before.

But I want to see Zach again. Tonight.

Lunchtime arrives, the trickle of customers becoming a steady flow, and by the time we're doing the end-of-day tasks at five-thirty p.m., I'm about ready to drop.

'That's all the tables done,' Ruthie breezes, grabbing a broom. 'I'll do the floors and then I've got to shoot.'

'Doing something nice after work?' I ask.

She grins. 'Got a date.'

For a moment, I wonder if Seth has finally mustered the courage to ask Ruthie out. Or maybe she's made the decision for him?

'And you're only telling me this at the end of the day? Denying me gossip, Ruthie?'

'Nothin' to tell, yet,' she replies, clearly loving the revelation. 'With any luck, Nico will change that.'

So, not Seth. Those two have been dancing around each other for the best part of a year, the longing looks between them impossible to ignore. Will they ever admit how they feel?

'Nico who?'

'He's on the lifeboat crew. Built like a tower, smile like a dream. His dad owns *La Mer* over near Porthminster, so he's not short of cash, either.'

'He sounds delightful.'

'He's *sex on legs*.'

'That too.' I smile, Ruthie's summation of her date pure gold. 'I'll do the floors. You head off.'

'Lifesaver! Cheers!' My assistant props the broom against the counter, heading round to give me a hug before she grabs her bag and hurries to the door. Flinging it open, she looks back at me. 'Talk to Seth.'

'I will.'

Will I?

It's enough to send Ruthie out of the door, my café falling into delicious silence. I close my eyes and take a long, slow breath, the knots in my shoulders protesting.

A memory of last night returns: of Zach Trevelyan's stare that seemed to reach into me. That moment of connection in the night-dark courtyard, our hands lightly joined . . .

It was impossibly lovely. But nowhere near enough.

My decision is as easy as the breath moving freely through my lungs: I won't lock the gate again tonight.

Twenty-Two

ZACH

Luke Pengelly is persistent – I'll give him that.

I'm not due to start work at Pengelly's until Saturday afternoon, but a phone call from Luke after my bakery round has me heading back out into the busy streets to the harbour-front restaurant.

More has been done since my training session, the only thing missing from the restaurant and bar are customers to fill it. It's impressive, I'll admit, the kind of place you gaze in the windows of as you pass, promising yourself a visit. I can see it now, as I sit at a table beside the large windows: the turned heads of passing visitors that quickly become small groups peering at the gold-framed menu display by the front door.

Grinning like a cat that stole all the cream, Luke raises his hand at the gathered admirers, chuckling when they return bemused smiles in his direction.

'We've got pull,' he says, as if he's always known Pengelly's would.

I guess that kind of confidence is essential when you've invested as much in a new business venture as Luke has. But it doesn't impress everyone, it seems. I mentioned my soon-to-be second job to Matt this morning, just before I left Downalong Bakery, and his reaction was not what I expected . . .

'Pengelly, huh? Can't say I'm surprised he slithered back.'

'What do you mean by that?'

My morning employer shook his head. 'He has form, is all.'

Of course that was an invitation to gossip I wasn't going to refuse, even in my sleep-poor state.

'Okay, I need more than that. Spill the tea.'

Matt didn't need any more encouragement, launching into a fulsome critique of the newest member of the St Ives hospitality community.

'Opened the biggest place in town, just shy of four years ago. Bragged to all and sundry that it would put St Ives *on the culinary map*, threw money around like seawater to get people coming in. Then, after six months, he just shut the whole thing down. Overnight job. Staff only found out when they saw the closure notice on the front door.'

'That's awful,' I replied, my seemingly sure foundations in my second job suddenly rocky.

'Not the best, no.' Matt's smile faded a little. 'It was his missus I felt sorry for. He shut up shop, left her with a ton of angry staff, suppliers and customers to contend with, then skipped off to shack up with some other woman. So all I'm saying is be careful. He'll give it the *Big I Am* and throw his cash around, but he can change course like the wind.'

Listening to Luke now, bragging about the three solid weeks of bookings Pengelly's already has, I wonder how much of it is for show. I like the guy – I think he has drive and vision, which I don't always get to see close at hand. But what Matt told me earlier has set a question mark hanging over everything Luke says.

There's another thing: I'm the only one he's called in today. I arrived expecting the other team members to be here as they were last time. But it's just me.

I wait for a lull in his self-aggrandising flow to ask why.

'Is nobody else in today?'

He pauses for a moment before his perma-smile returns. 'Scotty's off with some investors so he won't be in. Oh, sorry, you mean the others?'

'I thought they'd be here, too.'

'Nah. I'm just taking the opportunity to get to know you all. Individually, that is.'

I'm not completely convinced by his bright reply. 'What do you want to know?'

'I just wanted to know more about your former career. Pro surfer in our midst is a pretty big deal. So, did you win much?'

It isn't what I was expecting to have to talk about, but fine. I don't mind the question, especially not from my new employer, who seems so interested. And my achievements are still impressive, even if the end of my career wasn't.

'Yeah, I did. I was a pro champion, five years running.'

'Impressive. Just this country or . . . ?'

'Mostly the UK, some Europe. Did a few competitions in the US towards the end.'

Luke sits back in his seat, observing me with a mixture of respect and amusement. Is he seeing me now, and the slight limp I walk with, wondering how this body won so many competitions? 'So we'll have a celebrity under our roof.'

'I don't know about that.'

'No – hang on – this could play to our advantage. If I were to, say, contact my friend at the *Cornwall Daily News* for a feature, would you be up for appearing in it?'

My stomach lurches. I'm resigned to people in St Ives knowing what I'm doing, but a feature in a paper my former surf competitors will read?

'I – I'm not sure . . .'

He waves away my reply. 'Nothing national. Zanna Venn is local. She handles business and good news stories. She wouldn't know a hatchet job if she found a shelf-full of them in B&Q.' The snigger he unleashes at his own joke isn't attractive. 'I'm just saying, Zach, we're proud of our team at Pengelly's. And knowing we have a champ on the squad might bring us more business. Not every restaurant in the town can say they have a former surf pro on their team. We should capitalise on that.'

'Even so . . .'

'Yeah, whatever. Think it over, okay? It could be good for you as well as us.'

Walking home afterwards, I'm still uneasy. It's clear the *getting to know the team* initiative was nothing more than Luke wanting to get me to agree to free publicity. Which wouldn't be so bad if he'd just been honest about it in the first place. I don't buy that he's repeating the meeting with my fellow team members and I don't know how to feel about what he's done.

Matt's advice remains at odds with Luke's over-enthusiastic manner as I mull it over. I'm glad I talked to my bakery boss before going to Pengelly's. It's given perspective to Luke's sales pitch. I need that. I haven't always made the best decisions when it comes to people I've put my trust in.

My first surf manager stole eight months' worth of

competition winnings from me in my first year as a pro. He had been a good mate – or so I'd believed. When I discovered the fraud, he'd already left the country. I wasn't his only victim, but I couldn't believe a friend could have done that to me.

I don't want to think Luke Pengelly will be a contender for the list of bad judgements in my life, but his stunt today hasn't helped my fear.

I can't think about this now. My brain's too fried to manage much more than finding food and going to bed today. And while I want to go back to Sweet Reverie, to play the piano for Merryn, I suspect that as soon as I lie down I'll be out of action till morning.

Tomorrow night, though.

I just need to think of a way of letting Merryn know.

On my way home, I duck into Wharf Post Office and Toy Shop on Chy-an-Chy. They have a tiny room filled with cards just off the main shop floor. I have a feeling I'll find what I need there.

It takes five minutes of sleepy-headed searching before I find it: an art card, blank on the inside, the picture on its front a small marmalade kitten asleep on a piano keyboard. More ginger than my hair is, but I hope she'll get the reference.

I need a pen, too, and am about to head to the counter where there's a display of them, when I notice a revolving wire display unit filled with boho-style surf bead bracelets. If I can't play for Merryn tonight, maybe a gift for her will be the next best thing?

Turning the creaking display slowly, I search for one that will be perfect to slip into the card for her. I think of her sun-streaked hair, the blush of pink along her cheekbones, the warmth of her skin when I held her hand . . .

What colour are her eyes?

In the gloom of the courtyard I couldn't make it out. I saw their brightness, the conviction they projected when she told me she'd left the sign for me. The gentlest stare behind which I sensed stories I've yet to discover.

And then, I see it. The perfect one.

It's woven from pale yellow thread, beads the colour of the midnight sky flanking white ones flecked with silver. They shimmer amid the blue like the stars I imagine sparkled over us last night, hidden from view by the courtyard roof. At the centre is one single pale gold bead, as welcoming as a rising summer moon over the sea. It reminds me of the welcome I found – precious, bright and completely unexpected. Merryn was the serendipity I couldn't have foreseen; her welcome the gift I didn't know I needed.

It's *her*. Everything I want to express to her that I'll never find words for.

I glance over my shoulder in case anyone is watching. I haven't been tempted to wax lyrical over someone for a long time and I'm not sure I want anybody seeing this. I take it to the till with the card and select an *I'D RATHER BE IN ST IVES* pen from the display box on the counter. The friendly lady behind the counter doesn't bat an eyelid at my strange collection of purchases. Even still, heat prickles my neck as I hurriedly thank her and leave the shop.

Back at the studio, I stare at the blank inside of the card, willing the right words to appear. I need to write them, put the bracelet inside the card and deliver it to Sweet Reverie. I know they close at five p.m. today, so an hour beyond should make it clear of anyone else. My weariness might just afford me enough time to see out my plan, I reckon. I'm dangerously tired now and need sleep. But this has to happen first.

I force my straying mind back to last night, to the relief of playing and the ground shock of discovering Merryn there. How do I express what I felt – what I still feel – so she'll understand what she did for me?

My mind settles on the image of us in the courtyard, our hands joined together, the feeling of finding a kindred spirit when I'd convinced myself I was alone.

That's when the words arrive.

My pen captures them before they're gone.

Then, I slip the bracelet inside the card, seal the envelope, and write Merryn's name on the front. I push myself to my feet and head back out into St Ives.

I hope she understands. I hope it's enough.

Twenty-Three

MERRYN

I don't want to sleep, but I do, the call of my bed overwhelming when I return upstairs to the flat. I just about manage to stay awake long enough to drink a mug of tea and set an alarm for ten p.m. before sleep claims me.

My dreams are cluttered, racing from one thing to another, a constant tension underpinning them. I'm running, desperate to return home, frustrated when the road ahead of me stretches out to infinity.

When my alarm rouses me, darkness fills my room. The urge to turn over and fall back asleep is strong, but a sudden panic pushes it aside.

What if Zach has visited already? What if I've missed him?

I hurry downstairs, switching on the lights in the café this time. It's silent, save for the usual clicks and hums of the fridge behind the counter that are so familiar I don't hear them most of the time. When I look out into the courtyard, the piano is still beneath its cover, the stool where I left it earlier, empty of any player.

My heart hits the cold slate floor beneath my bare feet.

He wasn't going to return immediately, was he? Considering how exhausted I've been, and how fast sleep came after work, he's probably in his own bed now, attempting to make up the sleep deficit. To come back here on so little sleep would have been the worst idea.

He said he'll come back, I reassure my fretting mind. I have to trust that he will, but also that he'll take care of himself.

I've been thinking about what he said, that he doesn't have a permanent home right now. Does that mean he's staying with someone else, or is he all alone? And is he working, or relying on someone else's kindness to get by? I hope there's someone looking after him, although his willingness to break into a café after hours to seek refuge at an old piano suggests there isn't. The way he played, as if each note was a lifeline, makes me wonder what he's dealing with all by himself.

When Luke left me with the mess of the restaurant, I lived at Seth's place for four months, sleeping on a single futon in his cramped second bedroom. It was far from ideal and the combination of what I was dealing with and our forced proximity made for an uncomfortable time together. I was broken, scrabbling around to salvage whatever shards of my former life I could. Seth was amazing, despite the stress and extra upheaval of keeping me fed, watered and cared for. I don't know how I would have navigated those initial months without him.

I know that's why he's protective of me now, despite how much I've achieved since. I'll go to see him tomorrow, to clear the air. Despite my frustrations with him, he's my best friend. I miss him when he isn't around. I know he'll have been miserable today, too, with us not talking.

We do this occasionally. Blow up at each other, then hide away while the dust settles. But we always bounce back. At the end of the day, that's the best anyone can hope for.

Does Zach have a friend like Seth in his life?

Certain he isn't coming now, I turn off the café lights and make my way back to the stairs. I glance at the front windows, as I always do before going back up to my flat, my eyes following the line of glass to the front door. When I see the light coming through the stained-glass border around the door's panel, my gaze drops.

Something square and pale is lying across the doormat, bright in the shaft of streetlamp glow coming in from the street.

I hurry across the cold floor and bend down to pick it up.

It's an envelope, with what feels like a card inside. It's bulkier in the centre, bowing the surface of the envelope. When I turn it over in my hands, my breath stalls.

For Merryn x

I don't recognise the handwriting, but its arrival here, unexpectedly, in the dark, sets my pulse racing. I hurry upstairs and go straight into my bedroom, switching on my bedside lamp.

I get into bed, pulling the covers back over my legs. Settling my breathing, I open the envelope.

There's a card inside. I smile when I see the photo of a cute ginger kitten on it curled up asleep on piano keys. As I open the card, something slides out, landing on the bedsheets. I reach down to retrieve it, surprised when my fingers close around beads and woven thread.

A bracelet. Woven twists of braided yellow cotton, with beads caught between. Dark blue, like the sky at midnight, white with tiny sparkles of silver and a central bead of pale yellow.

It's beautiful.

I slip it onto my wrist, fastening the ties over my padding pulse, and lift my hand to admire the beads against my skin. They look at home there, as if it's where they were always destined to be.

Is this from Zach? Did he choose this for me?

I return to the card, reading the handwritten message inside it:

> **Merryn,**
> **I'm so sorry I can't play tonight.**
> **(Tiredness got the better of me, as I sus-**
> **pect it has you.)**
> **But I didn't want you to think I'd forgotten**
> **you. That's impossible.**
> **So this gift is for you.**
> **Can I play for you tomorrow?**
> **If it's okay, draw a smiley face on the sign**
> **by the gate. If not, leave it blank.**
> **I'll look for your invitation.**
> **Until then, take care. And thank you.**
> **Zach x**

My hand flies to my mouth, the new bracelet dancing against my wrist. It's perfect. The gift, his words and the heart behind them bring tears to my eyes.

I've wondered how we would do this, not having any way to contact each other unless he comes to Sweet Reverie. Now

I know how to extend the invitation. Until we can talk more and work out how we make this startlingly new thing happen, a simple smile on the blackboard will act as my secret signal to Zach. Nobody will suspect a smiley face drawn on the sign by the side gate. But we'll know.

I don't know what's happening here, but Zach's card and gift and his suggestion of a signal system gives it a hope and possibility it hasn't had before.

I love it. I love all of it.

I switch off my beside lamp and curl up beneath the sheets, impossibly happy.

On the pillow beside me, the bracelet on my wrist glints in the soft light from the street that pours in through the gap in my curtains, falling across my bed. For the first time in years, I feel I'm not alone here.

Heart full, I close my eyes, as thoughts of my secret friend pull me gently to my dreams.

Twenty-Four

ZACH

I dreamed of her last night.

Did she find my card and the bracelet I sent for her? I hope I chose the right one.

It's an early start again, but a better night's sleep has made a world of difference. An extra shift, too, which Matt has indicated might become permanent if I'm interested. I'm definitely interested – the more days I can fill with work, the better.

I load up the delivery crates, the delicious scent of the warm bakery soothing any nerves I might have harboured this morning. Merryn is in my thoughts and the reason for my smile as I work. When Matt comes out to the van with the final crates, he gives me an amused look.

'You win the lottery or something?'

It feels like I did. 'No,' I reply, my smile a cheeky betrayer.

Matt clocks it immediately – not that it's hard to miss. I feel like my entire body is glowing. 'Well, whatever you're on this morning can you save some for me? I could do with a smile like that.'

'Have a slice of your sourdough. That'll keep the smile in place all day.'

'Nice. Smooth. I hope you're using that line on your rounds.'

'My one and only catchphrase, boss.'

'Cheeky git!' He laughs, waving me off. 'Away with you.'

My delivery round is fun today, but then everything about the day feels good. Even though the weather is a drizzly sea fret that mists and fogs the van's windscreen. Even when unexpected roadworks on the Hayle bypass mean a twenty-minute convoluted diversion that introduces me to tiny, mud-covered roads I never knew existed. Even when a flock of sheep floods the road ahead, their apologetic farmer offering me suitably sheepish smiles as I become his flock's unofficial escort for a long, frustrating mile to their new grazing field. Nothing can steal my good mood today because of the promise of tonight.

When I return to St Ives and sign off at the end of my Downalong Bakery shift, it's all I can do not to run to Star Court to see if the signal I suggested to Merryn has made it onto the blackboard sign outside Sweet Reverie.

I hang back in the alleyway at the entrance to the street, as a group of laughing locals bundle into the café. I've seen some of them in Aggie's beach café, though their names escape me. One guy in particular is a builder, I seem to recall. But I could be mistaken about that, too.

When they're safely inside Sweet Reverie, I glance at the surf shop to make sure the kid I met before isn't looking out. I don't want to meet his boss again, either. *Seth.* I still don't know the deal with him and Merryn, but if there's a smile drawn on the sign by the courtyard gate at least I'll know she wants to see me. That'll stick in old Sethy's gullet, which is the best form of retaliation I can hope for after he chased me halfway up Tregenna Hill on Saturday night.

I check myself. I can't make this new thing with Merryn about getting one over on her friend, however much the prospect that they're more than friends might bite at me.

This has to be about us and Merlin.

Nobody else.

When I'm certain the coast is clear, I enter Star Court. Walking to the side gate seems to take an eternity, each step matching the thud of my heart. If Merryn can't see me tonight, it won't mean she never wants to, I remind myself, though I know not seeing the signal will be a kick. I pass the edge of Porthia Surf and focus on the blackboard sign, a step away.

I look and . . .

. . . it's *there*.

A simple smile in a small round circle, drawn in the same shiny gold chalk paint that Merryn's first invitation was, hiding at the bottom right-hand corner of the sign advertising evening openings starting tomorrow.

Satisfied, I keep walking, past Sweet Reverie and out of Star Court.

I'd forgotten about the evening openings. Wednesday, Thursday and Friday nights, closing at eleven p.m. What will that mean for future piano meetings?

Wait – I'm getting ahead of myself. There's nothing to say this will become a regular thing. Tonight will only be the first we've agreed together. It may not be possible to extend that.

The thing is, I hope it will.

How did I get here? Just a few days ago, I'd never spoken to Merryn Rowe, never played the piano in the café courtyard.

How have so many hopes piled up on top of what happened on Sunday night?

Needing to walk, I pass through the town and round the harbour towards Smeaton's Pier, taking the road to the left to Wheal Dream, where the St Ives Museum is, and the infamous 'invisible man' overlooking tiny Bamaluz Beach. Today he's sporting sunglasses, a yellow Eighties-style sun visor and bright orange and pink flowered Bermuda shorts, suspended by a clever system of invisible threads to look as if a ghostly body is wearing them, above a wooden box with blue and white striped slider sandals stuck to its top. Visitors are posing with him, his sudden discovery a source of great amusement.

It's one of the things I love about St Ives – the quirkiness you find around its streets. Like the secret cat drawn in the cement between the cobbles near Norway Stores that Mum always loved to spot, or the small plastic toy dinosaurs that randomly appear in the stone flowerbed planters that edge the harbour. Little glimpses of humour and whimsy that keep St Ives feeling like a real place, not a Cornish-themed Disneyland as many of the most popular fishing villages on this coast seem to have become.

I take the steep steps down around the cliff overlooking Bamaluz and out to St Ives Bay, my sneakers crunching on the sand deposited on the steps by countless feet from the town's beaches. Kids race up past me, salt-covered and sea-damp, trailed by weary parents carrying armfuls of beach stuff. Young couples canoodle on the large rocks at the edge of Porthgwidden car park; older couples stand on the shingle beach opposite, where teens are balancing stones in impossible-looking towers. The benches overlooking the small sweep of Porthgwidden

Beach are all occupied, bags and spades and towels resting beside them. Sandwiches already eaten, takeaway coffee from Aggie's place still in hand.

The beach café comes into view as I walk along the path edged with cast-iron lampposts that, as a kid, I believed came straight from Narnia. Beside it, Porthgwidden Beach hums with life, the sand rammed with holidaymakers. I wouldn't want to be jostling for space down there, but I like that it's busy. This beach is the one swimmers prefer, and on a day like today it beckons whole families into the sea.

I need to get back into the ocean. Maybe I could start by swimming here.

Maybe playing Merlin tonight will help me make up my mind.

So much of the jumble of thoughts, fears and issues fell into place on Sunday night as I sat at the piano. Like I knew it would. If I can't make sense of life in the water yet, the piano may well be my saving grace. That's if it continues to be available to me after tonight. I have a feeling Merryn understands that, without me having to explain it.

It's why I'm counting my blessings that I have her.

Well, I don't *have* Merryn. Not like that.

But the more I think of her, the more I hope I might.

Is it possible to fall in love with someone after one, impossibly late, conversation?

'Someone's happy,' Aggie says, when I arrive at her beach café. She's seated on a stool at the end of the driftwood bar, holding court as her staff buzz around making coffee and serving customers. She really should be resting, but Aggie Keats doesn't know the meaning of the word.

'Happy to see you,' I reply.

'Well of course you are, Zachy. But that's not what I meant.'

I might have known Aggie would read me so easily. 'Things are looking brighter.'

'Good. You all done for the day?'

'Yes. Surprised to see you here, though.'

Aggie receives this with an exasperated eye-roll. 'I've heard that from everyone today.'

'Maybe they have a point?'

'Maybe they're interferin' *bastards*.'

O-kay . . . 'Rest is important, though, Ag.'

'Rest is doin' my chuffin' head in,' she retorts. 'I don't do rest, Zachy. Never have. Sittin' on my bum goin' slowly mad in an empty flat? No thank you. Kieran tried to suggest it this mornin' and I reckon his ears are still stingin' from my reply.'

I wince on her partner's behalf.

'Anyway, you haven't answered my question. What's with the smile?'

'Just happy.'

'Spoilsport.' She tuts and hands me a coffee her assistant has just made. 'There you go. On the house.'

'It's okay, I'll pay.' I dig in my pocket and hand her the money. It's a point of principle: I've relied on the kindness of friends for too long now. Part of getting back on my feet is paying my way. 'And I have some money for Kieran, too.'

'Save it.' When I protest, she silences me with a raised eye-brow. 'You're doin' him a favour, lookin' after the studio.'

My mood dips. 'Except for the other day.'

'Don't sweat it, lover. We got the graffiti off the wall so no harm done. We all forget stuff, like you and your phone so

His Nibs couldn't contact you. Yesterday I found my socks in the fridge.'

'Yeah, but you have an excuse. You're pregnant.'

Her eyes narrow, mischief alive in her expression. 'You sure you're not? Might explain all your random smilin'.'

I love the joke. Love too that she's noticed the effect Merryn's signal has had on me. I won't tell Aggie – or anyone else – what's happening, though. It's just mine and Merryn's.

Having a good secret to hide is a blessing for me. I've avoided talking about the bad stuff – the injury, the decision to leave the pro-surfing circuit and how I lost everything in its wake – each one a secret shame I've carried, stuffing them away deep within myself.

The piano at Sweet Reverie is a secret I can finally treasure. And its owner.

I can't wait for tonight.

Twenty-Five

MERRYN

Has Zach seen the smile?

Drawing it on the blackboard sign was a thrill, the promise of what it would enable so exciting it was all I could do to keep from squealing aloud. Has he passed by the café today to check?

I don't know what time he'll arrive, either, which makes the waiting even more charged. Will he come to the courtyard from the gate entrance, or will he try the front door? How long should I wait for him to show?

Ruthie has watched me like a hawk all morning. I've felt her scrutiny hot at my back as I've moved through the café delivering orders. Have her suspicions been fuelled by what she sees?

I'm smiling more today. I can't help it. Zach's gift is on my wrist, its presence a bright reminder of what's happening.

What *is* happening, exactly?

I love the emergence of this new *thing* in my life, but I'm reeling myself in whenever I think about it. Because it would be too easy to read something into it that isn't there. Zach needs the piano. I need to hear it. Beyond that, who knows?

The lunch rush has passed, Ruthie has just returned from her break and I've made us each a mug of tea. Peace settles across the café, the lull something I look forward to on busy days.

'Grab something from the cake displays,' I offer, helping myself to one of the iced digestive biscuits covered with sweets that we keep for our younger customers to enjoy with their babyccinos and hot chocolates.

'Lush!' Ruthie descends on the final slice of salted caramel loaf with the most enthusiasm I've seen her muster today. 'This baby's mine!'

We're about to enjoy our sweet treats when the bell over the door heralds a new visitor. I smile at Ruthie's groan – it's a long-standing joke between us that customers must lurk just beyond the door, waiting for the exact moment we take a break to come barrelling in.

But this visitor hasn't been lurking outside, picking his moment to arrive.

At least, I hope he hasn't.

Seth's expression is pure apology, the routine we've replayed countless times before back in play.

'I'm good here,' Ruthie says, her cake a shield for the words meant only for me.

'You sure?'

She nods. 'Go.'

I edge past her, walking through the café and out to the courtyard, where none of the tables are occupied. Seth follows me, saying nothing. Instead of sitting at a table, I move a little way down the path leading to the side passage, out of view of any customers who may be watching. When I stop and turn, Seth pauses a few paces away.

'I'm a knob, Mer.' When I don't dispute the fact, he continues. 'I shouldn't have yelled at you. It's your business, not mine.'

'It is.'

'And that bloke . . .'

'. . . *Isn't* a threat.'

'Yeah. Probably.'

'Definitely.' He wilts a little in my stare. 'He was a customer, same as everyone else. I wouldn't dream of chasing someone out of your shop.'

'Fair point.'

We observe each other, still stung, but the ice is beginning to thaw.

'Can we stop this overprotective thing, please?' I ask. 'I don't need a battling knight. I just need you.'

He hefts a sigh. 'I need you, too. I've missed you.'

'Come here, you daft git,' I groan, bridging the gap between us to gather him up into a hug.

He relaxes in my arms. 'Sorry.'

'So am I. Can we move on now, please?'

'Sounds like a plan, bird.'

The hug is good, long overdue after our latest clash. But as he holds me I wonder if I'm finding it easier to forgive him because of the promise of tonight. Everything has felt easier since the card and bracelet arrived. Simpler to navigate. Lighter.

What would Seth say if he knew?

'Let's get back to being us, yeah?' he says, breaking the hug. 'I can't take the drama.'

'Me either. I have cake, if that helps?'

'Could bleddy murder some! See, I knew there was a reason I came round here.'

And we're back, the rhythm returned like it had never left. It's welcome and I'm relieved we aren't at odds anymore. It helps that thoughts of Zach are never far away from our chatter. Seth doesn't stay long, but it's long enough for me to trust we're back on an even keel.

By the time Ruthie and I close for the day, nerves are starting to nip at me. I say goodbye to her and turn back to face my quiet café. Do I wait here? Or go upstairs and hope I hear Zach's arrival?

Not knowing much about this arranged meeting is disconcerting. Most of my life revolves around known systems and schedules. The business dictates the majority of my time – more tomorrow, when the evening openings commence – and the rest of my time has to fit around that. And I think, after the shock and upheaval of the end of my marriage, with all that entailed for me, I've come to find safety in knowing exactly what lies ahead.

Tonight challenges that.

It shouldn't feel as important as it does. Yet I'm aware already of hopes and possibilities stretching way beyond one arranged meeting. The potential is what floors me. Why is that?

At seven p.m., I stop pacing the café and make myself go upstairs. I shower quickly and change, one ear listening out for a knock at the door or the first notes of a song being played in the courtyard. Usually I would put on music, or have the TV chatting away to itself for company. Not this evening.

I try to eat something, but my stomach is too full of nerves to accommodate a meal. Instead, I drink white tea to calm myself and pick up a book to read. As the minutes pass, I begin to lose myself in the story, only the occasional stab of concern breaking the narrative.

What if he hasn't seen the smile?

– Then he'll see it tomorrow. I might add a small 12 beneath to signify a time.

What if he's changed his mind?

– I glance at the bracelet on my wrist. I don't think he will.

What if I'm making a fool of myself?

– I'm not. At least, I hope I'm not . . .

I look up from my book, take a long, slow breath and try to find perspective. I'm just nervous. And this means so much because of my connection with the piano. Nothing more.

One glance at my watch reveals that it's now past ten p.m. That's okay, I tell myself, it's still early for Zach. Smiling at the memory of his own joke about the late hour of his first visit, I return to the story awaiting me in the open pages.

And then, I hear it.

The first notes of a song.

I throw my book aside and hurry downstairs.

Twenty-Six

ZACH

I can't stop smiling as I play the opening bars. I know Merryn will appear any minute and the waiting is delicious.

I could pretend that this is all about Merlin. That it's the pull of the *Play Me* piano lifting me up and making everything seem brighter. But that would be a lie.

It started with the piano.

But Merryn is the reason I'm smiling tonight.

I can't explain it, only that she's been on my mind. Everything hopeful and positive I've encountered since has somehow linked back to her. And now the notes beneath my fingers cast a spell, an enchantment that will summon her to my side.

We hardly know each other, bound only by the piano and this fragile arrangement now hanging on the appearance of a drawn smile on a blackboard. But I can't stop thinking about her, about the way the music I played made her shine. I never thought my playing, hidden from everyone in my life except those closest to me, was capable of that.

There's a click to my right. When I turn, she's there.

'Hi.'

'Evening.'

Our smiles are mirrors of each other.

'I wasn't sure if you'd seen the sign.'

'I checked this afternoon.'

'I hoped you might.' She moves to sit on the step between the courtyard and the café, where she sat before. 'Don't let me stop you. Play what you like.'

My fingers return to the keys, but it takes effort to wrench my eyes away from her. She's beautiful, her skin illuminated by the soft glow of the courtyard lights strung above us like stars. Her hair is down tonight, resting in soft waves on her shoulders. And her eyes sparkle as they watch me.

I didn't imagine how she made me feel. It's stronger now.

I pull my attention back to the melody, closing my eyes so they don't tempt me to look back to her. The music flows, a piece I learned one summer after hearing it through the tinny speakers of a beachfront café after a competition. I sought it out and taught myself the melody. As I play, memories of that time return, when I took life for granted. When the only restlessness that bothered me was the need to better my surf record.

So much has changed, but the song's ability to bring me peace remains.

Merryn doesn't make a sound. I can feel her attention on me, as tangible on my shoulder as if her hand was resting there. I wonder what the song means to my audience of one – if she recognises it as she did the folk song I played before, or if the tune is a new discovery.

As I play, I'm aware of how new this all is. Audiences have stilted my playing in the past, making me self-conscious, aware of every missed note and beat. I would shy away from playing when friends demanded a show, joking my way out of it, or playing a throwaway piece to shut them up. 'Chopsticks' to elicit groans, 'King of the Road' to invite a sing-song. Nothing personal. Nothing with any meaning.

Tonight, I want Merryn to hear the pieces that touch me most.

When the song comes to an end, I wait for a moment before daring to look at her.

She applauds; I bow.

And a soft silence settles between us.

When I imagined how tonight might play out, I didn't anticipate this. It's as if the courtyard is charged, as if every note, every breath has the potential to change everything.

'What next?' I ask, at last, because I need to speak and it's all I can think of.

'Whatever you want.'

'Fast? Slow? Techno remix?'

That makes her laugh. It's the loveliest sound . . .

Man, I have to pull this back. I'm getting carried away.

'Play the first song you fell in love with.'

Bloody hell.

'Put me on the spot, why don't you?' I laugh, willing my brain to focus, settling on a song my dad used to sing around the house, before he and Mum divorced and he moved away: 'Everyday' by Buddy Holly. It's a classic I'm sure she'll know – and when I look over my shoulder, she's nodding along.

'Do you sing?' she asks, when I reach the chorus for the second time.

'Not really. Do you?'

'No!' She gives a shrug. 'Maybe sometimes. Not tonight.'

I smile and return to the piano. 'Perhaps we should duet.'

I don't mind that she doesn't reply.

When the song ends, I move straight into a theme song from a film I've long forgotten and couldn't name if someone paid me. It's a slow, lilting melody that drifts around the courtyard, the notes returning to me despite it being years since I last played them. It calms me, the initial thrill of Merryn's arrival settling into something more meaningful.

'What song is that?'

'Something from a film,' I reply, wishing now that I'd committed the title to memory as I have the tune. 'Can't remember its name.'

'I like it.'

'Thanks.' I reach the final few bars and stop, pivoting on the stool to look at her. 'So, tell me about Merlin. You found him on a street?'

Merryn hugs her knees to her chest. 'On North Terrace. Seth and I were walking and saw it on the pavement.'

A stab of jealousy registers in my gut at the mention of his name. I dismiss it. 'Just left outside? Who does that?'

'I couldn't believe it either. The house it was outside is being developed, so I reckon they just gutted it and left Merlin on the pavement.'

'I suppose it's a good thing they left him to be taken, rather than chucking him in a skip,' I offer.

She smiles. 'There is that.'

'And you painted it?'

'With Seth, yes.'

Okay, I can't avoid this now. 'The guy who chased me.'

'Sorry about that. I ripped a strip off him about it, if it helps.'

Surprisingly, it does. But it doesn't answer the question I don't want to ask. 'You two seem close. From what I saw on Saturday night.'

'We are.'

'Close as in —' I hate what I'm going to ask '—together?'

She blinks. 'Oh.'

'I'm prying, sorry.'

'No, it's okay. I'm not with Seth. He's my best friend. He's also hopelessly in love with my assistant, Ruthie.'

Surf Shop Seth and the Scary Waitress? The image makes me laugh, instantly clamping a hand to my mouth. 'Sorry. That's some pairing.'

'It would be if either of them ever dare to admit how they feel.'

'Do you think they will?'

'Maybe.' Her smile is my reward. 'We'll have to warn the town if it happens.'

We lapse into easy silence, but secretly I'm punching the air. She's not with Seth. The connection I saw was friendship, which explains his overprotectiveness. If I had a friend as lovely as Merryn Rowe, I'd be a fierce defender, too.

I don't ask if she has anyone else. The fact we're here, together, arranged by a secret sign nobody else in St Ives knew about, is confirmation enough.

'Why don't you play something?' I ask, needing to switch the focus from everything I suddenly want to say.

'This is about you playing.'

'But Merlin's yours. And I'd like to hear you.'

Her reaction isn't what I expect. She shrinks back, her smile fading. 'I – can't.'

'Of course you can. I don't mind.'

'No, I can't, Zach. Don't ask me.'

It's so sharp, so at odds with the woman I'm slowly getting to know, that it knocks breath from me. What have I said? She rescued a piano, brought it here, and lovingly decorated it. The whole reason I'm here is that she wanted to share it with me. It makes no sense.

'Why?'

When she doesn't reply, I slide along the piano stool and pat the space beside me. 'Sit with me.'

'It's okay. I don't . . .'

'Sit with me, please? I won't make you play, I promise.' I hold out my hand, willing her to move. Maybe I should drop the subject, return to playing tunes for her. But I can't leave it while the strange atmosphere exists between us. I don't want this to be awkward, or something Merryn won't want to return to.

She considers my invitation for an age.

Then, just when I think I've blown this whole thing and she'll never ask me back, she stands and crosses the floor. When she sits beside me, the closeness is breathtaking.

I have to pull this back; convince Merryn to trust me.

'What can I play for you?' I ask.

'Anything.'

Placing my hands on the keys, I opt for the bravest thing I know to play. A piece of my own, one of the last tunes I wrote before I had to give up my home.

A song of the sea.

It's gentle and slow, a wistful memorial to the life I knew I was losing. I'd left the circuit and officially retired as a pro. All of my sponsorships had ended and I was staring at a future I hadn't planned. But the biggest loss to me was the sea herself. For months I'd tried going out with my board, but the pain in my knee sent me straight back to shore. The only thing I'd ever known about myself was slipping away – so I turned to the only other solace I had.

And 'Wavechaser' was the result.

It's a risk, even though my piano stool companion doesn't know any of its history. Playing 'Wavechaser' for Merryn feels like offering her a piece of my soul, presenting it to her with the fear she might refuse it.

Beside me, she listens, her eyes glazed as the music takes her somewhere far from the courtyard. Up close, the dark brown of her eyes seems endless.

It's intense and close, the connection undeniable.

A kiss in musical form.

Reddening, I stare pointedly at the keys, hoping Merryn doesn't read my thoughts, which seem as loud and obvious as if they were written in neon above my head.

When the piece ends, my fingers draw back from the keys, resting on the lip of the wooden surround.

'That's beautiful,' Merryn breathes.

You're beautiful, my mind replies. 'Thank you.'

'What's it called?'

'"Wavechaser".' It's the first time I've said it aloud, the act making it a real piece instead of a collection of notes I play about with.

'I haven't heard it before. Who wrote it?'

I take a breath. Nobody knows I write – not even Mum. I wish I'd told her before she passed away. One of many still-boxed regrets I'm not ready to unpack yet. 'I did.'

When I dare to look at her, Merryn is staring at me.

'It's beautiful, Zach.'

My heart swells. 'Thanks.'

'What made you write it?'

I wasn't expecting the question, but now she's asked, it was obvious it would happen. My nerves twist. I haven't talked to anyone about what happened, not beyond the shield of flippant replies designed to ward off any unwanted prying. But the way Merryn is looking at me – and my desire to keep her wanting me to be here – makes my choice clear.

'I was a pro surfer,' I begin, my voice hesitant, my heartbeat loud in my ears. 'But my knee was injured when my board hit it in a wipeout. I had to retire and lost pretty much everything because of it. I wrote 'Wavechaser' because I couldn't get back into the sea.'

She listens, holding me with her gaze.

'I don't know, I just needed to say what I was too scared to admit out loud. And my piano was the only place where I could make it make sense.'

'It's a love song,' she says.

Her words stop me dead. Helplessly, I stare back. 'I think it is.'

I want to say more, attempt to express exactly what her response means to me, but all I can think about is gazing at her. She's so close to me, the beginnings of a smile on her lips. I could be there in a breath . . .

Twenty-Seven

MERRYN

We're so close now, the still-warm memory of the love song he wrote to the sea sparkling in the air around us. I didn't expect him to be so honest with me, or share something so personal.

Did he do it because of how I reacted when he asked me to play?

The possibility draws me back to this moment, here, with Zach.

But should I kiss him?

I always said I wouldn't get involved with anyone again, not after Luke. To let anyone close to me after such a betrayal was unthinkable.

Or so I believed.

But lately I've watched my friends and customers falling in love, starting lives together, getting married, having kids. And from my vantage point behind the counter at Sweet Reverie, I've started to wish I could have what they do. I see how love brings people together, breaks barriers, offers hope. On Saturday night, I watched Jack and Nessie with Seren. And it was wonderful. Love brought them together, despite so many obstacles life threw in their way.

I hardly know Zach. But my heart wants to know him. He just shared his song with me – and the events that brought him to write it. The most intimate, private glimpse into his life. When I couldn't tell him about Grant, or why playing the piano is both my most longed for desire and my biggest fear.

He's all I see now, his breath dancing across my lips, our eyes closing as we move closer . . .

'I should go,' he whispers, so close that our lips almost touch. 'It's late.'

My heart contracts as his lips brush my cheek in a soft kiss. It's beautiful: gentle, unhurried and kind. But it isn't what I want. What I thought we both wanted.

'Of course.' Blushing, I pull away, the courtyard swimming a little as I regain my control. 'Thank you – for the song.'

A line forms between his eyebrows as he looks at me. 'I'll come back. If you want me to?'

'Yes,' I reply, the word carried on a rush of air.

'When?'

'I have the evening opening tomorrow.'

'Afterwards? Or another night?'

I should leave it until Saturday, when our first round of evening services are done. But can I wait that long to hear Zach play again?

'Tomorrow night, eleven-thirty. But I can't stay up for long.'

Relief blooms in his smile. 'Half an hour. Just tunes and chat. Sound good?'

I smile back, the moment passed between us. 'Sounds great.'

We stand, Zach closing the lid of the piano with such kindness and respect that it makes my heart ache. He must guess what it means to me, even if my *not playing* it is a mystery to him. That he treats it – and me – with such gentleness means the world.

I walk with him to the point where the courtyard meets the passage to the street. When I face him his gaze drops, warm fingers catching my wrist and lifting it up.

'You're wearing it.'

'I've worn it all day.'

His smile is impossibly lovely. 'It's you. Bright in the dark night.' Laughing, he shakes his head. 'Never thought I'd say that out loud.'

'You're very lyrical for a surfer.'

'*Former* surfer.'

'I don't think you cease to be one just because you stop competing,' I counter, daring to place my hand against his chest. 'You're still one – in here.'

His hand closes over mine. 'Maybe. So, tomorrow night?'

'Tomorrow night.'

He releases my hand and I watch him hurry away into the night.

Twenty-Eight

ZACH

I should have kissed her.

Why didn't I?

The question haunts me as I wait at a window table in Pengelly's, the smell of paint still fresh in the air and the clink of glass sounding from the bar, where three of my soon-to-be colleagues are unpacking bottles and glassware. I gaze out to the harbour, sparkling in the sun, the town beyond thrown into silhouette by the brightness of the light.

I had the opportunity to kiss her. We were too close to deny what was about to happen, sitting together at the piano she clearly loves so much, even if she won't play. Why did I pull back at the moment that could have changed everything?

There's so much I don't know about Merryn. But I know I wanted to kiss her. That should have been enough, shouldn't it?

I'm not sure I'll find answers here, in the almost-open restaurant. I'm nervous about the reason I'm sitting at the table instead of helping my colleagues. Turns out Luke didn't hang about when I said I didn't mind talking to his journalist friend. He's arranged an interview today, when I don't feel prepared for it and my mind would far rather think about Merryn.

Now it's imminent, I feel vulnerable.

What if my former surf buddies see this as proof that I've hit rock bottom? Or, worse, think the interview was my idea, a desperate bid for publicity from a has-been?

When I left the circuit, I refused to do any press interviews. I issued a statement announcing my retirement and didn't explain why. I thought now, with the story long since being newsworthy, I was in the clear.

But I hadn't banked on Luke Pengelly.

I should go. Say I've changed my mind.

But he's offered me seventy quid to be here.

I hate that money has become the weapon to override my personal boundaries. Time was when I could refuse point-blank if a promotional opportunity wasn't a good fit. Those days are well behind me, it would seem.

'Here she is! Our very own Lois Lane,' Luke declares, striding across Pengelly's.

When I look up, there's a woman standing by the door. She has a bag that looks half the size of her slung over her shoulder, a camera hanging around her neck. Her blonde hair is scraped back and held with a wooden clip, revealing large hoop earrings and a line of tiny studs in her ears. She raises a hand and breaks into a huge smile as Luke reaches her.

'So, what do you think?' he asks, arms spread wide to indicate his kingdom.

'It's amazing, Luke. And you've done all this in three weeks?'

He shrugs, his thousand-kilowatt smile on full display.

'Maybe four, if you count the structural stuff. But who's counting, eh? Point is, we'll be open for the summer, setting this town alight.'

'Not literally, I hope.'

They share snorts of laughter, before Luke beckons for her to follow him.

'Come and meet our very own surf star . . .'

I stand as they approach, pushing down my embarrassment and thinking instead of the money this has earned me. Funny, I never thought I'd sell out for seventy quid. And yet here I am, smiling like my pay packet depends upon it.

'Zan, meet Zach Trevelyan. Zan and Zach! There's a fated pairing if ever I heard one.'

The journalist smiles, offering me a handshake. 'Zanna Venn, *Cornwall Daily News*. It's good to meet you.'

'You too.'

'Sit, one and all,' Luke commands, raising his hand and clicking his fingers towards the bar. Hen, one of the soon-to-be bar staff, and owner of the only name I can remember from our first team meeting, scurries over with a tray.

'What can I get for you all?' she asks, shooting me a nervous smile.

'I'd love a coffee, cheers,' Zanna replies – and I'm struck by how kindly she makes her request. How she makes eye contact with Hen and speaks to her as if our new boss isn't watching her every move.

'Same for me,' Luke barks, not even making eye contact with Hen. 'And Zach?'

'Yeah, coffee's good for me. Thanks, Hen.'

I catch her grateful nod before she hurries away.

'New staff,' Luke says to Zanna, his eye-roll meant to invite her into the joke. It's not funny. He holds up a hand to me. 'No offence, Zach.'

I don't reply. Not that Luke even gives me the opportunity.

Zanna produces a voice recorder from her pocket and sets it on the table between us. 'So, Zach, you're a pro surfer turned barman. That's quite the career change.'

'Lots of surfers on the circuit work other jobs out of season,' I reply, careful to keep any hint of defensiveness from my tone. As soon as I knew this interview was inevitable, I started anticipating which questions I'd likely be asked. Better to be prepared than poleaxed, I reckon.

'And when did you retire as a pro?'

'A little over a year ago.'

'Can I ask why?'

'A knee injury.'

She looks up from the spiral-bound pad where she's taking additional notes. 'I'm sorry to hear that.'

'Thanks.'

Luke watches our exchange like a proud if slightly pushy parent. 'See? I told you Zan's good. Straight in there, all the questions asked, *boom-boom-boom*!'

The journalist shakes her head as she returns to her notes. 'Leave off, Luke. I'm just doing my job.'

'And a great job you do,' Luke replies, quick as a shot. He's fidgety today, excess energy bleeding out from him. If it were anyone else, I'd think he was nervous, but I can't imagine Luke gets nervous about anything. 'I'm going to check where our drinks are. Carry on, you two.'

And then he's off, heading for the kitchen. I hope Hen

isn't about to get an earful. His attitude needs sorting if he wants to keep the staff he's recruited. None of us have worked here long enough to feel any kind of loyalty to the place. If he isn't careful, he'll end up losing people before Pengelly's is even open.

Zanna blows out her cheeks. 'He's a lot. At least we can talk properly while he's away.'

'Have you known him long?' I ask, genuinely wondering how the kind-hearted, gently spoken reporter ever crossed paths with Luke.

'Since college,' she says. 'He's a bit of a git, but we always got on. And since I made senior reporter at the *CDN*, he's been a good source of stories.'

'Like this one?' Aware my nerves are showing, I plaster a bright smile over the cracks.

'Exactly.' She observes me for a moment. 'About the story – you don't need to worry, Zach.'

'I wasn't . . .'

'I cover good news and business stories. That's my remit, not dishing dirt on anyone. Just tell me what you're comfortable to share, okay? I won't go digging for anything else.'

It's a relief, I'll admit. I remember some of my friends being burned by journalists in the past, rocking up purporting to be covering competitions only to print intensely invasive, personal articles about their private lives. I don't mind people knowing I've retired, or that an injury took me out for good. Those things happen, every pro facing the danger of injury the longer their career lasts. But a less-than-flattering article showing my new life here as some kind of mighty comedown is my worst fear.

'Thank you,' I say, meaning it. 'So, what would you like to know?'

We talk about life on the road with competitions, about the championships I won and the titles I claimed. Zanna takes careful notes, pausing occasionally to clarify details. Her questions are straightforward and interesting, nothing to suggest a trap hidden within a clever enquiry. I relax a little as I watch her work, noting how much she thinks about the next question, so that the conversation feels exactly that: a natural, flowing exchange of information.

When she comes to the end of her questions, she asks if she can take some photos, suggesting we go outside to allow her to capture images of the restaurant.

'You don't have a photographer?' I ask, as we step out into the bright sun.

'Used to, but money's tight at work now. We all got sent on a one-day photojournalism course to learn how to take photos. It's far from ideal, but it is what it is.'

'You get to use a cool camera, though,' I offer, recognising the model she's using. I've seen similar at Kieran's studio.

She grimaces. 'It would be, if it didn't keep breaking. This one's been in the repair shop more than it's been on jobs with me.'

'I'm staying with a photographer,' I say, letting Zanna pose me in front of Pengelly's. 'Kieran Macklin – I don't know if you've heard of him?'

Zanna lowers her camera. 'Heard of him? He's only my hero!'

'Really?'

'Totally. I have so many of his editorials. The man is a ledge! Photos for *The Sentinel* travel section, *National Geographic*,

WildWorld travel magazine. He's won awards for all kinds of assignments.' She laughs, rubbing the back of her neck. 'Sorry, I'm a bit of a fan.'

'So I see. I could ask him to meet you, maybe?' Could I? Not sure I'm in a position to ask Kieran anything yet. But if it wins me favour with the journalist writing the piece that will make my new life public, it's worth a shot.

'I'd love that! Give me your number when we're done here, okay?'

'Of course.'

Zanna returns to her camera as Luke strides outside. I relax a little more, our unexpected connection below the radar of the restaurant owner a delicious secret I can hang on to. It feels good to know something Luke Pengelly doesn't.

'Okay, Miss Zee-de-Venn, I'm ready for my close-up! Where do you want me?'

Her wry glance at me puts me at ease far more than anything Luke could say.

After ten minutes of posing, changing position, discussing the best light, moving from the harbour road to the beach and back again, we're done. Luke is the consummate showman, handing flyers from his back pocket to the tourists who stop to watch the spectacle of our photoshoot.

'Opening Saturday. Come and check us out!'

'You look like you appreciate great food. You need to visit us on Saturday.'

'You haven't had the full St Ives experience till you've dined at Pengelly's!'

While he's doing his thing, Zanna moves beside me. 'I'd love to chat further, if you ever wanted to tell me more about your pro career. I'm always looking for local people to feature and I know many of our readers would love to hear your story.' She hands me her card.

And even though I swore I'd never do any interviews once I left the circuit, talking with the journalist has been a revelation. I didn't think I'd ever be comfortable talking about the life I've left, but reminiscing for this article has unearthed a connection I thought I'd lost. Sometimes, you need to be reminded of who you are, even if life has moved you on from where you found it.

'Might just do that,' I reply. 'Cheers, Ms Venn.'

'Zanna, please. It's been really good to talk to you, Zach.'

When Luke finally lets me go – an extra tenner in the folded notes he promised me – I head home. I have hours to kill before returning to Sweet Reverie tonight and I need sleep.

Talking with Merryn last night before *that* moment was the first time I've felt comfortable revisiting my past. I hadn't planned it, but in the light of what Luke had me do today it was providential. Would I have been as ready to discuss my surfing career with Zanna if I hadn't broken ground with Merryn?

The piano was key to it all. Reminding me of the song I wrote, daring me to open up to Merryn. Sitting at the keys unlocked something within me, almost as if the piano willed me to do it.

The almost-kiss, too, wouldn't have happened if Merryn wasn't sitting beside me, her strange reaction when I asked her to play the key that unlocked my own confession. What is it with her and the piano?

Maybe hearing me play made her fear a comparison of her

own skill would be made. Except I would never judge anyone for their playing. But she doesn't know that yet, does she? She doesn't know me, beyond the music I've played for her.

Is that why I held back?

I need to find out why the thought of playing the piano scares her. Unlocking that might unlock everything else.

I just have to work out how.

Twenty-Nine

MERRYN

In the two hours between the end-of-day closing and the start of our first proper evening opening, I just about manage a shower and a bite to eat before I'm back down in the café, making final checks. It's been busier today than I was expecting, and now the challenge of evening hours looms ahead like a behemoth.

I know this is what I want for Sweet Reverie, but it's a much greater undertaking than I'd anticipated.

With everything as ready as it can be, I wander through to the courtyard. I need a moment of stillness. A chance to settle myself before it begins. Seth and Murph are due to arrive in twenty minutes and then we'll be open, half of the tables booked for tonight already.

Merlin has been covered since we closed for the day, so I gently remove the sheet and fold it, stowing it behind the piano. The colours glow in the late afternoon sun that streams in through the courtyard's open sides, the paint strokes catching the light. Slowly, I sit on the piano stool, taking it all in.

Will I sit here with Zach again tonight?

His invitation to join him at the piano surprised me. It harked back to a time when I would have done anything to be invited to sit there. So I didn't think twice last night, the impulse as fresh as if it was the first time of asking.

Grant was nervous of letting me sit beside him, at first. Looking back, it must have been daunting, not only finding himself living with a woman he'd barely met, but also becoming an instant father figure to her daughter. His jokes didn't always land, his attempts at conversation stilted and over-thought. But sitting side by side at the piano changed everything. At the keys we found common ground, the jokes and anecdotes and chats working when the piano was their theme.

The piano lid is cool when my fingers rest on it, its presence soothing after the endless questions of the day. I promised myself I wouldn't think about Zach, or what almost happened last night. But who was I kidding? I could no more keep him from my thoughts than I could keep his hands from Merlin's keys.

Sitting here brings a perspective I haven't found yet. Almost as if Merlin is a gentle provocateur, coaxing thoughts from me. Is that what Zach experienced? Is it why he played me the piece that he wrote and opened up so unexpectedly about his life?

I have to admit that being so close to the music and the man playing it was like a long, cool drink after too many years spent in the desert. I knew I'd hear Merlin played if I put the piano here, but I never imagined I would sit beside the player as I did so many years ago.

It was wonderful.

It felt like coming home.

Gently, I lift the piano lid, resting it back against the upright panel of the case. Before me the keys glisten in the streak of low sun that falls across them. Promise. History. A thousand and one longed-for moments in ebony and ivory lines.

Sitting at Grant's piano made me fall in love with music. And while he lived with us, I dreamed of a future that would always include it. So much was lost when I lost him – not only my stepdad but also the dreams he encouraged me to have.

I think back to Grant's piano, of the way my small hands gravitated to the keys the second I was invited to play. Of what it felt like to make the piano sing. If I could recapture that confidence, that childlike impulse to make music . . .

My hands hesitate above the keys. They're so close I can almost feel them beneath my fingers. I think of Grant's invitation – of Zach's after it.

Go for it, birdie. Play us a song.

Play something for me.

If Grant had been in the courtyard last night, his voice would have joined with my new friend's, exhorting me to play. Would I have accepted the challenge as easily as I did as a child?

I can do this.

It won't mean letting go of Grant Henderson. It will be a tribute to what he meant to me.

I'm about to touch the keys when a sudden, unwelcome memory shoulders its way between Grant and Zach, an uninvited third player intent on crashing the party.

Autumn morning glass. Trails of condensation streaking its surface, like the tears staining my cheeks. Flaking paint peppered with swathes of black mould edging the window frame where I sit. And along the white lines of the potholed, car-flanked street beyond, a slow-moving wooden shape, trailed by a figure shouldering a large, battered rucksack. My reaching hand finding only an ice-cold barrier instead of human warmth, powerless to stop the man and the piano leaving my life. And below me, loud enough to bring neighbours' faces to their windows, the furious screams of a woman who wouldn't, couldn't be loved.

YEAH, THAT'S RIGHT, GET OUT! I DON'T NEED YOU IN MY LIFE, GRANT HENDERSON! I NEVER DID! GO – AND TAKE YOUR BLOODY MUSIC WITH YOU!

I never asked Grant to leave. Just like I never asked for the succession of useless bastards Mum dragged into our lives when he'd gone. The injustice of it still stabs me, my own powerlessness underlined by another failed attempt to play.

But how could I ever express that to Zach?

I can't push the memory aside before it's dragged my hands away from the keys, a too-familiar rush of failure and hurt my reward. Frustrated, I stand, leaving Merlin in his sunshine spotlight as I hurry back into the café.

I busy myself with final checks for tonight's opening, summoned to the front door twenty minutes later by a bright knock and the glimpse of two dopey grins pressed against the glass.

Seth and Murph fall in when I open the door, giggling like a couple of schoolkids. I get the feeling this evening is going to be fun with these two around, whether any customers arrive or not. Seth seems back to his usual self, too, which is a relief.

'We good?' he asks.

I smile. 'Always.'

And that's it, a line drawn and a return to the *us* I know and love, completed in a simple, three-word exchange.

Adrenaline is my friend as we launch into final preparations to open. When it subsides later tonight, I know the exhaustion it's holding back will crash in on me like a spring high tide, but I'm riding the wave for as long as I can.

Finally, at seven-thirty p.m., I stand by the front door, ready to turn the sign and welcome in our first evening customers. A rush of joy hits me when I see a gaggle of friendly faces grinning at me from the street, my secret fear that our first evening service would be quiet banished in an instant.

'Ready?' I ask.

Seth and Murph whoop and drum their hands on the counter, a drumroll for the next stage in Sweet Reverie's journey to officially begin. When they reach a crescendo, I flip the sign to OPEN and unlock the door.

The loveliest opening rush bursts into the café, hugs and best wishes exchanged as they pass me to go and find their tables. Lou and his wife Margie, Jack and Seren, Cerrie and her hunky Aussie Tom, plus several of our daytime regulars – the biggest compliment to our first night of evening trading.

'*See,*' Seth says, joining me behind the counter as the orders start to arrive. 'I told you your regulars would love it.'

'I'm so glad they're here. I knew they'd come through for me.'

'Wait!' He slaps a hand to his heart. 'Are you sayin' . . . could you mean . . . I was *right*?'

'*Maybe.*'

'Maybe isn't *really* an answer.' He cups a hand to his ear and leans closer to me. 'What was that, Mer? Didn't quite catch it . . .'

I roll my eyes and sing-song what he wants to hear. 'Yes, Seth, you were right.'

Delighted, he claps his hands. 'Finally she notices!'

I relax as the night goes on, relieved that our first one isn't a flop. And while I'm not so naive as to think this crowd will come to every one of our evening openings, it's a promising start.

It's always been a thrill watching people enjoying the café I dreamed into life. But tonight, it's even more so. From the upheaval and heartbreak of the mess Luke left, I built this welcoming, hopeful place. What has risen from the ashes of my previous life is more beautiful than I could have dared to hope it would be.

'This is so cool, Merryn,' Jack says, arriving at the counter to settle his bill. 'We've loved it.'

'Thank you. I hope you'll come again?'

He grins. 'Try and stop us! Next time we'll have to bring Nessie. She'll never forgive us if she finds out we came here without her, even though Grandad Dave will have spoiled her rotten tonight.'

'We'd love to see her. And she's welcome to play Merlin again if she likes.'

'She'll be over the moon to hear that. Piano lessons are her latest thing. Seren and I hear "Ode to Joy" so many times at the moment I reckon we both sing it in our sleep.' He laughs and looks back to his partner. 'Actually, I couldn't ask for your help with something, could I?'

'Of course.'

'Would you consider catering a beach picnic?'

'Oh.' I'm not expecting the question and it isn't a request I've had before. But if tonight has taught me anything, it's to be braver. 'We haven't done much outside catering before, but I could put together a quote for you?'

He flushes a little. 'Great. I'll pop the details to you in a day or so. And – um – keep it under your hat for me?' His glance back to Seren tells me everything I need to know.

'No problem.'

A beach picnic. No idea how we'd work the logistics of that, but it's an interesting challenge.

What other surprises might tonight hold for me?

Thirty

ZACH

Eleven-thirty takes an age to arrive. I do what I can to fill the time and distract my mind from checking my watch every five minutes. But I can't settle.

It shouldn't be as important as it feels: just chance to play the courtyard piano in the company of my newest friend. But there's a pull to be there that I haven't felt for a long time.

I used to feel it about the sea.

Waking up at first light, dressing at record speed and being in the water before the sun came up. Watching the tide and weather forecasts, obsessing over conditions, weighing up risks. What began with a love of the ocean became a compulsion, a need that, if not satisfied, left me hollow and frustrated.

And then it became my way of paying bills, bringing with it a whole new pressure to get in the water. I still loved it, but it was as if my board had passengers every time I went out. Bills, sponsors, industry pundits critical of my every move through the waves. Silence them once with a great performance, only to find them stubbornly seated on board for the next.

I went through about a year where competing was no longer

fun, where I had to drag myself into the sea and returning to dry land was a relief. I'd leave it till the last minute to get ready, often the last to arrive at a competition. Some of my surf mates started calling me Tardy Trev, a joke that quickly became a commentary on my pro career. I still won, the sponsors were still satisfied (mostly), but everything felt stilted and over-rehearsed, my body going through the motions but my head a million miles away.

It's almost time. I jump up from the studio sofa and start to get ready. As I'm putting on my sneakers, I glance down to my left where the curves of a wave tattoo rest above my ankle. A cresting wave, like the one featured in Katsushika Hokusai's famous woodblock print *The Great Wave off Kanagawa*, with two shining stars behind it. I had *The Great Wave* on a poster that followed me through various flats and apartments from the age of sixteen, and it still means a lot to me.

It was at the end of that disillusioned period of my career when I had the tattoo done. I'd debated having one for years, seeing so many of my fellow surfers sporting increasingly impressive inks. What swayed my decision was a competition in Portugal, where the top three competitors would win instant entry to a huge surf meet in Oahu, Hawaii. It was the one everyone wanted to win, the chance to surf in the biggest league competition bringing with it career-transforming prestige.

I went with a bunch of mates, all of us competing in the same class. I'd been struggling for a while, hating every session, super critical of everything I was doing, and the last thing I wanted was to be in the water. But as I stood on the beach watching my friends compete, I met an old Aussie dude who was working as a marshal. We got chatting and he revealed that he was a former champion, once ranked tenth in the world.

'That's what I want,' I'd said, surprised when he'd shook his head.

'That's what you tell everyone you want. But you don't feel it.'

How could he have known that, only minutes after meeting me?

When I questioned his incredibly snap judgement, he laughed. 'You can't kid a kidder, mate. I see it in your face now, and when you were out on the waves earlier. Point is, you don't want what really matters. Competitions, accolades, notches on your board, it's all meaningless if you don't want the wave.'

'What's that supposed to mean?' I asked.

'All that matters – all that ever has and ever should – is the next wave. And the next. And the next. If you aren't chasing the wave, you aren't moving forward. You aren't learning. You can have all the medals and firsts in the world, but they're meaningless unless you want the next wave.'

I crashed out of the competition, outclassed by the waves and the other competitors. It should have been well within my grasp, but I failed. I returned home questioning my future as a pro. Questioning everything in my life. That winter, I took myself to the sea every day I could. No training schedule, no tick-box list of achievements to log. Just me and the next wave.

It changed everything.

Through it all, I would gaze at the *Great Wave* print on my bedroom wall, remembering what the old surfer had told me. And by the spring, I finally understood.

So I got the tattoo.

I run my finger over it now, wondering which wave I'm chasing tonight.

Star Court is dark and still when I arrive, the side gate to the café courtyard unlocked as before. I still check there's nobody watching as I lift the latch, slipping into the side passage quickly. I'm nervous tonight, more nervous than I was last time. I'm conscious of every step, every breath, of the distance between the piano and me shrinking, the time I see Merryn getting closer.

How will she be with me tonight?

There's still the issue of our almost-kiss. I was the one who pulled away at the moment it should have happened. How will that have looked to her? I wasn't thinking of anyone but myself then – choosing self-preservation over the thing that everything in me wanted. I still don't know why.

She's waiting as I turn the corner and walk towards the piano. Sitting on the ledge between the courtyard and café, a lilac hoodie over her flowered dress. She looks tired, her smile brief and weary. I won't stay too long for her sake, even though I could remain chatting to Merryn Rowe all night.

'Hi,' I say.

'Hey.'

'How did the evening opening go?'

'Good, thanks. We had lots of people in and they all seemed happy. So, no complaints from me.' She stifles a yawn. 'Sorry. How was your day?'

'It was okay.' I take a seat on the old piano stool, sitting with my back to the instrument, all my attention on Merryn. 'I was interviewed for the *Cornwall Daily News*.'

She raises her eyebrows. 'Impressive.'

'Well, maybe. I'll wait and see what happens. Journalists can be tricky to judge before you see what they've written.'

'How come you were interviewed?'

'One of my new jobs found out I used to be a pro surfer. I think my boss wanted to cash in on my former success.'

'One of your new jobs?'

I laugh. 'This is my life now.'

'So what do you do?'

'I do early morning deliveries for a bakery and I'm about to start shifts at a restaurant on the harbour.'

Merryn smiles – and I swear the courtyard brightens in the soft light. 'That just makes you a local. Everyone has more than one job. Apart from me.'

'You have the evening openings. That must be like a second job.'

'I guess it is. So, you're going to be in the paper? I didn't realise Merlin has a celebrity player.'

'Hardly. But thanks for the compliment.' I gaze at her for a moment, what I want to say flanked by a hundred reasons not to go there. 'Look, about last night . . .'

Her eyes avoid mine. 'It's okay, you don't have to say anything.'

'I've been thinking about it all day. About you.'

'Honestly, Zach, we're good.'

It's only then I realise what she means – and what she thinks I'm referring to.

'No – I don't mean when we . . . When I . . . That's not what I'm talking about.'

She reddens. 'Oh. Sorry.'

'Don't apologise.' This isn't going how I wanted. I've embarrassed her within five minutes of arriving. How is she ever going to trust me enough to tell me why the piano scares her? I take a breath, calm my racing thoughts, and send Merryn the brightest smile I can.

This is the next wave.

She is my next wave.

And I want it more than I've wanted anything in a long time.

'When I asked you to play,' I begin, praying she doesn't cut me off before I've said what I need to, 'I didn't mean to scare you or offend you. But I feel like I did, by the way you reacted.'

'You didn't do either.' Her reply is so quiet I barely catch it all, her words directed resolutely at her feet.

'Then can I ask why?'

'It's complicated.'

'I guessed it was. Why have the piano here if you don't want to play it?'

'For my customers. For the café.'

Even she doesn't sound convinced. If I push now, I could ruin everything. She could demand I leave, with no future smiles drawn on the sign by the gate. But the more I've considered it today, the more convinced I've become that she might never have been asked this before; that maybe I was always supposed to gatecrash the courtyard in order to help her.

I understand the pull of the piano, the need to play, more than anybody else Merryn seems to have around her. Maybe if I ask . . .

'Honestly? I don't buy that.'

She's staring at me now, a glimpse of the steel I know she must have to make this place a reality breaking through. 'Excuse me?'

'I don't think the café or your customers are a strong enough reason to rescue an old piano from the street, to push it all the way back here, late at night, and to spend hours lovingly painting it as you have. Love is the reason for that. Like the song I played for you, last night: it has to come from the heart.'

She says nothing, her stare fixed on me.

I press on – because I've said too much now anyway to remain neutral on this. Backing down is no longer an option. I've chosen my wave and have no choice but to follow it all the way to shore. 'When you look at the piano, it's like you're gazing at someone you love. Maybe someone who hurt you, long ago. There's history, sadness, hope, all playing out at once. And maybe that's why you're scared to play. Because of the history. Or the strength of what you feel.'

Am I completely off with this? I can't read her expression. I might have read too much into her reluctance to play, but as I've spoken the words, my conviction that I'm right has grown.

Silence builds and intensifies between us, challenging my courage.

Have I blown it? Will she ask me to leave?

I long to fill the gap with chatter, to dispel the tension, but if I do that I could lose my only chance to reach her. So I wait. Hold my nerve. And watch Merryn's silent stare.

After what feels like forever, she closes her eyes. 'I lost someone. Years ago. He taught me to play.'

Someone *died*. Why didn't I work that out?

I redden. 'I'm so sorry.'

She's looking at her hands now, her fingers working the hem of her skirt. 'That song you played, the first night you came here – "Time Wears Awa" – he used to play it for my mum. Not that she ever appreciated it.'

'Who was he?' I don't know if I should ask, but she's talking now and I don't want to lose this moment.

'He dated my mum for a while. Moved in with us for two years and brought his piano with him.'

'And that's when he taught you to play?'

She nods. 'I used to sit beside him on the piano stool and he'd show me the notes. I thought it was the most—' she breathes a deep sigh as if the memory has pulled her back to the piano of her past '—*magical* thing I'd ever seen. Filling a room with music just by pressing the keys.'

'What was his name?'

'Grant. Grant Henderson. He was the manager of a bar Mum got drunk at. But I think he wanted to be a musician. It's all he ever talked about when he was with us.'

'When did he pass?'

A frown furrows her brow. 'He didn't, oh . . .' She looks up. 'He isn't dead. At least, I don't think he is.'

I have no idea what to say to that. She said she'd lost someone – and it was a time ago – so what else was I supposed to think? 'Sorry,' I manage, wishing I could shrink away.

'Mum chucked him out,' she says. 'And he left, taking his piano with him. I don't know what happened to him. I was nine years old when he went. He was the closest thing to a dad I ever knew.'

Now it makes sense. 'So that's why you wanted a piano. To feel close to him?'

'It sounds lame, I know.'

'No, it doesn't.'

She studies me, as if testing the water, working out if she can trust what she sees. 'Thank you.'

'But why not play? The music might bring you close to his memory.'

'No. I can't. I've tried.'

I move along the piano stool and pat the seat, as I did last night. Another chance to get this right, to reach Merryn, knowing the link between her and Merlin. 'Sit by me.'

'Zach, I can't.'

'You don't have to play. Just sit by me. Be closer to the music.'

In the stillness that follows, I swear my heart pauses.

And then she moves.

Beside me, Merryn sits, her gaze never leaving me.

I could sweep her into my arms right now. I'm shocked by the impulse – and the notion of sweeping *anyone* up. It's new and almost impossible to resist. But I can't lose focus, can't let this chance go.

I have an idea. I don't know if it will work, but I have to try.

Slowly, I place my fingers on the keys, making the first chord of the song Merryn told me reminds her of Grant Henderson. Then I turn to her.

'Put your hands on mine.'

'What?'

'You won't be playing. I will.'

I see the rise and fall of her chest become more pronounced. Her dark eyes grow wide. Does she trust me? Can I make this work for her?

'I don't think I can.'

'How will you know what's possible unless you try?'

She stares at my hands. Shifts her position. I hold my breath.

And then her left arm snakes under mine, the brush of her skin sending shockwaves across me as her fingers rest on top of my hand. Slowly, the fingers of her right hand join mine.

Heart in my mouth, air breath-held between us, I start to play.

Thirty-One

MERRYN

His fingers move slowly, warm beneath my own.

And as the song my heart loves begins to play beneath our fingers, I bite my lip to hold back tears.

It's a gentle rendition, the chord and melody changes deliberately slower to accommodate our joined hands. Every note brings me closer to Zach. Closer to the memory that's held me back from touching the piano keys.

If I play it alone, it means he won't come back.

I've never been able to express a reason why I couldn't play, only that it hurt too much to try. But now it arrives, clarion and undeniable.

It wrenches my heart in two, but here I'm not alone.

Zach is playing for us both.

It's tender and sweet, impossibly lovely and powerful as a lightning bolt.

'Time Wears Awa' fills the courtyard with its lovely sound, soothing away hurt, warming this space I've created to welcome others. Memories of the past swirl like the melody, dancing with the feeling of *this* moment: the sensation of warmth beneath my hands, the flow of movement as we travel together across the keys.

And safety. Complete, all-encompassing safety, in this single, astonishing act.

I'm not alone. I'm shaking, but I'm no longer scared.

And between us, the song plays.

My tears break free as we play, as the melody becomes stronger. I want to look at him, but I can't tear my gaze away from our hands together on the keys. I can hear Zach's breathing, feel the warmth of his body beside me. It's more intimate than the kiss we almost shared before. It's an all-encompassing caress: fingers and bodies, heartbeats and breath. I'm stunned by the intensity, exhilarated by the feeling.

He did this for me. Hardly knowing me at all. The first person I've told about Grant who actually listened, who cared enough to ask why I couldn't play.

When the song ends our hands become still. Neither of us speaks, the final echo of the notes ebbing away, replaced by the beat of my heart and the soft sound of our breathing.

I can't find words to express what Zach just did, but I need him to know.

I lift my head – and find his eyes intent on me.

Blue.

His eyes are startlingly blue.

A deep blue, like the colour of the bay on the sunniest days. It's a colour my heart knows, contained within a gaze I long to know.

In a heartbeat, our lips meet, our hands leaving the keys to find each other. I will all of my heart into our kiss, hoping Zach catches what this means to me. Tonight, he doesn't pull back, his arms drawing me closer. I'm surrounded and cradled, beside the piano that made all of this possible.

Swept into this single moment.

I reach out to steady myself, my right hand finding the curve on the piano above the point where the key block meets the outer case. My fingers settle in a smooth indentation in the centre of the wood . . . and my world shifts.

Shocked, I break our kiss, easing from Zach's embrace.

His smile disappears. 'What's wrong?'

'Nothing, it's just, there's something here.'

'Where?'

I move off the piano stool and crouch by the side of the cabinet, peering underneath.

It's *there*.

I blink twice, force my eyes to refocus. Because what can't possibly be there, *is*.

Zach is beside me now, following my move. 'Is that a heart?'

I nod, because a surge of emotion is claiming my throat, blocking any words I could offer.

'It's been carved into the wood.'

A pen-knife, scratching away at the dark varnish, splinters of pale wood revealed as they fall to the floor. A heart traced over and over, frantic lines deepening, the meaning clear. The tears that match my own: only his strange and alien. The first tears I ever see him cry. And behind it all, the slam and shatter of objects tossed down the stairs to the hard tiles of the hall floor below, a woman's furious screeching rising high over every other sound . . .

My own heart shattering like the belongings being hurled at the floor.

'I want to go with you.'

'You can't, birdie. I'm so sorry. I'd take you with me if I could.'

'She doesn't want me. You do.'

A pause in the carving. A hand, rough and warm, against my cheek.

'You've got to be here for your mum. Because I can't look out for her now.'

'What about me?'

The thin line of his lips – a grimace held, masquerading as a smile.

'See this heart? Put your finger here and I'll do the same.'

My finger finding the spiky centre of the heart. His index finger resting beside it.

'Now you're part of the piano's journey. Wherever I go, I'll take this with me. I promise, birdie. I'll never forget you.'

'Merryn?' Zach's voice now, soft and low, close to me.

'It's his,' I manage, before I'm overwhelmed, curling into his body where we kneel together on the courtyard floor.

Zach holds me for a long time. He says nothing, but the resolute beat of his heart where my head rests against his chest keeps me company. His arms are shields across my body, his hand cradles my head against him.

Outside my body, a calm settles. Inside my mind, a storm rages.

This has to be Grant's piano. But how? Could someone else have carved a heart, hidden in a corner of the cabinet – in exactly the same place, exactly the same shape?

It's been there all the time, during all the hours Seth and I spent painting it, and every day it's been in the courtyard as I've worked and dreamed and lived around it. Why did I never think to look?

Zach's gentle kiss on the top of my head makes me pull him

closer. He strokes my hair and eases us to a seated position, drawing me to rest against him.

I never thought to look for the carved heart because I never believed the piano could be Grant's. How could it be? There could be a hundred thousand pianos in Cornwall: any one of them might have ended up on the pavement outside that house. And that's assuming Grant remained in Cornwall. He'd come from Hereford, via Newcastle, Bristol and London, before rocking up in Penzance at the bar Mum was thrown out of. Any one of those places could have called him back.

'What's the story with the heart?' Zach's voice buzzes in his chest.

I lift my head, the initial wave of tears passed. 'Grant carved it on the day he left. We put our fingers there, side by side, and he said it made me part of the piano's journey wherever he took it.'

Zach's blue eyes dim a little. 'A touchpoint.'

'Yes.'

He nods. 'I had one on my board – the one I won my last major competition on.'

'A heart?'

'A wave. Like this.' He twists his ankle to reveal an intricate wave tattoo. It's instantly recognisable, although I can't say how I know it. 'It wasn't carved, though. My mate Xan is a pyrography artist. He burned it into the wood, to remind me of my mum.'

'Your mum loves the sea?'

His smile is instant, sad. 'She did, but that's not why I chose it. She passed away, three weeks before the competition.'

My heart contracts. Zach's reply is weighted with love and loss. I don't need to ask him if they were close, or if he loved her. It's there, in every syllable, every breath between the words.

I lost my mum, too, but I didn't know until the police arrived at my student flat. They'd found her passed out and unresponsive behind a pub – she'd passed away from a massive heart attack in the ambulance on the way to hospital. By then, she'd told me she didn't need me and I'd gladly left her alone, reasoning that she was never going to be what I needed her to be.

I won't tell Zach this – not now. I can see the love and loss for his mother washing across his lovely face.

All my life, I've envied people with that kind of familial love. I don't imagine it's always easy, but the concept was alien to me. I was the adult in our relationship from as early as I can remember: my own young hands holding my mother upright, my small arms bearing the weight of her lived years. It took me many years to understand Mum's inability to love me. She couldn't love because she didn't know how to. I don't think she loved herself a day in her whole life.

So to have been loved as a kid should be, by a mother who knew love; to have been supported and held and cherished, and *then* to have lost it, must be unthinkable.

'I'm sorry for your loss.' My words don't seem enough.

He nods. 'Thanks. She's why I'm in St Ives. I miss her, but I feel like she's closer here than anywhere.'

I don't say that for me St Ives was a sanctuary from all the crap with my mum, or that I had to fight to own it again after my marriage fell apart. For me, the town is the place I chose for myself, time and again.

Zach runs his finger over the carved heart. 'So this was a touchpoint for him? Your stepdad?'

'That's what he said. I think he was trying to offer me comfort while the massive upheaval was happening. He carved it just before he left. He couldn't stop Mum throwing him out, so he tried to make it easier for me.'

'And did it?'

His question stops me in my tracks. I've never considered this before, only seeing the hurt and betrayal and loss wrapped so tightly around my memories of the last day I saw Grant. Did knowing about the heart change my response to his leaving?

'No,' I reply, as much to myself as to Zach. 'I haven't thought about the heart for years. Maybe because it was never meant for me. Grant took it with him when he took the piano – *this piano*. There was never any question of me going with him.'

We lapse into silence. I rest my head against Zach, suddenly bone-weary. His arms fold around me again. I can't work out how we got here: from the kiss, to the discovery of the heart, to the revelation. But, while I'm scrambling to make sense of Merlin being Grant's piano, I'm relieved that Zach is with me. Without him – without the invitation, his beautiful act that brought me closer to the piano than I've been in years, or the kiss that still thrills me – I might never have found the carved heart.

'It's here with you now,' Zach says, at last, as if my thoughts were spoken aloud. 'Which means Grant may be closer than you think.'

Could it be a sign? My searches have all drawn blanks, but could finding Grant's piano mean he was closer to home than I realised? I want to believe it – but another thought wedges itself between the possibility. 'He abandoned it, though,' I counter. 'He would never do that. It can only mean he . . . he had no use for it anymore.'

I don't want to think the worst, but the Grant Henderson I

knew could never be parted from his beloved instrument. The only way he would let it go would be if the decision was out of his hands. Or if his hands had no more need of it.

As long as I've been searching, the prospect that he might have died has never been far away. It would explain the blanks I've drawn and now the piano he left behind. But I don't want to think he isn't alive: even if I never find him, I want to believe that he's somewhere happy, living a good life. Even if I can't be part of it. I want that for him.

'No, hear me out,' Zach insists. 'If the piano is in St Ives, it means Grant was here, too. Someone must know something about what happened to him. You know how gossip travels in town. If Grant lived on North Terrace, someone must know about it.'

I leave the warmth of his arms and study his face. His eyes are alive now, darting between Merlin and me, a thousand thoughts behind each movement.

'What are you saying?'

He smiles – and possibility floods back in. 'I'm saying that if you want to find out, I'm here. I'll help you find him.'

PART THREE

'Everything Has Changed' (Taylor's Version)

– Taylor Swift feat. Ed Sheeran

Thirty-Two

ZACH

I didn't want to leave her last night.

After everything that happened, I didn't want her to be alone. I offered to sleep on the sofa in her flat above Sweet Reverie – honestly meaning to stay there, not use it as a reason to gain an invite into her home. But she refused.

So I returned to the studio, light-headed and giddy with the suddenness of everything. I don't remember going to bed but I guess I must have, because I jolted awake at the sound of my alarm at four-thirty a.m.

That kiss was everything.

Whatever happened after it, I would have done without question. Because being with Merryn changed everything.

But now I'm on my bakery delivery route, trying to wrap my head around the bold suggestion I made. How the hell am I going to help Merryn find the man who owned the piano?

What if he's dead?

She said as much herself, stopping short of actually giving the possibility voice. But honestly, why else would a man who had taken the piano with him everywhere he went leave it in a house due for development? I've seen the street where Merryn found the piano. There's a run of three houses there that I can't remember anyone having lived in. Right in the middle of the boutique B&Bs and luxury holiday rentals that dominate the street, their tangled gardens and empty windows at odds with their glamorous, expensive neighbours. It was only a matter of time before a developer snapped them up. It's a surprise that it's taken so long for it to happen.

I guess we should start in the street. Even if nobody can remember Grant Henderson, they might be able to tell us how long the house has been empty. Perhaps the developer will tell us when they acquired the property. From there, we can maybe track down the original owner or landlord and see where that takes us.

I could be setting Merryn up for a fall. The last thing I'd ever want to do. But if she wants to look for this guy, I'm going to make sure she isn't doing it alone.

And then there's the kiss.

Kisses, as it turned out.

She pulled me in for another when we stood at the end of the passageway – a lingering, intense kiss we both leaned into, despite the late hour and the exhaustion of the night's events.

On my way back to Downalong Bakery, I take a detour to drive down North Terrace. It's easy to spot the houses currently being renovated: scaffolding surrounds them and the middle building is missing a roof. A large *BROTHERSON DEVELOPMENTS* banner has been hung across the scaffolding. Maybe they would know who occupied the houses they're now developing?

The idea sparks a plan.

I'm not due to meet Merryn until late again tonight, following the evening opening. But this can't wait.

By the time my shift at the bakery is complete, I know where I'm going.

*

The smile that Merryn sends me when I walk into Sweet Reverie is the best reward. The frosty glare from her café assistant, not so welcoming.

'Hope you're *payin'* this time.' She pouts, standing protectively close to Merryn.

'It's okay, Ruthie. You two need a proper introduction anyway. So, Zach, this is Ruthie, my assistant. Ruthie, this is Zach, my . . . *friend.*'

The pause is interesting, although not a cause for concern. What should we call each other now? We've shared two amazing kisses and I've played piano for her. Does that mean we're together? Or heading towards it?

Ruthie gives me the briefest nod. 'Just as long as he's not goin' to skip out on us, I have no objections.'

I wasn't aware we needed her approval, but okay. 'Nice to meet you.'

'Same, I s'pose. What can I get for you?'

'Merryn, actually.'

Ruthie readies a return volley, but Merryn intervenes.

'I'm all yours.' There's a definite sparkle in her eyes as she says it. I feel like we're kids, sneaking around behind our parents' backs. It's a thrill I want to hang on to.

'Have you taken your break yet?'

'No.'

'Any chance I can whisk you away for half an hour when you do?'

Merryn looks to Ruthie, who responds with a shrug. 'I don't see why not. I'll be ready in about twenty minutes? Please, take a seat.'

'Okay. Can I order a coffee and maybe a slice of chocolate cake, please?' I risk a wink at her assistant, who scowls back. 'I'm happy to pay upfront, if you like.'

'Might be an idea.'

'That won't be necessary,' Merryn says, pointedly. 'I'll bring it over to you.'

She's gorgeous.

I find a table midway down the café and watch her at work. I'm struck by how many of her customers she knows. She shares a joke, a smile – whatever it takes to make people feel at home. For the obvious holidaymakers she offers kind words and recommendations for things to do. Nothing dims her light. It's amazing.

The coffee is good and the chocolate cake better, finally pacifying the grumble my stomach has had since I set out for work in the pre-dawn light. And then, Merryn is at my table, bag slung across her body, smile trained on me alone.

'Ready.'

It's a ten-minute walk from Star Court to North Terrace, the road rising steeply away from the town centre. Our hands bump together as we walk, each collision causing self-conscious smiles. When we pass the tiny Royal Cinema, I dare to take her hand. Her smile as her fingers lock with mine is the best thing in my day.

I never imagined that returning to St Ives, as lost and rud-derless as I was, might lead to finding someone like Merryn. Love, like everything else in my life, seemed a luxury I could ill afford.

But this feels right.

We reach the house, today a hive of activity with two *Brotherson Developments* vans parked outside. A long green plastic chute has been fixed to the scaffolding, bricks and roof tiles being thrown down it into a waiting skip.

'Excuse me,' I call to a huge bear of a bloke, wearing a yellow hi-vis gilet and dusty blue hard hat, who's loading sand into a rolling concrete mixer. 'Excuse me?'

The builder turns, dislodging an ear bud. 'Wasson?'

'Do you know who the landlord was of this place before Brotherson Developments acquired it?'

'Not the foggiest,' he calls back over the noise of the con-crete mixer.

'Any idea who might?'

'Hang on.' He steps over a pallet of bricks and moves to the side of one of the vans, banging on the side with his gloved fist. 'Boss! Visitor!'

The side door of the van slides open and a tall, handsome bloke gets out. He instantly breaks into a smile when he sees us, walking straight past me to hug Merryn. I'm so surprised I'm just left there, gawping on the pavement.

Merryn breaks free from the hug, laughing. 'Sorry, Zach, meet Jack Dixon, one of our very good customers.'

Now I see it. In his work clothes, I didn't recognise him: the dad of the girl who bumped into me at the evening opening celebration. 'Hi. You work for Brotherson Developments?'

'For my sins.' Jack grins.

'Are you working on this house?'

'Not usually, no. Our regular foreman is off sick, so I'm stepping in.'

'Maybe you can help us,' Merryn says, glancing at me.

'Sure, if I can.'

'The piano we have at Sweet Reverie . . .'

'Merlin? Nessie can't stop talking about it.'

'That's so sweet,' Merryn replies, her smile as bright as the summer sun. 'Thing is, Seth and I found Merlin here, outside this house, a few weeks ago. It had a *Free To A Good Home* sign on it. I've just discovered it was once owned by someone my mum dated, way back when I was a kid. We lost touch, but if his piano is here it means he was, too. I was just wondering if you know who the owner of this place was before Brotherson bought it?'

'Wow, okay.' Jack leans against the van. 'Like I said, this isn't my project, but I can certainly do some digging back at the office. You want to track him down?'

'Yes.' I hear the resolve in her reply.

'More power to you. What was the guy's name?'

'Grant Henderson.'

'Okay, cool.' He pulls a pencil from behind his ear and a small notebook from his back pocket, scribbling down the name. 'Leave it with me and I'll see what I can do. Oh, while you're here, remember that picnic I asked if you could cater?'

'Yes?'

He gives a sheepish smile. 'Any chance you could do it this Sunday?'

'*This* Sunday?'

'Yeah. Sorry. I was going to leave it till the end of summer, but Seren's best mate is expecting and she's due literally any day. I'd hate for her not to be there.'

'At the picnic?'

'Mm-hm. So, what do you reckon? Is it a goer?'

That seems like ridiculously short notice to me, but Merryn is clearly considering the logistics.

'If we scale back on the food, make it sandwiches, scones and cakes instead of canapés and a hot buffet, I think it's possible. I'll have to see if Ruthie will be available, but I'll make it work.'

'Yes! Beauty!' Jack punches the air and gathers Merryn into another enormous hug, much to the amusement of his colleagues on the building site. 'Cheers for this, Mer. It's going to be epic!'

'Is that something you can do at such short notice?' I ask her, as we're walking back down into the town. Her hand is back in mine, swinging between us, the point where our skin connects deliciously warm.

'It'll be a challenge,' she admits. 'But Jack and Seren have supported the café from the beginning. And if I can make it work, who knows what else might come of it?'

'Seems a lot of work for a beach picnic, though.'

'That's because it's not just a beach picnic.' Her smile is enigmatic, as if there's a secret code I'm unaware of.

'What do you mean?'

She laughs and squeezes my hand. 'Nothing. Come on, I need to rescue Ruthie before the afternoon tea crowd descends.'

I watch her as we walk towards Star Court, this incredible woman who can tap into hope at will. Knowing where she came from, and what she dealt with at an age no kid should ever have to, makes her all the more amazing.

I'm falling for her, fast. There's no point denying it: when it comes to Merryn Rowe, I'm in. Wherever this takes us.

Which makes me all the more determined to find Grant Henderson.

Thirty-Three

MERRYN

'*This* Sunday?' Ruthie repeats, incredulous at the request. 'Jack Dixon's havin' a laugh!'

'I said we could do it.'

I brace myself for her reply.

'Ridiculous, Mer! That's what this is! We can't do that menu in two days!'

'That's why we're changing it,' I reply. 'Sandwiches. Scones. Empire oceans.'

Her glare softens a little at my mention of the new menu. It's simple, easy to prepare in batches but still infused with Sweet Reverie's character. Our empire ocean biscuits will be the killer touch: homemade treats that are fast becoming our bestselling sweet option this summer. Inspired by Scottish empire biscuits, they're made from two rounds of buttery vanilla shortcake sandwiched with raspberry jam, topped with white icing. But where traditional empire biscuits are finished with a glacé cherry or jelly tot sweet on top, ours have a swirl of blueberry icing on top of the white, to resemble a cresting wave. Perfect for the setting, the company and the occasion.

'But I can't be there to do it,' she says.

'Please, Ruthie. I'll give you double time.'

She shakes her head. 'It's not the money, Mer. I'm doin' a craft fair with Mum, over in Porthleven. I promised her, months back.'

'Could someone else help?' I know I sound panicked and I wish I didn't, but we need this gig and it could open up so many possibilities for the business. I should have checked with Ruthie first before agreeing, but Jack caught me off-guard and I was keen to show him Sweet Reverie could handle it.

'No can do. Sorry, Mer. Mum's paid for the table and she can't take all that stuff on her own.' She sets a conciliatory hand on my arm. 'I can help with all the food prep, and maybe Murph or Jenna could come with you.'

'But I need them here.' I hadn't expected any problems, caught up in the joy of being with Zach and the thrill of the search for Grant. My mind races with logistical puzzles – I could transport the food to the beach by myself, but would I be able to set it up and serve everyone single-handedly?

'How about Zach?' Ruthie says.

'What? No, I don't think I could ask him.'

'I reckon he'd do just about anythin' you asked him, judgin' by his big old dopey face when he saw you today.' My assistant folds her arms. 'Besides, it's the least he can do to make up for runnin' out on his order.'

'He's said sorry for that.'

'That ain't the point, Mer! You're the carrot that can get him to do stuff. That's the beauty of relationships! So *ask* him.'

I set about putting preparations in place, busying myself with lists and schedules to get the food ready, while trying not to think about the risk of asking Zach. It feels too soon, too sudden to be seeking his help, when he's already doing so much aiding my search for Grant. But later that evening, when we're sitting together beside Merlin, I dare to ask the question.

'Ruthie can't do Sunday,' I begin, 'for the picnic. We're fine getting everything ready, but I need Murph and Jenna to hold the fort here. I can't afford to lose a day's trading. So I was wondering – and please don't feel you have to agree – could you help me? At the picnic? I mean, if not I'll just do it myself, but . . .'

'Yes,' he says, his smile broadening when I stop gabbling and look up at him.

'Really?'

He strokes a gentle finger over the contour of my cheek. 'Of course. I'd love to.'

*

Gwithian Beach is a blustery beauty on Sunday morning, the thunder of waves and wind tempered by the salt air rush and warm, sparkling sunshine bathing everything in sight. It's been too long since I visited, despite being just around the bay from St Ives.

I'll make more time to explore the landscape when the summer season ends, I promise myself, lugging crates from the van I hired and following Zach down the steep, sandy path over the dunes to the beach.

I still can't believe he agreed to help me. I keep sneaking glances at my handsome assistant for the day, amazed at how quickly he's become part of my life. He's charming and sunny and acts like nothing is too much trouble for him. I love that. Even if my head is taking longer to accept it than my heart.

My team have been great, too – another blessing I'm counting in this. As planned, we started preparations yesterday, making items that could be kept chilled in the fridge overnight and baking batch upon batch of cheese scones, a favourite speciality of ours, which Jack had specifically requested. At six this morning, the final push began. With the help of Murph and Jenna, we cut sandwiches, assembled salads and baked extra empire ocean biscuits, each one dotted with tiny gold sugar stars around the cresting wave on top.

Ruthie, Murph and Jenna have speculated in recent days about why Jack Dixon organised this and why so many of our friends have been invited. His plea for us to keep talk of it from Seren has only added to the suspicion. So, when he meets us on the beach, uncharacteristically flustered, I sense our theories might be correct.

'We're just going to be out by the shoreline,' he tells us. 'So, if you and the gang could hang back here, by the dunes, that would be great.'

'Leave it to us,' I assure him. 'Do you have everything you need?'

'I think so.' He pats his pocket, then instantly reddens when he realises he's given the game away. 'You can't tell anyone.'

'Your secret's safe with me.' I smile, even though I suspect most of the guests for the impromptu beach picnic, at the place where Jack and Seren's love story began, have probably sussed the reason behind it.

He hurries off to fetch Seren and Nessie from the nearby

caravan park where he and his daughter once lived. They're visiting Jeb, the owner, who I suspect is in on Jack's plan, too.

'Is he doing what I think he's doing?' Zach whispers to me, his arm sliding around my shoulder as we watch Jack jogging away.

'Wait and see,' I reply, leaning into his warm body.

We set out a stack of cosy blankets from a Cornish blanket company in St Ives, woven in random shades that match the surrounding landscape. Adwenna, who manages the shop, donated them to Jack as a gift for the occasion. They sell some of Seren's gorgeous seaglass jewellery alongside the blankets and wanted to be part of this *completely innocuous* picnic. We have a crate of champagne delivered by the bottle shop on Fore Street and stunning glass platters to serve food on from the fused glass workshop next to St Ia's Church.

Everything here speaks of love.

It's moving to see it. And to be beside Zach is an added gift.

Seren and Jack are loved by so many in the community, their journey to find each other the stuff of local legend. Seren's father once ran a gallery in Cyril Noall Square, just off Fore Street, and much of the love locals had for him has passed naturally to his daughter.

We have twenty guests due at any moment, so Zach and I lay out the random rug blankets across the sand at the base of the dunes, weighing down the corners with rocks and scattering cushions around them for comfort.

I'm excited and nervous, witnessing Sweet Reverie's first foray into catering that could prove providential if it's a success. Having a catering arm of the business would mean a secondary source of income for the months when visitor numbers to the café lessen. It's an opportunity I'm determined to make the most of.

'Does it matter that we're in view?' Zach asks, as we unpack the last of the crates and stack them in a natural dip in the dune, pulling a green tarpaulin over them.

'I don't think so. We'll have to keep everyone quiet while Jack's doing whatever it is he's doing.'

He laughs. 'I love how everyone's acting like it isn't obvious what's about to happen.'

I smile back. 'We all want it to work. I just hope nobody's let the secret slip to Seren.'

'They won't. It's so sweet. And they'll love the food. This is such a cool thing you're doing, Merryn. I'm glad I could be here for you.'

I link my arm with his. 'Me too. Okay, I think we're ready.'

'And just in time,' he says, looking up to the path between the dunes, where a stream of people are descending.

It takes a while for us to settle the picnic party, furnishing them all with fruit punch and cheese nibbles while we wait for Jack to appear. Nerves are building in my stomach: not just for us, but for Jack, too.

And then, we see them.

Out at the shoreline, where the light meets damp sand in a dazzle of white. Silhouetted against the huge rolling waves, Jack and Seren walk, hand in hand, Nessie dancing and weaving around them. When they come level with us, staring out to sea, we see Jack stop and point at something on the beach. Seren looks down, her hand flying to her mouth. As she's looking at whatever is on the beach, Jack drops to one knee in the sand, Nessie skipping about behind him.

Zach and I, and the gathered picnic party, hold our collective breaths, and then we see Seren nod, Jack rising to scoop her up in his arms. Spontaneously, we all jump to our feet and cheer, causing the newly engaged couple to look over and head across the sand to join us.

It's the loveliest moment I've witnessed. I catch Zach wiping a tear away as we move to welcome the newly engaged couple.

It's so different to the proposal I had. Not on a stunning beach, with a line of beautiful seaglass pieces leading to a collage of stars surrounding the message WILL YOU MARRY ME? picked out in pebbles and driftwood, as Jack did for Seren – but in the busy kitchen of a Falmouth restaurant where Luke and I were working together. Across the din between saucepans and plates, he yelled his proposal to me. Days later, the head chef promoted Luke to his second-in-command, citing his ability to take initiative as the reason, while I carried on as a sous chef.

I don't want to remember that anymore. For so long I held on to the moment as proof of a time when we were good together. Looking at it now, I wonder. Did Luke only propose like he did to catch the attention of our head chef?

I dismiss the thought as Zach and I serve champagne to the delighted party. The food is a success, our outside styling loved by all. Having Zach beside me is the loveliest bonus, his faith in me and what I do as bright as the sun this afternoon. And the sight of two people completely in love, surrounded by a tight-knit group of friends, gives me the shot of hope I need.

Pushing memories of Luke firmly from my mind, I lean into the joy of this moment.

The past is gone, I tell myself. I have a new life now. One I've worked hard for, that I owe only to myself. New openings, new friends, new possibilities. And whatever Zach Trevelyan is going to bring me.

It's more than I could have dared to imagine. And I'm loving it.

When we return to the empty café – now cleaned and prepared for tomorrow's trading – Zach helps me put everything away. We're tired but buzzing, the best kind of weary after a triumph of an event.

'I have been waiting to do this all day,' he says, pulling me in for a long, slow kiss. I melt into it, the thrill overriding my aching limbs and tired mind. We rise and fall as we hold each other close, the sweet delay of the day rewarded.

When he pulls back, I reach up to stroke his hair, sand-soft beneath my fingers.

'Stay,' I say, never more certain of anything before.

His kiss is the perfect reply.

Thirty-Four

ZACH

Merryn Rowe is fast becoming the best thing that's happened to me. Working alongside her at the proposal picnic – and what happened when we returned to her home – confirmed it for me.

I haven't felt this way about someone for a long time. I might never have felt as much for someone. It's thrilling and terrifying how quickly I've fallen for her. And I sense that she feels the same.

It makes me want to do whatever I can to make her happy – including assisting her in the search for Grant Henderson.

But the news from Jack Dixon, when it comes, is frustrating.

The previous landlord had the house on the market for thirteen months after giving his tenants notice. Hours after the sale to Brotherson Developments went through, he suffered a major heart attack, underwent surgery and never woke up from the anaesthetic.

It feels like a dead end, not helped by my own door-to-door enquiries that drew blanks at every turn.

I need to think of something else.

In the meantime, my shifts at Pengelly's have begun in earnest, two extra shifts already under my belt when the launch attracted a sold-out crowd for the first weekend.

When I arrive, Luke greets me at the door, brandishing a newspaper.

'Seen this? It's a triumph!'

He hands it to me – and I see Zanna Venn's piece about me. The photo of us in front of Pengelly's takes up half a page, a fortuitously placed advert for the restaurant underneath.

I've been dreading how this might turn out. Nice though Zanna was, I've learned to my cost that you never trust what journalists say until you see what they print.

This is a good surprise.

It's not every restaurant in West Cornwall that can boast a former national and European champion, but Pengelly's on St Ives Harbour can do just that. Zach Trevelyan, recently retired from the pro-surfing world, is forging a new path serving delicious food and local ales and spirits to visitors and locals alike.

Pengelly's, the brainchild of local restaurateur Luke Pengelly and business partner, Scott Mayfield, opened last week to packed tables and rave reviews. Billed as the go-to destination for foodies, it promises a locally sourced, seasonal menu supporting local food and drink providers across the south-west.

'We knew we had a gem in Zach when he applied to join the team,' Luke Pengelly told the Cornwall Daily News, *'but learning of his stellar pro-surfing career confirmed it.'*

Trevelyan plays down his starry status, but is clearly relishing his new role. 'I've always loved a challenge, and I'm excited to see what happens.'

'Perfect, huh?' Luke beams. 'And she got in all the info I gave her. This is going to bring the punters in!'

Later, in the welcome silence of the studio, I look again at the copy of the paper Luke gave me. Zanna promised she'd write something positive and she did.

So what could she do with a real story?

Beside the newspaper is the business card she gave me.

Before me, the proof I need that she would do justice to whatever story she was given.

I make the call before I can think better of it, or question whether I should take this to Merryn first. The call connects but directs immediately to voicemail.

I take a deep breath before I leave my message.

'Zanna, hi, it's Zach Trevelyan. Thanks for the article about Pengelly's – it's great. Luke is over the moon. Listen, I might have a story for you . . .'

*

It happens with surprising speed.

Merryn loves the idea, as does Zanna. Before I know it, we're all gathered around a table in Sweet Reverie, a voice recorder placed between Merryn and Zanna, a notebook and pen ready beside it.

'How is this going to work?' Nerves play in Merryn's question.

'We'll just chat,' Zanna assures her. 'I'll take notes of everything alongside the recording and I'll check every detail with you before I include it.'

'Right. And this will be a piece in the paper?'

The journalist folds her hands on the table. 'More than that.

An appeal, championed by the *Cornwall Daily News*, across print and online media. We add to the story as the search goes on, seek support and help from our readership across the county and build this into the biggest human interest story the paper's ever covered.'

'But if we don't find him . . .'

'Then it'll add to the mystery. My editor loves it and, trust me, Frank doesn't get excited about a story often.'

I squeeze Merryn's hand where it rests on my knee under the table. 'This could work. I really believe it.'

Her gaze is still as she looks at me, the slightest hint of uncertainty in her eyes. 'If you're with me, I'll be fine.'

I would kiss away every concern from her right now if we didn't have an interview to record. There will be time for that when Zanna leaves. 'Ready?'

She nods. 'Let's do it.'

Thirty-Five

MERRYN

The article goes live next day, the print edition appearing a day after it's published online. And then – nothing. For a whole, agonising week.

Zanna assures me this is to be expected. 'It takes a while for word to get out,' she says, when I call her for an update. 'People need time to think about things, ask their friends, remember back. Keep the faith, okay?'

I know things take time and I keep reminding myself how quickly wheels have been set in motion. That the new campaign has three years of my own fruitless searches behind it. But with every day, my fears grow. What if he doesn't want to be found? Or what if he's no longer here?

'We're just trying doors,' Zach reassures me, as we're curled up together in bed. 'I know it's tough, waiting it out. But things arrived at the right time – me and Zanna and the newspaper search. Maybe that was for a reason. Maybe Grant is waiting to be found.'

In his arms, his heartbeat strong against my ear, I could believe anything was possible.

It doesn't stop the fears, though.

And there's the small detail of Zach working for my ex-husband to contend with. I haven't said anything to Zach because it's a job he needs and it isn't any of my business. But it kicks me every time he's waxing lyrical about Luke. I get it: I was as blown away by Luke's confidence and iron-clad self-belief as everyone else. It was only when what he wanted stopped being me that I saw it for what it was. Selfishness. An absolute unwillingness to take any responsibility for his actions. He won't ever change, so why even try to challenge it?

All the same, I wonder if Luke has said anything to Zach about being married to me. He probably doesn't even know we're together. But when he reads Zanna's article about my search for Grant, there's no way he'll be able to ignore it.

Luke told me to forget about looking for my stepdad. But now I am – and his 'star' employee is not only helping me search for Grant, but is also my new lover.

I don't know how he'll take that, and if it will make problems for us.

But before I can worry about that, there's someone else who definitely needs to know.

We're eight days into the appeal, when I decide to tell Seth about Zach and me. I suspect he knows already, the mention of Zach in Zanna's launch piece impossible to ignore.

I wait until I've finished work for the day and the café is prepared for the morning, before I venture round to Porthia Surf. Seth is cashing up when I walk in, his head bowed over the till.

'We're closed,' he says, not looking up.

'I know.'

He raises his eyes to meet me and lets out a sigh. 'Hey, Mer.'

'I haven't seen you for a couple of days. Everything good?'

He shrugs. 'Busy, you know.'

'Okay.' Why doesn't his reply feel genuine? 'Can we chat? I brought coffee and pie.'

Instantly, he brightens. 'Well, in that case, you can head upstairs, if you like. Place is a pit but it's home sweet home till September. Find somewhere to sit and I'll be up in five.'

The flat above Porthia Surf is a mirror-image layout to mine, which always makes me feel like I've entered a parallel universe. That and the fact that it's a weird combination of mismatched furniture and piles of boxes of stock. Seth only stays here during peak season, when he can rent out his flat and make over a thousand pounds a week from it. I have quite a few friends in town who do this, the income from high summer holiday rentals enough to cover mortgages for the next few months.

This place is pure Seth: a story behind every piece of furniture and soft furnishing. The armchair came from his nan's house when she passed away, still sporting the handmade crochet triangle across the high back cushion. He pulled the brightly coloured rug from a skip, in surprisingly good condition, and he found the slightly wonky bookcase in a flea market over in Padstow, years ago. Even the teapot he loves to bits came from a craft sale in the Guildhall, reduced because the stallholder didn't think anyone could love its garish yellow, turquoise and burgundy checkerboard design.

Where my flat has one large bedroom, Seth's is divided into one decent-sized room and one tiny boxroom – the room I slept in while I was renovating my building. I feel a wash of nostalgia when I look over to it from my perch between stacks of surfing magazines on the old saggy sofa. I dealt with so much in this cramped, eccentrically furnished space. This is where my dream of Sweet Reverie was born. I will forever be grateful for the tough but rewarding months spent here.

Ten minutes later, Seth jogs upstairs, his hand raised in apology. 'Sorry, bird, my cash-countin' skills are off today.'

'I see you're settled in,' I say, handing him the box of pie as he evicts a magazine pile to sit beside me.

'Yep.' He grins as he looks around the unconventional space. 'I mean, it's not Tregenna Castle, but it'll do.' He takes a large bite of white chocolate and strawberry pie. 'So, anythin' you want to tell me? Or any*one*?'

I swallow a groan. Of course he knows. My best guess is Ruthie, but anyone who was at Jack and Seren's proposal picnic could have mentioned it to him. Our friendship circle is small and tight-knit: not much escapes the grapevine.

'I'm with Zach,' I say slowly, watching his expression carefully.

He nods, his attention held by the slice of pie. 'How long?'

'Couple of weeks? It's still very new.'

'The pro surfer.'

'Yes. He used to be.'

'I should send Flynn round. He'd be over the moon.' His expression doesn't betray his opinion. 'Ruthie says he was the bloke who skipped out without payin' for his tea and biscuits.'

'He was embarrassed. That's why he ran.'

'Hm.'

'But he's an amazing musician,' I insist. 'And – he's helping me to look for Grant.'

I see Seth's shoulders stiffen.

I was expecting to.

Seth's always known about my search for Grant, largely because I started it again during the months I was lodging with him here. After years of Luke telling me I was wrong to assume Grant would even remember me, let alone want me back in his life, I sought Seth's support when I decided to search again. He gave it, of course, but not as enthusiastically as I thought he would.

I haven't mentioned it since I moved into my place, the search becoming my own private mission. I wonder if he's seen the *Cornwall Daily News* campaign, or the article that launched it. Ruthie's been careful not to share her opinion on it, beyond smiling at customers who have wished me luck with the search, but might she have been more candid with Seth?

'Say something,' I urge, when the pause becomes uncomfortable.

'Not for me to say.'

'I'm asking.'

He hefts a sigh. 'I just . . . I don't think it's a good idea, Mer. I never have. People go out of our lives for a reason.'

'Because my mum threw him out.'

'Or maybe he didn't want to be found. Too messy, too much water under the bridge. It's been years, bird. Don't you think he'd have come lookin' for you if that's what he'd wanted?'

After Zach's unwavering support, Seth's words hurt. Out of everyone, I hoped he'd understand.

'I thought you believed in signs.'

'I do.'

'Finding his piano – the actual piano I learned on – is a sign I can't ignore.'

'And three years of searchin' with no sign of the bloke?'

'I was on my own before. I'm not now.'

'Zach.' He scoffs.

'Yes, Zach. And the paper, and the campaign.' I don't understand the scowl this earns me. 'Okay, what?'

'Nothin'.'

'You don't get to say that, Seth. If you've something to say . . .'

'I just think it's weird.'

'What's weird?'

He shifts on the sofa so he's facing me. 'You haven't mentioned the bloke for years and then this surfer turns up and all of a sudden you're launchin' a big campaign? This isn't you, Mer. Jumpin' into things without thinkin' them through, hookin' up with complete strangers.'

'I've been looking for Grant since I left Luke. And Zach isn't a stranger.'

'You've only known him five minutes!'

Where is this coming from? And if Seth had such an issue with Zach, why didn't he tell me? My guess is that he's known for a while, his responses far too considered to be a knee-jerk reaction. 'I'm really happy, Seth.'

He stares back. Whatever else he might think about my life and the choices I'm making, he has to see that. Even customers who hardly know me have commented on it this week. 'I get that. And I'm happy for you.'

'It doesn't sound like it.'

'I think he's untested. I mean, he's kippin' at a mate's place, he's left the surf circuit and what is he even plannin' to do?'

'I wasn't aware he had to submit a five-year plan in order to date me.' I put down my coffee cup. 'I should go.'

'No – Mer – wait.' His hand is on my arm. 'I don't want you to get hurt.'

'I'm not going to.'

'You don't know that. And I've been there, remember? I saw what that bastard Pengelly did to you. I don't want your lovely heart to get broken again. And searchin' for Grant is a bad idea. You don't know what his life has been like, or what kind of person he is. You were a little kid when you knew him. How can you be sure he's someone you can trust?'

'I know it,' I insist, fighting a lump that's taken residence in my throat. I only have my instinct to trust, which Seth can't feel like I can. I know Grant: I know the dad he was for me when he didn't have to be. I don't think someone would change from that, even with the passage of time.

Besides, if I stop believing Grant wanted to be as present in my life as he was, where does that leave me?

'I don't want to argue with you,' I say, struck by a strong desire to leave Seth's place. 'You don't have to agree with me. I just thought, as my friend, you should know what I'm doing – with Zach and with Grant.'

'Thanks for tellin' me. Don't leave, Mer. Stay and chat a bit? About other stuff?'

'I'm tired,' I reply, done with this now. 'I'll see you tomorrow.'

He's still staring after me when I leave.

Thirty-Six

ZACH

Merryn is quiet when we meet next day. When I ask her if she's okay, she asks if we can go for a walk. Of course I agree. I don't care where we are as long as we're there together.

The sudden dimming of her light is a shock to see. I know waiting for news on Zanna's newspaper campaign is tough for her, but this feels like something more. With no particular destination in mind, we wander through the streets, the glow of the sunset sky washing the rows of fishermen's cottages with the softest gold. It's one of those perfect summer evenings, when the air is still, the heat of the day is past and the town settles itself for the night to come.

Perhaps predictably, we end up at Porthmeor. It's particularly lovely when the sun is setting, the crowds who have camped on the beach all day are gone, replaced by groups of happy visitors and locals wandering down for a gentle evening stroll. The sea is on the way back in, but doesn't seem in a hurry to make it up the beach. Gone is the swell of recent days, the waves smaller and gentler, although I know that can often be an illusion. You never underestimate the sea, especially on the Meor.

When we reach the sand we kick off our shoes, walking hand in hand across the still-warm beach.

'What's up?' I ask at last, trusting the magic of this place to do its stuff.

She leans a little against my arm. 'I had a run-in with Seth.'

I'm no longer concerned that she and Seth are together, but I understand how close they are as friends. Suddenly, her quiet mood makes sense. 'What about?'

'The search. And you. But mostly the search.'

'Thinks I'm not good enough for you, does he?'

'He's just being protective. But he thinks I shouldn't be looking for Grant.'

'Why?'

'I don't know. I wish I did.'

I glance down at her. 'Is he worried you won't find him?'

'I think he's worried I will.'

I stop walking. She looks up at me – and I see the hurt her so-called best friend has caused. Who stamps on the dreams of someone they care about? 'Why would he be concerned about that? If he knows what Grant means to you?'

'Seth thinks there's a good reason why I've never been able to find him. That he has some awful secret, or didn't care about me like he said he did. He thinks I'm approaching this like a child, trusting someone who's been out of my life for years.'

I can see his point and, sure, there are risks that the man Merryn has held in such high regard for most of her life might not be worthy of his throne. But isn't the point to help her find him and then deal with whatever else is revealed?

'Ignore him,' I say, as we start to walk again towards the tideline. 'I'm here for you. That's all that matters.'

We fall back into silence as we near the sea. The sand beneath our feet transforms from soft and dry to ridged and damp. It's the familiar feeling I've missed – the anticipation as the waves reach out to me. My heart aches as we near the sea.

'You want to be out there, don't you?' Merryn asks, her fingers squeezing mine where they are joined.

'I miss it,' I admit, because to deny how I feel to Merryn is unthinkable now.

'You could teach me to surf.' When I look at her, she's smiling. 'I've always wanted to learn.'

'You didn't do it as a kid?'

'No. Mum was scared of the water, so she kept me away. I only learned to swim because of lessons at school. By the time I moved out, it felt too late to learn to surf. At the grand old age of seventeen.' She laughs, shaking her head. 'What little we know when we're kids, eh?'

I remember the certainty of my teens, the cockiness that made me believe the world was at my feet. I don't think I'd recognise my younger self now. I'd probably find him highly annoying and want to push him into the sea. 'I was a dick when I was seventeen.'

'But great at surfing?'

'Oh yeah, the best.' I bask in her smile and the break in tension as the sky above us turns orange and pink.

'Teach me to surf, Zach,' she says, her soft request almost lost amid the rumble of the incoming tide.

'I don't think I—'

'I don't know what you were like as a surfer before. I have nothing to compare it with. I won't judge you, or bemoan things you can't do that you did in the past.'

'My mate Jakey works at the surf school. I could arrange a lesson for you with him?'

My suggestion is silenced by her hand leaving mine, her arms wrapping around my waist.

'I want you to teach me. You've helped me so much with the piano – with the search for Grant. And even if we don't find him, I feel closer to making peace with my past. Let me help you get back into the water.'

I'm blindsided by her request. All I can do is stare at the rolling waves, emotion stealing my words, as Merryn nestles against my chest.

*

I'm still considering her request the next day. Aggie clocks the conundrum the moment she arrives at the studio to drop off a cake she somehow 'over-ordered' at her coffee hut. She's been doing that regularly since I've been here, the same bright excuse trotted out as if the whole of St Ives couldn't see what she's really doing.

Not that I'm likely to complain, though. Free cake is never a thing to refuse.

'Right,' she says, lowering herself gingerly onto the studio couch. 'Stick the kettle on and then tell me what's playin' on that mind of yours.'

I've always believed Aggie has a sixth sense but the addition of pregnancy hormones has sent it stratospheric. I love how she knows stuff as much as I hate it: there's no hiding when Aggie Keats is on your case.

So, tea made and duly delivered, I flop down beside her. 'Merryn wants me to teach her to surf.'

My friend nods and says nothing.

Understanding my cue to continue, I comply. 'And she's being really lovely, asking me to do that. But I don't think I . . .'

'But you're crappin' yourself,' Aggie interjects, in her own succinct style.

'I haven't been properly out there since the accident.'

'Which makes it a perfect time to try.' Her pierced eyebrow rises as she observes me. 'Because if not now, when?'

'When I'm ready.'

The raspberry she blows sends ripples dancing across the surface of her tea. 'Bollocks, Zachy. If you wait till you're *ready* you'll never do it. You're scared. It will hurt. You'll probably have to learn how to do things all over again. But don't you think doin' it with someone who's new to the gig – who wouldn't know surf technique if she tripped over it – is the perfect way to get back in the water?'

I hate it when she makes sense like that. How am I supposed to argue?

'If I let her down—'

'How are you goin' to do that, exactly, hmm? Teach her with the board the wrong way up?'

'Ag—'

'No, Zach, I'm sorry. You've been stuck on land for too long. Jakey says . . .'

I stare at her. 'How do you know what Jakey says?'

She stares back like I've just told her the sea is zebra-striped. 'I am the eyes and ears of the town. There's nothin' I don't hear or see. Besides, Jakey Lowen's long been a fan of my saffron buns.' She sniggers. 'Sorry. Point is, I know he's invited you out with the Meor gang. And he wants you to teach the nippers in his classes.'

'I can't, Ag.'

'Yes, you can. You care about the girl. You love the sea. It's bleddy simple when you look at it like that.'

And when I look at it from Aggie's perspective, it finally is.

Thirty-Seven

MERRYN

It's the first time I've been in a wetsuit for more years than I care to count and it feels a little strange as I emerge from the surf school changing room. Jakey Lowen grins at me, taking in the sight of me in neoprene.

'Looks good on you, maid!'

'Um, cheers?' Nerves dance in my reply.

Jakey catches it and pats my arm. 'Don't sweat it, dude. Trev's the best in the biz. Seriously. Even with a dodgy knee.'

There's something really lovely about the way his eyes shine when he says this, the smile he wears brightening more when Zach sprints across the sand towards us. I don't know their history, beyond the fact that they competed on the same circuit for a while, but it's clear how much they respect one another.

It's a window into Zach's life that I wasn't expecting, and I like it.

I'm so glad he accepted my request. Even if it means I'm now well out of my comfort zone, with the waves looking scarily big from the shore. I silently thank Ruthie for holding the fort at Sweet Reverie this morning to let me do this. I suspect she only agreed so she can have first dibs on the gory details when I return.

'Sorry, sorry,' Zach puffs, reaching us. 'Matt had a last-minute order so I had to drive it over for him.' He grins at me. 'So are you ready for this?'

'Are you?' I laugh.

A flicker of something dims his smile for just a moment and then he's back. 'As I'll ever be. Now, boards.'

Jakey is already prepared, with two boards resting against the surf school wall. They look enormous, but Zach assures me they'll be fine.

We practise on the sand first, as I've seen countless classes from the surf school doing over the years. It's a regular sight on Porthmeor Beach, but I never thought I'd be the one jumping to my feet on a beached board. It feels strange at first, but after a while I start to get the hang of it, aware that doing this on moving waves will be a world away from the safe foundation of the sand.

Jakey watches Zach as we repeat the standing drill. The wince Zach makes every time he moves to a crouching position is impossible to ignore. I wonder if he's having second thoughts. His eyes drift to the surf every time he's standing on the board, the sight robbing his smile.

His greatest love is the waves. But will his body allow him to reclaim it?

Jakey grins at us. 'Okay, kids, enough of that. Ready to get in the sea?'

We tuck our surfboards under our arms and head down towards the distant surf. The tide has turned, but much of Porthmeor Beach is exposed as the waves begin to slowly reclaim the bay. A strengthening breeze is whipping the peaks of the waves, causing sunlit bursts of sea spray to lift into the air. Despite the warm summer day, the water temperature is decidedly chilly. I'm glad of the wetsuit, the shock of the water making my hands and feet sting.

I notice Jakey watching Zach from the shore, a look of pure pride on his face. I hope Zach sees it, too, as we wade out into the waves.

Zach is quiet beside me as we go deeper, only speaking to direct me to sit up on the board. It takes a couple of attempts to achieve, my hands and body out of sync as I grapple with the wet surfboard. But on my third attempt, I make it up, rewarded by Zach's smile as we bob with the waves.

'You make that look easy.'

'Funny,' I grin back. 'It's cool up on the board, though.'

'It is.'

'How are you doing?' I ask, aware of his thoughts being far away from where we are. I can see what it means to him, but can only imagine the battle he's faced to get here.

'Okay, actually. Good. So the question is, are you ready to catch a wave?'

'If you'll show me how it's done.'

Zach grins and starts to explain the process to get me up on the board. Wait for the right wave, push into it, follow it to shore. Lying on the board for the first few tries, then attempting to stand.

'You'll fall off a lot,' he says. 'But that's part of the fun. Feel the rhythm of the waves, try to let that guide you.'

It's only when we start trying – and I start failing – to follow the waves that I understand what he means. The sea has a rhythm beyond the waves on the surface. I feel the pull of the current as it races to shore, the swell and ebb beneath the board.

'It's like music,' I say, breathless from the effort.

'Exactly like that,' he replies, his blue eyes bright. 'Only you feel it with your whole body, your senses and your instinct. It's just learning to coordinate your body and board to take advantage of it.'

'You say that like it's easy,' I reply, loving the smile this elicits.

'Better take me at my word, then, Mer. Let's go again.'

Thirty-Eight

ZACH

It's when Merryn first catches a wave that emotion hits me.

I follow, a board's length behind her, jumping up to my feet before I've even thought about it. My knee hates me but the instinct is there, as bright and immediate as it always was.

Instantly, I'm back at home on the board, salt on my lips and the breeze kissing my cheeks. I thought I'd lost this when my career ended. I'm painfully aware of the changes in my body from my pro-surf days – the thing I'd dreaded facing most – but the swell of joy from being back out among the waves overrides any sense of loss I might feel.

It's beautiful. New. And I'm here because of *her*.

I watch Merryn slowly discovering how her body can move on the water, making all the slips and recalibrations I did when I first tried a board as a kid. It's like seeing myself as I was then, way before surfing became my entire life. The frustration, the laughter, the glimpses of euphoria when something clicks. It was those tiny snapshots of success that became intoxicating, dragging me out into the sea every time, determined to chase the joy.

When what you love becomes your identity, your career, and your reason to get out of bed, it's easy to lose sight of what made you fall for it in the beginning. For years I went through the motions, pushing myself further, never settling for where I found myself.

This time, I have no expectations. The biggest barrier is gone – getting my body back in the waves – and for the first time in forever I let go and just *feel*. It's a revelation.

We stay out for an hour, until Merryn is beginning to tire and my whole body aches. We tandem-ride one last wave to shore, Merryn shakily standing on her board for most of the way, and land back on the beach.

'You did it!' I yell, gathering her into my arms and kissing her sea-salt lips.

'So did you!' She smiles, her cold fingers brushing my hair from my face.

'I couldn't have done it without you.' Emotion balls in my throat. 'Thank you.'

Merryn folds herself into my body, her warmth meeting the coolness of our wetsuits. 'You belong out there,' she murmurs against me.

When she says it, I can believe it again.

'And thus the Mighty Trev was restored to the waves!' Jakey jogs out to greet us, high-fiving us both then grabbing me for a huge, back-slapping hug.

'Loved it, mate,' I manage, as he squeezes the air out of me.

'So come back. Join us at the surf school. The kids will adore you.'

My stomach twists. 'I don't know.'

'You should,' Merryn agrees.

I love their faith in me, but I'm not there yet. I need to process the step I took today before I can think of what comes next. 'Just give me time, yeah?'

Jakey is undeterred, chatting happily to us about the school as we return to the building. Kids race past us, boards in tow, their bare feet slapping against wet sand as the waves beckon them. I see their passion and joy and I want so much to be part of it. But teaching? It was easy to help Merryn out there, knowing she had no prior experience and nothing to compare my instruction to, but would kids who've had the best teachers already see my flaws and limitations?

'Tell him, Merryn,' Jakey pleads, when we're back beside the surf school building. 'I reckon he'll listen to you.'

'Okay, Jakey.' Her smile full of fun and mischief, she turns to me. 'Zach.'

'Yes.'

'In the nicest possible way, get in the sea!'

'Get in the sea! Classic!' Jakey laughs. 'Get in the sea! Get in the sea!'

Merryn joins in and I groan as the two of them start to dance around me. Other beach visitors look over and smile, an audience I hadn't banked on witnessing my good-natured humiliation.

I feign embarrassment, but inside I'm buzzing.

I did it.

I got back out there.

And the beautiful woman giggling and dancing a circle in the sand around me is the reason.

I don't know what the next step is, but with Merryn in my corner I'm not terrified to discover it.

Thirty-Nine

MERRYN

Ten days after the appeal went live – just as I was beginning to think it wasn't going to work – things start to happen.

Calls and emails begin to trickle into the *Cornwall Daily News* office – sightings of Grant, claims from supposed exes, stories from former employers. As the days pass, the trickle becomes a steady stream, Zanna and her colleagues following up each potential new lead.

Zanna reports back as often as she can, occasionally coming to the café for in-person briefings. She's buoyed by the response so far and her editor is delighted. Updates of the *Cornwall Daily News* campaign receive record numbers of hits for their website, easily smashing their previous top stories for engagement.

With every positive sign, my hope becomes a little stronger. And with every late-night meeting with Zach, my feelings for him increase. We're closer since our surfing lesson, the experience binding us to each other. Watching him reclaim his greatest love is beautiful.

He plays Merlin tonight as I sit beside him; stealing kisses between tunes. I still can't touch the keys: it's become a point of principle now the search is officially underway. Until I know for certain – or the search fails to find Grant – I won't say goodbye.

After a while, Zach starts to play a slow, gentle song his mum used to sing to him and his sister. He's forgotten the title and the words, but the shy, gentle way he hums the melody close to me is much better than anything he could perform.

'I love that,' I murmur, leaning my head against his arm as he plays.

'Elowen and I would catch her singing it to herself when she thought nobody was watching. It was her song and singing it made her feel better. Even at the end, when she couldn't dance around her kitchen as she used to, she still hummed it to herself every day.'

'She sounds wonderful.'

'She was. She would have loved you.' He dips his head as I look up, our kiss lingering, unhurried.

'Side gate was open so I just . . .'

We spring apart, to see Seth standing at the edge of the courtyard.

'What are you doing here?' I ask, nerves shivering through my question. Seth knows about us but this is the first time he's seen us together.

'I heard the music from the flat and I thought—' he runs a hand through his hair '—I thought it was you.'

'Zach's the one playing,' I reply.

'Figures.'

'What's that supposed to mean?' Zach asks – and I feel a spark of uncomfortable energy ignite between them.

'Okay, easy tiger! I'm not here to spoil your fun.'

They eyeball each other as the courtyard falls silent.

'Was there something you wanted?' I rush, on edge now.

'Yeah, actually, while Zach's here. I don't think this search for Grant Henderson is wise. I've tried to ignore my reservations, but I can't. You're goin' to get hurt, Mer, and I wouldn't be your friend if I didn't warn you.'

'How do you know she'll get hurt?' Zach counters.

'Because the guy clearly doesn't want to be found.'

'And you've deduced that how, exactly?'

'Zach,' I warn, my hand resting on his shoulder.

'No, he's out of line. There have been sightings, Seth. Several. Zanna and the *Cornwall Daily News* team are investigating them now. I'd say we're on exactly the right path.'

'You would.'

'Sorry?'

'Seth – Zach's right. The search is gaining momentum now. Zanna thinks they're onto something.'

'Zanna just wants a juicy story.' He jabs a finger towards Zach. 'And *he* wants to bask in the glory of it.'

Zach's on his feet now. 'You're talking bollocks, mate.'

'I'm not your *mate*.'

'It's what I want, Seth,' I return, aware I'm now on a precipice between two colliding storms.

'Yeah, *Seth*, this is none of your business.'

'It is when my best friend is being played.'

'Excuse me?'

'I said *played*, you failed surfer.'

'Come here and say that again.'

'Oh, I would, if I didn't think you'd run away like a snivellin' little kid . . .'

'Seth, stop it!'

'You jealous, Hartley?'

'Of you?' He snorts. 'Do me a favour.'

'That's exactly what this is.' Zach squares up to him, leaning a little closer. 'You don't want Merryn to rely on anyone except you. It's pathetic.'

'She's relied on me for years before you blew into town.'

I can't believe what I'm hearing. Are they seriously squabbling over me like I'm a trophy?

'Stop it!' I yell.

'Tell him, not me.' Seth is inches from Zach now. 'I'm not the one usin' a memory of a random guy to get you into bed.'

'And I'm not the one who failed to help her find him for years.'

'Enough, both of you!' I hate this. I'm not even sure it's about me now, the two of them posturing like complete idiots.

'You've got a bleddy nerve, Trevelyan. You appear out of nowhere, disrupt Mer's event, see an opportunity in her, then slither back like the snake you are. Foolin' her. Gettin' her to agree to this public humiliation in the *Daily News*, like some desperate maid too thick to work out that the bloke didn't care about her . . .'

'Get out, Seth,' I growl, shocked by what he really thinks of the appeal to find Grant.

'I ain't leavin', Mer. Not until he admits it.'

'Admit what? That I care for her? That I want her to find this guy? That I want to be by her side when it happens?' Zach throws up his hands in mock surrender. 'Guilty as charged!'

'What's it for, Zachy? One more shot at glory? So you can pretend you still matter?'

'Oh, I matter. Unlike you.'

'I said, enough!' I push between them. 'Seth, go home. Zach, I think you should, too.'

'He's being a dick.'

'You both are!' I'm stung by the way they've casually commandeered me and my search for Grant to use as cheap ammunition against each other. The words they've said can't be taken back. 'I will not be collateral damage in your stupid little row. Get out, both of you.'

Zach's scowl fades for a moment. 'Mer, I'm sorry. I'm just trying to defend you.'

'I don't want to be defended like that.'

Minutes ago I wanted to be as close as I could to Zach. Now, I just want to be alone. How has so much changed in so little time?

'Okay. I'll give you some space. See you tomorrow.'

He tries to kiss me, but I look away. I feel his wounded stare seeking my attention, but he's hurt me and I don't have the will to deal with it now. The calmness of the evening has been shattered, the promise of time with Zach stolen by a stupid, unnecessary fight.

He's almost at the door when my so-called best friend calls after him. 'Run away, Trevelyan, like the washed-up little coward you are.'

I don't even see it start, the speed with which Zach charges at Seth shocking. He slams his fist into Seth's stomach, knocking air from him as he tumbles back, crashing into a table and sending the chairs propped up on its surface scattering across the floor.

I yell at them to stop, but they're not listening.

Seth scrambles to his feet and lunges at Zach, his punch

aimed at Zach's eye. He yelps and covers it with one hand, the other raised to defend himself from the blows Seth rains down on his torso.

They crash through the courtyard, displacing tables and upending chairs. Seth snatches one up and swings it like a hammer. There's a sudden explosion, a splintering of wood and an agonising metallic clang.

Shocked, Seth steps back – and my heart splinters like the gaping hole in the right side of the piano. The wave and stars I painted there smashed away.

It breaks something within me.

'Get out,' I say.

'Mer, I didn't mean to . . .'

I don't look at Seth. Or Zach. My beautiful, hopeful piano, that found its way back to me, sits broken and scarred, shards of wood and smashed keys strewn like shrapnel around its feet. *Grant's* piano – the only link to him I have.

'Get . . . *out* . . .' I bite the syllables like bitter bullets as they leave me.

'He owes you an apology,' Zach begins. 'You should . . .'

'You smashed the one thing of his I still have,' I fire back. 'I don't want anything from you now. Either of you.'

'You don't mean that . . .'

'Get out! And don't come back!'

They say nothing as they shuffle towards the café door. Zach opens it and looks back, but I stare through him.

'I'm sorry.' He frowns, walking out.

As he leaves, Seth turns, holding his arms out to me. 'He went for me. You saw it, clear as day. The bloke's a liability, bird. You should steer clear.'

'You too.'

'What?'

Shaking with rage so strong it scares me, I walk towards him, Seth tripping as he scrambles out of my reach. 'Go. Leave me alone. We are done, Seth. You can't come back from this.'

'But if I just . . .'

'GET OUT!'

I slam the door after him, locking the bolts and stumbling back through to the courtyard as hot tears flood my face. Merlin's broken body is where they left it, an unfair casualty of their stupid war.

Carefully, I lean down and pick up every piece of wood and every broken key from the sawdust-covered slate, cradling each one like a treasured former promise. Flecks of paint fall across my palm, fragments of what can never again be part of the piano. Splashes of saltwater drop between them, joining in rivulets that follow the contours of my skin.

It feels like a death.

Like losing Grant all over again.

Only this time, Zach and Seth are gone, too. Sent packing from my life because their petty squabble destroyed my faith in them. I can't count on them any longer.

And I don't know where to go from here.

PART FOUR

'Oh Woman Oh Man'

– LONDON GRAMMAR

Forty

ZACH

What was I thinking? I fell right into Seth Hartley's plan, blinded by my own rage. He knew he was spouting lies, but that was the point, wasn't it? To goad me. To make me attack him.

And now Merryn hates me.

She couldn't even look at me.

What have I done?

The last thing I see as I crash out of the café is Seth turning back to Merryn, arms outstretched like a wounded child. I don't see her push him out.

My eye feels ready to burst out of its socket, the right hook Hartley threw connecting with sickening accuracy. The skin beneath is already starting to swell. I'm going to look attractive for my bakery round tomorrow. I feel bruises rising across my chest and my right fist feels like I slammed it into a brick wall. I'll pay for it in the morning – but the greatest debt is already past resolution.

The hurt in her eyes.

The anger and betrayal.

I never thought I'd be responsible for either in Merryn.

There are people in the streets I stagger down but they

might as well be ghosts for all the attention I pay them. All I can focus on is my own stupidity.

I don't want to go back to the studio, but I don't trust myself to be anywhere else. St Ives doesn't need to see my battered face or broken pride tonight. So I push my body back through town, every step heavy with shame. I'll get something on my eye and lock myself away until morning. Better for everyone if I'm not around.

I see the blaze of lights when I turn up the private road to the studio, spilling out across the rain-damp tarmac.

Great. The last thing I need.

Kieran's car is parked beside the building. He hasn't done a night session for weeks. Why choose tonight, of all nights?

He's going to take one look at me and chuck me out. His acceptance of me is still tenuous – I've yet to feel confident in it. This will tip him over the edge.

Bloody Seth Hartley! I might lose everything because of what he did. And he knew that, didn't he? That was the aim all along. Rid Merryn of me and get her all to himself as he's clearly long dreamed of.

He was asking her for a hug.

She wasn't yelling at him to leave.

Have I been fooling myself that she wants me?

I reach the front door to find it already ajar. A sudden yell from inside makes me dash in, discarding any thought of my own self-preservation.

Aggie is on the floor, half-propped against the orange sofa, her features creased in pain. She's clutching her belly, her hands spread wide either side of her bump.

'Ag!' I race to her side, throwing her arm over my shoulder as I lift her to the seat. 'Lean on me, okay? Steady now.'

'Bleddy kids,' she wails, grasping for the sofa arm as I strip off my hoodie and roll it into a makeshift cushion to prop against her back. 'I told 'em they'd to hang fire till the weekend, but did they listen to me?'

'We need to get you to hospital,' I rush, wincing as she grips my right hand. 'Where's Kieran?'

'I sent him out.'

'What for?'

'You had nothin' in your cupboards! How are you supposed to work two jobs if you're not eatin'? *Aargh* . . .'

'Try and breathe. Don't speak.'

She raises an eyebrow. 'You do know you're talkin' to me? And what the hell happened to your face?'

'It doesn't matter. We need to find Kieran. Does he have his phone with him?'

'He always has it.'

I pull my phone from my pocket, wincing at the large crack across the screen where I fell on it in the café. There's still a display and a signal, both of which I can work with. I find Kieran's number as Aggie wails beside me, praying he doesn't see my name on the caller ID and ignore the call.

On the final ring, it connects.

'I'm stuck in the Co-op because of you,' Kieran barks in my ear. 'Do you even know how to shop?'

'Aggie's in labour,' I rush. 'You need to get back here and get her to hospital.'

'Stay with her!' he yells, and I hear him running before the line goes dead.

'What did he say?'

'He's on his way.'

'Well, he better bleddy *leg it*.'

I risk a smile, despite my aching face and rising panic. A hundred potential catastrophes race through my mind, none of them anything I feel confident to deal with. Should we call an ambulance? Where is the nearest hospital? Is there time to get Aggie to it? How quickly are twins born? What happens if the babies arrive before Kieran gets here?

Completely out of my depth, I sit beside Aggie, rubbing her back because it seems like a good thing to do.

'Just breathe. That's right. Good. Breathe.'

'Are you tellin' me or yourself?'

'Ag, you're in labour. It's kind of a big deal.'

'Like your face.'

'Don't worry about me. Just try to relax.'

'Okay, I get it. None of my business.'

'Thank you.'

Where the hell is Kieran? I'm trying to stay in control, but my heart is crashing in my chest.

'I just wouldn't like to see the state of the other bloke.'

I groan. '*Ag*.'

'Humour me, yeah? I'm a ratty pregnant woman in severe pain. Now is not the time for me to hear a *no*.'

When she puts it like that, how can I refuse? 'What do you want to know?'

'Which bastard tried to punch your eyeball out of the other side of your head?'

'You don't know him.'

'Does it matter? Name and shame, Zachy-Boy. I need the distraction.'

'Merryn's friend, Seth. He owns the surf shop next door to her café and he's *everywhere . . .*'

'In love with her, eh?'

'Not in love. Thinks he has a God-given right to protect her, though. Like a stupid overprotective brother. And I got in the way.' My eye throbs as a reminder of just how much in the way I was. 'He came in while we were together, shouting the odds. Accusing me of exploiting the search to get close to Merryn. Of lying to her.'

'And then he hit you?'

'No. He just kept on and on, not letting up. In the end I just went for him.' I pat the edge of my eye. 'This is what I got for it.'

She groans again, and I grab my phone.

'I'm calling an ambulance.'

As I stand, the door to the studio bursts open, Kieran skidding across the floor to kneel by his partner's side.

'How are you? Have your waters broken? How far apart are the contractions? Are you doing your breathing?'

'I'm in labour and it bleddy hurts! Now stop yellin' at me, unless you want an eye that looks like his.' She jabs an angry thumb towards me.

Kieran looks up. 'What happened?'

'We need to get her to hospital,' I urge.

'But we don't have the bag. Or the birth plan. Or the mood music she wanted.'

'Do you have your car keys?'

'Should the babies be coming now? I thought we had three more weeks.'

He's not even listening. And judging by his jabbering, he's in no state to drive.

'Give me your keys,' I demand.

'What?'

'The keys, Kieran! I'll drive. You get in the back with Aggie and look after her.'

'You can't drive my car!'

There's a loud cry from Aggie that silences us. 'Argh! Would you just give him the bleddy keys!'

By some minor miracle, I manage to shepherd them both out of the studio, take Kieran's keys and get all of us into the car. I'm too buzzed with adrenaline to think about anything except this journey. It's forty minutes away – one of the things people don't always consider when dreaming of living in Cornwall. At this late hour the roads should be clear, but I don't dare trust that. I won't be complacent, or allow any thoughts of what happened earlier to intrude on the journey. Aggie and her babies just need me to drive.

It's a white-knuckle journey from St Ives to Truro, but we make it, Kieran rushing Aggie into the Royal Cornwall Hospital while I park. In the race to get here, we didn't discuss what I'd do once they were in the hospital, so I wait in the car, trying to get as comfortable as I can. Until I hear from Kieran, I'm stuck.

What if I'm here all night? I didn't stop to consider the possibilities before. I have a five-thirty start at Downalong Bakery and the small issue of a huge black eye to explain. I can't go running into the hospital asking for Kieran because he's more than a little busy right now.

To cover my bases, I send Matt a text, explaining where I am and what's happening. If the worst happens and I'm here until morning, at least he'll know and I'll still have a job to return to.

I'm wrung out, my body is protesting and, nice though Kieran's car is, I'm not relishing spending hours waiting in it.

And then, there's Merryn.

The fight in Sweet Reverie seems an age ago now, only my bruises reminding me of how recent it was. I want to call her, but what would I say? I lashed out at Seth when I should have held my tongue. That he engineered the whole thing to get me to attack him is immaterial. I should have had more control – and I should have put Merryn first.

Now he's got the upper hand and I'm out in the cold.

Unless I . . .

The bright, blue-white glow of my phone interrupts my thoughts, a message from Matt displayed on the cracked screen.

You hero!
Just spoke to Kieran.
You can drop his car keys off at the hospital's main desk. I'm on my way to pick you up.
Hang tight!

Two hours later, I'm back at the studio, finally in my own bed. Thoughts of Merryn won't leave me alone, but I need sleep. Matt was great about driving me back to St Ives, but I still need to make sure I'm ready for work in the morning.

I can't think about it all now.

Exhausted, hurting and emptied out of emotion, I close my eyes.

Forty-One

MERRYN

We have a writers' group in the courtyard today. They've been writing there all morning, while Ruthie and I keep them supplied with tea, coffee and cakes.

We've shut the door between them and the rest of the café, creating a cool little sanctuary for them to write in. It's surprisingly calming to watch them at work.

'Any chance there's more of your empire oceans?' asks Polly Kim, a local author and one of our regulars. 'The last lot disappeared in seconds.'

'Good job I made a second batch this morning.' I smile. 'I'll bring them to you.'

'Lifesaver! I think they may become the secret weapon for every retreat party I bring here.'

The group today are guests on Polly's latest venture: four- and five-day writing retreats in the B&B she runs up in Towednack, a village in the beautiful hills above St Ives. One of the activities is a morning of writing in St Ives, followed by an afternoon exploring the town. I was only too happy to welcome her guests here. It's a positive after so much drama, reminding me again of how special Sweet Reverie is.

I wonder what stories will be dreamed up in our lovely courtyard, and whether Merlin might feature in some of them. He's more than worthy of starring in his own story, even in his current sorry state.

As I start to load a plate with empire ocean biscuits, a sudden memory returns of Zach's wave tattoo, with its two tiny stars. Annoyed, I push it aside. I don't need to think of him today, or why he hasn't made any attempt to apologise or return. Three days have passed since I threw him and Seth out. It's too long to mean nothing.

'They're like gannets!' Ruthie puffs, handing me an empty platter that, until thirty seconds ago, was stacked with slices of cake. 'Is Penny starvin' them up at her place?'

'Food helps concentration, apparently.'

'It helps our profits.' Ruthie chuckles. 'So who are we to judge?'

'I'll get these to the poor hungry loves,' I say, enjoying the joke, as the bell above the café door heralds the arrival of more customers.

But my assistant's smile has vanished. 'You have *got* to be kiddin'.'

I follow the frown her direction is aimed in, over to the front door. Seth is standing there, half over the threshold, as if he might vaporise to dust should he fully enter. I'm not altogether sure that would be a bad thing.

'Can we talk?' he asks, glancing nervously into the café.

'We're busy.'

'Merryn, please.'

'Go if you need to,' Ruthie offers, through gritted teeth, taking the plate of empire oceans from me. 'But don't you give that bastard an inch.'

The customers nearest the door are watching now. I won't have Seth disrupting the relaxed café atmosphere I've worked so hard to establish.

'I won't be long,' I say, resting my hand on Ruthie's shoulder as I pass.

'Take all the time you need, Mer. Give him hell.'

I walk outside, Seth following a few steps behind. Star Court is busy as it has been all week, a crush of bodies, boards and dogs as people try their best to navigate a path around each other. I walk away from the café and the surf shop, not wishing to have a scene in front of either business. Whatever else may have happened, we don't need disruptions that could deter trade.

I walk through the narrow passageway that connects Star Court with the streets beyond, turning down a side road to a small patch of brambles and grass beside a run of garages. If we're going to have a shouting match, there'll be no audience for it here.

He's pale when I face him, dark smudges of shadow below his eyes. I've seen that look before, the little-boy-lost expression he thinks wins arguments.

Not this one.

'Well?' I ask, my arms crossing as a shield.

'Can we stop fightin'? I've been doing my nut over what happened. I haven't slept. I can't have you thinkin' bad of me, Mer. I just couldn't let that man take advantage of you anymore.'

Of course this was never going to be a straightforward

apology. Seth rarely admits he's wrong, even when the evidence to the contrary is overwhelming.

'Really? You're starting with that?'

'I was tryin' to protect you.'

'By beating him up?'

A direct hit. I stand my ground. There is no way I am backing down just to protect his precious ego.

'He pushed my buttons. You saw it!'

'What I saw was you accusing him of all kinds of rubbish and then throwing punches when he didn't like it.'

'He threw them too,' he whines. The worst possible reply, because it puts flame to a touchpaper, reigniting the anger I've tried so hard to push away.

'If you just want to repeat this rubbish, I'm going.'

'No, Mer – *wait*.' He drops his head. 'I shouldn't have punched the bloke. And it shouldn't have happened at your place.'

'It shouldn't have happened at all. Zach was helping me, Seth, not leading me on. And yes, the search has become more public than I expected, but if it means we find Grant, what the hell does it matter?'

'I just don't think you should get your hopes up. This guy was in your life for two years. I know you had it tough with your mum, but pinnin' all your hopes on some random dude she dated is only ever going to lead to disappointment.'

I've heard enough. 'I didn't expect you to understand.'

I start to leave, but Seth steps into my path. 'You're right: I don't. I didn't have a childhood like yours, so I don't know what you went through. But if everyone is out there lookin' for this guy and he still hasn't come forward, doesn't that tell you somethin'?'

'There have been sightings.'

'Or cranks contacting the newspaper, looking for their thirty seconds of fame.'

'His piano is here. *He* was here.'

'And he left it behind. Maybe he doesn't want to be found, like he didn't want that piano. Someone has to say this, Mer. Zach has you chasin' a dream. That journalist, too. But both of them have a vested interest in draggin' you along for the ride.'

'They want to help me. Which is more than you do.'

'They don't care about you.'

'And neither do you.'

'You know that's not true.'

'You attacked someone I care about. And between you, you broke the piano that means the world to me.'

'I know. I'm sorry.'

'*His* piano. The one that connects me to the single happy season of my childhood. This is what you don't understand, Seth: Grant may have only been in my life for a short time, but he brought hope back, where there was none. He made me believe in better things. And that was what got me away from Mum in the end. It made it possible for me to leave. And the piano was a symbol of that. It was proof that I was loved. That I would be thought about, long after Mum dispensed with Grant.'

'I – I had no idea.'

'And you destroyed the only tangible link I have to the first person who believed in me. It came back into my life like a gift, and you smashed it to pieces.'

'I want to repair the piano.'

'You've done enough.'

'No, please, Mer. Let me put this right.'

'And Zach?'

He raises his eyes to the blue sky above. 'I can't do anythin' about him. But if he comes back – if he apologises to you, too – I won't stand in your way.'

If he comes back. I bite back my tears. Because he hasn't come back, has he? It's been three days and he hasn't even tried to contact me. And I won't beg.

Seth sees my struggle, hurrying back to me. 'Let me make this right? You're my best mate, Mer. I can't stand not havin' you in my life. I'm sorry.'

It doesn't undo the damage. But I've missed Seth, despite what he did. So I nod and let him hug me, tired now of the drama I never invited into my life.

'Thank you,' he breathes into my hair. 'You won't regret this.'

I hope I don't.

Forty-Two

ZACH

My eye is healing, the bruising changing colour as the days pass. But every time I look in the mirror, I'm reminded of what I've lost.

Shifts at Downalong Bakery merge into evenings at Pengelly's. I wake up to go to one and crash back to bed when the other ends. The summer is nearly over and soon I'll have to consider what I want to do when work is not so forthcoming. Or if I even stay here.

Being so close to Merryn yet so far from her is killing me. I don't know how long I can withstand it.

A mate over in Wales got in touch last week after someone sent him a link to Zanna's article about me and Pengelly's. He's crowdfunding a surf centre in a former slate quarry somewhere in the North Wales mountains and is looking for instructors. I could move there, find accommodation cheaper than anything on offer in Cornwall, and be teaching when it opens in the spring.

Maybe a new start is what I need.

One light in all of it is a certain pair of tiny twins – Freddie and Iris Macklin. After a long labour and a few worrying weeks in and out of hospital, they're home with Aggie and Kieran. I was cautious about going over, not wanting to get in the way of the new family, but the babies' mother's summons, delivered in classic Aggie Keats style, put paid to my plan to keep a respectful distance.

'Everybody's beggared off and bleddy left me. I don't need space, I need sanity. Get your 'ansum butt over here. And bring cake.'

I arrive at their apartment with two large Downalong Bakery paper carrier bags, stuffed with as many baked treats as Matt could squeeze in. I have flowers from the tiny florist in St Andrew's Steet, a tub of Aggie's beloved Shipwreck honeycomb swirled ice cream from Moomaid of Zennor and two super-soft teddies from Laff Kids on Fore Street.

Aggie greets me at the door, a twin cradled in each arm. 'Bleddy hell, Zachy, and there was me thinkin' *I* was weighed down!'

She ushers me in, expertly navigating a gauntlet of new-born-related obstacles: two baby carriers, a folded double pram frame and a washing basket beneath a clothes airer filled with row upon row of tiny babygrows. I just about manage to follow without trashing the lot. It's a relief to make the safety of a sofa, its back draped in a rainbow of freshly washed muslins. It's chaotic but strangely ordered – and suits Aggie down to the ground.

'How are you?' I ask, as she settles into a wide love seat without waking the twins.

'Buzzin'. Knackered. Bored out of my skull.' She gives a weary grin. 'But I love 'em to death. Can't really think how life was before. That might be the lack of sleep, mind.'

'I brought half of Downalong Bakery from Matt and a tub of Shipwreck, so the sugar alone should help.'

'Let's hope. Do you want one?'

'A pastry?'

'A baby.'

I'm thrown. 'I – er – not right now. I mean, one day, maybe. I wouldn't rule it out.'

Aggie snorts with laughter, the twin in her left arm stirring. 'I meant one of *these*, you daft-head!' She adopts a super-posh accent to mock my mistake further. 'Would you care to hold one of these two most excellent infants, Mr Trevelyan?'

I can't remember the last time I held a baby. There seem to be so many components to the act, any one of which might end in disaster. But Aggie asked, which means she trusts me. I can't say no to her.

'I'd love to,' I reply.

'Right. Budge up, buttercup.'

She joins me on the sofa, gently handing me Iris – who I am only able to confidently identify thanks to the *MAID* printed on her babygrow, where Freddie, still with his mum, sports one that reads *MAW*, the Cornish word for boy.

The tiny girl settles into the crook of my arm, Aggie adjusting the position of her daughter's head so it's properly supported. Iris is soft and warm, her body curled up as she sleeps, the strange sensation of the weight of her body setting my mind on high alert.

I'm speechless, hardly daring to breathe.

Such a precious bundle of life containing a whole world of potential, entrusted to my care. If I'm aware of the enormous responsibility of protecting her, how on earth is it for her parents?

I'm surprised when tears prickle the corners of my eyes.

'Oh, Zachy! It's okay.'

'I'm fine.' I sniff, laughing at my own soppiness.

'Pretty major, huh?' She observes me like a proud big sister. 'Iris is the feisty one. Not that you'd know it now. Lungs so strong they can hear her at Land's End when she wails. Freddie is like his dad, so laid-back he's in the middle of last week.'

'You can tell that much about them already?'

'Oh yeah. But then I've always been a bona fide *sensei* when it comes to sussin' people out. Talkin' of which, tell me what's happenin' with Merryn.'

The whip-fast subject change floors me, stealing my breath and any clever words I might try to hide behind. 'Nothing,' I manage. 'She doesn't want to see me.'

'Says who?'

'Says the woman who threw me out of her café, weeks ago.'

'Pfft, *details*. She was protectin' her business and her heart while you and that surf berk were busy trashin' them. Did you go back and apologise? I'm guessin' not.'

'I didn't want to cause her pain.'

'Oh, for heaven's sake, what kind of lame excuse is that?'

Iris stretches out a sleepy leg, then folds it back in. Not wanting to wake her, I drop my voice to a whisper. 'What else do you want me to do?'

'Grow a bleddy pair of balls and own it,' she snaps. 'What's she goin' to think if you slink off like a loser at the first sign of trouble? You can't claim to love the bird if you aren't ready to fight for her.'

'I never claimed to love her . . .' I begin, but Aggie Keats fixes me with a stare that could freeze the sun.

'You are holdin' my precious girl, half of my whole world. Don't you dare utter lies while she's in your arms. You love Merryn, Zachy. Admit it. And not bein' with her is crushin' you alive.'

Being a sleep-deprived new mum has only sharpened Aggie's powers, it seems.

'How do I get her to listen to me?'

'You do somethin' about it, instead of wallowin' like a sad hippo.'

Held safe in the crook of her arm, Freddie opens his eyes, grizzling a little.

'Wasson, 'ansum? Your Uncle Zachy's being a *sad* old *hippo* again, in't he? Yes he is. A proper stubborn sad old hippo.'

'Don't tell him that!'

'My Freddie knows I speak the truth. My Iris, too. No messin' with my kids, thank you very much.'

If they're anything like their brilliant mother, they'll be terrifying. 'Sorry.'

She relents, with a long sigh. 'Don't give in so easy, lover. Fight for her. Show her you're not givin' up. And do it soon. Because if you don't, you'll lose her forever.'

Forty-Three

MERRYN

There's still no news. Nothing concrete, anyway.

Fifteen recorded sightings in the Penwith area, every one of them drawing a blank. Zanna calls me daily now, updating me on what she's found. Her editor is loving the interest in the story, so he's given her permission to pursue it as a special assignment.

But still, we're no closer to finding Grant.

I don't know what's worse: knowing he's been seen close to St Ives or realising that, even with the story becoming so well known, he hasn't come forward. What if he doesn't want to be found? What if his reasons for abandoning the piano are the same reasons he doesn't want to find me? What if he's breaking free from the past, of which I'm only a tiny part?

To a kid, two years feels like a lifetime. To Grant, it was a short episode in a life that otherwise didn't include me. He and Mum were never going to work: he wanted peace and security, while Mum wanted to rail at the world. He couldn't have taken the brunt of her pain and anger indefinitely. She was always going to push him away, the fate of every relationship she ever encountered.

What if being reunited with me would mean dragging all that baggage back for him?

At least I have the busiest weeks of the summer to distract me. We're into August now, always the most intense part of the summer holidays, and St Ives is heaving. Long queues form every day while people wait for tables, the takeaway line snakes out into Star Court, and Ruthie and I barely have time to exchange two words as we race to fulfil orders. I've roped Murph and Jenna in, too. They're alternating shifts through the week to give us extra help.

With the frantically busy days and three evenings, I hardly have time to think.

But I miss Zach.

At night, after closing, the piano sits alone in the courtyard, silent and still. Since the repairs were completed, customers have resumed playing Merlin during the evening openings – we're getting quite the roster of regular players who bring their own flavours of music to the courtyard. I've even persuaded Murph to do a few tunes when service isn't so busy. He's developing an impressive repertoire of music. It's lovely to see.

But it isn't the music Zach played. The way his character spoke through every note, the deeper meaning I sensed behind each song he selected. It isn't being played just for me. It's only now I don't have it that I realise why Zach's playing meant so much: it was only ever meant for me. Even if there was a room full of customers. He was expressing his love for me through every song, a secret language just meant for us.

I fell in love with the man I discovered through his music.

And now it hurts to hear anyone else play.

At least there's a truce of sorts with Seth. After his apology and the repair he arranged for Merlin, the ground between us has become a little less rocky. I'm not sure I've forgiven him for the fight yet. But he's still here, where Zach isn't. Is that what matters, in the end? Who leaves and who remains?

With no evening opening tonight, I decide to take a walk. I've been hiding within the café walls since the fight, I realise now, when I've no need to. St Ives is my town, the place I love the most. It's time I got out to enjoy it.

It's a glorious evening, the kind St Ives is famous for but so many of us working over the summer don't get to see. I revel in it as I leave Star Court, enjoying the buzz of Fore Street with its lights and life and colour as I wander along it. I buy chips from The Balancing Eel takeaway, then walk up through the streets of Downalong, heading for Porthmeor Beach.

The sea greets me the moment I reach the sand, a sea-salt blast of air and sound. The tide is quite a way out, beginning its slow progression back up the beach, the waves beyond crested white. Over by the rocks on the Island side, several groups have gathered to drink and see the sunset. I pass the pockets of friends, moving down the beach to find a spot where I can watch the tide come in without being overlooked.

I wonder how many starry-eyed visitors to St Ives believe that if they lived here they'd spend all their days on the town's beaches. I used to dream of that, too, when I was living in Penzance. If I could afford to live and run a business in St Ives, I thought, it would be like the kind of perfect existence you see in lifestyle magazines. It *is* wonderful here, but it's surprising how often you can take for granted what's right outside your door. Life doesn't stop because you're lucky enough to live somewhere beautiful.

I eat and enjoy the view as the sea makes its lazy way up the beach. The sun sets, replaced by a clear night-blue sky that glows above ink-dark waves. Stars appear and the breeze becomes cooler. I needed this – to be somewhere other than Sweet Reverie, where too many concerns await me at every turn.

For a moment, I wish Zach was here. I see the ghosts of us out in the sea, the memory of our surf lesson that meant so much to both of us. I wish I could return to how we were then. But he stayed away after the fight and that speaks volumes. Could we have been happy together? I'll never know.

When the last of the light has gone, I leave Porthmeor and head home. The stillness of the café welcomes me, the buzz from the fridge a familiar sound as I round the tables to reach the stairs to my flat.

I make myself a mug of spiced apple tea and settle on the sofa upstairs, knowing full well I'm likely to fall asleep there. It's only when I'm curled up in the cushions, drink in hand, that I notice a message on the screen of my phone.

Sorry for the late message. I have news.
Call me when you get this.
Zan x

Shaking, I call her.

'Merryn hi! I'm so glad you got my message.'

'What's happened?'

'Okay, are you sitting down?'

My nerves twist, my pulse kicking into gear. 'Yes.'

'We've found him.'

I can hardly breathe. 'He's come forward?'

'No. But I know where he's working. It's a confirmed lead.'

'Where?'

'A bar. In Carbis Bay.'

My brain is racing now, processing the news. Carbis Bay is the next village around the bay from St Ives, ten minutes' drive at best, or one stop on the coastal rail line. And there are fewer bars there than in St Ives.

'Which bar?'

'Mariner's.'

The name hits me like a speeding train.

Not just any bar in Carbis Bay. *Mariner's* – the bar owned by Graham Jacobs, who I've known for years.

Luke's uncle.

Grant Henderson is working at Luke's uncle's bar, just two miles away from where we found his piano. There's no way Luke wouldn't have known about it. And all the time Luke told me not to search for Grant, he knew exactly where he was.

Forty-Four

ZACH

Without Merryn, my days morph into one another, time passing like sand through my fingers. I do my Downalong Bakery rounds in the morning, then head to Pengelly's. My shifts cover most days now, extra hours to meet the high season demand. Keeping busy is what motivates me, I tell myself, but I know that's a smokescreen. I'm avoiding thoughts of Merryn by throwing myself into work. Just like I threw myself into competitions when I lost Mum.

My life might have changed, but my default coping mechanisms haven't.

Fight for her . . . And do it soon . . .

Aggie's advice has buzzed around my head like a summer wasp since I went to see her. I want to fight for Merryn. I want her to know I love her. But have I left it too long to return?

'Zach.'

Hen is staring at me when I bump back from my thoughts. We're unloading newly washed glasses from the dishwasher, stowing them on the shelves beneath the bar. I realise I've had a pint glass in my hand for a while, drips of warm water running down my arm.

'Sorry,' I rush, quickly shelving the glass.

'Don't sweat it,' she returns, nudging my arm. 'But next time I want help emptying the dishwasher I'll avoid asking you, okay?'

'Might be wise.'

She glances over her shoulder. 'Luke's off out in a sec. Can we chat when he goes?'

'Yeah, sure.' There's something about my work colleague's tone that sounds off. Of all the Pengelly's team, Hen is the one I joke around with the most. She's ace, a fine art student on her summer break from Plymouth Uni. Her humour is something I rely on to keep us going through the busy shifts, but her usual smile is starkly absent now.

Half an hour later, Luke leaves. He's been bullish all afternoon and it's a relief to be away from it, if only for a while. I seek out Hen, who has been unpacking crates of mixers in the stockroom out back.

'What's going on?' I ask.

She folds her arms across her apron as if a chill has entered the space. 'I think we have a problem. With Luke.'

'Clichés getting too much again?' I joke.

She doesn't smile. 'I think he's doing something dodgy.'

'How do you mean?'

'Have you noticed he always replaces bottles on the optics?'

I can't say I have. But then shifts at Pengelly's have been so full-on recently I've barely been able to think, let alone notice anyone else.

'Well, he does,' Hen continues, not waiting for my reply. 'And the thing is, I'm not convinced he's changing them.'

'But I've seen the spirits running out,' I counter. 'The Glenfiddich twelve-year-old emptied in less than a week.'

'The contents emptied.' I can't work out her tone, or what she's trying to say.

'And the bottle.'

'*Not* the bottle,' she corrects. 'I noticed the label had a scratch across the bottom before and after Luke changed it. If it was a new one, why would it be in exactly the same place?'

'Hen, you're not making any sense.'

'Okay, look.' Exasperated, she grabs my sleeve, dragging me through to the restaurant and behind the bar. She jabs a sunset-yellow-painted fingernail at the bottle in question. Sure enough, there's a deep, horizontal scratch across the bottom third of the label.

'Are you sure it was there before?'

'Positive. It's the kind of random thing I notice. Anyway, I did an experiment. The vodka was almost finished, so I put a tiny dot of nail varnish on the back of it. Luke changed it this morning – and look.'

We move along to the Smirnoff optic and Hen twists the bottle. Sure enough, a small dot of yellow varnish is on the side.

'So he's refilling the optic bottles?'

'Exactly. And get this: there's a red van that visits once a week. Luke always goes to collect the order. Like, he's really protective over it.'

'Our regular supplier's vans are blue,' I say, the conundrum becoming clear. 'You think he's bringing in dodgy spirits?'

Hen nods. 'Put it like this: he doesn't want anyone else handling the bottles or the red van deliveries, but he's happy to let us do everything else. Doesn't that strike you as odd?'

'Have any customers questioned the taste of their drinks?'

'Most of them are three sheets to the wind by the time their food arrives,' Hen replies. 'But one bloke last week sent his single malt back. He said the water we put in it was off, but what if it was the whisky?'

The question becomes an itch for the rest of my shift. Luke returns and I watch him, striding around the restaurant as the perfect host, all warm compliments and loud welcomes. A few times he gravitates towards the bar, and I see him squinting at the line of optics. But that could mean anything.

All the same, the idea that he might not be what I thought refuses to leave me. I've had a sense of it before, in his over-blown confidence and attitude towards some of the team, but this seems to confirm it.

I get home just after midnight, the evening shift extended to accommodate a large party of late diners. I'm exhausted, which suits me fine. Collapsing in my bed, I have no time or energy to think of Merryn before I succumb to deep, dreamless sleep.

*

When I wake next morning, I discover I've missed a text. After an extended shift at Downalong Bakery followed by an early evening shift at Pengelly's, I was barely able to get back to the studio and eat something before I crashed out. I'd just wanted to keep busy, to have a hope of escaping the endless cycle of thoughts about Merryn and what might have been.

But the text has dragged me right back to it.

Hi Zach, I have news.
Call me as soon as you get this.
Zan x

My first two attempts to call Zanna go straight to voicemail. The third informs me the user is busy. I pace the studio, thankful at least that I don't have work today. What does 'news' mean? Has Zanna found him? Or has she discovered something Merryn won't want to know?

Finally, just after nine a.m., my call connects.

'Hi, Zach, sorry, it's been manic here since seven.'

'What's the news?'

I will the best news to answer my question – that he's been found alive and well, that he wants to see Merryn. I can't be with her as I long to be, but I still hope for the best. She's spent most of her life without the one person she wanted to be part of it. That should be rectified. How that relates to me is irrelevant.

'I've found Grant Henderson.'

I punch the air, checking myself when I realise what I've done. At least I'm alone in the studio this morning and won't have to explain my reaction to anyone else.

'Awesome! Where?'

'In Carbis Bay.'

'Wow, that's . . . close.'

'I know. And to think he's been at a bar there all this time we've been searching. It's pretty amazing.'

'Which bar in Carbis?'

'Mariner's. Do you know it?'

I smile against my phone. Do I know Mariner's? It was only my illegal drinking venue of choice with the surf crowd when I was sixteen. I officially had three eighteenth birthday parties in the beachfront establishment, with only the last one being genuine. How the landlord never worked it out is a mystery.

Was Grant Henderson working there back then?

I dismiss the thought. Hardly anyone in the bars and pubs around here works in the same place for years. Bar staff are like the shifting sands on Porthmeor and Porthminster beaches: ever moving, never settling. I've done it myself over the years, the ease of finding bar jobs meaning I could pick up a bit of work anywhere we went.

'Does Merryn know?'

'I spoke to her last night. I'm heading over to pick her up now and we're going over to Mariner's. Do you want to come?'

My heart sinks like a stone. 'It's for Merryn to do, I think.'

'Yeah, but you made it happen, Zach.'

She doesn't know. About the fight, about Merryn asking me to leave. About how I've stayed away because I couldn't bear it if she threw me out again.

'All the same, this is Merryn's journey to complete.' Do I sound magnanimous? Or scared? 'But could you keep me posted?'

'Will do. This is a good thing, Zach. You started a beautiful thing for Merryn – and look what we've achieved!'

I don't feel I've achieved anything, other than causing pain to Merryn and damaging the piano that brought us together. I miss her, with every breath, with every day that goes by without me seeing her. But it's a necessary separation. I let my pride and competitiveness take over when Seth was throwing his weight around. I don't want to think about how quickly I lost sight of what mattered.

But she's found Grant now – or will do, when Zanna drives her over to the bar. That's one thing I can be proud of. What happens next for them is none of my business.

With nothing to distract me at home, I go out into St Ives.

Having two jobs is a blessing I won't take for granted, but it's a lot. I've begun to appreciate days off like today in a way I never did before. I'll grab some breakfast and then head out of town to join the cliff path. A walk will do me good, I think. Blow the conflicting thoughts from my head and put some distance between me and the town.

Merryn is getting what she most wanted. I have to be happy for her, even if I wish we were travelling to Carbis Bay together. Walking in the opposite direction is the safest thing for me to do.

Matt grins at me when we meet at the counter of Downalong Bakery.

'You do know it's your day off?'

'What can I say? I just can't keep away.'

He laughs. 'So, what'll it be?'

'A rosemary focaccia, one cronut and a bag of the shortbread stars, please.'

'Definitely day-off food,' Matt says, jotting down a list of the prices on a brown paper bag before going to fetch my order. When I hand over the money, he pauses before taking it, studying me in the unnervingly quiet way of his. 'You could always enjoy your breakfast with a coffee in the back, if you're up for it?'

It's an invitation I'm not expecting, and one I won't turn down.

He lifts the hatch in the counter and I follow him through, smiling at Lottie, one of the bakery shop team, as she moves to take Matt's place.

The kitchen bears the ghost-scents of Matt's early morning baking, an aroma that's now become familiar for me. Over in the corner, the coffee machine is already at work. We pull up a stool each at the stainless steel prep table and Matt fetches coffee, returning with two mugs and a bowl of buttery baked pastry scraps, the best perk of working for the bakery.

'Dig in,' he says, grabbing a handful for himself.

'Cheers.'

We eat and drink in companiable silence for a while, the calmness of the bakery kitchen working its magic on my thought-muddled head. Matt told me once that you should be able to tell a baker's kitchen by the character it has. It's certainly true for him, this kitchen infused with the character of its owner: steady, organised, a place of hard work tempered by the confidence and experience that makes it seem unhurried.

'So, what's on your mind?' he asks.

'Sorry?'

'You don't buy cronuts and shortbread stars unless you're trying to distract your head from something.'

'Are you psychoanalysing my bakery choices?' I laugh.

'Bakers are like bartenders, barbers and priests,' he replies, without a hint of sarcasm. 'We cater to people's innermost needs and facilitate honest conversations – like this one, for example.'

'I never had you down as a guru of baked goods.'

He smiles. 'Well, now you know. So, what's going on?'

I don't intend to tell him anything, but the coffee and still-warm pastry begin to work their magic. Little by little, it all comes out: Merryn, my late-night piano playing, our kisses, the fight and the news from Zanna this morning. Matt listens without comment, considering my flood of information over slow sips of coffee.

When I reach the end, I wait for his reply.

'Okay.'

'Okay? That's it?'

'Chill your beans, mate. First thing, I wouldn't have guessed you played the piano. Nice one. Always fancied having a go myself. Second, if you love Merryn so much, why haven't you gone back there?'

'She asked me to leave.'

'That night. Not forever. And maybe that's why you're struggling now.'

'I'm not struggling.'

'Yeah, you are. You just spilled your guts in my bakery. That doesn't happen unless you're battling it.'

'She's found Grant now, so she'll be fine.'

Matt raises a bushy eyebrow. 'Or *maybe* she'll need friends now more than ever to help her work through it all. Sounds like there's a lifetime of stuff centred around this guy. She won't discard it all just because she found him. And if you love her—'

'—I don't.'

'Yeah, you do.'

I stare at him as it sinks in.

I *love* her. Of course I do. It's why she's on my mind, all the time.

But what good does it do me? She threw me out. She's getting on with her life.

'If you love her, you'll be there for her. End of. *Bleddy* fight for the woman, Zach. Because if you don't you'll regret it, every day of your life.'

There's something about the way he says this, an uncharacteristic shadow of emotion behind his laid-back air.

'Sounds like you know what you're talking about,' I risk.

This is my boss, after all. I've told him more than I've ever told anybody I've worked for, but I don't want to overstep the mark.

'Yeah, well, life kicks you in the bum sometimes.'

He doesn't elaborate and I don't push him. It's enough to know he understands.

'Maybe I'll go to see her when she's met Grant,' I say, a thought spoken aloud more than a part of the conversation.

'You should,' Matt replies. 'Where did you say he'd been found?'

'Mariner's, in Carbis Bay?'

Matt chuckles. 'There's a blast from the past. Many nights of my misspent youth wasted there.'

'You and me both. Mostly underage.'

'Same. It's a wonder the owner didn't get done for it. I reckon half of his customers were under eighteen when I was going there.'

Surprised by our shared history, a thought occurs to me. 'Does the same bloke own it now?'

'Lefty Hughes? Nah, he went off years ago. He got done for running charity raffles and keeping the money for himself.'

'No way!'

'Yeah. It was all over the news down here. Massive scandal. I'm surprised you didn't see it.'

'I was competing then.' So much was missed during those years. I'm only beginning to realise that. 'So, who owns it now?'

'Graham – oh, what's his surname? I know him from the Chamber of Commerce stuff and he's involved in fundraising for the lifeboat, too. Graham . . . Graham . . . Jacobs! That's it. Cool dude, very involved with the community. And he doesn't nick charity money, so, you know, a bonus all round.'

The name is vaguely familiar, though I can't say why. 'I think I've heard of him.'

'You'll probably know his nephew better, seeing as you work for him.'

'You?'

'The *other* one? Total git who you seem to like.'

Realisation dawns. 'Graham is Luke's uncle?'

'Small world, huh? At least he's stuck around for years. Jury's still out on whether Lukey-boy is going to do the same this time.'

'I wonder if Luke knows Grant.' The thought rocks me: two pieces of my world colliding.

'Probably.' Matt sits back, a hand to his beard. 'Hang on, your girl, the one you've been hiding from . . .'

'I'm not hiding.'

'Yeah, you are. What's her surname?'

'Rowe.'

'Merryn Rowe . . .' He slaps a hand to his forehead. 'Oh my good Lord. *That's* why I didn't make the link.'

'What link?'

'I thought her name was familiar, but I couldn't work out why. I didn't know her as Rowe before.'

'Wait – you know Merryn?'

'Yeah. Crazy I didn't realise until now. I didn't know her as Merryn Rowe: I knew her as Merryn Pengelly.'

'She's related to Luke?'

Matt blesses me with a pitying look. 'Not related, mate. *Married*.'

'What?'

'Or was. Remember I told you about his other place? The missus he dumped and left to deal with it all?'

My heart is in my throat as everything falls into place.

No.

But she knew I was working for Luke. Why didn't she say?

It hits me like a speeding train: all the times I talked about Luke with Merryn, thinking his only flaw was cockiness and being a bit brash with his staff. Saying I found his confidence inspiring. Merryn heard all my chatter about the guy who trashed her heart and destroyed her life. How did she bear that in silence?

My rose-tinted view of Luke has already gone after what Hen told me about the dodgy refilled bottles in the optics. But this? This is horrific. If he knew Grant was working at his uncle's bar – and I can't imagine he didn't, knowing how everyone knows everyone else's business around here – why did he keep it from Merryn?

I remember during the interview with Zanna that Merryn was asked why she'd only started looking for Grant in the last three years. She'd said her former partner had dissuaded her, but then she'd asked Zanna not to include it. Her former partner being Luke.

'I've got to go,' I say, all thoughts of today's walk abandoned. 'Thanks for the coffee.'

Matt frowns as I stand. 'You're welcome. Are you okay?'

'I'm good. I'll see you tomorrow.'

I don't wait for his reply, snatching up the bakery bag and hurrying out.

I know Merryn won't be at Sweet Reverie. But another possibility presents itself as I dash through town.

Seth Hartley.

He was against Merryn searching for Grant, despite knowing

what it meant to her. Why? Could it be that he, like Luke, knew where her former stepfather was?

I thunder into Star Court, past Sweet Reverie and the blackboard sign, its surface achingly empty, and the side passage gate left open for the day's trade. I hope Merryn is being reunited with Grant right now, or that Luke's uncle tells them where they can find him.

But I'm not here to see her.

I head straight for Porthia Surf, the place I haven't revisited since my awkward flight from there at the start of summer. Before I knew about the piano, or Merryn, or the person she was searching for.

How much has changed in one summer.

This time, I don't hesitate, or try to figure out what to say. I just storm in, not caring what the startled customers who spring back from me think.

He's there, behind the counter, wide eyes quickly narrowing when he sees it's me.

'Get out.'

'I want a word with you.'

'You're disruptin' my customers. Turn around and go.'

'No chance.'

He gives a bitter laugh, squaring up to me as the new kid serving beside him shrinks back into a rack of T-shirts. 'You really don't know when to give up, do you? I'm not interested, boy. Now get the hell out of my shop.'

'Grant Henderson,' I growl. 'You know where he is.'

He blinks. 'Nobody knows where he is.'

'I think you lied to Merryn. For years, maybe.'

'I care about Merryn. I would never lie to her.'

'He's been found.' His shock registers immediately. Good. But I'm not finished. 'Zanna found him. She's taking Merryn over now. To Mariner's in Carbis Bay.'

'Mariner's?'

'Luke Pengelly's uncle's bar. That why you kept telling Merryn not to look for her stepdad, is it? Because you and Luke knew where he was?'

His expression grows thunderous. 'Outside.'

I fold my arms, the fight far from over. 'I'm not moving till I get answers.'

'I won't do it in here. I have customers,' he bites back, teeth gritted.

'Good. They should know what a lying bastard you are.'

'Right. Out the back.' He storms through an archway at the back of the shop and I follow, ready for whatever he swings at me. We arrive in a stock area and he turns in a corner filled with boxes. 'You have no right stormin' in here, shoutin' your mouth off in front of my customers.'

'And you have no right calling yourself Merryn's friend when you're lying to her.'

'I didn't know!'

'I don't believe you.'

'Believe what you want. How certain is Zanna that Grant's there?'

'She said he'd been found.'

He swears and looks up to the single lightbulb in the stockroom ceiling. 'I had no idea.'

I stare back, not knowing whether to trust him. 'Why tell her not to look for Grant, then, if you didn't know he was in Carbis?'

'Because she'd been hurt enough.' When he looks at me, the fight is gone. 'You don't know what she went through, when that bastard Pengelly left her. I put her back together. I got her thinkin' of the future again. The thought that anyone else could shatter her like Pengelly did was too much. I couldn't bear to let her go through that.'

It makes sense. I don't want it to, but it does.

'That wasn't your choice to make.'

'It wasn't yours, either. But you still pushed her into it.'

'It worked! The search was successful.'

'At what cost? What happens if she meets him and he doesn't remember, hm? Or if he doesn't want her in his life? Have you any idea what that would do to her?'

'I would be there for her. I would make things right . . .'

'So you say. How often have you been back since it all kicked off, eh? Oh, that's right, you haven't. Because, unlike me, you're a coward who's too shit-scared to apologise.'

He might as well have punched me. I slump against the wall. I haven't been there for her, have I? Before the search bore fruit, when she was alone and wondering if he would ever be found? Aggie was right: I should have fought for her. And if I go back now, will she think it's just because Grant has been found? To bask in the victory instead of standing beside her through the storm?

'Then you have to be there for her,' I reply. 'Because I don't want her to be alone.'

He observes me for the longest time. 'I will.'

I believe he will be. I walk back through the shop, past the nervous assistant and the goggling customers, out into Star Court.

I've left it too late to make things right with Merryn. I didn't fight for her when I should have. What she needs now is time to get to know Grant again, surrounded by her friends. And Seth, while an obnoxious idiot, is a good friend. She's obviously forgiven him. It's only me left out in the cold.

I glance at Sweet Reverie as I pass.

I can only wish her well. And hope that Grant Henderson – and Seth – prove worthy of the trust she's placed in them.

There's nothing for me here now. I won't visit Star Court again.

Forty-Five

MERRYN

I'm shaking.

As Zanna drives us out of St Ives, fear threatens to overwhelm me. I grip my hands together in my lap, willing them not to betray my nerves. I paced my flat for hours last night, trying in vain to reconcile the flailing threads of everything I've discovered.

Luke lied to me.

Grant has been just around the bay, all the time I was married and all the years I've searched for him since.

But if he's been so near for so long, why didn't he respond to the appeal that apparently half of Cornwall has seen? Is that my answer before we even get to Carbis Bay?

'How are you doing?' Zanna asks. It's meant to be a straightforward question, but I hear the tremor of nerves in her voice; see how tightly her hands grip the steering wheel.

'I'm terrified.'

'Me too,' she admits, in a rush of relieved air. 'But this is huge, Mer. You're going to see him. Today!'

I return her excited smile as best I can, feeling like a fraud.

This isn't how I imagined it would be.

I thought I'd be better prepared, that he would come forward and we would meet, with no questions surrounding how it happened. That I would enter our reunion well rested and excited for what lay ahead. That I'd be finally freed from the questions I've carried for decades of my life.

'I called Zach, by the way. He says he's crossing everything for us.'

I'd assumed she would tell him, but hearing her say it sends a fresh flood of sadness over me. We should be here together. Without Zach suggesting the search, this wouldn't be happening. He did that for me, not to score points or try to force his way into my life. He understood from that first night when I told him about Grant, and he didn't let go until he'd made a way forward for me to find him.

But he isn't here. He hasn't returned after the fight, not even to apologise for the damage done to Merlin.

That tells me everything I need to know.

And as for Luke, I had to stop myself from storming round to Pengelly's last night to tell him what I knew. But I'm so incandescently furious about his betrayal that I knew my anger would derail everything I want to say to him. It's there now, the moment I think of it, tempered only by my fear of the meeting Zanna and I are speeding towards.

I'll wait until this is over and my molten fury has set like cold, hard steel. Then I'll tell him exactly what I think of him.

Luke Pengelly isn't going to know what hit him.

My whirring thoughts cease the moment the sign for Carbis Bay comes into view, *PORTHREPTOR*, its Kernewek name, written in proud capitals beneath, as all village signs in this part of Cornwall have. I've seen it countless times, but today it feels providential.

'Nearly there,' Zanna says. 'It's going to be great.'

I hope she's right.

Mariner's bar is set down a steep hill, over the bridge the coastal train runs beneath and down to the picturesque bay with its golden sand and perfect curve of turquoise-edged sea. It's been there forever, as familiar a sight to generations of teenagers as the famous outline of St Ives harbour. It was the place passed in whispers between local kids, the ultimate goal to score a drink there a rite of passage famous even over in Penzance, where I spent my teenage years. A bus to Carbis Bay – or a train if you could afford it – followed by a night in the beachfront bar, rolling home in the early hours.

It's beautiful in the mid-morning sunshine, scatters of tiny white sparkles dancing across the gentle waves of the bay. The bar is open already, taking full advantage of the summer trade from the nearby hotel and self-catering apartments. Will Grant be working this morning?

'Did you call ahead?' I ask, as we park and leave the car.

'I thought it best not to,' Zanna replies. 'He may not even be working. But the owner will be.'

My heart sinks. Luke's uncle, someone I've always respected. Graham Jacobs knows everything that happens in Carbis Bay and St Ives, being on every business and community committee going. There's no way he wouldn't have seen the news reports. And he knows me well enough to have made the link.

Has he been complicit in hiding Grant, too?

We leave the sand-covered beach road and head onto the weathered boardwalk leading to Mariner's. Rope handrails loop between wooden struts either side of the walkway, salt-encrusted and swinging in the morning breeze. At night the uprights glow, the LED strips hidden in them a curving path of tiny lighthouses guiding drinkers to the delights of the bar.

We climb the steps leading to the main bar area, its open sides bedecked with maritime flags of all colours and shapes. Several of the high tables are occupied, holidaymakers making the most of the bottomless brunch menu. Chat and laughter mingle with the smooth jazz soundtrack from the speakers behind the bar and the constant call of seagulls spying targets for their next raid.

Behind the bar, a grey-haired man is serving cocktails, head bowed over the glass he's filling.

Is that him?

I will my racing heart to slow, forcing air into my lungs as I try to match the barman with the younger man I remember. I can't reconcile the two, but am I mistaken? As we reach the bar, he looks up – and my questions vanish. It isn't Grant.

He comes over to us, his too-bright smile and pronounced Eastern European accent final proof, if I needed it. But I'm scanning Mariner's and I already know Grant isn't here.

'Ladies, what can I get for you?'

'We're looking for someone who works here,' Zanna says.

I'm glad she's taken the lead.

The smile tightens. 'Oh?'

'Grant Henderson. Is he working today?'

'I . . . don't know this person.'

Zanna nods. 'Okay. I know he works here. He's not in any trouble. In fact, he's going to want to talk to us. It's good news?'

The barman has backed away a little, his hands held in surrender. 'All the same, I don't know him.'

'Problem, Dragan?'

An older man with an impressive sweep of pure white hair approaches from behind the faltering barman. I see him register me immediately, a broad smile appearing as quickly as he has.

'Merryn! What a delight!'

'They're looking for someone, boss.'

'That's okay,' Graham Jacobs smooths, clamping a hand on the barman's shoulder. 'I'll take it from here.'

He waits until Dragan scurries away before he turns back to us. 'I didn't expect to see you for bottomless brunch but please, you and your friend should enjoy it. On the house.' His wink at Zanna turns my stomach.

'We didn't come for that,' I say, not caring how dismissive it sounds.

'Hi,' Zanna says, thrusting her hand across the bar. 'Zanna Venn, *Cornwall Daily News*. We're looking for an employee of yours. Grant Henderson?'

Graham's smile never moves. 'You've been misinformed, I'm afraid.'

Zanna is undeterred. 'I have a trusted source who confirmed Grant works here.'

'Then they're mistaken.'

'It's for me,' I say, hoping that might tip the balance in our favour. 'I've been looking for him. He lived with my mum a long time ago. Was my stepdad for that time. I have the piano he used to own.'

'I've seen the reports.'

'Then why didn't you tell me? You know where I am.'

He exacts a sigh, leaning on the bar pulls as if he's about to divulge a valuable secret. 'Fact is, he doesn't go by that name anymore.'

I feel Zanna's eyes on me as I take this in. 'What name does he use?'

'Guy Henson. Something to do with when he worked as a musician. Had to change his name because there was already someone using his on the club circuit.'

'So you do know him.' Zanna eyeballs him. 'And you know Merryn. Why did you conceal the fact that he was employed here?'

'Because it's none of my business!' He glances at the nearest table of customers who have looked up from their bottomless cocktails, flashing a reassuring smile in their direction before turning back to us. 'Look, I don't want any trouble. Luke told me not to get involved.'

Another gut punch. What else has Luke done to scupper our search?

'I'm asking you – as a friend,' I say, fixing him with a stare he can't look away from. 'Does he work here?'

He flags a little. 'He did. Until yesterday.'

'What?'

'He handed in his notice. We'd not had the best of weeks and a stag party came in. They started a fight and I think it was too much for him. He said he wanted to leave and I gave him a week's wages to ease the transition. What else could I do? Someone like him, Merryn, he's never going to settle. Still chasing the music dream, only working in bars to pay his way.'

'Do you have an address for him?' Zanna asks.

'He was staying with friends in Carbis. But he's gone.'

'Give us their address, then.'

'I can't do that.'

'Why not?'

'Why should I?' He rounds on Zanna, anger flaring now. 'And what gives you the right to demand confidential employee information?'

'Because we've been searching for him, which you are apparently well aware of.' Her coolness is a study in control. 'And because it concerns someone you – and your nephew – know well. Don't be *that* person who stands in the way of a beautiful reunion at the eleventh hour, Mr Jacobs. Especially when you rely on the support of the *Cornwall Daily News* for the many, *many* community projects you're concerned with.'

'Is that a threat? Because I have your editor's number. And Mariner's spends a considerable sum advertising in your news rag. One call and you'll be out on your ear.'

We're losing him. No amount of righteous anger is going to stop Graham Jacobs walking away, taking whatever he really knows with him. I can't let that happen.

'I've always respected you,' I say, the effort to keep my tone light considerable. 'You were good to me when I was married to Luke. Grant – or Guy, if that's his name now – was the closest thing to a father I ever knew. When Seth and I found his piano, I knew it was a sign. I lost my mum years before she drank herself into a premature grave. I need to find Grant to tell him he changed my life. I don't want anything more than that.'

He doesn't reply, but I see his jaw working.

'We just need an address,' Zanna says, softer than her last volley. 'Even if he's no longer there.'

'He doesn't want to be found,' he says. 'You need to let this go.'

Stunned, I watch him walk away.

Beside me, Zanna swears.

The laughter and light-hearted conversation of Mariner's becomes a mocking, relentless backdrop to the dead end we've reached.

'Come on,' Zanna says, her arm clamping across my shoulders. 'Let's get you out of here.'

We don't talk on the slow drive back, our progress hampered by an open-topped double-decker bus that appears to be stopping at every bus stop on the road into St Ives. It's only when Zanna's ageing Fiesta has navigated the warren of narrow backstreets to reach the alley that leads to Star Court that she speaks.

'I'm so sorry, Merryn. I should have double-checked my source before dragging you over there.'

'You weren't to know.' I manage a brief smile. She's as gutted on my behalf as I feel. With so many people doing their utmost to obstruct my search, her allyship means the world. I won't have her feeling a failure because others have vested interests in keeping Grant and me apart. 'Thanks, Zan. For everything.'

'This isn't over,' she insists. 'Let me talk to my editor. There has to be something else we can do to find Grant. I'll call you as soon as I have more, okay?'

'Okay. Thank you.'

I leave the car and wave her off. My heart is shattered as I turn and walk down the alleyway to Star Court, my hope in tatters. I need to get back to Sweet Reverie. Ruthie and Murph have been holding the fort for me and they'll need a break. I need distraction, too, despite my body begging for rest.

Luke lied.

Graham too.

Grant – or Guy – doesn't want to be found.

Each one an insult, an emotional blow that stings as if it were physical.

And Zach? Will he care when Zanna tells him we hit another roadblock, as she's bound to do? Will it make him come back here?

Too many questions I can't answer. All I know is, he isn't here now.

I stare at the buildings in Star Court – Porthia Surf, Sweet Reverie and the Dydh Da deli, which is now advertising its grand opening in three weeks' time. This should be a happy place, the foundation of everything we've worked to build. For most of the summer, I've believed magic can happen here. The piano, the link to Grant, falling in love with Zach, believing that was enough. Now, I'm not sure of any of it.

A group of wetsuit-clad teens bursts out of Porthia Surf, catching my attention. Immediately, the anger I've pushed down all morning surges back, an unstoppable wave that engulfs me.

Seth caused the row that pushed Zach away.

Seth did his best to dissuade me from the search. Did he know where Grant was, like Luke did?

Hurt and fury, betrayal and loss power me straight into the shop.

I don't recognise the young assistant behind the counter, his wide-eyed horror evident as I approach.

'Seth's out the back,' he squeaks, as if he can tell by the way I've entered the shop that his boss is my chosen target.

'Thanks,' I bark as I aim for the stockroom.

Seth is hunched over an open box on the small folding table

where he packs online orders, cellophane-wrapped T-shirts in piles around him.

'Did you know?'

His head snaps upright. 'Hang on, Mer . . .'

'You said I shouldn't look for Grant. Did you know where he was?'

'No, bird, I swear.'

'Zanna took me to Mariner's. Grant was working there until yesterday. Luke knew. His uncle said Grant changed his name.'

'I didn't know. Did you find him?'

'Graham wouldn't tell us.' Emotion balls in my throat, tears threatening to fall.

'Maybe it's best to let it go.'

'How? How do I get past this?'

'I'll help you.' He holds his arms out to me but I refuse to yield.

'I don't want you to.'

He stares at me. 'Why?'

'Because you never wanted me to look for Grant.'

'I just didn't want you to get hurt.'

'But you knew what it meant to me. What I've been through. I never needed you to agree with me, Seth, just support me.'

'I'm here now,' he protests.

But I don't want to hear it. I'm hurt and angry and over-whelmed by everything. 'I need to be alone.'

'Mer . . .'

I don't wait for his reply.

I just walk out.

I'm done with everything. With Seth, with Zach, with Grant – or whatever he's calling himself now. It's time I put myself first.

In Star Court, I stop beside Sweet Reverie, the business I built from nothing, and love more than my heart can contain. This is what matters now. I have the piano, which returned to me, and is now mine. The carved heart beneath its cheek reminds me of who I was; its presence in the business I poured my heart into is proof of what's possible. That has to be my focus.

And nothing else.

Forty-Six

ZACH

Zanna called me this morning. None of what she told me was hopeful.

'We've hit a dead end,' she said, her usual upbeat chatter dulled and weary. 'My editor Frank is getting antsy about me spending so much time on the story.'

'Can you stall him? Find new ways of reporting the search?'

'I'd love to, but he's not budging. And I don't want to face facts, Zach, but it looks like Grant, or Guy as he's calling himself now, just doesn't want to be found. I'm not giving up, I promise. But I have to put this on the back burner for now or my job could be on the line.'

She's done so much for Merryn that I couldn't argue. 'It's okay, Zan, I know you've done everything you can.'

'I wish it was better news. Look after Merryn, yeah? She's had a kicking with all the crap about her ex.'

I said I would. She doesn't need to know I'm no longer in Merryn's life. Seth as good as said she'd forgiven him, and he said he'd look out for her. That's the best I can hope for.

All the same, I miss her. My stupid heart won't give up hope, even though the universe is yelling at it to quit.

I push it aside as I walk to Pengelly's. The one place in St Ives I don't want to be.

I don't want to work there, or be within ten feet of Luke.

But this late in the season, with my living situation still uncertain beyond the end of the summer, I can't just quit.

Besides, I want to push him a little. Find out what he really knows about Grant. It means pretending I like the guy and don't want to smash his fake-smiling, smug face into the nearest table. But if he lets slip something that could help Merryn, my act will be worth it.

Pengelly's is busy when I arrive, Zanna's piece about the restaurant in the *Cornwall Daily News* still bringing in customers. We have a handful of regulars already – who are good tippers at the bar, it transpires – and word seems to be spreading.

Luke is like a strutting cockerel, proudly parading around for all to see. Pretty quickly everybody on the team has adopted what we've dubbed *the Pengelly Eye-roll*, a shorthand to share whenever our employer is being a dick. It's been a kind of gentle mock before, but today it has a definite edge, for me and for Hen, who is still watching Luke like a hawk.

'Another bottle refilled,' she hisses as we pass one another with orders from the kitchen. 'Gin, this time.'

'Are you sure?'

'Positive. The marks are still on the bottle.'

I avoid chatter with Luke as much as possible, which is easier today with the crush of customers to serve. At one point, he takes a seat at the bar and opens a copy of the *Cornwall Daily News*. I can't tell whether it's the new edition or the original piece about Pengelly's as I hurry past.

He must know though. Zanna said Luke's uncle had threatened to pull advertising from the paper if they didn't leave. And it was his nephew's former wife asking: that would have been cause enough to make Graham tell Luke, wouldn't it?

There's a lull around four p.m., giving us a chance to breathe as we reset the restaurant for the early evening service. Luke's unbridled good mood is grating on me now, my last reserves of goodwill running on empty. Is he in such a good mood because he knows what happened at Mariner's?

After ten minutes of watching his entitled bravado, I need to get out of there. I gabble something about taking my break and head outside.

The harbour is packed as always but the later afternoon hour has brought a relaxed vibe to the groups on the benches and rows of deckchairs that line the harbour-side. The air is fresher here, the shade the surrounding buildings send across the cobbled street providing respite from the sun. I lean against the cool wall between Pengelly's and the gallery next door and wish myself anywhere but here.

I can't do it.

I thought I could push everything aside and just get on with the job. But who was I kidding? Luke Pengelly is a lying, entitled bastard, who thought so little of Merryn that he dumped her, left her with the wreck of his last business venture and trashed her heart. And, as if that weren't enough, he stood in the way of the most wonderful woman in the world finding her stepdad.

How the hell am I supposed to work with him now?

A rumble from my right summons my attention. A flash of red, pulling to a halt, displacing a group of tourists who were gathered there.

I watch the driver get out of the van and amble across to the ice-cream parlour he's parked beside. The moment he's out on the street, I recognise him: the other delivery guy who always asks for Luke.

Leaving my vantage spot, I follow him.

There's a queue inside the parlour, the generous air conditioning pacifying the waiting customers. As I join them, the delivery guy looks back. A flicker of recognition passes his features as he smiles.

'Wasson, mate?'

'All right. You?'

'Swelterin' in that tin can.'

'I can imagine. Ice cream's the best solution, right?'

'Always.' He moves to turn back towards the queue, but I push my advantage.

'Busy round?'

'Manic.' His eyes narrow and for a minute I think he's sussed me.

'I do early mornings,' I say, thanking my stars for the coincidence.

He raises an eyebrow. 'Oh?'

'For Downalong Bakery. Delivering bread and cakes.'

Now he's interested. 'You hit those roadworks on the Hayle bypass?'

'Total nightmare,' I sympathise, pushing my luck. 'And don't get me started on the four-way lights on the A3074.'

The road to Carbis Bay. A thought's occurred to me and I need to test it.

'Bleddy nightmare,' he agrees.

'So, where does your round take you?'

'All over, bro. Here, Hayle, Marazion, Newlyn. Carbis . . .'

My hunch proved, I mirror his eye-roll. 'The big hotel in the bay?'

'Nope. The bar near it? Mariner's?'

'Go there often?'

''Bout once a week.' The woman ahead of him passes with her ice cream, causing the delivery guy to turn back to the counter.

I slip back out onto the busy harbour, heart thudding hard.

If the red van delivers to Luke's uncle's bar as well as Pengelly's, chances are Graham Jacobs is accepting the same dodgy alcohol as his bastard of a nephew. Luke clearly doesn't care about Merryn, but he gives more than a damn for his precious new business.

I've got him.

But first, I need to find out what else he knows.

'Had a bit of sun, have you?' Luke jokes, his smile noticeably tight.

'Just needed ten minutes of fresh air,' I reply. 'It's refreshing out there.'

'I'll bet.' I notice the *Cornwall Daily News* folded beneath his arm. 'Can I have a word?'

'Of course.'

'Walk with me,' he says, clearly imagining himself as a character from *The West Wing*.

I follow him out to the stockroom, squashing my irritation down. I want to hear this. Hear his slimy attempt to lie.

'Problem, boss?' I ask. I can hear the sarcasm barely hidden beneath my question. Can he?

'The search, in the *Daily News*. Zanna Venn says it was your idea.'

'It was.'

'Can I ask why?'

'Someone I care about is looking for her stepdad. I knew Zanna could help.'

'You care about her?'

I fix my stare directly on him. 'Yes. Merryn is amazing. Merryn Rowe, from Sweet Reverie, over in Star Court?'

I catch his flinch the moment I say her name.

'Can't say I recognise it.'

Liar.

'Oh? I'm surprised. Everyone loves her in St Ives.'

'I doubt that. St Ives is bigger than you think.'

You are a bloody liar . . .

I want to launch myself at him, pummel him into the ground. But I hold my nerve. I want Luke Pengelly to dig his own trap.

'I hear they found him,' I say, scrutinising every move of his expression. 'Grant Henderson.'

Another flinch. He isn't smiling now, the bravado gone.

'Funny, it says in here they're scaling back the search.' He brandishes the paper like a weapon.

'Yeah, well, they say that to keep the story to themselves, don't they? Protect their big scoop for when the sweet reunion happens.'

'You should stay away from Merryn.'

It's not what I expect him to say and it takes me a moment to respond. 'I thought you said you didn't know her?'

'She's a mess. With a mess of a life. Truth is, she doesn't know what she wants. She won't listen to anyone speaking reason.'

'And you know this because . . . ?'

He inches closer, chest puffed out. 'I was married to her, mate.'

And there it is.

'Surprised she didn't mention me, considering how close

Zanna says you are,' he continues, thinking he's got one over on me, believing he's delivering a devastating blow.

'She mentioned a rat of an ex. She didn't bother giving him a name.'

'Watch what you're saying, Zach,' he warns. 'Remember who's paying your wages.'

Is that what he thinks will work? Threatening me? Does he believe I care so much for this job that I'd abandon Merryn to keep it?

My heart slams against my chest. I don't have Merryn, but Luke doesn't know that. I won't ever give her up, even if she never speaks to me again. I love her. She's changed my life, first with the piano she rescued, then the friendship she offered. She got me back in the sea. She made me believe life was good again, after months spent adrift, hardly knowing who I was.

I owe her everything. And I'm hers, no matter what.

Luke Pengelly isn't fit to even mention her name.

In that moment, my choice is clear.

I won't work for the man who caused Merryn so much pain and trouble. I care about her too much. So I square up to him, aware that my answer will throw all of the plans I'd made into question. 'You can shove your job, then.'

The Pengelly smile slips.

'You don't pay me enough to abandon Merryn.'

'Okay, what will it take? Twenty pounds an hour? Twenty-five?'

It's pathetic – and now I see him for who he really is. I can't believe it's taken this long.

'You can shove your money.'

He follows me out through the restaurant, stares from the few remaining diners following our course to the door.

'Don't think you can come back,' he hisses.

'Don't expect me to.'

Indignation carries me onto the road and powers me away from Pengelly's. It lasts until I'm halfway round the harbour.

Then the weight of what I've done lands fully on me.

I just quit the best-paid job I had. And we only have a few more weeks of the summer season. My chances of scoring another job are slim at best; of finding one that pays as well practically non-existent.

I flop on a bench and cover my eyes with my hands.

It's a disaster. But I did the right thing. Luke Pengelly can get in the sea.

Get in the sea . . .

A sudden memory returns of being in the waves off Porthmeor Beach, with Merryn laughing beside me. She did what I'd failed to do since my career ended: get me back out there. Without that act of love from her, I might never have dared to go out on my board again.

Get in the sea, Zach! Get in the sea!

Her and Jakey Lowen, dancing delighted circles around me in the sand, celebrating what we did . . .

I may have lost her, but she left me with a gift I haven't fully appreciated until now.

Finding Jakey's number in my phone, I make a call.

'Trev! 'Bout bleddy time you called me! Wasson, dude?'

I take a breath, imagine Merryn smiling beside me. 'That offer to do some stuff at the surf school – is it still on?'

His fulsome expletive makes me laugh. 'You serious?'

'As I'll ever be. I just quit Pengelly's, so I have a bit of time on my hands.'

'Hired, mate! Come over to mine and we'll thrash out the details. And bring beer. Time for a bleddy great celebration!'

On my way to his place, I take a detour. At the entrance to Star Court, I stop. I won't go in, but there's something I want to do.

I wonder what Merryn is doing now. I hope she's okay.

I wish I could sneak into the courtyard tonight, to play Merlin and be close to her.

Checking nobody else is within earshot, I do the next best thing. My inexplicable necessity.

'I love you,' I whisper to the wind, praying it skims the courtyard cobbles and carries my words through the open window of Sweet Reverie.

I love you, Merryn.

And I'm sorry.

Forty-Seven

MERRYN

This evening is quieter than our previous openings. Some empty tables remain between those occupied by our regular customers. It was always going to happen, the momentum of our first few weeks of the new hours impossible to maintain long term.

I'm not worried, even though Murph and Jenna keep shooting concerned glances in my direction as they serve food. Tonight, I'm glad of the calm. There's a soothing, laid-back atmosphere in the café and courtyard, helped by Thorsten, one of our newest customers, playing soothing classical pieces on Merlin. It feels like the first time I've been able to breathe during evening service since we began.

I haven't heard any more from Zanna since she called me to say the search was being moved down the list of *Cornwall Daily News* priorities. It was inevitable, given the dead end we'd found at Mariner's. I won't beg Luke to tell me where Grant is – that's if he even knows. So that's it. Nothing more I can do.

When the summer is over and the half-term weeks are done in October, I think I might go away for a few days, somewhere quieter, away from St Ives. I haven't taken a holiday for three years and it's time I changed that. I need space and time to process everything this summer has brought.

For now, I'll focus on the last of the summer trade and making the evening hours the best they can be. They'll stop at the end of September, so we should make the most of them.

'He's good,' Murph says, nodding at the piano player.

'He's *hot*,' Jenna says, bursting into giggles as soon as she's said it.

Murph nods. 'No denying that.'

'Maybe you should ask for his number, Jenna.'

She receives my suggestion with shock. 'No way! I wouldn't know what to say to him.'

'You say, "You're hot. Give us your number?"' Murph replies, as no-nonsense as ever.

'I can't do that!'

'Well, unless you're using telepathy, how else will he know?'

'I have an idea,' I say, going behind the counter and fetching two of our empire ocean biscuits. 'Take these to Thorsten, say they're on the house because you love his playing and see what happens.'

'I can do that!' she squeaks, hurrying out to the courtyard.

Murph and I watch as she reaches the piano, Thorsten smiling up at her as she delivers the biscuits.

'Ah, young love,' Murph observes.

'Or, the power of two free empire oceans.'

'That'd swing it for me.'

It's good to see more people finding – or contemplating – new happiness in Sweet Reverie. Even if my own chance was lost in the fight that damaged Merlin and the silence with Zach that followed.

I wonder what he's doing tonight. I hope he's finding something that brings him peace as much as playing the piano did.

We reach the end of the evening, the final stragglers lingering over the dregs of their drinks as we start the end-of-day tasks around them. I'm tired, looking forward to having the place to myself at last.

The bell above the door chimes, making me look over from the table I'm cleaning – and my heart sinks to the newly swept floor.

Luke offers an apologetic grin as he walks over to me.

'We're about to close,' I say, quietly. I could tear him to pieces for his betrayal over Grant, but I don't want any of our remaining customers to sense any kind of tension between us.

'I know. I thought we might chat?'

'I've got a ton of jobs to do.'

'Then I'll wait? Please, Merryn, I just want to talk.'

I catch Jenna and Murph watching us with interest, eyes like saucers. Of course they don't know. They just see a new, good-looking man talking to me, not my ex-husband who just betrayed me all over again with what I've discovered.

The final group of customers leave, Luke stepping back with that super-friendly smile of his as they walk out. He isn't going until we've talked, is he? Thinking on my feet, I call over to my assistants.

'You guys can head off, if you like.'

'Really, boss? We haven't done the bins or stacked the chairs.'

'It's fine, Murph. Go. Thanks for tonight.'

Neither Jenna or Murph need any more coaxing, both rushing to collect their things and hurrying out.

The door closes – and we're alone, the final rings of the bell echoing around the café.

'Turn the sign, please.'

He does as he's told. A ghost of a similar sign returns uninvited, stuck to a restaurant door in the heart of Fore Street, where he'd promised me the risk was worth taking. I'm still stunned by the speed with which he abandoned that business – and me. I don't wish him back, but I regret ever agreeing to that place. The memory of the fallout from his selfish decision still haunts me – facing angry staff, suppliers and landlords with no answers to give them. I'll never do that again.

Anger burns my stomach, but I won't give him the satisfaction of seeing it. Whatever he wants to say to me will be more lies piled on the rest. He'll dig a hole ten feet deep and never realise.

'You'll have to make this quick,' I tell him, busying myself with upending chairs onto the tables. 'I've got a lot to do.'

'Of course.' He picks a piece of pale green seaglass from the filled jar I keep on the counter, holding it up to the light. 'This is cool. You always loved this stuff.'

I stiffen, memories I don't want springing back. Our hands reaching for the same piece of smoothed beach treasure five years ago, then our eyes meeting . . . 'It's for the customers,' I rush, packing my response away. 'Visitors take a piece and regulars bring their finds from the beach to refill the jar.'

'Mermaid treasure.' His eyes meet mine, a world away from the first time. 'For luck.' He smiles, the piece of seaglass dancing between his fingers. I don't want to see it, but I do. 'I remember you loved the green pieces most. But the one that brought you to me was deep blue . . .'

I've heard that soft, suggestive tone of his voice too many times, burned by its lies too often to be fooled now. 'What do you want?'

'I just wanted to see how you were.'

'Why?'

'You know – after that piece in the *Cornwall Daily News*. Ending the search and all that.'

I would be completely naive if I thought Luke hadn't heard about that, however much I hoped the news might pass him by. 'I'm fine.'

'I'm just wondering why you decided to look for that guy now.'

Is he serious? The chair in my hands pauses, midway from the floor to the table. 'I've been looking for him for three years.'

'Well, I . . .' He falters, the veneer slipping. 'It just took me by surprise. I mean, we talked about it before and you didn't look for him then.'

You didn't talk to me about it, Luke. You lied through your white veneered teeth and kept on lying . . .

I say nothing, resuming my work.

He sits pointedly on the only chair at the table that I haven't stacked yet. 'Anyway, I read the news about the search being scaled back today and, I don't know, I thought you might need a friend.'

'I don't need you.'

He laughs. 'No, you probably don't. But I thought I'd offer.'

'What do you want, Luke?'

'Just to say that I'm sorry, for the record. Finding the piano, as you did, and it being the one you had as a kid – that's got to inspire a load of hope. To have it dashed . . .'

'It isn't dashed,' I retort.

'Actually, I got all the details from an employee of mine. Zach Trevelyan? I believe you know him?'

I breathe hard against the stab of pain. 'He's a good friend.'

'Sounded like more than that, the way he talked about you.'

What is that supposed to mean?

'He's been a great support,' I state, willing it to be enough to stop Luke mentioning Zach again.

'If I didn't know any better, I'd say the bloke was in love with you.'

'Which is none of your business.'

He holds up his hands as if I've trained a gun on him. 'I never said it was.'

I regroup, not wanting to give my ex any more ammunition he can use against me. 'Thanks for your concern, I'm fine. Now, if you don't mind?'

He glances at the door, then back at me. 'Look, I just wanted to say, I think it's a good job you didn't find Grant.'

'What?'

'I always thought there was a good reason he wasn't part of your life.'

'Well, what you think doesn't matter,' I shoot back.

He leans back in his chair, looking too comfortable to consider leaving. 'That's as may be. But I think I was right. He always struck me as the sort who made a ton of promises he couldn't keep. He said he'd look after your mother, but then he left at the first sign of trouble.'

'Mum threw him out. He didn't have a choice.'

'Okay, maybe not then. But giving you all that time and energy and then just leaving you behind? Doesn't sound like you were a priority to him.'

'Oh and you'd know all about that, wouldn't you?' I don't want this conversation. I never invited Luke's opinion and I don't need this.

'*And* back to that.' He raises his eyes to the ceiling. 'Because it's always about what I did, isn't it?'

That's it. I can't be civil any longer.

'What you did? I thought I knew what you did, but it was the tip of the iceberg, wasn't it?'

'What?'

'You lied to me. You knew Grant was working for your uncle all along.'

His mouth flaps open, but I don't give him the chance to reply.

'You knew where he was. And yet you belittled me, every time I mentioned him. You made me feel like a silly child for even wanting to look.'

He reaches for me. 'I wanted to keep you safe . . .'

I swat his hand away. 'Don't give me that! You didn't want anyone else in my life!'

'Maybe I didn't. Maybe I knew you needed me more than some waster from your past.'

The truth. Spoken after so long as if it never mattered at all. He wanted control of me. I didn't have family to interfere, so he hid the only other person who could influence my life. 'He was my stepdad. I had a right to find him.'

'He left. And didn't bother trying to find you. Fact is, you don't know him. He's not the saviour you make him out to be.'

'I should be the one to decide that. Not you.'

'Merryn, sweetheart, you don't know what you'd be getting into.'

'Oh? Like I didn't know I'd married a lying bastard? How is Holly, by the way? The great love of your life you trashed mine to be with?'

He blanches. 'I'm not – we're not . . .'

It should feel like a victory, knowing she's kicked him to the kerb. But I'm floored by the pointlessness of it. 'Get out.'

'I care about you!' he blurts. 'I never should have left you . . .'

'No. You don't get to do this. Get out!'

'Please? You don't need Zach Trevelyan. And Grant doesn't want to be found. He never did. Every promise he ever made you was a lie. I knew what was best for you then and I know it now . . .'

'Where is Grant?'

'I . . . can't . . .'

'Where is he?'

'I don't know. He left – Graham says he moved away.'

I've heard enough. 'Go away, Luke. I don't need you. I never did.'

I stand my ground, dizzy with adrenaline, as Luke moves to the door. He doesn't look back as he leaves.

I take a moment to catch my breath before I return to the end-of-day tasks, each one a meditation now, the familiarity soothing. I lock the door, wipe down the counter and carry the rubbish sacks through to the bins hidden behind a fence panel at the end of the side passage.

Luke *isn't* right about Grant. He never promised me anything he couldn't give. There were plenty of promises he could have made to the bright-eyed kid sitting beside him at the piano. He could have promised to make things better with Mum, or to come back to fetch me. But Grant did none of those things.

All he promised was that the piano connected us, and that I'd never be forgotten.

But as I return to my flat and try to settle before bed, doubts creep in.

He said the piano connected us, then abandoned it in a house due for renovation.

He promised he'd never forget me, but when he had the chance to see me again, he didn't come forward. Does he even remember the child he only knew for a while?

I'm here, with the piano he didn't care enough to keep.

And I feel more alone than I ever have.

Luke is wrong. So why can't I shake what he said?

Forty-Eight

ZACH

I'm loading the delivery van when I see her. Not wanting another confrontation, I try my best to hide behind the van door, but it's too late.

Ruthie has seen me and is bearing down like a thunderstorm.

'Oi! Surf dude!' Her voice shatters the stillness of the street. 'I want a word with you!'

What is she even doing out here at five-thirty in the morning? She's too early to start work at Merryn's place and she doesn't strike me as someone who gets up before it's absolutely necessary. She has a bag slung over her shoulder and is wearing blue denim dungarees with the bottoms rolled up to calf height, a red and white striped T-shirt beneath and white platform sneakers slapping against the cobbles – looking like an angry yet stylish pirate.

Thank goodness she has no cutlass. My head would be rolling under the van in one stroke.

'Hey,' I reply, knowing she won't be pacified by my attempt at friendliness.

'Why haven't you been to see Merryn?'

I can only gawp back at her.

She folds her arms and stares me down. 'Well?'

'She asked me to leave, after the fight.'

'And you listened?'

'I did what she wanted.'

'You trashed her piano! What did you expect her to say?'

I have had nowhere near enough caffeine to deal with this yet. 'She threw me out. I took that as a pretty big hint.'

'Don't be cute with me,' she hisses.

'I wasn't trying to be.'

'She's alone.'

'She has Seth.'

'She told Seth she doesn't want him around,' Ruthie returns.

'That's between them.'

'Well, I'm talkin' about you, you blockhead. You left her, when she needed you most. She's been kicked by that bleddy news story and abandoned by you. And then she found out Luke did the dirty on her, knowin' where that fella was all the time.'

'I know, I quit my job at Pengelly's when I found out.'

'Well, Big Woop for you.'

I shake my head, wishing this conversation would go away. 'Look, I know you mean well, but I have a van to pack and I'm already late for my round.'

'Go and see her.'

'I can't.'

'Make it right. You hurt her. Merryn's been an angel to me and I see when she's hurtin'. So you and Seth need to get over your shit and put her first for a change.'

She says it like it's the easiest fix in the world. Like it's nothing.

'I told Seth to look after her. The rest doesn't concern me.'

'Doesn't it?' Ruthie groans. 'Idiots, the pair of you. Maybe she needs you both? So bin your bleddy pride, grab him by the scruff of his thick neck and make this right!'

And then she's gone, leaving me dazed by the van, her words ringing in my ears.

I set off on my delivery round, Ruthie's words a frustrating soundtrack stuck on repeat. When I've done my final stop, I pull into a layby at the top of a hill and get out of the van. There's a gate across a lush green paddock, the land dropping away to a thin ribbon of blue, sparkling sea. Reception is good here, so I call Zanna.

'Zach? Is everything okay?'

'Hi Zan. Yes – well, no. Can I ask a question about when you and Merryn went to Mariner's?'

'Sure, fire away.'

'Did you get the impression that Graham Jacobs knew more about where Grant is than he told you?'

There's a pause, the sound of bleating sheep and a rising skylark rushing in from the landscape surrounding me. Then, a soft sigh. 'Actually, I did. I wanted to push it when we got back, but my editor's on the warpath so I had to lay low.'

'What did Graham say, exactly?'

'That Grant had wanted to leave and he'd given him a week's wages as a goodwill gesture.'

Goodwill gesture my arse. 'Do you think Graham paid him off?'

'I don't know. But he tried his best to dissuade us from looking for Grant. He insisted the bloke had changed his name to Guy Henson and left the county. We hit a dead end. I did wonder if maybe Graham's nephew had expressed a desire for Grant not to be found. Merryn told me he was her ex.'

I grimace against the phone. Knowing Luke, I wouldn't put it past him, but how would I ever prove it? 'Doesn't say much for Grant that he'd rather take the money and run than meet the woman who was looking for him.'

'Depends on how much money we're talking,' Zanna says. 'People do all kinds of things if they're desperate for cash. Also, you don't know what kind of pressure Graham or his son put on Grant. What if they convinced him that meeting Merryn would do more harm to her than good?'

I can see that happening. 'Can you talk to your editor? Ask him to let you dig a bit deeper?'

'I'd love to, Zach, but my hands are tied. Frank won't budge, and Graham spends a lot of money advertising with the *Daily News* – too much to risk losing it. Frank's threatening to demote me to Community Pages for taking Merryn to Mariner's. Believe me, if I could find another way to get to Graham without it jeopardising the paper's income, I would.'

That's when it hits me: a way forward that keeps Zanna's job safe and gets us straight to the people that matter. But I can't do it alone. There's someone I need back on my side.

*

'Back for more, Trevelyan?'

It's the kind of reception I was expecting, walking back into Pengelly's like I'd be welcome. But I'm convinced this is the only way to make things right for Merryn. And if it means butting heads with the cheating, devious owner of the restaurant, so be it. Besides, I have something he won't be expecting.

And I can't believe I'm saying this, but I'm glad I have Seth Hartley beside me.

I wasn't certain he'd come. But when I told him what Luke had said – and what else I know – any hostility he might have had towards me vanished.

'Let's go and get the bastard . . .'

'Bring a friend, did you?' Luke asks now, eyeing Seth. 'How sweet.'

'Tell us where Grant Henderson is,' I state, keeping my voice as steady as I can.

'I told you, I don't know.'

'Let me put it another way, Pengelly,' Seth seethes beside me. 'You're going to tell us where Grant is.'

'Ooh, are you going to make me, Hartley?'

'If necessary.'

Some of the diners are staring now. Luke's eyes flick to them.

'Out the back.'

'Here is fine.'

'Please?' He's squirming now. It's rewarding to see.

'I've got a better idea,' I say, Seth's nod confirmation that he's with me. 'Why don't you come with us?'

'No can do, boys. I have a restaurant to run . . .'

'We're fine here, boss,' Hen calls from the bar. I want to hug her.

He's flushed now, clearly wanting us gone but not wishing to cause a scene. 'If you have something to say . . .'

'Oh, we do. I'm just wondering if you're happy for your

customers to hear where you source your spirits from. And your uncle over in Carbis Bay. Lovely red delivery van . . .'

I see the whites of his eyes, the colour draining from his face.

'Where?' he croaks.

'Wherever you've stashed Grant,' Seth growls, happy to play henchman. 'Get your keys, Lukey-boy. You're driving.'

Forty-Nine

MERRYN

Ruthie has been like a warrior queen since she arrived this morning. I don't know what's behind it, but I'm too nervous to ask. Better to let her stomp around like St Ives' answer to Boudicca than to attract her ire. When it comes to my assistant, the path of least resistance is definitely the preferable route.

Even still, it's a welcome distraction for me today. Luke's visit last night unsettled everything. My head doesn't believe a word of what he said, but my battered heart is vulnerable to doubt.

If Grant knew I was looking for him, and chose to leave the place he knew he'd be found – money or no money as part of that decision – it should tell me everything I need to know. I just can't quite let go of his ghost, of the memory of the kind-hearted man who always found time for me. Until I can, I'm always going to wonder what might have been.

'Table 14 wants more tea,' Ruthie says, leaving the counter with two toasted paninis.

'On it,' Murph says, leaping out of her way. Over by the hot water urn, I see him pause for a steadying breath.

'I can take those over,' I gently offer.

He shakes his head. 'No fear, boss. I have my orders.'

'You can say no, you know.'

'And risk losin' my head? Not likely! Mood she's in today, if she yells *jump*, I'm bleddy well jumpin'!'

I welcome a family as they arrive, holding open the door for the suntanned mother to manoeuvre a huge pushchair inside.

'Cheers,' she pants. 'I swear this thing'll be the death of me.'

'There's space beside the counter if you want to leave it there, once you and your little one are settled?' I offer, waving at the bright-eyed toddler observing me.

'Could I? That'd be amazing!'

I look over to Murph, but he's way ahead of me, fetching a wooden high chair from the stack beside the chained-off stairs to my flat and following the customers over to their chosen table. Ruthie appears the other side, with a pot of colouring pencils and a small stack of paper, blessing a startled Murph with an approving glance.

'There are baby change facilities in the toilet out in the courtyard and if you need any food or bottles warming we can do that for you,' I say, aware that we're now crowding the table. Murph takes the hint and slopes back to the counter, Ruthie turning towards the courtyard, order pad in hand.

'You're angels, the lot of you,' the woman breathes, flopping down onto her seat. 'You wouldn't believe the hassle we've had, lugging that pushchair everywhere. Anyone would think we'd brought a sherpa tank with us. And pushing it over all those cobbles.'

'I can imagine. Now, relax, take a look at the menu and give us a wave when you're ready to order. No rush.'

I love the calm that settles over customers once they're seated in Sweet Reverie. Over the last three years, I've learned to recognise the change when people feel comfortable. When this place was just a dream and a seemingly impossible to-do list to get it off the ground, I hoped I could create a sanctuary in the heart of St Ives. Somewhere people would associate with calm and fun, a place to consider theirs, wherever they had travelled here from. It doesn't work for everyone, of course, especially in the summer months, when people are stressed and frustrated and paying far too much for their holiday homes. But most of our visitors seem happy here.

Today, at least, the nicer kind of customers are prevalent.

Which is probably for the best, considering Ruthie appears ready for a fight.

I wait until all the seated orders are done before broaching the topic with her. 'You look like you need a cuppa,' I say, guiding her behind the counter. 'Come and keep me company for five minutes.'

She accepts, joining me at the urn. I nod at Murph, who quickly plates an empire ocean biscuit and slides it cautiously along the worktop towards her.

'I saved you this,' he mutters. 'Because you deserve it.' Treat delivered, he hurries back out.

Ruthie watches him through narrowed eyes. 'Weird.'

'Kind,' I argue. 'He's been scared of you all morning.'

'Me? Why?'

I hand her a large mug of tea. 'Because you've been like a Valkyrie.'

'Like the Amy Winehouse song?' Her smile cracks almost immediately. 'I'm messin' with you, Mer. Your face!'

She's proud of the joke, so I'm happy to let her have it. 'It's a bit hard to tell today.'

She takes a large bite of her empire ocean biscuit, wiping crumbs from her lips. 'That scary?'

'*That* scary. Are you okay?'

'I'm good. Not as good as these biscuits, though. What's different with them?'

'Murph baked them.'

'Get out of town!'

'He did. Decorated them, too.' I glance at what remains of her biscuit. 'That one had a smiley face iced on it, to try to cheer you up.'

'Did it?' She stops chewing, eyes growing wide. '*Did* it?'

'It did. Which you might have noticed if you hadn't been ripping the place up.'

She winces at that. 'I didn't mean to. It's just that I sorted somethin' today, before I came in. I'm still fired up about it. And before you ask, no, I'm not tellin'. But it's been on my mind.'

'I'm sure whatever it was needed to be dealt with.'

She observes me as she drinks tea. 'Yeah, I reckon it did. Sorry, Mer. I'll cool it now . . .'

Over her shoulder, I see Zanna Venn in the open doorway.

'Take a moment, okay? Enjoy your tea.'

Leaving Ruthie, I hurry over to the reporter. 'Hey, good to see you. Did your editor let you out of the newsroom for good behaviour?'

'Something like that.' Her smile is fleeting, gone too soon, her usual joviality dulled. 'Can we have a chat?'

Instantly, I'm tense, my body on alert. This isn't a social call.

It's something urgent that demands delivery in person. 'There's a table free by the piano.'

Zanna accepts and I follow her through the café to the courtyard. We sit, and I watch her hands writhing and twisting on the mosaic table top. Eventually, they become still as she looks at me.

'Frank's cancelling the assignment,' she says, my worst fears confirmed. 'Numbers are falling online and there just isn't the interest to keep it going. He's moving me on to the community pages desk, so it's WI groups and rotary functions for the foreseeable.'

'Can you appeal? Ask him to reconsider?'

'Not if I want to keep my job.' She shakes her head. 'I'm so sorry, Merryn. I've tried keeping stuff going under his radar, but he's cottoned on.'

'Or someone made him stop you,' I say, remembering the open threats Graham Jacobs threw at Zanna when we went to see him.

'Or that.'

'Why don't they want me to find him? What is it to them, anyway?'

Zanna shrugs. 'I wish I knew. But this is as far as I can go. I shouldn't even be here. I made up some bollocks about interviewing a knit'n'natter group just so I could get out of the office.'

It's funny and heartbreaking at the same time, the release of the joke tempered by the finality of our position.

'Well, thank you. For everything.'

'I just wish it was more.'

So do I. But I won't tell her that.

I see her out, exchanging vague promises to stay in touch

that I recognise as the escape routes they really are. It's unlikely we'll speak again. But I won't regret asking for her help, or making the public appeal.

It's the final glimmer of hope, extinguished. The last roll of the dice. I can't fight it, or demand a different outcome.

It's time to face facts: I won't find Grant Henderson.

Heart shattered, I force a smile into place and return to my customers.

PART FIVE

'Rainbow'

– Kacey Musgraves

Fifty

ZACH

He's in Hayle.

Literally up the road from Carbis Bay.

Talk about hiding in plain sight.

As I guessed, Luke takes us straight to the pub Grant has found work in, owned by a good friend of Graham, no less. Luke can't meet my eye as we walk in. He knows how crooked the arrangement is. How long would he have kept the truth from Merryn if she hadn't found out? I know the answer to that and it makes Luke Pengelly even more of a git than I thought he was.

Unlike the constant crush of every pub, bar and restaurant in St Ives, The Lobster Pot is practically empty. Just a few regulars installed at their tables, half-drunk pints ignored in front of them. It's an old-fashioned seafarer's inn, not a contrived theme pub cashing in on the tourist trade. Horse brasses still line the dark-stained oak beams that prop up the ceiling, old tattered fishing nets looped between them.

A grey-haired man is collecting glasses at the far end of the pub. Lean and tall, the skin of his arms tanned to the colour of toffee by years spent in the Cornish sun. He's dressed in a faded blue T-shirt and jeans that seem too big for him, the waistband slung low and a silver chain hanging from the belt loops. His grey hair is pulled back into a stubby knot, thick and wiry with no sign of skin beneath. He's nodding to himself as he stacks the glasses in a crate. Beneath the burr of a talk radio station, I think I can hear him humming a tune.

Luke nods in his direction, confirming he's the one we're here to see.

Grant Henderson doesn't look like a man in hiding. Or someone who doesn't want to be found. He's relaxed, at ease in his vintage surroundings. It's a world away from Mariner's. Has this new arrangement worked better for him?

We reach the bar and Seth picks up a beer mat, tapping its edge against the scratched wood. The noise catches Grant's attention, his face falling when he sees us.

'I don't want no trouble,' he calls.

'No trouble, mate. Just a word.'

There's a rustle of plastic strip curtain behind the bar and a squat, tattooed man appears. He has thinning red hair and no discernible neck, a large mermaid tattoo on his right bicep. Whether he's the landlord of The Lobster Pot or not, I wouldn't want to get on the wrong side of him.

'Wasson, boy?'

Grant's mouth drops open, fear flashing in his stare. 'I ain't asked them to come.'

The landlord snorts. 'Trouble followin' you round, is it? That's not what I took you on for.' His neckless head snaps round, the scowl instantly softening into gold-tooth-peppered grin.

It's *terrifying*. I think I preferred the scowl . . .

'Mr Pengelly, a pleasure to see you. And your – *friends*. What'll you have?'

Beside me, Luke breaks into a smile. 'Bit early for me, Silas. We just need a quick word with Mr Henson.'

So, Graham was telling the truth. Grant is using Henson instead of Henderson.

'He's needed in the bar,' Silas returns, the slightest edge of threat in his reply.

'Ten minutes,' Luke soothes. 'Twenty at most.'

Grant is watching this exchange from behind the shield of the glasses crate, his head switching between the landlord and Luke.

Silas makes a sound like seawater sucked through a channel worn into rock. 'Lunch rush will be in soon.'

I scan the faded interior of the pub, trying to imagine what a lunch rush looks like here. Two old men and a plate of cheese cobs?

'Fifteen minutes,' Luke replies, his ever-so-benevolent smile unwavering. 'If the – er – *rush* arrives while we're talking, of course we'll let you have him.'

The bushy eyebrows of the landlord drop. 'Ten minutes. And take it out the back. I won't have my regulars disrupted.' He nods at the scant few customers, none of whom appear to have even registered we're here.

Grant drags his feet to join us, pointing at a door to the left of the bar. 'Snug's in there.'

'Lead the way,' Luke replies, so brightly I wonder what threat it might conceal.

We follow Grant through the door, down a small corridor and another door, emerging in a tiny room with an ancient-looking hearth on one side and a small curve of bar counter on the other. Two tables, four upholstered stools and a two-cushion bench seat have been squeezed into the space. Grant takes the bench, while Luke, Seth and I perch on the stools.

'I don't want trouble,' Grant repeats, his back pressed against the bench as if he might slip through the wall behind.

'No trouble,' Seth says. 'Zach here just wants to ask a couple of questions.'

His pale eyes flick to me.

'Hey, I'm Zach,' I say, as warmly as I can. My proffered hand returns to my side, unshaken. 'And this is Seth. We're nothing to do with Luke. Or Graham. We're here for my friend.'

'Friend? Which friend? I don't know either of you.'

'Merryn Rowe.'

The flinch is impossible to miss. I press on regardless, aware that time is short, wanting to get this right for Merryn.

'She was the daughter of a woman you dated.' I suddenly realise I've never asked Merryn for her mother's name. 'Back in Penzance, about thirty years ago? You moved in with her and Merryn and stayed for about two years.'

'Don't remember.' His wary stare isn't fixed on me.

I glare at Luke, who appears to have lost his charming smile on the journey to the snug. '*Tell* him.'

Another eye-roll. I hope he's hating this, being put in his place in front of someone he may well have intimidated into silence. 'He knows it all, Grant. You're free to talk.'

So Guy Henson is only a name for others to call him. He's still Grant behind it all.

Grant brings a many-ringed hand up to rub at his eyes. 'Of course I remember. Chirpy little thing she was, bright as a button. How I imagine her mum was, before life kicked her.'

I try to imagine Merryn as a chirpy little girl, delighting in a new friend in the home that proved so tough for her to grow up in.

'You loved her mum?'

He shrugs. 'I tried to.'

'You brought your piano,' I prompt. 'She begged you to teach her to play. And you did.'

The pale eyes mist a little.

'On the day you left, you carved a heart under the right curve of the piano case. The part that's called the cheek? You promised Merryn you would never forget her.'

'I said a lot of things to get out of tough situations. When kids are there, too . . .'

'Do you know she's been looking for you?'

His mouth snaps shut.

'She found your piano, left on the pavement in North Terrace, St Ives, beside a house gutted for renovation,' I continue, willing him to respond to it. He's been evasive at best, and I can't read his reaction as I speak. 'She took it back to the café she owns. It has pride of place there.'

'Did she?' He swallows hard, casting another nervous glance at Luke. 'Not that it's any of my business.'

'It's your piano!' Frustration is fraying the edge of my words. I have to pull back, or I could blow my chance. 'Why didn't you respond to the appeal in the newspaper?'

'I didn't read it.'

'Try again with the truth.'

'I don't have to take this!'

He's suddenly on his feet, his escape plan scuppered by the stools on which Seth and I are sitting, barring his route.

'Sit down,' I say, repeating softer, 'Sit down, Grant. Please?'

'I'll stand, if it's all the same.'

'You need to understand what that piano means to her. What you mean to her.'

'That's sweet of the kid, but I was in her life for such a short time.'

'And you changed everything for her! How she saw herself, how she viewed life with her mother, the hope she discovered – because you were the first person to believe in her.'

Luke is watching me now, his expression clouded.

'But two years . . .'

'She was seven years old when you moved in, mate. Two years feels like a lifetime at that age.'

Grant's eyes flick from me to Luke. 'This true?'

Seth leans a little so that his face is level with Luke.

Luke swallows hard. 'Every word.'

'And she's been looking for me? In the paper?'

'Yes,' I reply. 'You didn't know?'

'I did, but—' he keeps a careful eye on Luke '—I was advised not to reply.'

'Who by?'

'Mr Jacobs. And Mr Pengelly . . .'

It's as I suspected. 'Why?'

'I just thought it best.' Luke's weary concession is a surprise, but I don't have time to question him on it.

'I wasn't asking you,' I bark, turning back to the startled barman. 'Why didn't you feel you could answer the appeal?'

Grant slumps. 'My life – it's been a mess. All the plans I had, all the doors I tried. One kick after another. Nobody needs that crap. Specially not that girl.' He wipes his forehead with the back of his hand. I notice a faded rising sun motif tattooed on the underside of his wrist. 'I remember her, poor kid. Like a little shadow, everywhere I went. Smart as a whip, she was. Learned every song I taught her in no time. I wanted to leave the piano for her, but Marcia would have smashed it to tinder if I had. Kind of thing that woman would have done, just to make a point. I always hoped the kid would get away from her.'

'She did,' I say.

'And her ma?'

'Passed away, a few years back.'

He nods. 'I hope she found peace. Reckon her girl needs good stuff now. No shit from the past to get in the way.'

'She just wants to meet you. To say thank you.'

He's shaking his head, hands wringing the cloth he carried in from the bar. 'I can't. Sorry.'

He edges past me and waits for Luke to lean back to allow him to pass.

Is that it? We just let him leave?

'She can't play the piano without you!'

It rushes out of me, a final, last-breath attempt to change his mind.

Grant freezes in the doorway.

'She's tried, over and over in her life. I've seen it happen. She can't touch the keys, even though it's what she longs for most. Because she never stopped waiting for you to come back. And the moment she plays without you, she'll have to let you go.'

Grant's knuckles grow white where he grips the doorframe.

'If you care for Merryn at all,' I say, my voice thick with emotion, the dying moments of our time already past, 'if she ever meant anything to you, meet her. Just once. No press, nobody else there. So she can say goodbye and finally move on.'

It's all I have. I've told him everything I know. Now one decision remains – and neither Luke, Seth nor I can make it.

If Grant declines, it's over. I'll never tell Merryn I saw him, and I'll swear Seth to secrecy, too. What we know about the illegal alcohol at Pengelly's and Mariner's will ensure Luke never talks about it, either. Somehow, I'll try to reach Merryn again, if she'll let me. If she won't, I'll leave her to get on with her life.

'How?'

Grant has turned back into the snug.

Luke says nothing.

I look to Seth, but he holds up his hands. 'Don't look at me, Zach. This is your gig.'

I flail for a moment in view of the victory. But then it comes to me. A flash of inspiration; the perfect solution. 'I have an idea . . .'

Fifty-One

MERRYN

I lie awake in darkness, trying to calm my racing mind enough to sleep.

But it's no use.

I've turned the facts over and over, searching for any glimpse of hope, like sifting pebbles at the tideline, seeking seaglass buried beneath. But there is no hope.

Zanna can't help me. The newspaper has halted the search. Grant doesn't want to found. I'm not ready to talk to Seth about everything yet, and Zach is gone, never to return. Everything that brought me hope this summer seems broken and worthless. Even the piano has become a reminder that the promise Grant made to me with the small carved heart was one he couldn't keep.

I passed Merlin before I turned off the café lights tonight, his bright colours shrouded in the grey sheet. A spectre of a dream that once meant the world.

There are no answers, nothing I can find in the darkness of my room or the corners of my consciousness that can change the truth.

Luke's assertion that Grant didn't care about me seems proven, even though my ex-husband is the last person on earth I want to be right about this. His damning indictment of Grant's character refuses to leave, buzzing around my ears like a mosquito. I have nothing to counter it with because I have no evidence to the contrary.

I sit up, reach for the glass of water beside my bed, and drink.

When Mum was at her most desperate, I would have countless nights like this. Lying awake and scared in a tangle of bedsheets, seeking solutions that weren't there to be found. Hearing her voice racked by sobs through the too-thin walls, or the constant wail of her on the phone to some loser or other, begging them to listen; knowing that, if I made a sound, the full weight of her hurt, frustration and self-hate would fall on me.

A teacher at my primary school once told me that the best sea captains know the safest course to steer when a storm hits isn't around it, but through it. Going against every human instinct to avoid danger, charting a path through the heart of the storm. It's stayed with me all my life, because as a young kid too scared to admit what was happening at home for fear of being taken from my mother, it spoke to where I was.

Not around, but through.

The skill is in knowing the storm you face. In forging ahead when all seems lost.

I wonder what would have happened if Mum had learned that skill. She was too battered by life and broken in her mind to realise she still had power to steer a better course. I wish she'd seen that, before she ran out of time.

I still have time. And I'm not her.

I'm not Grant, either. I don't run from trouble, even when

the impulse to escape is overwhelming. I didn't run from the fallout of my divorce and I won't run from this.

All is not lost, however easy it is to assume that.

I have my business, thriving this year after the step of faith it took to extend our opening hours. I have the piano that miraculously returned to my life, now a fixture of the café. My expanded team of Murph, Jenna and Ruthie have breathed new life into Sweet Reverie, bringing possibility and positivity with them. And slowly, I'm learning to trust the good stuff, instead of fearing it might all be taken from me.

I won't let what happened this summer steal everything.

I steady my thudding heart with a deep inhale, my body aching and settling as I release the breath. Then I lie back down, pulling the sheets around me. It doesn't matter if I sleep, I tell myself: I'm just going to close my eyes and rest. Stop trying to avoid the storm in my mind and chart a course through it instead.

Slowly, I begin to drift, spaces appearing between the conflicting thoughts like clouds parting after rain. My bed is comfortable once again, its soothing softness drawing me in.

And then, I hear it.

A sound from beyond my room.

A gentle rhythm, a soft lilt.

I'm imagining it. A ghost of a memory, drifting through my semi-consciousness. I shift position, burying my head in my pillow.

But the sound continues.

It can't possibly be what it was before. The side gate is locked, the café, too. Merlin is silent and still beneath his cover. There's no way the piano is playing.

Unless . . .

Could Zach have returned? Might this be his apology? Quiet, understated, powerful, knowing what the piano means to me?

Slowly, the music modulates, the disparate notes merging together. And the melody it forms is unmistakable.

I'm out of bed in a heartbeat, pulling on my hoodie and a pair of shorts, hurrying through my flat to the staircase, where at the bottom step the softest light glows.

Tears flood my view, but I stab them away with the cuff of my sleeve.

The main café remains in darkness, but the courtyard is bathed in warm white light.

'Time Wears Awa' fills the air, willing me towards it. It's gentler than Zach played it before, the altered cadence striking a chord within me that I can't quantify. It's familiar yet different, timeless yet brand new.

The slate floor is cold beneath my feet, but the welcome that draws me is as warm as sun-baked sand.

He's here. He came back. Zach hasn't forgotten me.

I reach the door at the boundary between café and courtyard.

And breath leaves my body.

Zach is here. But he's standing beside Merlin, his hands nowhere near the keys. His eyes are still as he observes me.

And he's not alone.

At the piano, a grey-haired man sits, tanned arms bent at the elbows, fingers travelling over the keys. The hunch of his shoulders, the position he adopts on the piano stool, are all immediately recognisable.

My legs shake beneath me. I grab the door to steady myself.

The sound it makes halts the music.

Grant Henderson's hands leave the keys. Slowly, he looks towards me. And the years between my stolen views on the stairs in my childhood home and this moment on the courtyard's threshold melt away.

'Hey, birdie.' His voice is deeper than I remember, its peripheries cracked by time.

'You came.'

'Zach said you wanted to see me.'

There are a thousand and one things I stored up in his name over the years, tiny treasures of observance, dream and hope stacked together, ready to share with him, awaiting his return. Now he's here, in the place I thought I'd never see him, my words fail me.

He shifts a little on the stool and reaches his arm towards me. 'Come and sit with me. Like you used to.'

Does he even remember? Or has Zach relayed my memories to him? As I walk towards the piano, I realise it doesn't matter. This is the moment I've longed for. I won't let it pass by.

Beside him, I risk a smile. 'What are you going to play?'

'Might as well carry on with this one, I reckon.' His fingers form the opening chords I know well, the memory of my hands resting on Zach's the night we first kissed flooding back. Slowly, Grant plays, the soft pulse of his breath in time with the music a feature I'd forgotten. Not a whisper or an exhalation, but something in between.

I can feel Zach's eyes on me as Grant plays, but I can't look up from the keys for fear that the vision might vanish as easily as it appeared. Zach brought Grant here? How is that possible?

Abruptly, the song ends. When I look at Grant, he's smiling. 'Time for you to play now.'

'I – I can't,' I rush, fear surging like an ocean swell.

Even though Grant is here, the thought of touching the keys still overwhelms me. I don't know why. Maybe it's the terror of good things snatched away. That if I dare to play now, it will herald another broken promise, another door slammed.

I thought I'd left the uncertainty of my childhood behind. But here I am, once again, poleaxed by it.

'You know the notes to play. You know the song. So play it, Merryn. Forget everythin' else – it doesn't matter once the music takes over.' He strokes the keys, his eyes sad. 'This old girl was escape for me. No matter what else was goin' on around me – earthquakes, shouts, people comin' at me – it all went away the moment I played.'

'Why did you throw it out?'

It's the question that's dominated my thoughts, more than anything else I want to know. And now it's out there, awaiting an answer.

'Life got in the way, birdie. Like it does with me. The land-lord was sellin' up, so I had to go. Only place I found to rent couldn't fit a piano. Money was tight, my options were limited and I was scared if I didn't take the flat in Carbis I'd never find anythin' else I could afford.' He holds my gaze, as he did so many years before. 'I reckoned the old girl had served her time with me, been shifted from pillar to post too often. Pianos don't like to travel much and she put up with more than she should have.'

'So you left it?'

'I asked the landlord to find her a home and he said he would. I didn't reckon he'd sling her out onto the street.'

It makes sense. But there's another question, one I've

imagined asking for years. Now the time is here, I'm not sure how to ask.

'Did you know I was looking for you?'

His eyes dip from mine. 'I did.'

'Why didn't you reply?'

'I was told not to.' He stops, a sigh escaping. 'I believed Luke was right to say it. My life isn't what I wanted it to be. I've made a mess of so much. You were one of the good things I did. I thought it best left in the past.'

It hurts my heart, but I finally have the truth. 'So what changed?'

He pats Merlin. 'This old darlin'. You gave her a home, when I'd had to leave her.'

'Maybe it's a good thing you did.'

I look up. Zach's smile is gentle, maybe a little cautious. 'Why?'

'Because the piano brought you to me. And brought Grant back. You were right when you said it had its own magic. Look what it's done.'

Zach is here. The piano is here, restored from the fight. And Grant completes the picture. A triptych of magic, brought together in the heart of Sweet Reverie.

'Play, birdie,' Grant says, his arm nudging me. 'We ain't going anywhere.'

The keys shine in the glow of the courtyard lights. Battered and repaired, a thousand stories below each note. History and the here and now. Memory and possibility. All meet where my hands now tentatively rest.

If I play, this doesn't end.

If I play, a new chapter will begin.

Around me, the people I love most are willing the music to start. The man who taught me to play, who was a dad when I needed one. And the man I love.

Whatever's gone before – whatever wrongs and injustices, whatever misunderstandings and mistakes – is immaterial. It's time to leave it all behind.

The first note I play sends a shockwave through my heart. The spell broken, more notes follow. Slowly, the melody builds, the strangeness of my adult hands on the keys soon settling as muscle memory forged a lifetime ago takes over. 'Time Wears Awa' sings from beneath my fingers, the song bringing release and hope in a flood. My tears follow suit, but I don't stop to wipe them away.

It's the escape Grant described, but something more besides. Healing. Restoration. A heart-hug of hope.

When my hands retreat from the keys, Grant's arm around my shoulder steadies me. Zach kneels beside the piano stool, his warm fingers gently brushing tears from my cheeks.

'I should have come back,' Zach says, the deep ocean blue of his eyes sparkling like sunshine on waves. 'I should have fought harder for you.'

'It doesn't matter. You made this happen.'

'I love you,' Zach says. 'I always will.'

'I love you, too,' I reply.

And the magic is complete.

I don't hesitate. My hands find his face, drawing him close. I will everything that fills my heart into our kiss, pulling him close, as the pieces of my life deftly join together. I'm found and loved, given new life like the piano beside us. And love surrounds us all.

Summer nights in St Ives are strange beasts. But tonight is a good one.

It's where the magic returned, where rifts healed.

And where my heart finally found its home.

I don't know what lies ahead. But for the first time, my past has no say in it. Wrapped in Zach's embrace, reunited with Grant, with the piano that began it all making the music my heart longed for, I'm ready to sail right through.

Acknowledgements

Thank you for visiting Sweet Reverie.
The proprietor offers her most sincere thanks to:

STARTERS

Editor Extraordinaire:

PRIYAL AGRAWAL

Accompanied by:

MANPREET GREWAL, EMMA PICKARD,
FELICIA HU, KOM PATEL, GRACE MARSHALL, MAREN LANDSNES

Followed by:

HELENA NEWTON & MICHELLE BULLOCK

MAINS

Specially Selected Agent:

HANNAH FERGUSON

The Real Deal:

MY LOVELY BOB AND FABULOUS FLO

SWEET TREATS TO FOLLOW

Sweet Reverie
(named by LUCY HUDSON)

Empire Ocean Biscuits
(designed by ERIN KATHLEEN WILLIAMSON)

A Bevvy of Supportive Sweethearts:

CLAIRE SMITH & A.G. SMITH, CRAIG HALLAM, KATY AND
WILLIAM BALDWIN, TEAM SPARKLY, CHRIS CALLAGHAN,
CL TAYLOR, KIM CURRAN, IAN WILFRED, MICK ARNOLD,
FAB NIGHT IN CHATTY THING LOVELIES INCLUDING
VICTORIA ASPLUND, CLAIRE ROWLANDS AND SIAN
SANDWITH, THE DICKINSON, WHITE AND DAVIS CLANS,
AND SUPPORTERS OF MY SPARKLY NEWS AND
WRITEFOXY SUBSTACKS.

Menu lovingly prepared in honour of
the wonderful people of St Ives, Cornwall.

Thank you for your custom.
New treats are on the way. Visit us again soon!

Book Playlist

Music is such a huge part of every story I write – even more so with this book. Here are the songs that inspired the story from initial idea to finished novel.

Merryn & Zach's theme: 'Simple Things (Piano Version)' – Teddy Swims

- 'Brand New Day (Radio Edit)' – Joshua Radin
- 'Find Me' – Sigma feat. Birdy
- 'Everything Has Changed (Taylor's Version)' – Taylor Swift feat. Ed Sheeran
- 'Oh Woman Oh Man' – London Grammar
- 'Rainbow' – Kacey Musgraves
- 'Everything Will Be Alright' – Bernhoft
- 'Stargazing' – Myles Smith
- 'Starting Now' – Brandy
- 'You'll Get By' – Show of Hands
- 'Only For You' – Tors
- 'No Hopers, Jokers & Rogues' – Fisherman's Friends
- 'Northern Attitude' – Noah Kahan & Hozier
- 'Heaven' – Cian Ducrot

ONE PLACE. MANY STORIES

Bold, innovative and
empowering publishing.

FOLLOW US ON:

@HQStories